DUEL OF MAGIC

Too stunned even to be afraid, Garion watched as the Devil Agrinja and the Devil Horja closed on each other, clawing and tearing out chunks of scaly flesh with their awful jaws. The earth shook beneath their feet as they fought. But their full, burning hatred was directed at the two humans who had invoked them and now drove them to destroy each other.

This was magic, not sorcery. Garion shuddered, remembering that his grandfather had admitted that he was not proficient at magic.

Belgarath was sweating. Droplets of perspiration trickled down his face. The incantations which controlled the Devil Agrinja rippled endlessly from his tongue. The slightest faltering of either the words or the image he held in his mind would break his power over the beast he had summoned.

Then the Devil Agrinja would turn upon him and destroy him!

By David Eddings

THE BELGARIAD

Published by Ballantine Books

"THEY'RE *GOOD*! IN FACT, THEY'RE
FABULOUS. MORE! MORE! MORE!"
—Anne McCaffrey

"EDDINGS' *BELGARIAD* IS
EXACTLY THE KIND OF
FANTASY I LIKE. IT HAS MAGIC,
ADVENTURE, HUMOR, MYSTERY
AND A CERTAIN DELIGHTFUL
HUMAN INSIGHT."
—Piers Anthony

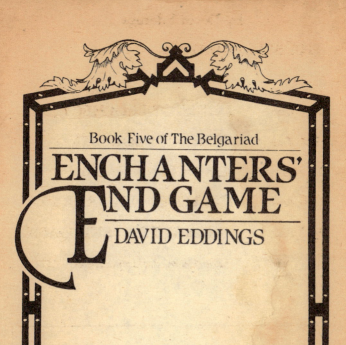

Book Five of The Belgariad

ENCHANTERS' END GAME

DAVID EDDINGS

A Del Rey Book

BALLANTINE BOOKS • NEW YORK

And finally,
for Leigh, my beloved wife,
whose hand and thought have touched
every page,
and who has joined me in this making
—even as she joins me in all that
I do.

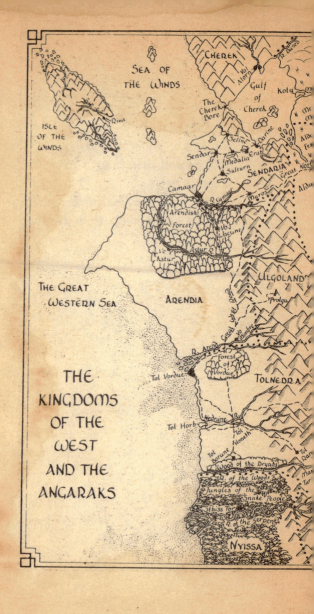

THE
KINGDOMS
OF THE
WEST
AND THE
ANGARAKS

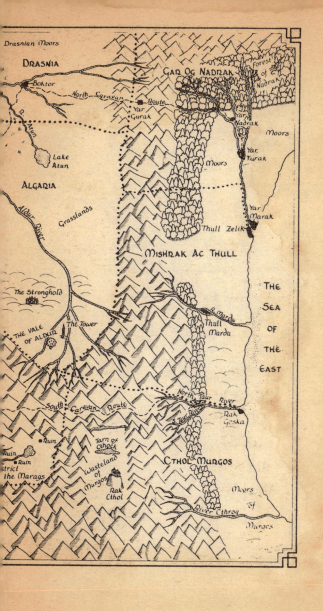

Drasnian Moors

DRASNIA

Boktor

North Caravan Route

Yar Gurak

R. Mrin

Lake Atun

ALGARIA

Aldur River

Grasslands

The Stronghold

THE VALE OF ALDUR

The Tower

South Caravan Route

Ruin

Ruin District the Marags

Tarn of Cthok

Wasteland of Murgos

Rak Cthol

GAR OG NADRAK

Forest of Nadrak

Yar Nadrak

Moors

Yar Turak

Moors

Yar Marak

Thull Zelik

MISHRAK AC THULL

R. Mardu

Thull Mardu

North Taur River

Taur River

Rak Goska

CTHOL MURGOS

THE SEA OF THE EAST

Moors of Murgos

River Cthrog

Murgos

Prologue

Being an account of beginnings—and endings.
— Excerpts from *The Book of Torak**

HEAR ME, YE Angaraks, for I am Torak, Lord of Lords and King of Kings. Bow before my Name and worship me with prayers and with sacrifices, for I am your God and I have dominion over all the realms of the Angaraks. And great shall be my wrath if ye displease me.

I was, before the world was made. I shall be, after the mountains crumble into sand, the seas dwindle to stagnant pools, and the world shrivels and is no more. For I was before time and shall be after.

From the timeless reaches of Infinity, I gazed upon the

---

*Editor's Note: This version, said to be from the dread *Book of Torak*, is one of several circulated among the Nadraks. Since only the high Grolims were permitted official copies of the work, it is impossible to establish that this version is authentic, though internal evidence suggests that much of it may be. A true copy of the complete *Book of Torak* is believed to be in the library of King Anheg of Cherek, but this was not available for comparison.

future. And I beheld that there were two Destinies and that they must rush toward each other from the endless corridors of Eternity. Each Destiny was Absolute, and in that final meeting, all that was divided should be made one. In that instant, all that was, all that is, and all that was yet to be should be gathered into one Purpose.

And because of my Vision, I led my six brothers to join hands to make all that is, in fulfillment of the needs of the Destinies. Thus we set the moon and the sun in their courses and we brought forth this world. We covered the world with forests and grasses and made beasts, fowls, and fishes to fill the lands and skies and waters which we had made.

But our Father took no joy in this creation which I had caused to be. He turned his face from our labor to contemplate the Absolute. I went alone into the high places of Korim, which are no more, and I cried out to him to accept what I had made. But he rejected the work I had caused to be and turned from me. Then I hardened my heart against him and went down from that place, fatherless evermore.

Once more I counseled my brothers, and we joined our hands and brought forth man to be the instrument of our will. We created man as many peoples. And to each people, we gave a choice to select among us the one who should be their God. And the peoples chose from us, save only that no people chose Aldur, who was ever contrary and discontented that we would not grant him dominion. Then Aldur withdrew himself from among us and sought to entice our servants away from us with enchantments. But few were they who accepted him.

The peoples who were mine called themselves the Angaraks. I was well pleased with them and I led them to the high places of Korim, which are no more, and to them I revealed the nature of the Purpose for which I had caused the world to be.

Then they worshipped me with prayers and offered burnt offerings unto me. And I blessed them, and they prospered and grew numerous. In their gratitude they raised up an altar to me and there made sacrifice to me of their fairest maidens and a portion of their bravest youths. And I was well pleased with them and again I blessed them, so that they prospered above all other men and multiplied exceedingly.

Now the heart of Aldur was filled with envy for the worship that was given to me, and he was driven with despite for me. Then did he conspire against me within the secret places of his soul, and he took up a stone and breathed life into it, that it might thwart my Purpose. And in that stone he sought to gain dominion over me. Thus Cthrag Yaska came to be. And there was eternal enmity sealed within Cthrag Yaska against me. And Aldur sat apart with those whom he called his disciples and plotted how the stone should give him dominion.

I saw that the accursed stone had divided Aldur from me and from his other brothers. And I went to Aldur and remonstrated with him, begging that he lift the wicked enchantment from the stone and take back the life he had breathed into it. This I did that Aldur might no longer be divided from his brothers. Yea, I did even weep and abase myself before him.

But already the evil stone had gained possession over the soul of Aldur, and he had hardened his heart against me. And I saw then that the stone which Aldur had created would forever hold my brother in thralldom. And he spoke slightingly to me and would have driven me forth.

Then for the love I bore him and to save him from the evil course which my Vision revealed, I struck my brother Aldur down and took from him the accursed rock. And I bore Cthrag Yaska away to bend my will upon it and to still the malice within it and quell the wickedness for which it was created. So it was that I took the burden of the thing which Aldur had created upon myself.

Aldur was wroth with me. He went to our brothers and spoke to them falsely against me. And each of them came to me and spoke slightingly to me, commanding that I return to Aldur that which had twisted his soul and which I had taken to free him from the enchantment of it. But I resisted.

Then they girded for war. The sky was blackened with the smoke of their forges as their peoples beat out weapons of iron to spill the blood of my Angaraks upon the ground. When the year turned, their hosts marched forth and onto the lands of the Angaraks. And my brothers loomed tall in the forefront of the hosts.

Now was I greatly loath to lift my hand against them. Yet

I could not permit that they should despoil the lands of my people or loose the blood of those who worshipped me. And I knew that from such war between my brothers and me could come only evil. In that struggle, the Destinies I had seen might be sent against each other before it was time, and the universe be shaken apart in that meeting.

And so I chose that which I feared, but which was less evil than the danger I foresaw. I took up the accursed Cthrag Yaska and raised it against the earth itself. And in me lay the Purpose of one Destiny, while the Purpose of the other was affixed within the stone Aldur had created. The weight of all that was or will be was upon us, and the earth could not bear our weight. Then did her mantle rend assunder before me, and the sea rushed in to drown the dry land. Thus were the peoples separated one from the other, that they might not come upon each other and their blood be spilled.

But such was the malice which Aldur had wrought within the stone that it smote me with fire as I raised it to divide the world and prevent evil bloodshed. Even as I spoke the commands unto it, it burst into dreadful fire and smote me. The hand with which I held it was consumed and the eye with which I beheld it was blinded. One half of my face was marred by its burning. And I, who had been the fairest among my brothers, was now abhorrent to the eyes of all, and I must cover my face with a living mask of steel, lest they shun me.

An agony filled me from the evil that was done me, and pain lived within me, which could never be quenched until the foul stone could be freed of its evil and could repent of its malice.

But the dark sea stood between my people and those who would come against them, and my enemies fled in terror of that which I had done. Yea, even my brothers fled from the world which we had made, for they dared no longer come against me. Yet still did they conspire with their followers in spirit form.

Then I bore my people away to the wastelands of Mallorea and there caused them to build a mighty city on a sheltered place. They named it Cthol Mishrak, as a remembrance of the suffering I had undergone for them. And I concealed their city with a cloud that should ever be above it.

Then I had a cask of iron forged, and in it I bound Cthrag Yaska, that the evil stone should never again be free to unleash its power to destroy flesh. For a thousand years and still another thousand years I labored, contending with the stone that I might release the curse of malice which Aldur had laid upon it. Great were the enchantments and words of power which I cast at the obdurate stone, but still its evil fire burned when I came near to it, and I felt its curse lying ever upon the world.

Then Belar, youngest and most rash of my brothers, conspired against me with Aldur, who still bore hatred and jealousy within his soul toward me. And Belar spoke in spirit to his uncouth people, the Alorns, and set them against me. The spirit of Aldur sent Belgarath, the disciple in whom he had most wholly instilled his despite, to join with them. And the foul counsel of Belgarath prevailed upon Cherek, chief of the Alorns, and upon his three sons.

By evil sorcery, they passed the barrier of the sea I had caused to be and they came like thieves in the night to the city of Cthol Mishrak. By stealth and low cunning, they crept through my tower of iron and made their way to the chest that held the evil stone.

The youngest son of Cherek, whom men called Riva Irongrip, had been so woven about with spells and enchantments that he could take up the accursed stone and not perish. And they fled with it to the west.

With the warriors of my people I pursued them, that the curse of Cthrag Yaska not again be loosed upon the land. But the one called Riva raised the stone and loosed its evil fire upon my people. Thus the thieves escaped, bearing the evil of the stone with them into their lands of the west.

Then I pulled down the mighty city of Cthol Mishrak, that my people must flee from its ruins. And I divided the Angaraks into tribes. The Nadraks I set in the north to guard the ways in which the thieves had come. The Thulls, broad of back for the bearing of burdens, I set in the middle lands. The Murgos, fiercest of my people, I sent to the south. And the most numerous I kept with me in Mallorea, to serve me and multiply against a day when I should have need of an army against the west.

Above all these peoples I set the Grolims and instructed them in enchantments and wizardry, that they be a priesthood to me and watch over the zeal of all others. And them I instructed to keep my altars burning and to be unceasing in their sacrifices to me.

Belgarath, in his wickedness, had sent Riva with the accursed stone to rule an island in the Sea of Winds. And there Belar caused two stars to fall to earth. From these, Riva forged a sword and set Cthrag Yaska into its pommel.

And when Riva gripped that sword, the universe shuddered about me, and I cried out, for my Vision had opened to me, revealing much that had been hidden before. I saw that Belgarath's sorcerous daughter should in time be my bride, and I rejoiced. But I also saw that a Child of Light would descend from Riva's loins, and he would be an instrument of that Destiny which opposed that other Destiny which gave me my Purpose. Then would come a day when I must wake from some long sleep to face the sword of the Child of Light. And upon that day, the two Destinies would clash, with only one victor alive and one Destiny thenceforth. But which was not revealed.

Long I pondered this Vision, but no more was revealed. And a thousand years passed, and even more.

Then I called to me Zedar, a wise and just man who had fled from the malice of Aldur's teachings and had come unto me with an offer of service. And I sent him to the court of the Serpent People who dwelt among swamps in the west. Their God was Issa, but he was ever lazy and he slept, leaving the people who called themselves Ny-Issans to the sole rule of their queen. And to her Zedar did make certain offers, which were pleasing to her. And she sent her assassins as emissaries to the court of Riva's descendants. There did they slay all of that line, save only one child who chose to drown himself in the sea.

Thus did the Vision err, for what Child of Light can be born when none remain to bear him?

And thus have I assured that my Purpose shall be served and that the evil of Aldur and his brothers shall not destroy the world which I caused to be created.

The Kingdoms of the West which have harkened unto the counsel and beguilements of wicked Gods and evil sorcerers will be brought unto the dust. And I will harry those who sought to deny me and confound me and multiply their suffering. And they shall be brought low and they shall fall before me, offering themselves as a sacrifice upon my altars.

And the time shall come when I have Lordship and dominion over all the earth, and all peoples shall be mine.

Hear me, ye peoples, and fear me. Bow down before me and worship me. For I am Torak, forever King of Kings, Lord of Lords, and God alone to this world which I have caused to be.

Part One

GAR OG
NADRAK

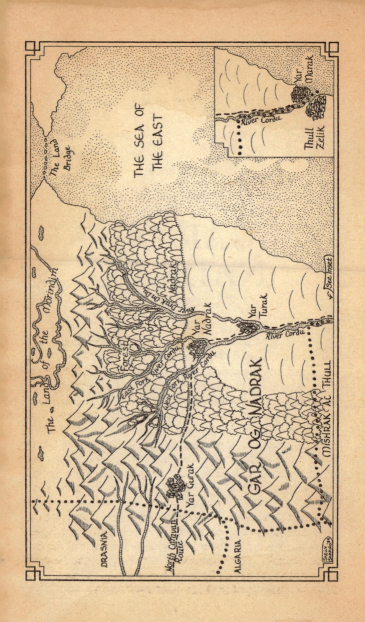

Chapter One

THERE WAS, GARION decided, something defi-
nitely mournful about the sound of mule bells. The mule was
not a particularly loveable animal to begin with, and there was
a subtle difference to his gait that imparted a lugubrious note
to a bell hung about his neck. The mules were the property of
a Drasnian merchant named Mulger, a lanky, hard-eyed man
in a green doublet, who—for a price—had allowed Garion,
Silk, and Belgarath to accompany him on his trek into Gar og
Nadrak. Mulger's mules were laden with trade goods, and
Mulger himself seemed to carry a burden of preconceptions
and prejudices almost as heavy as a fully loaded mule pack.
Silk and the worthy merchant had disliked each other at first
sight, and Silk amused himself by baiting his countryman as
they rode eastward across the rolling moors toward the jagged
peaks that marked the boundary between Drasnia and the land
of the Nadraks. Their discussions, hovering just on the verge
of wrangling, grated on Garion's nerves almost as much as the
tiresome clanging of the bells on Mulger's mules.

Garion's edginess at this particular time came from a very specific source. He was afraid. There was no point in trying to conceal that fact from himself. The cryptic words of the Mrin Codex had been explained to him in precise detail. He was riding toward a meeting that had been ordained since the beginning of time, and there was absolutely no way he could avoid it. The meeting was the end result of not one, but *two* distinct Prophecies, and even if he could persuade one of them that there had been a mistake someplace, the other would drive him to the confrontation without mercy or the slightest consideration for his personal feelings.

"I think you're missing the point, Ambar," Mulger was saying to Silk with that kind of acid precision some men use when talking to someone they truly despise. "My patriotism or lack of it has nothing to do with the matter. The well-being of Drasnia depends on trade, and if you people in the Foreign Service keep hiding your activities by posing as merchants, it won't be long before an *honest* Drasnian isn't welcome anywhere." Mulger, with that instinct that seemed inborn in all Drasnians, had instantly recognized the fact that Silk was not what he pretended to be.

"Oh, come now, Mulger," Silk replied with an airy condescension, "don't be so naïve. Every kingdom in the world conceals its intelligence activities in exactly the same way. The Tolnedrans do it; the Murgos do it; even the Thulls do it. What do you want me to do—walk around with a sign on my chest reading 'spy'?"

"Frankly, Ambar, I don't care what you do," Mulger retorted, his lean face hardening. "All I can say is that I'm getting very tired of being watched everyplace I go, just because you people can't be trusted."

Silk shrugged with an impudent grin. "It's the way the world is, Mulger. You might as well get used to it, because it's not going to change."

Mulger glared at the rat-faced little man helplessly, then turned abruptly and rode back to keep company with his mules.

"Aren't you pushing it a little?" Belgarath suggested, lifting his head from the apparent doze in which he usually rode. "If you irritate him enough, he'll denounce you to the border guards, and we'll never get into Gar og Nadrak."

"Mulger's not going to say a word, old friend," Silk assured him. "If he does, he'll be held for investigation, too, and there's not a merchant alive who doesn't have a few things concealed in his packs that aren't supposed to be there."

"Why don't you just leave him alone?" Belgarath asked.

"It gives me something to do," Silk replied with a shrug. "Otherwise I'd have to look at the scenery, and eastern Drasnia bores me."

Belgarath grunted sourly, pulled his gray hood up over his head, and settled back into his nap.

Garion returned to his melancholy thoughts. The gorse bushes which covered the rolling moors had a depressing gray-green color to them, and the North Caravan Route wound like a dusty white scar across them. The sky had been overcast for nearly two weeks, though there was no hint of moisture in the clouds. They plodded along through a dreary, shadowless world toward the stark mountains looming on the horizon ahead.

It was the unfairness of it all that upset Garion the most. He had never asked for any of this. He did not *want* to be a sorcerer. He did not *want* to be the Rivan King. He was not even sure that he really *wanted* to marry Princess Ce'Nedra— although he was of two minds about that. The little Imperial Princess could be—usually when she wanted something—absolutely adorable. Most of the time, however, she did not want anything, and her true nature emerged. If he had consciously sought any of this, he could have accepted the duty which lay on him with a certain amount of resignation. He had been given no choice in the matter, though, and he found himself wanting to demand of the uncaring sky, "Why me?"

He rode on beside his dozing grandfather with only the murmuring song of the Orb of Aldur for company, and even that was a source of irritation. The Orb, which stood on the pommel of the great sword strapped to his back, sang to him endlessly with a kind of silly enthusiasm. It might be all very well for the Orb to exult about the impending meeting with Torak, but it was Garion who was going to have to face the

Dragon-God of Angarak, and it was Garion who was going to have to do all the bleeding. He felt that the unrelieved cheerfulness of the Orb was—all things considered—in very poor taste, to say the least.

The border between Drasnia and Gar og Nadrak straddled the North Caravan Route in a narrow, rocky gap where two garrisons, one Drasnian and one Nadrak, faced each other across a simple gate that consisted of a single, horizontal pole. By itself, the pole was an insubstantial barrier. Symbolically, however, it was more intimidating than the gates of Vo Mimbre or Tol Honeth. On one side of the gate stood the West; on the other, the East. With a single step, one could move from one world into a totally different one, and Garion wished with all his being that he did not have to take that step.

As Silk had predicted, Mulger said nothing about his suspicions to either the Drasnian pikemen or the leather-clad Nadrak soldiers at the border, and they passed without incident into the mountains of Gar og Nadrak. Once it passed the border, the caravan route climbed steeply up a narrow gorge beside a swiftly tumbling mountain stream. The rock walls of the gorge were sheer, black, and oppressive. The sky overhead narrowed to a dirty gray ribbon, and the clanging mule bells echoed back from the rocks to accompany the rush and pounding gurgle of the stream.

Belgarath awoke and looked around, his eyes alert. He gave Silk a quick, sidelong glance that cautioned the little man to keep his mouth shut, then cleared his throat. "We want to thank you, worthy Mulger, and to wish you good luck in your dealings here."

Mulger looked at the old sorcerer sharply, his eyes questioning.

"We'll be leaving you at the head of this gorge," Belgarath continued smoothly, his face bland. "Our business is off that way." He gestured rather vaguely.

Mulger grunted. "I don't want to know anything about it," he declared.

"You don't, really," Belgarath assured him. "And please

don't take Ambar's remarks too seriously. He has a comic turn of mind and he says things he doesn't always mean, because he enjoys irritating people. Once you get to know him, he's not quite so bad."

Mulger gave Silk a long, hard look and let it pass without comment. "Good luck in whatever it is you're doing," he said grudgingly, forced to say it more out of courtesy than out of any genuine good feeling. "You and the young man weren't bad traveling companions."

"We are in your debt, worthy Mulger," Silk added with mocking extravagance. "Your hospitality has been exquisite."

Mulger looked directly at Silk again. "I don't really like you, Ambar," he said bluntly. "Why don't we just let it go at that?"

"I'm crushed." Silk grinned at him.

"Let it lie," Belgarath growled.

"I made every effort to win him over," Silk protested.

Belgarath turned his back on him.

"I really did." Silk appealed to Garion, his eyes brimming with mock sincerity.

"I don't believe you either," Garion told him.

Silk sighed. "Nobody understands me," he complained. Then he laughed and rode on up the gorge, whistling happily to himself.

At the head of the gorge, they left Mulger and struck off to the left of the caravan route through a jumble of rock and stunted trees. At the crest of a stony ridge, they stopped to watch the slow progress of the mules until they were out of sight.

"Where are we headed?" Silk asked, squinting up at the clouds scudding past overhead. "I thought we were going to Yar Gurak."

"We are," Belgarath replied, scratching at his beard, "but we'll circle around and come at the town from the other side. Mulger's opinions make traveling with him just a bit chancy. He might let something slip at the wrong time. Besides, Garion and I have something to take care of before we get there." The old man looked around. "Over there ought to do," he said, pointing at a shallow green dale, concealed on the far side of the ridge. He led them down into the dale and dismounted.

Silk, leading their single packhorse, pulled up beside a small pool of spring water and tied the horses to a dead snag standing at its edge.

"What is it that we have to do, Grandfather?" Garion asked, sliding out of his saddle.

"That sword of yours is a trifle obvious," the old man told him. "Unless we want to spend the whole trip answering questions, we're going to have to do something about it."

"Are you going to make it invisible?" Silk asked hopefully.

"In a manner of speaking," Belgarath answered. "Open your mind to the Orb, Garion. Just let it talk to you."

Garion frowned. "I don't understand."

"Just relax. The Orb will do the rest. It's very excited about you, so don't pay too much attention to it if it starts making suggestions. It has a severely limited understanding of the real world. Just relax and let your mind sort of drift. I've got to talk to it, and I can only do that through you. It won't listen to anybody else."

Garion leaned back against a tree; in a moment he found his mind filled with all manner of peculiar images. The world he perceived in that imagining was tinged over with a faint blue haze, and everything seemed angular, as if constructed out of the flat planes and sharp edges of a crystal. He caught a vivid picture of himself, flaming sword in hand, riding at great speed with whole hordes of faceless men fleeing out of his path. Belgarath's voice sounded sharply in his mind then. "Stop that." The words, he realized, were not directed at him, but instead at the Orb itself. Then the old man's voice dropped to a murmur, instructing, explaining something. The responses of that other, crystalline awareness seemed a trifle petulant; but eventually there seemed to be an agreement of some kind, and then Garion's mind cleared.

Belgarath was shaking his head with a rueful expression. "It's almost like talking to a child sometimes," he said. "It has no conception of numbers, and it can't even begin to comprehend the meaning of the word danger."

"It's still there," Silk noted, sounding a bit disappointed. "I can still see the sword."

"That's because you know it's there," Belgarath told him. "Other people will overlook it."

"How can you overlook something that big?" Silk objected.

"It's very complicated," Belgarath replied. "The Orb is simply going to encourage people not to see it—or the sword. If they look very closely, they might realize that Garion's carrying *something* on his back, but they won't be curious enough about it to try to find out what it is. As a matter of fact, quite a few people won't even notice Garion himself."

"Are you trying to say that Garion's invisible?"

"No. He's just sort of unremarkable for the time being. Let's move on. Night comes on quickly up in these mountains."

Yar Gurak was perhaps the ugliest town Garion had ever seen. It was strung out on either side of a roiling yellow creek, and muddy, unpaved streets ran up the steep slopes of the cut the stream had gouged out of the hills. The sides of the cut beyond the town had been stripped of all vegetation. There were shafts running back into the hillsides, and great, rooted-out excavations. There were springs among the diggings, and they trickled muddy water down the slopes to pollute the creek. The town had a slapdash quality about it, and all the buildings seemed somewhat temporary. Construction was, for the most part, log and uncut rock, and several of the houses had been finished off with canvas.

The streets teemed with lanky, dark-faced Nadraks, many of whom were obviously drunk. A nasty brawl erupted out of a tavern door as they entered the town, and they were forced to stop while perhaps two dozen Nadraks rolled about in the mud, trying with a fair amount of success to incapacitate or even maim each other.

The sun was going down as they found an inn at the end of a muddy street. It was a large, square building with the main floor constructed of stone, a second storey built of logs, and stables attached to the rear. They put up their horses, took a room for the night, and then entered the barnlike common room in search of supper. The benches in the common room were a bit unsteady, and the tabletops were grease-smeared and littered with crumbs and spilled food. Oil lamps hung smoking on chains, and the smell of cooking cabbage was overpowering. A fair number of merchants from various parts of the world sat at their evening meal in the room—wary-eyed men in tight little groups, with walls of suspicion drawn around them.

Belgarath, Silk, and Garion sat down at an unoccupied table and ate the stew brought to them in wooden bowls by a tipsy servingman in a greasy apron. When they had finished, Silk glanced at the open doorway leading into the noisy taproom and then looked inquiringly at Belgarath.

The old man shook his head. "Better not," he said. "Nadraks are a high-strung people, and relations with the West are a little tense just now. There's no point in asking for trouble."

Silk nodded his glum agreement and led the way up the stairs at the back of the inn to the room they had taken for the night. Garion held up their guttering candle and looked dubiously at the log-frame bunks standing against the walls of the room. The bunks had rope springs and mattresses stuffed with straw; they looked lumpy and not very clean. The noise from the taproom below was loud and raucous.

"I don't think we're going to get much sleep tonight," he observed.

"Mining towns aren't like farm villages," Silk pointed out. "Farmers feel the need for decorum—even when they're drunk. Miners tend on the whole to be somewhat rowdier."

Belgarath shrugged. "They'll quiet down in a bit. Most of them will be unconscious long before midnight." He turned to Silk. "As soon as the shops open up in the morning, I want you to get us some different clothing—used, preferably. If we look like gold hunters, nobody's going to pay very much attention to us. Get a pick handle and a couple of rock hammers. We'll tie them to the outside of the pack on our spare horse for show."

"I get the feeling you've done this before."

"From time to time. It's a useful disguise. Gold hunters are crazy to begin with, so people aren't surprised if they show up in strange places." The old man laughed shortly. "I even found gold once—a vein as thick as your arm."

Silk's face grew immediately intent. "Where?"

Belgarath shrugged. "Off that way somewhere," he replied with a vague gesture. "I forget exactly."

"Belgarath," Silk objected with a note of anguish in his voice.

"Don't get sidetracked," Belgarath told him. "Let's get some sleep. I want to be out of here as early as possible tomorrow morning."

The overcast which had lingered for weeks cleared off during the night; when Garion awoke, the new-risen sun streamed golden through the dirty window. Belgarath was seated at the rough table on the far side of the room, studying a parchment map, and Silk had already left.

"I thought for a while that you were going to sleep past noon," the old man said as Garion sat up and stretched.

"I had trouble getting to sleep last night," Garion replied. "It was a little noisy downstairs."

"Nadraks are like that."

A sudden thought occurred to Garion. "What do you think Aunt Pol is doing just now?" he asked.

"Sleeping, probably."

"Not *this* late."

"It's much earlier where she is."

"I don't follow that."

"Riva's fifteen hundred leagues west of here," Belgarath explained. "The sun won't get that far for several hours yet."

Garion blinked. "I hadn't thought of that," he admitted.

"I didn't think you had."

The door opened, and Silk came in, carrying several bundles and wearing an outraged expression. He threw his bundles down and stamped to the window, muttering curses under his breath.

"What's got you so worked up?" Belgarath asked mildly.

"Would you look at this?" Silk waved a piece of parchment at the old man.

"What's the problem?" Belgarath took the parchment and read it.

"That whole business was settled years ago," Silk declared in an irritated voice. "What are these things doing, still being circulated?"

"The description *is* colorful," Belgarath noted.

"Did you see that?" Silk sounded mortally offended. He turned to Garion. "Do I look like a weasel to you?"

"—an ill-favored, weasel-faced man," Belgarath read, "shifty-eyed and with a long, pointed nose. A notorious cheat at dice."

"Do you *mind*?"

"What's this all about?" Garion asked.

"I had a slight misunderstanding with the authorities some years ago," Silk explained deprecatingly. "Nothing all that serious, actually—but they're *still* circulating that thing." He gestured angrily at the parchment Belgarath was still reading with an amused expression. "They've even gone so far as to offer a *reward*." He considered for a moment. "I'll have to admit that the sum is flattering, though," he added.

"Did you get the things I sent you after?" Belgarath asked.

"Of course."

"Let's change clothes, then, and leave before your unexpected celebrity attracts a crowd."

The worn Nadrak clothing was made mostly of leather—snug black trousers, tight-fitting vests, and short-sleeved linen tunics.

"I didn't bother with the boots," Silk said. "Nadrak boots are pretty uncomfortable—probably since it hasn't occurred to them yet that there's a difference between the right foot and the left." He settled a pointed felt cap at a jaunty angle. "What do you think?" he asked, striking a pose.

"Doesn't look at all like a weasel, does he?" Belgarath asked Garion.

Silk gave him a disgusted look, but said nothing.

They went downstairs, led their horses out of the stables attached to the inn, and mounted. Silk's expression remained sour as they rode out of Yar Gurak. When they reached the top of a hill to the north of town, he slid off his horse, picked up a rock, and threw it rather savagely at the buildings clustered below.

"Make you feel better?" Belgarath asked curiously.

Silk remounted with a disdainful sniff and led the way down the other side of the hill.

Chapter Two

THEY RODE FOR the next few days through a wilderness of stone and stunted trees. The sun grew warmer each day, and the sky overhead was intensely blue as they pressed deeper and deeper into the snowcapped mountains. There were trails of sorts up here, winding, vagrant tracks meandering between the dazzling white peaks and across the high, pale green meadows where wildflowers nodded in the mountain breeze. The air was spiced with the resinous odor of evergreens, and now and then they saw deer grazing or stopping to watch them with large, startled eyes as they passed.

Belgarath moved confidently in a generally eastward course and he appeared to be alert and watchful. There were no signs of the half-doze in which he customarily rode on more clearly defined roads, and he seemed somehow younger up here in the mountains.

They encountered other travelers—leather-clad Nadraks for the most part—although they did see a party of Drasnians laboring up a steep slope and, once, a long way off, what appeared to be a Tolnedran. Their exchanges with these others were brief and wary. The mountains of Gar og Nadrak were at best sketchily policed, and it was necessary for every man who entered them to provide for his own security.

The sole exception to this suspicious taciturnity was a garrulous old gold hunter mounted on a donkey, who appeared out of the blue-tinged shadows under the trees one morning. His tangled hair was white, and his clothing was mismatched, appearing to consist mostly of castoffs he had found beside this trail or that. His tanned, wrinkled face was weathered like a well-cured old hide, and his blue eyes twinkled merrily. He joined them without any greeting or hint of uncertainty as to his welcome and began talking immediately as if taking up a conversation again that had only recently been interrupted.

There was a sort of comic turn to his voice and manner that Garion found immediately engaging.

"Must be ten years or more since I've followed this path," he began, jouncing along on his donkey as he fell in beside Garion. "I don't come down into this part of the mountains very much any more. The streambeds down here have all been worked over a hundred times at least. Which way are you bound?"

"I'm not really sure," Garion replied cautiously. "I've never been up here before, so I'm just following along."

"You'd find better gravel if you struck out to the north," the man on the donkey advised, "up near Morindland. Of course, you've got to be careful up there, but, like they say, no risk, no profit." He squinted curiously at Garion. "You're not a Nadrak, are you?"

"Sendar," Garion responded shortly.

"Never been to Sendaria," the old gold hunter mused. "Never been anyplace really—except up here." He looked around at the white-topped peaks and deep green forests with a sort of abiding love. "Never really wanted to go anyplace else. I've picked these mountains over from end to end for seventy years now and never made much at it—except for the pleasure of being here. Found a river bar one time, though, that had so much red gold in it that it looked like it was bleeding. Winter caught me up there, and I almost froze to death trying to come out."

"Did you go back the next spring?" Garion couldn't help asking.

"Meant to, but I did a lot of drinking that winter—I had gold enough. Anyway, the drink sort of addled my brains. When I set out the following year, I took along a few kegs for company. That's always a mistake. The drink takes you harder when you get up into the mountains, and you don't always pay attention to things the way you should." He leaned back in his donkey saddle, scratching reflectively at his stomach. "I went out onto the plains north of the mountains—up in Morindland. Seems that I thought at the time that the going might be easier out on flat ground. Well, to make it short, I ran across a band of Morindim and they took me prisoner. I'd been up to my ears in an ale keg for a day or so, and I was far gone when they took me. Lucky, I guess. Morindim are superstitious, and they thought I was possessed. That's probably all that saved my life. They kept me for five or six years, trying to puzzle out the meaning behind my ravings—once I got sober and saw the situation, I took quite a bit of care to do a lot of raving. Eventually they got tired of it and weren't so careful about watching me, so I escaped. By then I'd sort of forgotten exactly where that river was. I look for it now and then when I'm up that way." His speech seemed rambling, but his old blue eyes were very penetrating. "That's a big sword you're carrying, boy. Who do you plan to kill with it?"

The question came so fast that Garion did not even have time to be startled.

"Funny thing about that sword of yours," the shabby old man added shrewdly. "It seems to be going out of its way to make itself inconspicuous." Then he turned to Belgarath, who was looking at him with a level gaze. "You haven't hardly changed at all," he noted.

"And you still talk too much," Belgarath replied.

"I get hungry for talk every few years," the old man on the donkey admitted. "Is your daughter well?"

Belgarath nodded.

"Fine-looking woman, your daughter—bad-tempered, though."

"That hasn't changed noticeably."

"Didn't imagine it had." The old gold hunter chuckled, then hesitated for a moment. "If you don't mind some advice, be careful in case you plan to go down into the low country," he said seriously. "It looks like things might be coming to a boil down there. A lot of strangers in red tunics are roaming about, and there's been smoke coming up from old altars that haven't been used for years. The Grolims are out again, and their knives are all new-sharpened. The Nadraks who come up here keep looking back over their shoulders." He paused, looking directly at Belgarath. "There've been some other signs, too," he added. "The animals are all jumpy—like just before a big storm— and sometimes at night, if you listen close, there's something like thunder way off in the distance—like maybe from as far off as Mallorea. The whole world seems to be uneasy. I've got a hunch that something pretty big's about to happen— maybe the sort of thing *you'd* be involved in. The point is that *they* know you're out here. I wouldn't count too much on being able to slip through without somebody noticing you." He shrugged then, as if washing his hands of the matter. "I just thought you'd like to know."

"Thank you," Belgarath replied.

"Didn't cost me anything to say it." The old man shrugged again. "I think I'll go that way." He pointed off to the north. "Too many strangers coming into the mountains in the last few months. It's starting to get crowded. I've about talked myself out now, so I think I'll go look myself up a bit of privacy." He turned his donkey and trotted off. "Good luck," he threw back over his shoulder by way of farewell and then he disappeared into the blue shadows under the trees.

"You're acquainted with him, I take it," Silk observed to Belgarath.

The old sorcerer nodded. "I met him about thirty years ago. Polgara had come to Gar og Nadrak to find out a few things. After she'd gathered all the information she wanted, she sent word to me, and I came here and bought her from the man who owned her. We started home, but an early snowstorm caught us up here in the mountains. He found us floundering along, and he took us to the cave where he holes up when the snow gets too deep. Quite a comfortable cave really—except that he insists on bringing his donkey inside. He and Pol argued about that all winter, as I recall."

"What's his name?" Silk asked curiously.

Belgarath shrugged. "He never said, and it's not polite to ask."

Garion, however, had choked on the word "bought." A kind of helpless outrage welled up in him. "Somebody *owned* Aunt Pol?" he demanded incredulously.

"It's a Nadrak custom," Silk explained. "In their society, women are considered property. It's not seemly for a woman to go about without an owner."

"She was a *slave*?" Garion's knuckles grew white as he clenched his fists.

"Of course she wasn't a slave," Belgarath told him. "Can you even remotely imagine your Aunt submitting to that sort of thing?"

"But you said—"

"I said I bought her from the man who owned her. Their relationship was a formality—nothing more. She needed an owner in order to function here, and he gained a great deal of respect from other men as a result of his ownership of so remarkable a woman." Belgarath made a sour face. "It cost me a fortune to buy her back from him. I sometimes wonder if she was really worth it."

"Grandfather!"

"I'm sure she'd be fascinated by that last observation, old friend," Silk said slyly.

"I don't know that it's necessary to repeat it to her, Silk."

"You never know." Silk laughed. "I might need something from you someday."

"That's disgusting."

"I know." Silk grinned and looked around. "Your friend took quite a bit of trouble to look you up," he suggested. "What was behind it?"

"He wanted to warn me."

"That things were tense in Gar og Nadrak? We knew that already."

"His warning was a great deal more urgent than that."

"He didn't *sound* very urgent."

"That's because you don't know him."

"Grandfather," Garion said suddenly, "how did he manage to see my sword? I thought we'd taken care of that."

"He sees *everything*, Garion. He could glance once at a tree and tell you ten years later exactly how many leaves were on it."

"Is he a sorcerer?"

"Not as far as I know. He's just a strange old man who likes the mountains. He doesn't know what's going on because he doesn't *want* to know. If he really wanted to, he could probably find out everything that's happening in the world."

"He could make a fortune as a spy, then," Silk mused.

"He doesn't want a fortune. Isn't that obvious? Any time he needs money, he just goes back to that river bar he mentioned."

"But he said he'd forgotten how to find it," Garion protested.

Belgarath snorted. "He's never forgotten anything in his life." Then his eyes grew distant. "There are a few people like him in the world—people who have no interest whatsoever in what other people are doing. Maybe that's not such a bad trait. If I had my life to live over, I might not mind doing it his way." He looked around then, his eyes very alert. "Let's take that path over there," he suggested, pointing at a scarcely visible track angling off across an open meadow, littered with bits of log bleached white by sun and weather. "If what he says is true, I think we'll want to avoid any large settlements. That path comes out farther north where there aren't so many people."

Not long afterward the terrain began to slope downward, and the three of them moved along briskly, riding down out of the mountains toward the vastness of the forest of Nadrak. The peaks around them subsided into forested foothills. Once they topped a rise, they were able to look out at the ocean of trees lying below. The forest stretched to the horizon and beyond, dark green beneath a blue sky. A faint breeze was blowing, and the sigh of its passage through the mile upon mile of trees below had a kind of endless sadness to it, a regretful memory of summers past and springs that would never come again.

Some distance up the slope from the forest stood a village, huddled at the side of a vast, open pit that had been gouged, raw and ugly, in the red dirt of the hillside.

"A mine town," Belgarath noted. "Let's nose about a bit and see what's going on."

They rode warily down the hill. As they drew closer, Garion could see that the village had that same temporary kind of appearance he had noticed about Yar Gurak. The buildings were constructed in the same way—unpeeled logs and rough stone—and the low-pitched roofs had large rocks laid on them to keep the shingles from blowing off during the winter blizzards. Nadraks seemed not to be concerned about the external appearance of their structures; once the walls and roofs were completed, they appeared quite content to move in and devote their attentions to other matters, without attending to those final finishing touches which gave a house that look of permanence that a Sendar or a Tolnedran would feel absolutely necessary. The entire settlement seemed to reflect an attitude of "good enough" that offended Garion, for some reason.

Some of the miners who lived in the village came out into the dirt streets to watch the strangers ride in. Their black leather clothing was stained red by the earth in which they dug, and their eyes were hard and suspicious. An air of fearful wariness hung over the whole place, seasoned with a touch of defiant bellicosity.

Silk jerked his head toward a large, low building with a crude painting of a cluster of grapes on a sign banging in the breeze by the double doors at the front. A wide, roofed porch surrounded the building, and leather-garbed Nadraks lounged on benches along the porch, watching a dogfight in progress out in the middle of the street.

Belgarath nodded. "But let's go around to the side," he suggested, "in case we have to leave in a hurry."

They dismounted at the side porch, tied their horses to the railing, and went inside.

The interior of the tavern was smoky and dim, since windows seemed to be a rare feature in Nadrak buildings. The tables and benches were rough-hewn, and what light there was came from smoking oil lamps that hung on chains from the rafters. The floor was mud-stained and littered with bits of food. Dogs roamed at will under the tables and benches. The smell of stale beer and unwashed bodies hung heavy in the air, and, though it was only early afternoon, the place was crowded. Many of the men in the large room were already far gone with drink. It was noisy, since the Nadraks lounging at the tables or stumbling about the room seemed all habitually to speak at the top of their voices.

Belgarath pushed his way toward a table in the corner where a solitary man sat bleary-eyed and slack-lipped, staring into his ale cup.

"You don't mind if we share the table, do you?" the old man demanded of him in an abrupt manner, sitting down without awaiting a reply.

"Would it do any good if I did?" the man with the cup asked. He was unshaven, and his eyes were pouchy and bloodshot.

"Not much," Belgarath told him bluntly.

"You're new here, aren't you?" The Nadrak looked at the three of them with only a hint of curiosity, trying with some difficulty to focus his eyes.

"I don't really see that it's any of your business," Belgarath retorted rudely.

"You've got a sour mouth for a man past his prime," the Nadrak suggested, flexing his fingers ominously.

"I came here to drink, not fight," Silk declared in a harsh tone. "I might change my mind later, but right now, I'm thirsty." He reached out and caught the arm of a passing servingman. "Ale," he ordered. "And don't take all day."

"Keep your hands to yourself," the servingman told him. "Are you with him?" He pointed at the Nadrak they had joined.

"We're sitting with him, aren't we?"

"You want three cups or four?"

"I want one—for now. Bring the others what they want, too. I'll pay for the first time around."

The servingman grunted sourly and pushed his way off through the crowd, pausing long enough to kick a dog out of his way.

Silk's offer seemed to quiet their Nadrak companion's belligerence. "You've picked a bad time to come to town," he told them. "The whole region's crawling with Mallorean recruiters."

"We've been up in the mountains," Belgarath said. "We'll probably go back in a day or so. Whatever's happening down here doesn't interest us very much."

"You'd better take an interest while you're here—unless you'd like to try army life."

"Is there a war someplace?" Silk asked him.

"Likely to be—or so they say. Someplace down in Mishrak ac Thull."

Silk snorted. "I've never met a Thull worth fighting."

"It's not the Thulls. It's supposed to be the Alorns. They've got a *queen*—if you can imagine such a thing—and she's moving to invade the Thulls."

"A *queen*?" Silk scoffed. "Can't be much of an army, then. Let the Thulls fight her themselves."

"Tell that to the Mallorean recruiters," the Nadrak suggested.

"Did you have to *brew* that ale?" Silk demanded of the servingman, who was returning with four large cups.

"There are other taverns, friend," the servingman replied. "If you don't like this one, go find another. That'll be twelve pennies."

"Three pennies a cup?" Silk exclaimed.

"Times are hard."

Grumbling, Silk paid him.

"Thanks," the Nadrak they were sitting with said, taking one of the cups.

"Don't mention it," Silk said sourly.

"What are the Malloreans doing here?" Belgarath asked.

"Rounding up everyone who can stand up, see lightning, and hear thunder. They do their recruiting with leg-irons, so it's a little hard to refuse. They've got Grolims with them too, and the Grolims keep their gutting knives out in plain sight as a sort of a hint about what might happen to anybody who objects too much."

"Maybe you were right when you said we picked a bad time to come down out of the mountains," Silk said.

The Nadrak nodded. "The Grolims say that Torak's stirring in his sleep."

"That's not very good news," Silk replied.

"I think we could all drink to that." The Nadrak lifted his ale cup. "You find anything worth digging for up there in the mountains?"

Silk shook his head. "A few traces is all. We've been working the streambeds for free gold. We don't have the equipment to drive shafts back into the rock."

"You'll never get rich squatting beside a creek and sifting gravel."

"We get by." Silk shrugged. "Someday maybe we'll hit a good pocket and we'll be able to pick up enough to buy some equipment."

"And someday maybe it will rain beer, too."

Silk laughed.

"You ever thought about taking in another partner?"

Silk squinted at the unshaven Nadrak. "Have you been up there before?" he asked.

The Nadrak nodded. "Often enough to know that I don't like it—but I think I'd like a stint in the army a lot less."

"Let's have another drink and talk about it," Silk suggested.

Garion leaned back, putting his shoulders against the rough log wall. Nadraks didn't seem to be so bad, once you got past the crudity of their nature. They were a blunt-spoken people and a bit sour-faced, but they did not seem to have that icy animosity toward outsiders he had noted among the Murgos.

He let his mind drift back to what the Nadrak had said about a queen. He quickly dismissed the notion that any of the queens staying at Riva might, under any circumstances, have assumed such authority. That left only Aunt Pol. The Nadrak's information could have been garbled a bit; but in Belgarath's absence, Aunt Pol *might* have taken charge of things—although that was not like her, at all. What could possibly have happened back there to force her to go to such extremes?

As the afternoon wore on, more and more of the men in the tavern grew reeling drunk, and occasional fights broke out—although the fights usually consisted of shoving matches, since few in the room were sober enough to aim a good blow. Their companion drank steadily and eventually laid his head down on his arms and began to snore.

"I think we've got just about everything we can use here," Belgarath suggested quietly. "Let's drift on out. From what our friend here says, I don't think it'd be a good idea to sleep in town."

Silk nodded his agreement, and the three of them rose from the table and made their way through the crowd to the side door.

"Did you want to pick up any supplies?" the little man asked.

Belgarath shook his head. "I have a feeling that we want to get out of here as soon as possible."

Silk gave him a quick look, and the three of them untied their horses, mounted and rode back out into the red dirt street. They moved at a walk to avoid arousing suspicion, but Garion could feel a sort of tense urgency to put this raw, mud-smeared village behind them. There was something threatening in the air, and the golden late afternoon sun seemed somehow shadowed, as if by an unseen cloud. As they were passing the last rickety house on the downhill edge of the village, they heard an alarmed shout from somewhere back near the center of town. Garion turned quickly and saw a party of perhaps twenty mounted men in red tunics plunging at a full gallop toward the tavern the three of them had just left. With a practiced skill, the scarlet-clad strangers swung down from their horses and immediately covered all the doors to cut off an escape for those inside.

"Malloreans!" Belgarath snapped. "Make for the trees!" And he drove his heels into his horse's flanks. They galloped across the weedy, stump-cluttered clearing that surrounded the village, toward the edge of the forest and safety, but there was no outcry or pursuit. The tavern appeared to contain enough fish to fill the Mallorean net. From a safe vantage point beneath spreading tree limbs, Garion, Silk, and Belgarath watched as a disconsolate-looking string of Nadraks, chained together at the ankle, were led out of the tavern into the red dust of the street to stand under the watchful eyes of the Mallorean re- cruiters.

"It looks like our friend has joined the army, after all," Silk observed.

"Better him than us," Belgarath replied. "We might be just a little out of place in the middle of an Angarak horde." He squinted at the ruddy disk of the setting sun. "Let's move out. We've got a few hours before dark. It looks as if military service might be contagious in this vicinity, and I wouldn't want to catch it."

Chapter Three

THE FOREST OF Nadrak was unlike the Arendish forest lying far to the south. The differences were subtle, and it took Garion several days to put his finger on them. For one thing, the trails they followed had no sense of permanence about them. They were so infrequently traveled that they were not beaten into the loamy soil of the forest floor. In the Arendish forest, the marks of man were everywhere, but here man was an intruder, merely passing through. Moreover, the forest in Arendia had definite boundaries, but this ocean of trees went on to the farthest edge of the continent, and it had stood so since the beginning of the world.

The forest teemed with life. Tawny deer flickered among the trees, and vast, shaggy bison, with curved black horns shiny as onyx, grazed in clearings. Once a bear, grumbling and muttering irritably, lumbered across the trail in front of them. Rabbits scurried through the undergrowth and partridges exploded into flight from underfoot with a heart-stopping thunder of wings. The ponds and streams abounded with fish, muskrat, otter, and beaver. There were also, they soon discovered, smaller forms of life. The mosquitoes seemed only slightly smaller than sparrows, and there was a nasty little brown fly that bit anything that moved.

The sun rose early and set late, dappling the dark forest floor with golden light. Although it was midsummer now, it was never exactly hot, and the air was rich with that smell of urgent growth common to the lands of the north, where summer was short and winter very long.

Belgarath seemed not to sleep at all once they entered the forest. Each evening, as Silk and Garion wearily rolled themselves in their blankets, the old sorcerer threaded his way back into the shadowy trees and disappeared. Once, several hours past dusk on a night filled with starlight, Garion awoke briefly and heard the loping touch of paws skittering lightly across a leaf-carpeted clearing; even as he drifted back to sleep, he understood. The great silver wolf who was his grandfather roamed the night, scouring the surrounding forest for any hint of pursuit or danger.

The old man's nocturnal roamings were as silent as smoke, but they did not pass unnoticed. Early one morning, before the sun rose and while the trees were still hazy and half-obscured by ground fog, several shadowy shapes drifted among the dark trunks and stopped not far away. Garion, who had just risen and was preparing to stir up the fire, froze half-bent over. As he slowly straightened, he could feel eyes on him, and his skin prickled peculiarly. Perhaps ten feet away stood a huge, dark gray wolf. The wolf's expression was serious, and its eyes were as yellow as sunlight. There was an unspoken question in those golden eyes, and Garion realized that he understood that question.

"One wonders why you are doing that?"

"Doing what?" Garion asked politely, responding automatically in the language of wolves.

"Going about in that peculiar form."

"It's necessary to do it."

"Ah." With exquisite courtesy the wolf did not pursue the

matter further. "One is curious to know if you don't find it somewhat restricting," he noted however.

"It's not as bad as it looks—once one gets used to it."

The wolf looked unconvinced. He sat down on his haunches. "One has seen the other one several times in the past few darknesses," he said in the manner of wolves, "and one is curious to know why you and he have come into our range."

Garion knew instinctively that his answer to that question was going to be very important. "We are going from one place to another," he replied carefully. "It is not our intention to seek dens or mates in your range or to hunt the creatures that are yours." He could not have explained how he knew what to say.

The wolf seemed satisfied with his response. "One would be pleased if you would present our esteem to the one with fur like frost," he said formally. "One has noted that he is worthy of great respect."

"One would be pleased to give him your words," Garion responded, a bit surprised at how easily the elaborate phrasing came to him.

The wolf lifted his head and sniffed at the air. "It is time for us to hunt," he said. "May you find what you seek."

"May your hunt be successful," Garion returned.

The wolf turned and padded back into the fog, followed by his companions.

"On the whole, you handled that rather well, Garion," Belgarath said from the deep shadows of a nearby thicket.

Garion jumped, a bit startled. "I didn't know you were there," he said.

"You should have," the old man replied, stepping out of the shadows.

"How did he know?" Garion asked. "That I'm a wolf sometimes, I mean?"

"It shows. A wolf is very alert to that sort of thing."

Silk came out from under the tree where he had been sleeping. The little man's step was wary, but his nose twitched with curiosity. "What was that all about?" he asked.

"The wolves wanted to know what we were doing in their

territory," Belgarath replied. "They were investigating to see if they were going to have to fight us."

"Fight?" Garion was startled.

"It's customary when a strange wolf enters the hunting range of another pack. Wolves prefer not to fight—it's a waste of energy—but they will, if the situation demands it."

"What happened?" Silk asked. "Why did they just go away like that?"

"Garion convinced them that we were just passing through."

"That was clever of him."

"Why don't you stir up the fire, Garion?" Belgarath suggested. "Let's have some breakfast and move on. It's still a long way to Mallorea, and we don't want to run out of good weather."

Later that same day, they rode down into a valley where a collection of log houses and tents stood beside a fair-sized stream at the edge of a meadow.

"Fur traders," Silk explained to Garion, pointing at the rough settlement. "There are places like this on just about every major stream in this part of the forest." The little man's pointed nose began to twitch, and his eyes grew bright. "A lot of buying and selling goes on in these little towns."

"Never mind," Belgarath told him pointedly. "Try to keep your predatory instincts under control."

"I wasn't even considering anything," Silk protested.

"Really? Aren't you feeling well?"

Silk loftily ignored that.

"Wouldn't it be safer to go around it?" Garion asked as they rode across the broad meadow.

Belgarath shook his head. "I want to know what's going on ahead of us, and the quickest way to find out is to talk to people who've been there. We'll drift in, circulate for an hour or so and then drift on out again. Just keep your ears open. If anyone asks, we're on our way toward the north range to look for gold."

There were differences between the hunters and trappers who roamed the streets of this settlement and the miners they

had met in the last village. They were more open for one
thing—less surly and distinctly less belligerent. Garion surmised that the enforced solitude of their occupation made them
appreciate companionship all the more during their infrequent
visits to the fur-trading centers. Although they drank probably
as much as the miners, their drinking seemed to lead more
often to singing and laughter than to fighting.

A large tavern stood near the center of the village, and they
rode slowly along a dirt street toward it. "Side door," Belgarath
said tersely as they dismounted in front of the tavern, and they
led their horses around the building and tied them at the porch
railing.

The interior of the tavern was cleaner, less crowded, and
somewhat lighter than the miners' tavern had been, and it
smelled of woods and open air instead of damp, musty earth.
The three of them sat at a table not far from the door and
ordered cups of ale from a polite servingman. The ale was a
rich, dark brown, well chilled, and surprisingly inexpensive.

"The fur buyers own the place," Silk explained, wiping foam
from his upper lip. "They've discovered that a trapper is easier
to bargain with if he's a little drunk, so they make the ale cheap
and plentiful."

"I suppose that makes sense," Garion admitted, "but don't
the trappers know that?"

"Of course they do."

"Why do they drink before they do business, then?"

Silk shrugged. "They like to drink."

The two trappers seated at the next table were renewing an
acquaintanceship that obviously stretched back a dozen years
or more. Their beards were both touched with gray, but they
spoke lightheartedly in the manner of much younger men.

"You have any trouble with Morindim while you were up
there?" one was asking the other.

The second shook his head. "I put pestilence-markers on
both ends of the valley where I set out my traps," he replied.
"A Morind will go a dozen leagues out of his way to avoid a
spot that's got pestilence."

The first nodded his agreement. "That's usually the best

way. Gredder always claimed that curse-markers worked better; but as it turned out, he was wrong."

"I haven't seen him in the last few seasons."

"I'd be surprised if you had. The Morindim got him about three years ago. I buried him myself—what was left of him anyway."

"Didn't know that. Spent a winter with him once over on the headwaters of the Cordu. He was a mean-tempered sort of a man. I'm surprised that the Morindim would cross a curse-marker, though."

"As near as I could judge, some magician came along and uncursed his markers. I found a dried weasel foot hung from one of them with three stems of grass tied around each toe."

"That's a potent spell. They must have wanted him pretty badly for a magician to take that much trouble."

"You know how he was. He could irritate people ten leagues away just walking by."

"That's the truth."

"Not any more, though. His skull's decorating some Morind magician's quest-staff now."

Garion leaned toward his grandfather. "What do they mean when they talk about markers?" he whispered.

"They're warnings," Belgarath replied. "Usually sticks poked into the ground and decorated with bones or feathers. The Morindim can't read, so you can't just put up a signboard for them."

A stooped old trapper, his leather clothing patched and shiny from wear, shuffled toward the center of the tavern. His lined, bearded face had a slightly apologetic expression on it. Following after him came a young Nadrak woman in a heavy, red felt dress belted about the waist with a glittering chain. There was a leash about her neck, and the old trapper held the end of the tether firmly in his fist. Despite the leash, the young woman's face had a proud, disdainful look, and she stared at the men in the tavern with barely concealed contempt. When the old trapper reached the center of the room, he cleared his throat to get the attention of the crowd. "I've got a woman I want to sell," he announced loudly.

Without changing expression the woman spat upon him.

"Now you know that's just going to lower your price, Vella," the old man told her in a placating tone of voice.

"You're an idiot, Tashor," she retorted. "No one here can afford me—you know that. Why didn't you do what I told you to and offer me to the fur buyers?"

"The fur buyers aren't interested in women, Vella," Tashor replied in that same mild tone. "The price will be better here, believe me."

"I wouldn't believe you if you said the sun was going to rise tomorrow, you old fool."

"The woman, as you can see, is quite spirited," Tashor announced rather lamely.

"Is he trying to sell his wife?" Garion demanded, choking on his ale.

"She isn't his wife," Silk corrected. "He owns her, that's all."

Garion clenched his fists and half-rose, his face mottled with anger, but Belgarath's hand closed firmly about his wrist. "Sit down," the old man ordered.

"But—"

"I said sit down, Garion. This is none of your business."

"Unless you want to buy the woman, of course," Silk suggested lightly.

"Is she healthy?" a lean-faced trapper with a scar across one cheek called to Tashor.

"She is," Tashor declared, "and she's got all her teeth, too. Show them your teeth, Vella."

"They aren't looking at my teeth, idiot," she told him, looking directly at the scar-faced trapper with a sultry challenge in her black eyes.

"She's an excellent cook," Tashor continued quickly, "and she knows remedies for rheumatism and ague. She can dress and tan hides and she doesn't eat too much. Her breath doesn't smell too bad—unless she eats onions—and she almost never snores, except when she's drunk."

"If she's such a good woman, why do you want to sell her?" the lean-faced trapper wanted to know.

"I'm getting older," Tashor replied, "and I'd like a little peace and quiet. Vella's exciting to be around, but I've had all the excitement I need. I think I'd like to settle down some-place—maybe raise some chickens or goats." The bent old trapper's voice sounded a trifle plaintive.

"Oh, this is impossible," Vella burst out. "Do I have to do everything myself? Get out of the way, Tashor." Rudely, she pushed the old trapper aside and glared at the crowd, her black eyes flashing. "All right," she announced firmly, "let's get down to business. Tashor wants to sell me. I'm strong and healthy. I can cook, cure hides and skins, tend to common illnesses, bargain closely when I buy supplies, and I can brew good beer." Her eyes narrowed grimly. "I have not gone to any man's bed, and I keep my daggers sharp enough to persuade strangers not to try to force me. I can play the wood-flute and I know many old stories. I can make curse-markers and pes-tilence-markers and dream-markers to frighten off the Morin-dim and once I killed a bear at thirty paces with a bow."

"Twenty paces," Tashor corrected mildly.

"It was closer to thirty," she insisted.

"Can you dance?" the lean trapper with the scarred face asked.

She looked directly at him. "Only if you're seriously inter-ested in buying me," she replied.

"We can talk about that after I see you dance," he said.

"Can you hold a beat?" she demanded.

"I can."

"Very well." Her hands went to the chain about her waist, and it jingled as she unfastened it. She opened the heavy red dress, stepped out of it, and handed it to Tashor. Then she carefully untied the leash from about her neck and bound a ribbon of red silk about her head to hold back her wealth of lustrous, blue-black hair. Beneath the red felt dress, she wore a filmy rose-colored gown of Mallorean silk that whispered and clung to her as she moved. The silk gown reached to midcalf, and she wore soft leather boots on her feet. Protruding from the top of each boot was the jeweled hilt of a dagger, and a third dagger rode on the leather belt about her waist. Her

gown was caught in a tight collar about her throat, but it left
her arms bare to the shoulder. She wore a half-dozen narrow
gold bracelets about each wrist. With a conscious grace, she
bent and fastened a string of small bells to each ankle. Then
she lifted her smoothly rounded arms until her hands were
beside her face. "This is the beat, scar-face," she told the
trapper. "Try to hold it." And she began to clap her hands
together. The beat was three measured claps followed by four
staccato ones. Vella began her dance slowly with a kind of
insolent strut. Her gown whispered as she moved, its hem
sighing about her lush calves.

The lean trapper took up her beat, his callused hands clapping together loudly in the sudden silence as Vella danced.

Garion began to blush. Vella's movements were subtle and
fluid. The bells at her ankles and the bracelets about her wrists
played a tinkling counterpoint to the trapper's beat. Her feet
seemed almost to flicker in the intricate steps of her dance, and
her arms wove patterns in the air. Other, even more interesting,
things were going on inside the rose-colored, gossamer gown.
Garion swallowed hard and discovered that he had almost
stopped breathing.

Vella began to whirl, and her long black hair flared out,
almost perfectly matching the flare of her gown. Then she
slowed and once again dropped back into that proud, sensual
strut that challenged every man in the room.

They cheered when she stopped, and she smiled a slow,
mysterious little smile.

"You dance very well," the scar-faced trapper observed in
a neutral voice.

"Naturally," she replied. "I do everything very well."

"Are you in love with anyone?" The question was bluntly
put.

"No man has won my heart," Vella declared flatly. "I haven't
seen a man yet who was worthy of me."

"That may change," the trapper suggested. "One goldmark."
It was a firm offer.

"You're not serious," she snorted. "Five goldmarks."

"One and a half," he countered.

"This is just *too* insulting." Vella raised both hands up in the air, and her face took on a tragic expression. "Not a copper less than four."

"Two goldmarks," the trapper offered.

"Unbelievable!" she exclaimed, spreading both arms. "Why don't you just cut my heart out and have done with it? I couldn't consider anything less than three and a half."

"To save time, why don't we just say three?" He said it firmly. "With intention that the arrangement become permanent," he added, almost as an afterthought.

"Permanent?" Vella's eyes widened.

"I like you," he replied. "Well, what do you say?"

"Stand up and let me have a look at you," she ordered him.

Slowly he unwound himself from the chair in which he had lounged. His tall body was as lean as his scarred face, and there was a hard-muscled quality about him. Vella pursed her lips and looked him over. "Not bad, is he?" she murmured to Tashor.

"You could do worse, Vella," her owner answered encouragingly.

"I'll consider your offer of three with intentions," Vella declared. "Have you got a name?"

"Tekk," the tall trapper introduced himself with a slight bow.

"Well then, Tekk," Vella told him, "don't go away. Tashor and I need to talk over your offer." She gave him an almost shy look. "I think I like you, too," she added in a much less challenging tone. Then she took hold of the leash that was still wrapped around Tashor's fist and led him out of the tavern, glancing back over her shoulder once or twice at the lean-faced Tekk.

"That is a *lot* of woman," Silk murmured with a note of profound respect.

Garion found that he was able to breathe again, though his ears still felt very hot. "What did they mean by intention?" he quietly asked Silk.

"Tekk offered an arrangement that usually leads to marriage," Silk explained.

That baffled Garion. "I don't understand at all," he confessed.

"Just because someone owns her doesn't give him any special rights to her person," Silk told him, "and those daggers of hers enforce that. One does *not* approach a Nadrak woman unless one's tired of living. *She* makes that decision. The wedding customarily takes place after the birth of her first child."

"Why was she so interested in the price?"

"Because she gets half," Silk shrugged.

"She gets half of the money every time she's sold?" Garion was incredulous.

"Of course. It'd hardly be fair otherwise, would it?"

The servingman who was bringing them three more cups of ale had stopped and was staring openly at Silk.

"Is something wrong, friend?" Silk asked him mildly.

The servingman lowered his eyes quickly. "Sorry," he mumbled. "I just thought—you reminded me of somebody, that's all. Now that I see you closer, I realize that I was mistaken." He put down the cups quickly, turned, and left without picking up the coins Silk had laid on the table.

"I think we'd better leave," Silk said quietly.

"What's the matter?" Garion asked him.

"He knows who I am—and there's that reward notice that's being circulated."

"Maybe you're right," Belgarath agreed, rising to his feet.

"He's talking with those men over there," Garion said, watching the servingman, who was in urgent conversation with a group of hunters on the far side of the room and was casting frequent looks in their direction.

"We've got about a half a minute to get outside," Silk said tensely. "Let's go."

The three of them moved quickly toward the door.

"You there!" someone behind them shouted. "Wait a minute!"

"Run!" Belgarath barked, and they bolted outside and hurled themselves into their saddles just as a half-dozen leather-garbed men burst out through the tavern door.

The shout, "Stop those men!" went largely unheeded as they

galloped off down the street. Trappers and hunters as a breed were seldom inclined to mix themselves in other men's affairs, and Garion, Silk, and Belgarath had passed through the village and were splashing across a ford before any kind of pursuit could be organized.

Silk was swearing as they entered the forest on the far side of the river, spitting out oaths like melon seeds. His profanity was colorful and wide-ranging, reflecting on the birth, parentage, and uncleanly habits of not only those pursuing them, but of those responsible for circulating the reward notice as well.

Belgarath reined in sharply, raising his hand as he did. Silk and Garion hauled their horses to a stop. Silk continued to swear.

"Do you suppose you could cut short your eloquence for a moment?" Belgarath asked him. "I'm trying to listen."

Silk muttered a few more choice oaths, then clamped his teeth shut. There were confused shouts far behind them and a certain amount of splashing.

"They're crossing the stream," Belgarath noted. "It looks as if they plan to take the business seriously. Seriously enough to chase us, at any rate."

"Won't they give up when it gets dark?" Garion asked.

"These are Nadrak hunters," Silk said, sounding profoundly disgusted. "They'll follow us for days—just for the enjoyment of the hunt."

"There's not much we can do about that now," Belgarath grunted. "Let's see if we can outrun them." And he thumped his heels to his horse.

It was midafternoon as they rode at a gallop through the sunlit forest. The undergrowth was scanty, and the tall, straight trunks of fir and pine rose like great columns toward the blue sky overhead. It was a good day for a ride, but not a good day for being chased. No day was good for that.

They topped a rise and stopped again to listen. "They seem to be falling behind," Garion noted hopefully.

"That's just the drunk ones," Silk disagreed sourly. "The ones who are serious about all this are probably much closer.

You don't shout when you're hunting. See—look back there."
He pointed.

Garion looked. There was a pale flicker back among the
trees. A man on a white horse was riding in their direction,
leaning far over in his saddle and looking intently at the ground
as he rode.

"If he's any kind of tracker at all, it will take us a week to
shake him off," Silk said disgustedly.

Somewhere, far off among the trees to their right, a wolf
howled.

"Let's keep going," Belgarath told them.

They galloped on then, plunging down the far side of the
rise, threading their way among the trees. The thud of their
horses' hoofs was a muffled drumming on the thick loam of
the forest floor, and clots of half-decayed debris spattered out
behind them as they fled.

"We're leaving a trail as wide as a house," Silk shouted to
Belgarath.

"That can't be helped for now," the old man replied. "We
need some more distance before we start playing games with
the tracks."

Another howl drifted mournfully through the forest, from
the left this time. It seemed a bit closer than the first had been.

They rode on for another quarter of an hour and then they
suddenly heard a great babble of confusion to the rear. Men
were shouting with alarm, and horses squealed in panic. Garion
could also hear savage growls. At Belgarath's signal, they
slowed their horses to listen. The terrified squeals of horses
rang sharply through the trees, punctuated by their riders' curses
and frightened shouts. A chorus of howls rose from all around.
The forest seemed suddenly full of wolves. The pursuit behind
them disintegrated as the horses of the Nadrak reward hunters
bolted with screams of sheer panic in all directions.

With a certain grim satisfaction, Belgarath listened to the
fading sounds behind them. Then, his tongue lolling from his
mouth, a huge, dark-furred wolf trotted out of the woods about
thirty yards away, stopped, and dropped to his haunches, his
yellow eyes gazing intently at them.

"Keep a tight grip on your reins," Belgarath instructed quietly, stroking the neck of his suddenly wild-eyed mount.

The wolf did not say anything, but merely sat and watched.

Belgarath returned that steady gaze quite calmly, then finally nodded once in acknowledgment. The wolf rose, turned, and started off into the trees. He stopped once, glanced back over his shoulder at them, and raised his muzzle to lift the deep, bell-toned howl that summoned the other members of his pack to return to their interrupted hunt. Then, with a flicker he was gone, and only the echo of his howl remained.

Chapter Four

THEY RODE EAST for the next several days, gradually descending into a broad, marshy valley where the undergrowth was denser and the air noticeably more humid. A brief summer shower rolled in one afternoon, accompanied by great, ripping crashes of thunder, a deluge of pounding rain, and winds that howled among the trees, bending and tossing them and tearing leaves and twigs from the underbrush to whirl and fly among the dark trunks. The storm soon passed, however, and the sun came out again. After that, the weather continued fair, and they made good time.

Garion felt a peculiar sense of incompleteness as he rode and he sometimes caught himself looking around for missing friends. The long journey in search of the Orb had established a sort of pattern in his mind, a sense of rightness and wrongness, and this trip felt wrong. Barak was not with them, for one thing, and the big, red-bearded Cherek's absence made Garion feel oddly insecure. He also missed the hawk-faced, silent

48

Hettar and the armored form of Mandorallen riding always at the front, with the silver-and-blue pennon snapping from the tip of his lance. He was painfully lonely for Durnik the smith and he even missed Ce'Nedra's spiteful bickering. What had happened at Riva became less and less real to him, and all the elaborate ceremony that had attended his betrothal to the impossible little princess began to fade in his memory, like some half-forgotten dream.

It was one evening, however, after the horses had been picketed and supper was over and they had rolled themselves in their blankets to sleep, that Garion, staring into the dying embers of their fire, came at last to face the central vacancy that had entered his life. Aunt Pol was not with them, and he missed her terribly. Since childhood, he had felt that, so long as Aunt Pol was nearby, nothing could really go wrong that she could not fix. Her calm, steady presence had been the one thing to which he had always clung. As clearly as if she stood before him, Garion could see her face, her glorious eyes, and the white lock at her brow; the sudden loneliness for her was as sharp as the edge of a knife.

Everything felt wrong without her. Belgarath was here, certainly, and Garion was fairly sure that his grandfather could deal with any purely physical dangers, but there were other, less obvious perils that the old man either did not consider or chose to ignore. To whom could Garion turn when he was afraid, for example? Being afraid was not the sort of thing that endangered life or limb, but it was still an injury of sorts— and sometimes a deeper and more serious kind of injury. Aunt Pol had always been able to banish his fears, but now she was not here, and Garion was afraid and he could not even admit it. He sighed and pulled his blankets more closely about him and slowly drifted into a troubled sleep.

It was about noon some days later when they reached the east fork of the River Cordu, a broad, dirty brown flow running through a brushy valley in a generally southerly direction toward the capital at Yar Nadrak. The pale green, waist-high brush extended back several hundred yards from either bank of the river and was silt-smeared by the high waters of the spring runoff. The sultry air above the brush was alive with clouds of gnats and mosquitoes.

A sullen boatman ferried them across to the village standing on the far bank. As they led their horses off onto the ferry landing, Belgarath spoke quietly. "I think we'll want to change direction here," he told them. "Let's split up. I'll go pick up supplies, and the two of you go find the town tavern. See if you can get some information about passes leading up through the north range into the lands of the Morindim. The sooner we get up there, the better. The Malloreans seem to be getting the upper hand here and they could clamp down without much warning. I don't want to have to start explaining my every move to Mallorean Grolims—not to mention the fact that there's a great deal of interest in Silk's whereabouts just now."

Silk rather glumly agreed. "I'd like to get that matter straightened out, but I don't suppose we really have the time, do we?"

"No, not really. The summer is very, very short up north, and the crossing to Mallorea is unpleasant, even in the best weather. When you get to the tavern, tell everybody that we want to try our luck in the gold fields of the north range. There's bound to be somebody around who'll want to show off his familiarity with trails and passes—particularly if you offer to buy him a few drinks."

"I thought you said you knew the way," Silk protested.

"I know *one* way—but it's a hundred leagues east of here. Let's see if there's something a little closer. I'll come by the tavern after I get the supplies." The old man mounted and went off up the dirt street, leading their packhorse behind him.

Silk and Garion had little trouble finding someone in the smelly tavern willing to talk about trails and passes. Quite to the contrary, their first question sparked a general debate.

"That's the long way around, Besher," one tipsy gold hunter interrupted another's detailed description of a mountain pass. "You go *left* at the falls of the stream. It saves you three days."

"I'm telling this, Varn," Besher retorted testily, banging his fist down on the scarred table. "You can tell them about the way you go when I'm finished."

"It'll take you all day—just like that trail you're so fond of. They want to go look for gold, not admire scenery." Varn's long, stubbled jaw thrust out belligerently.

"Which way do we go when we get to the long meadow up on top?" Silk asked quickly, trying to head off the hostilities.

"You go right," Besher declared, glaring at Varn.

Varn thought about that as if looking for an excuse to disagree. Finally he reluctantly nodded. "Of course that's the only way you *can* go," he added, "but once you get through the juniper grove, you turn left." He said it in the tone of a man anticipating contradiction.

"*Left?*" Besher objected loudly. "You're a blockhead, Varn. You go *right* again."

"Watch who you're calling a blockhead, you jackass!"

Without any further discussion, Besher punched Varn in the mouth, and the two of them began to pummel each other, reeling about and knocking over benches and tables.

"They're both wrong, of course," another miner sitting at a nearby table observed calmly, watching the fight with a clinical detachment. "You keep going straight after you get through the juniper grove."

Several burly men, wearing loose-fitting red tunics over their polished mail shirts, had entered the tavern unnoticed during the altercation, and they stepped forward, grinning, to separate Varn and Besher as the two rolled around on the dirty floor. Garion felt Silk stiffen beside him. "Malloreans!" the little man said softly.

"What do we do?" Garion whispered, looking around for a way of escape. But before Silk could answer, a black-robed Grolim stepped through the door.

"I like to see men who are so eager to fight," the Grolim purred in a peculiar accent. "The army needs such men."

"Recruiters!" Varn exclaimed, breaking away from the red-garbed Malloreans and dashing toward a side door. For a second it looked as if he might escape; but as he reached the doorway, someone outside rapped him sharply across the forehead with a stout cudgel. He reeled back, suddenly rubber-legged and vacant-eyed. The Mallorean who had hit him came inside, gave him a critical, appraising glance, and then judiciously clubbed him in the head again.

"Well?" the Grolim asked, looking around with amusement. "What's it to be? Would any more of you like to run, or would you all prefer to come along quietly?"

"Where are you taking us?" Besher demanded, trying to pull his arm out of the grip of one of the grinning recruiters.

"To Yar Nadrak first," the Grolim replied, "and then south to the plains of Mishrak ac Thull and the encampment of his Imperial Majesty 'Zakath, Emperor of all Mallorea. You've just joined the army, my friends. All of Angarak rejoices in your courage and patriotism, and Torak himself is pleased with you." As if to emphasize his words, the Grolim's hand strayed to the hilt of the sacrificial knife sheathed at his belt.

The chain clinked spitefully as Garion, fettered at the ankle, plodded along, one in a long line of disconsolate-looking conscripts, following a trail leading generally southward through the brush along the riverbank. The conscripts had all been roughly searched for weapons—all but Garion, who for some reason had been overlooked. He was painfully aware of the huge sword strapped to his back as he walked along; but, as always seemed to happen, no one else paid any attention to it.

Before they had left the village, while they were all being shackled, Garion and Silk had held a brief, urgent discussion in the minute finger movements of the Drasnian secret language.

—*I could pick this lock with my thumbnail*—Silk had asserted with a disdainful flip of his fingers. —*As soon as it gets dark tonight, I'll unhook us and we'll leave. I don't really think military life would agree with me, and it's wildly inappropriate for you to be joining an Angarak army just now—all things considered.*—

—*Where's Grandfather?*—Garion had asked.

—Oh, I imagine he's about.—

Garion, however, was worried, and a whole platoon of "what-ifs" immediately jumped into his mind. To avoid thinking about them, he covertly studied the Malloreans who guarded them. The Grolim and the bulk of his detachment had moved on, once the captives had been shackled, seeking other villages and other recruits, leaving only five of their number behind to escort this group south. Malloreans were somewhat different from other Angaraks. Their eyes had that characteristic angularity, but their bodies seemed not to have the singleness of purpose which so dominated the western tribes. They were burly, but they did not have the broad-shouldered athleticism of the Murgos. They were tall, but did not have the lean, whippetlike frames of the Nadraks. They were obviously strong, but they did not have the thick-waisted brute power of Thulls. There was about them, moreover, a kind of disdainful superiority when they looked at western Angaraks. They spoke to their prisoners in short, barking commands, and when they talked to each other, their dialect was so thick that it was nearly unintelligible. They wore mail shirts covered by coarse-woven red tunics. They did not ride their horses very well, Garion noted, and their curved swords and broad, round shields seemed to get in their way as they attempted to manage their reins.

Garion carefully kept his head down to hide the fact that his features—even more than Silk's—were distinctly non-Angarak. The guards, however, paid little attention to the conscripts as individuals, but seemed rather to be more interested in them as numbers. They rode continually up and down the sweating column, counting bodies and referring to a document they carried with concerned, even worried expressions. Garion surmised that unpleasant things would happen if the numbers did not match when they reached Yar Nadrak.

A faint, pale flicker in the underbrush some distance uphill from the trail caught Garion's eye, and he turned his head sharply in that direction. A large, silver-gray wolf was ghosting along just at the edge of the trees, his pace exactly matching theirs. Garion quickly lowered his head again, pretended to stumble, and fell heavily against Silk. "Grandfather's out there," he whispered.

"Did you only just notice him?" Silk sounded surprised. "I've been watching him for the last hour or more."

When the trail turned away from the river and entered the trees, Garion felt the tension building up in him. He could not be sure what Belgarath was going to do, but he knew that the concealment offered by the forest provided the opportunity for which his grandfather had doubtless been waiting. He tried to hide his growing nervousness as he walked along behind Silk, but the slightest sound in the woods around them made him start uncontrollably.

The trail dipped down into a fair-sized clearing, surrounded on all sides by tall ferns, and the Mallorean guards halted the column to allow their prisoners to rest. Garion sank gratefully to the springy turf beside Silk. The effort of walking with one leg shackled to the long chain which bound the conscripts together was considerable, and he found that he was sweating profusely. "What's he waiting for?" he whispered to Silk.

The rat-faced little man shrugged. "It's still a few hours until dark," he replied softly. "Maybe he wants to wait for that."

Then, some distance up the trail, they heard the sound of singing. The song was ribald and badly out of tune, but the singer was quite obviously enjoying himself, and the slurring of the words as he drew closer indicated that he was more than a little drunk.

The Malloreans grinned at each other. "Another patriot, perhaps," one of them smirked, "coming to enlist. Spread out, and we'll gather him up as soon as he comes into the clearing."

The singing Nadrak rode into view on a large roan horse. He wore the usual dark, stained leather clothing, and a fur cap perched precariously on one side of his head. He had a scraggly black beard, and he carried a wineskin in one hand. He seemed to be swaying in his saddle as he rode, but something about his eyes showed him not to be quite so drunk as he appeared. Garion stared at him openly as he rode into the clearing with a string of mules behind him. It was Yarblek, the Nadrak merchant they had encountered on the South Caravan Route in Cthol Murgos.

"Ho, there!" Yarblek greeted the Malloreans in a loud voice. "I see you've had good hunting. That's a healthy-looking bunch of recruits you've got there."

"The hunting just got easier." One of the Malloreans grinned at him, pulling his horse across the trail to block Yarblek's way.

"You mean me?" Yarblek laughed uproariously. "Don't be a fool. I'm too busy to play soldier."

"That's a shame," the Mallorean replied.

"I'm Yarblek, a merchant of Yar Turak and a friend of King Drosta himself. I'm acting on a commission that he personally put into my hands. If you interfere with me in any way, Drosta will have you flayed and roasted alive as soon as you get to Yar Nadrak."

The Mallorean looked a trifle less sure of himself. "We answer only to 'Zakath," he asserted a bit defensively. "King Drosta has no authority over us."

"You're in Gar og Nadrak, friend," Yarblek pointed out to him, "and Drosta does whatever he likes here. He might have to apologize to 'Zakath after it's all over, but by then the five of you will probably be peeled and cooked to a turn."

"I suppose you can prove that you're on official business?" the Mallorean guard hedged.

"Of course I can," Yarblek replied. He scratched at his head, his face taking on an expression of foolish perplexity. "Where did I put that parchment?" he muttered to himself. Then he snapped his fingers. "Oh, yes," he said, "now I remember. It's in the pack on that last mule. Here, have a drink, and I'll go get it." He tossed the wineskin to the Mallorean, turned his horse and rode back to the end of his pack string. He dismounted and began rummaging through a canvas pack.

"We'd better have a look at his documents before we decide," one of the others advised. "King Drosta's not the sort you want to cross."

"We might as well have a drink while we're waiting," another suggested, eyeing the wineskin.

"That's one thing we can agree on," the first replied, working loose the stopper of the leather bag. He raised the skin with both hands and lifted his chin to drink.

There was a solid-sounding thud, and the feathered shaft of an arrow was quite suddenly protruding from his throat, just at the top of his red tunic. The wine gushed from the skin to pour down over his astonished face. His companions gaped at him, then reached for their weapons with cries of alarm, but it was too late. Most of them tumbled from their saddles in the sudden storm of arrows that struck them from the concealment of the ferns. One, however, wheeled his mount to flee, clutching at the shaft buried deep in his side. The horse took no more than two leaps before three arrows sank into the Mallorean's back. He stiffened, then toppled over limply, his foot hanging up in his stirrup as he fell, and his frightened horse bolted, dragging him, bouncing and flopping, back down the trail.

"I can't seem to locate that document," Yarblek declared, walking back with a wicked grin on his face. He turned the Mallorean he had been speaking to over with his foot. "You didn't really want to see it anyway, did you?" he asked the dead man.

The Mallorean with the arrow in his throat stared blankly up at the sky, his mouth agape and a trickle of blood running out of his nose.

"I didn't think so." Yarblek laughed coarsely. He drew back his foot and kicked the dead man back over onto his face. Then he turned to smirk at Silk as his archers came out of the dark green ferns. "You certainly get around, Silk," he said. "I thought Taur Urgas had finished you back there in stinking Cthol Murgos."

"He miscalculated," Silk replied casually.

"How did you manage to get yourself conscripted into the Mallorean army?" Yarblek asked curiously, all traces of his feigned drunkenness gone now.

Silk shrugged. "I got careless."

"I've been following you for the last three days."

"I'm touched by your concern." Silk lifted his fettered ankle and jingled the chain. "Would it be too much trouble for you to unlock this?"

"You're not going to do anything foolish, are you?"

"Of course not."

"Find the key," Yarblek told one of his archers.

"What are you going to do with us?" Besher asked nervously, eyeing the dead guards with a certain apprehension.

Yarblek laughed. "What you do once that chain's off is up to you," he answered indifferently. "I wouldn't recommend staying in the vicinity of so many dead Malloreans, though. Somebody might come along and start asking questions."

"You're just going to let us go?" Besher demanded incredulously.

"I'm certainly not going to feed you," Yarblek told him.

The archers went down the chain, unlocking the shackles, and each Nadrak bolted into the bushes as soon as he was free.

"Well, then," Yarblek said, rubbing his palms together, "now that that's been taken care of, why don't we have a drink?"

"That guard spilled all your wine when he fell off his horse," Silk pointed out.

"That wasn't my wine," Yarblek snorted. "I stole it this morning. You should know I wouldn't offer my own drink to somebody I planned to kill."

"I wondered about that." Silk grinned at him. "I thought that maybe your manners had started to slip."

Yarblek's coarse face took on a faintly injured expression.

"Sorry," Silk apologized quickly. "I misjudged you."

"No harm done." Yarblek shrugged. "A lot of people misunderstand me." He sighed. "It's a burden I have to bear." He opened a pack on his lead mule and hefted out a small keg of ale. He set it on the ground and broached it with a practiced skill, bashing in its top with his fist. "Let's get drunk." he suggested.

"We'd really like to," Silk declined politely, "but we've got some rather urgent business to take care of."

"You have no idea how sorry I am about that," Yarblek replied, fishing several cups out of the pack.

"I knew you'd understand."

"Oh, I understand, all right, Silk." Yarblek bent and dipped two cups into the ale keg. "And I'm as sorry as I can be that your business is going to have to wait. Here." He gave Silk one cup and Garion the other. Then he turned and dipped out a cup for himself.

Silk looked at him with one raised eyebrow.

Yarblek sprawled on the ground beside the ale keg, comfortably resting his feet on the body of one of the dead Malloreans. "You see, Silk," he explained, "the whole point of all this is that Drosta wants you—very badly. He's offering a reward for you that's just *too* attractive to pass up. Friendship is one thing, but business is business, after all. Now, why don't you and your young friend make yourselves comfortable? This is a nice, shady clearing with soft moss to lie on. We'll all get drunk, and you can tell me how you managed to escape from Taur Urgas. Then you can tell me what happened to that handsome woman you had with you down in Cthol Murgos. Maybe I can make enough money from this to be able to afford to buy her. I'm not the marrying kind, but by Torak's teeth, that's a fine-looking woman. I'd almost be willing to give up my freedom for her."

"I'm sure she'd be flattered," Silk replied. "What then?"

"What when?"

"After we get drunk. What do we do then?"

"We'll probably get sick—that's what usually happens. After we get well, we'll run on down to Yar Nadrak. I'll collect the reward for you, and you'll be able to find out why King Drosta lek Thun wants to get his hands on you so badly." He looked at Silk with an amused expression. "You might as well sit down and have a drink, my friend. You aren't going anywhere just now."

Chapter Five

YAR NADRAK WAS a walled city, lying at the juncture of the east and west forks of the River Cordu. The forests had been cleared for a league or so in every direction from the capital by the simple expedient of setting fire to it, and the approach to the city passed through a wilderness of burned black snags and rank-growing bramble thickets. The city gates were stout and smeared with tar. Surmounting them was a stone replica of the mask of Torak. That beautiful, inhumanly cruel face gazed down at all who entered, and Garion suppressed a shudder as he rode under it.

The houses in the Nadrak capital were all very tall and had steeply sloping roofs. The windows of the second storeys all had shutters, and most of the shutters were closed. Any exposed wood on the structures had been smeared with tar to preserve it, and the splotches of the black substance made all the buildings look somehow diseased.

There was a sullen, frightened air in the narrow, crooked streets of Yar Nadrak, and the inhabitants kept their eyes low-

ered as they hurried about their business. There appeared to be
less leather involved in the clothing of the burghers of the
capital than had been the case in the back country, but even
here most garments were black, and only occasionally was there
a splash of blue or yellow. The sole exception to this rule was
the red tunic worn by the Mallorean soldiers. They seemed to
be everywhere, roaming at will up and down the cobblestoned
streets, accosting citizens rudely and talking loudly to each
other in their heavily accented speech.

While the soldiers seemed for the most part to be merely
swaggering bullies, young men who concealed their nervousness at being in a strange country with an outward show of
bluster and braggadocio, the Mallorean Grolims were quite
another matter. Unlike the western Grolims Garion had seen
in Cthol Murgos, they rarely wore the polished steel mask, but
rather assumed a set, grim expression, thin-lipped and narrow-
eyed; as they went about the streets in their hooded black robes,
everyone, Mallorean and Nadrak alike, gave way to them.

Garion and Silk, closely guarded and mounted on a pair of
mules, followed the rangy Yarblek into the city. Yarblek and
Silk had kept up their banter during the entire ride downriver,
exchanging casual insults and reliving past indiscretions. Although he seemed friendly enough, Yarblek nonetheless remained watchful, and his men had guarded Silk and Garion
every step of the way. Garion had covertly watched the forest
almost continually during the three-day ride, but he had seen
no sign of Belgarath and he entered the city in a state of jumpy
apprehension. Silk, however, seemed relaxed and confident as
always, and his behavior and attitude grated at Garion's nerves,
for some reason.

After they had clattered along a crooked street for some
distance, Yarblek turned down a narrow, dirty alleyway leading
toward the river.

"I thought the palace was that way," Silk said to him, pointing toward the center of town.

"It is," Yarblek replied, "but we aren't going to the palace.
Drosta's got company there, and he prefers to do business in
private." The alleyway soon opened out into a seedy-looking

street where the tall, narrow-looking houses had fallen somewhat into disrepair. The lanky Nadrak clamped his mouth shut
as two Mallorean Grolims rounded a corner just ahead and
came in their direction. Yarblek's expression was openly hostile
as the two approached.

One of them stopped to return his gaze. "You seem to have
a problem, friend," the Grolim suggested.

"That's my business, isn't it?" Yarblek retorted.

"Indeed it is," the Grolim replied coolly. "Don't let it get
out of hand, though. Open disrespect for the priesthood is the
sort of thing that could get you into serious trouble." The black-
robed man's look was threatening.

On a sudden impulse, Garion carefully pushed out his mind
toward the Grolim, probing very gently, but the thoughts he
encountered showed no particular awareness and certainly none
of the aura that always seemed to emanate from the mind of a
sorcerer.

"Don't do that," the voice in his mind cautioned him. *"It's
like ringing a bell or wearing a sign around your neck."*

Garion quickly pulled back his thoughts. *"I thought all
Grolims were sorcerers,"* he replied silently. *"These two are
just ordinary men."* But the other awareness was gone.

The two Grolims passed, and Yarblek spat contemptuously
into the street. "Pigs," he muttered. "I'm starting to dislike
Malloreans almost as much as Murgos."

"They seem to be taking over your country, Yarblek," Silk
observed.

Yarblek grunted. "Let one Mallorean in, and before long
they're underfoot everywhere."

"Why did you let them in to begin with?" Silk asked mildly.

"Silk," Yarblek said bluntly, "I know you're a spy, and I'm
not going to discuss politics with you, so quit fishing for information."

"Just passing the time of day," Silk replied innocently.

"Why don't you mind your own business?"

"But this *is* my business, old friend."

Yarblek stared hard at him, then suddenly laughed.

"Where are we going?" Silk asked him, looking around at

the shabby street. "This isn't the best part of town, as I recall."

"You'll find out," Yarblek told him.

They rode on down toward the river where the smell of floating garbage and open sewers was quite nearly overpowering. Garion saw rats feeding in the gutters, and the men in the street wore shabby clothing and had the furtive look of those who have reason to avoid the police.

Yarblek turned his horse abruptly and led them into another narrow, filthy alleyway. "We walk from here," he said, dismounting. "I want to go in the back way." Leaving their mounts with one of his men, they went on down the alley, stepping carefully over piles of rotting garbage.

"Down there," Yarblek told them, pointing at a short, rickety flight of wooden stairs leading down to a narrow doorway. "Once we get inside, keep your heads down. We don't want too many people noticing that you're not Nadraks."

They went down the creaking steps and slipped through the doorway into a dim, smoky tavern, reeking of sweat, spilled beer, and stale vomit. The fire pit in the center of the room was choked with ashes, and several large logs smoldered there, giving off a great deal of smoke and very little light. Two narrow, dirty windows at the front appeared only slightly less dark than the walls around them, and a single oil lamp hung on a chain nailed to one of the rafters.

"Sit here," Yarblek instructed them, nudging at a bench standing against the back wall. "I'll be right back." He went off toward the front part of the tavern. Garion looked around quickly, but saw immediately that a pair of Yarblek's men lounged unobtrusively beside the door.

"What are we going to do?" he whispered to Silk.

"We don't have much choice but to wait and see what happens," Silk replied.

"You don't seem very worried."

"I'm not, really."

"But we've been arrested, haven't we?"

Silk shook his head. "When you arrest somebody, you put shackles on him. King Drosta wants to talk to me, that's all."

"But that reward notice said—"

"I wouldn't pay too much attention to that, Garion. The reward notice was for the benefit of the Malloreans. Whatever Drosta's up to, he doesn't want them finding out about it."

Yarblek threaded his way back through the crowd in the tavern and thumped himself down on the grimy bench beside them. "Drosta should be here, shortly," he said. "You want something to drink while we're waiting?"

Silk looked around with a faint expression of distaste. "I don't think so," he replied. "The ale barrels in places like this usually have a few drowned rats floating in them—not to mention the dead flies and roaches."

"Suit yourself," Yarblek said.

"Isn't this a peculiar sort of place to find a king?" Garion asked, looking around at the shabby interior of the tavern.

"You have to know King Drosta to understand," Silk told him. "He has some rather notorious appetites, and these riverfront dives suit him."

Yarblek laughed in agreement. "Our monarch's a lusty sort of fellow," he noted, "but don't ever make the mistake of thinking he's stupid—a little crude, perhaps, but not stupid. He can come to a place like this, and no Mallorean will take the trouble to follow him. He's found that it's a good way to conduct business that he prefers not to have reported back to 'Zakath."

There was a stir near the front of the tavern, and two heavy-shouldered Nadraks in black leather tunics and pointed helmets pushed their way through the door. "Make way!" one of them barked. "And everybody rise!"

"Those who are *able* to rise," the other added dryly.

A wave of jeers and catcalls ran through the crowd as a thin man in a yellow satin doublet and a fur-trimmed green velvet cloak entered. His eyes were bulging and his face was deeply scarred with old pockmarks. His movements were quick and jerky, and his expression was a curious mixture of sardonic amusement and a kind of desperate, unsatisfied hunger.

"All hail his Majesty, Drosta lek Thun, King of the Nadraks!" one drunken man proclaimed in a loud voice, and the others in the tavern laughed coarsely, jeering and whistling and stamping their feet.

"My faithful subjects," the pockmarked man replied with a gross smirk. "Drunks, thieves, and procurers. I bask in the warm glow of your love for me." His contempt seemed directed almost as much at himself as at the ragged, unwashed crowd.

They whistled in unison and stamped their feet derisively.

"How many tonight, Drosta?" someone shouted.

"As many as I can." The king leered. "It's my duty to spread royal blessings wherever I go."

"Is that what you call it?" someone else demanded raucously.

"It's as good a name as any," Drosta replied with a shrug.

"The royal bedchamber awaits," the tavern owner declaimed with a mocking bow.

"Along with the royal bedbugs, I'm sure," Drosta added. "Ale for every man not too drunk to swill it down. Let my loyal subjects drink to my vitality."

The crowd cheered as the king pushed toward a stairway leading to the upper storeys of the building. "My duty awaits me," he proclaimed, pointing with a grand gesture up the stairs. "Let all take note of how eagerly I go to embrace that stern responsibility." And he mounted the stairs to the derisive applause of the assembled riffraff.

"What now?" Silk asked.

"We'll wait a bit," Yarblek replied. "It would be a little obvious if we went up immediately."

Garion shifted uncomfortably on the bench. A very faint, nervous kind of tingle had begun just behind his ears, a sort of prickling sensation that seemed to crawl over his skin. He had an unpleasant thought or two about the possibility of lice or fleas migrating from the scum in the tavern in search of fresh blood, but dismissed that idea. The tingling did not seem to be external.

At a table not far away, a shabbily dressed man, apparently far gone in drink, had been snoring with his head buried in his arms. In the middle of a snore he raised his face briefly and winked. It was Belgarath. He let his face drop back onto his arms as a wave of relief swept through Garion.

The drunken crowd in the tavern grew steadily more rowdy. A short, ugly fight broke out near the fire pit, and the revelers at first cheered, then joined in, kicking at the two who rolled about on the floor.

"Let's go up," Yarblek said shortly, rising to his feet. He pushed through the crowd and started upstairs.

"Grandfather's here," Garion whispered to Silk as they followed.

"I saw him," Silk replied shortly.

The stairs led to a dim upper hallway with dirty, threadbare carpeting on the floor. At the far end, King Drosta's two bored-looking guards leaned against the wall on either side of a solid door.

"My name's Yarblek," Silk's friend told them as he reached the door. "Drosta's expecting me."

The guards glanced at each other, then one tapped on the door. "That man you wanted to see is here, your Majesty."

"Send him in." Drosta's voice was muffled.

"He isn't alone," the guard advised.

"That's all right."

"Go ahead," the guard said to Yarblek, unlatching the door and pushing it open.

The king of the Nadraks was sprawled on a rumpled bed with his arms about the thin shoulders of a pair of dirty, scantily dressed young girls with tangled hair and hopeless-looking eyes. "Yarblek," the depraved monarch greeted the merchant, "what kept you?"

"I didn't want to attract attention by following you immediately, Drosta."

"I almost got sidetracked." Drosta leered at the two girls. "Aren't they luscious?"

"If you like the type." Yarblek shrugged. "I prefer a little more maturity."

"That's good, too," Drosta admitted, "but I love them all.

I fall in love twenty times a day. Run along, my pretties," he told the girls. "I've got some business to take care of just now. I'll send for you later."

The two girls immediately left, closing the door quietly behind them.

Drosta sat up on the bed, scratching absently at one armpit. His stained and rumpled yellow doublet was unbuttoned, and his bony chest was covered with coarse black hair. He was thin, almost emaciated, and his scrawny arms looked like two sticks. His hair was lank and greasy, and his beard was so thin that it was little more than a few scraggly-looking black hairs sprouting from his chin. The pockmarks on his face were deep, angry red scars, and his neck and hands were covered with an unwholesome, scabby-looking rash. There was a distinctly unpleasant odor about him. "Are you sure this is the man I want?" he asked Yarblek. Garion looked at the Nadrak King sharply. The coarseness had gone out of his voice, and his tone was incisive, direct, the tone of a man who was all business. Garion made a few quick mental adjustments. Drosta lek Thun was not at all what he seemed.

"I've known him for years, Drosta," Yarblek replied. "This is Prince Kheldar of Drasnia. He's also known as Silk and sometimes Ambar of Kotu or Radek of Boktor. He's a thief, a swindler, and a spy. Aside from that, he's not too bad."

"We are delighted to meet so famous a man," King Drosta declared. "Welcome, Prince Kheldar."

"Your Majesty," Silk replied, bowing.

"I'd have invited you to the palace," Drosta continued, "but I've got some house guests with the unfortunate habit of sticking their noses into my business." He laughed dryly. "Luckily, I found out very soon that Malloreans are a priggish race. They won't follow me into places like this, so we'll be able to talk freely." He looked around at the cheap, gaudy furnishings and red draperies with a sort of amused toleration. "Besides," he added, "I like it here."

Garion stood with his back against the wall near the door, trying to remain as unobtrusive as possible, but Drosta's nervous eyes picked him out. "Can he be trusted?" the king demanded of Silk.

"Completely," Silk assured him. "He's my apprentice. I'm teaching him the business."

"Which business? Stealing or spying?"

Silk shrugged. "It amounts to the same thing. Yarblek says you wanted to see me. I assume it has something to do with current matters rather than any past misunderstandings."

"You're quick, Kheldar," Drosta replied approvingly. "I need your help and I'm willing to pay for it."

Silk grinned. "I'm fond of the word pay."

"So I've heard. Do you know what's going on here in Gar og Nadrak?" Drosta's eyes were penetrating, and his veneer of gross self-indulgence had fallen completely away.

"I *am* in the intelligence service, your Majesty," Silk pointed out.

Drosta grunted, stood up, and went to a table where a decanter of wine and several glasses stood. "Drink?" he asked.

"Why not?"

Drosta filled four glasses, took one for himself and paced nervously about the room with an angry expression. "I don't *need* any of this, Kheldar," he burst out. "My family's spent generations—centuries—weaning Gar og Nadrak away from the domination of the Grolims. Now they're about to drag us back into howling barbarism again, and I don't have any choice but to go along with it. I've got a quarter of a million Malloreans roaming around at will inside my borders and an army I can't even count poised just to the south. If I raise so much as one word of protest, 'Zakath will crush my kingdom with one fist."

"Would he really do that?" Silk asked, taking a chair at the table.

"With just about as much emotion as you'd feel about swatting a fly," Drosta replied. "Have you ever met him?"

Silk shook his head.

"You're lucky," Drosta told him with a shudder. "Taur Urgas is a madman, but, much as I hate him, he's still human. 'Zakath is made out of ice. I've *got* to get in touch with Rhodar."

"Ah," Silk said. "*That's* what this is all about, then."

"You're a nice enough fellow, Kheldar," Drosta told him dryly, "but I wouldn't go to all this trouble just for the pleasure of your company. You've got to carry my message to Rhodar. I've tried to get word to him, but I can't catch up with him. He won't stay in one place long enough. How can a fat man move so cursed fast?"

"He's deceptive," Silk said shortly. "Exactly what have you got in mind?"

"An alliance," Drosta replied bluntly. "My back's against the wall. Either I ally myself with Rhodar, or I get swallowed up."

Silk carefully set down his glass. "That's a very large suggestion, your Majesty. In the present situation, it's going to take a great deal of fast talking to arrange."

"That's why I sent for you, Kheldar. We're staring the end of the world right in the face. You've got to get to Rhodar and persuade him to pull his army back from the Thull border. Make him stop this insanity before it goes too far."

"Making my uncle do things is a little beyond my abilities, King Drosta," Silk replied carefully. "I'm flattered that you think I've got that much influence with him, but things have usually been the other way around between us."

"Don't you understand what's going on, Kheldar?" King Drosta's voice was anguished, and he gesticulated almost wildly as he spoke. "Our only hope of survival lies in not giving the Murgos and the Malloreans any kind of reason to unite. We should work to stir up trouble between them, not to provide them with a common enemy. Taur Urgas and 'Zakath hate each other with a passion so intense that it's almost holy. There are more Murgos than grains of sand and more Malloreans than stars. The Grolims can babble their gibberish about the awakening of Torak until their tongues fall out, but Taur Urgas and 'Zakath have taken the field for just one reason—each of them wants to destroy the other and make himself overking of Angarak. They're headed directly toward a war of mutual extinction. We can be rid of both of them if we just don't interfere."

"I think I see what you mean," Silk murmured.

"'Zakath is ferrying his Malloreans across the Sea of the East to his staging area near Thull Zelik, and Taur Urgas has the southern Murgos massed near Rak Goska. Inevitably, they're going to move on each other. We've *got* to stay out of the way and let them fight. Make Rhodar pull back before he spoils everything.'"

"Have you talked with the Thulls about this?" Silk asked.

Drosta snorted with contempt. "What's the point? I've tried to explain this to King Gethell, but talking to him is like talking to a pile of manure. The Thulls are so afraid of the Grolims that all you have to do is mention Torak's name and they go all to pieces. Gethell's a Thull through and through. There's nothing between his ears but sand."

"There's just one problem with all of this, Drosta," Silk told the agitated monarch. "I can't carry your message to King Rhodar."

"Can't?" Drosta exploded. "What do you mean, you *can't?"*

"My uncle and I aren't on the best of terms just now," Silk lied smoothly. "We had a little misunderstanding a few months ago, and about the first thing he'd do, if he saw me coming, is have me put in chains—and I'm almost certain things would go downhill from there."

Drosta groaned. "We're all doomed then," he declared, seeming to slump in on himself. "You were my last hope."

"Let me think a moment," Silk said. "We might be able to salvage something out of this yet." He stared at the floor, chewing absently on a fingernail as he turned the problem over in his mind. "*I* can't go," he concluded. "That's obvious. But that doesn't mean that somebody else couldn't."

"Who else would Rhodar trust?" Drosta demanded.

Silk turned to Yarblek, who had been listening to the conversation intently with a worried frown. "Are you in any kind of trouble in Drasnia at the moment?" he asked.

"Not that I know of."

"All right," Silk continued. "There's a fur dealer in Boktor —Geldahar's his name."

"Fat man? Sort of cross-eyed?" Yarblek asked.

"That's him. Why don't you take a shipment of furs and

go to Boktor? While you're trying to sell Geldahar the furs, tell him that the salmon run is late this year."

"I'm sure he'll be fascinated to hear that."

"It's a code-word," Silk explained with exaggerated patience. "As soon as you say that, he'll see to it that you get into the palace to see Queen Porenn."

"I've heard that she's a lovely woman," Yarblek said, "but that's a long trip just to see a pretty girl. I can probably find a pretty girl just down the hall."

"You're missing the point, Yarblek," Silk told him. "Porenn is Rhodar's queen, and he trusts her even more than he used to trust me. She'll know that I sent you, and she'll pass anything you tell her on to my uncle. Rhodar will be reading Drosta's message three days after you ride into Boktor. I guarantee it."

"You'd let a *woman* know about all this?" Drosta objected violently. "Kheldar, you're insane. The only woman safe with a secret is one who's had her tongue cut out."

Silk shook his head firmly. "Porenn's in control of Drasnian intelligence right now, Drosta. She already knows most of the secrets in the world. You're never going to get an emissary through an Alorn army to Rhodar, so forget that. There'll be Chereks with him, and they'll kill any Angarak on sight. If you want to communicate with Rhodar, you're going to have to use Drasnian intelligence as an intermediary, and that means going through Porenn."

Drosta looked dubious. "Maybe," he concluded after a moment's thought. "I'll try anything at this point—but why should Yarblek get involved? Why can't *you* carry my message to the Drasnian queen?"

Silk looked a trifle pained. "That wouldn't be a good idea at all, I'm afraid," he replied. "Porenn was rather central to my difficulties with my uncle. I'm definitely unwelcome at the palace just now."

One of King Drosta's shaggy eyebrows shot up. "So *that's* the way it is." He laughed. "Your reputation's well-earned, I see." He turned to Yarblek. "It's up to you, then. Make the necessary arrangements for the trip to Boktor."

"You already owe me money, Drosta," Yarblek replied

bluntly, "the reward for bringing in Kheldar, remember?"

Drosta shrugged. "Write it down someplace."

Yarblek shook his head stubbornly. "Not hardly. Let's keep your account current. You're known as a slow payer, once you've got what you want."

"Yarblek," Drosta said plaintively, "I'm your king."

Yarblek inclined his head somewhat mockingly. "I honor and respect your Majesty," he said, "but business is business, after all."

"I don't carry that much money with me," Drosta protested.

"That's all right, Drosta. I can wait." Yarblek crossed his arms and sat down in a large chair with the air of a man planning to stay for quite some time.

The king of the Nadraks stared at him helplessly.

Then the door opened and Belgarath stepped into the room, still dressed in the rags he had worn in the tavern downstairs. There was no furtiveness about his entrance, and he moved like a man on serious business.

"What *is* this?" Drosta exclaimed incredulously. "Guards!" he bawled, "get this drunken old man out of here."

"They're asleep, Drosta," Belgarath replied calmly. "Don't be too harsh with them, though. It's not their fault." He closed the door.

"Who are you? What do you think you're doing?" Drosta demanded. "Get out of here!"

"I think you'd better take a closer look, Drosta," Silk advised with a dry little chuckle. "Appearances can be deceiving sometimes, and you shouldn't be so quick to try to throw somebody out. He might have something important to say to you."

"Do you know him, Kheldar?" Drosta asked.

"Just about everybody in the world knows him," Silk replied. "Or *of* him."

Drosta's face creased into a puzzled frown, but Yarblek had started from his chair, his lean face suddenly pale. "Drosta!" he gasped. "Look at him. Think a minute. You know who he is."

Drosta stared at the shabby-looking old man, and his bulging eyes slowly opened even wider. *"You!"* he blurted.

Yarblek was still gaping at Belgarath. "He's been involved in it from the very beginning. I should have put it together down in Cthol Murgos—him, the woman, all of it."

"What are you doing in Gar og Nadrak?" Drosta asked in an awed voice.

"Just passing through, Drosta," Belgarath replied. "If you're quite finished with your discussion here, I need these two Alorns. We have an appointment, and we're running a little behind schedule."

"I always thought you were a myth."

"I like to encourage that as much as I can," Belgarath told him. "It makes moving around a lot easier."

"Are you mixed up in what the Alorns are doing?"

"They're acting more or less on my suggestions, yes. Polgara's keeping an eye on them."

"Can *you* get word to them and tell them to disengage?"

"That won't really be necessary, Drosta. I wouldn't worry too much about 'Zakath and Taur Urgas, if I were you. There are more important things afoot than their squabbles."

"So *that's* what Rhodar's doing," Drosta said in sudden comprehension. "Is it really that late?"

"It's even later than you think," the old sorcerer answered. He crossed to the table and poured himself some of Drosta's wine. "Torak's already stirring, and the whole matter's likely to be settled before the snow flies."

"This is going too far, Belgarath," Drosta said. "I might try to maneuver my way around Taur Urgas and 'Zakath, but I'm *not* going to cross Torak." He turned decisively toward the door.

"Don't do anything rash, Drosta," Belgarath advised him calmly, sitting in a chair and taking a sip of his wine. "Grolims can be most unreasonable, and the fact that I'm here in Yar Nadrak could only be viewed as the result of some collusion on your part. They'd have you bent backward over an altar and your heart sizzling in the coals before you ever got the chance to explain—king or no king."

Drosta froze in his tracks, his pockmarked face going very pale. For a moment, he seemed to be struggling with himself.

Then his shoulders slumped and his resolution seemed to wilt. "You've got me by the throat, haven't you, Belgarath?" he said with a short laugh. "You've managed to make me outsmart myself, and now you're going to use that to force me to betray the God of Angarak."

"Are you really all that fond of him?"

"Nobody's fond of Torak. I'm *afraid* of him, and that's a better reason to stay on the good side of him than any sentimental attachment. If he wakes up—" The king of the Nadraks shuddered.

"Have you ever given much thought to the kind of world we'd have if he didn't exist?" Belgarath suggested.

"That's too much to even wish for. He's a God. No one could hope to defeat him. He's too powerful for that."

"There are things more powerful than Gods, Drosta—two that I can think of offhand, and those two are rushing toward a final meeting. It probably wouldn't be a good idea to put yourself between them at this point."

But something else had occurred to Drosta. He turned slowly with a look of stunned incredulity and stared directly at Garion. He shook his head and wiped at his eyes, like a man trying to clear away a fog. Garion became painfully aware of the great sword strapped across his back. Drosta's bulging eyes widened even more as the realization of what he was seeing erased the Orb's suggestion that his brain not record what stood in plain sight before him. His expression became awed, and desperate hope dawned on his ugly face. "Your Majesty," he stammered, bowing with profound respect.

"Your Majesty," Garion replied, politely inclining his head

"It looks as if I'm forced to wish you good luck," Drosta said in a quiet voice. "Despite what Belgarath says, I think you're going to need it."

"Thank you, King Drosta," Garion said.

Chapter Six

"DO YOU THINK we can trust Drosta?" Garion asked Silk as they followed Belgarath along the garbage-littered alley behind the tavern.

"Probably about as far as we could throw him," Silk replied. "He was honest about *one* thing though. His back's to the wall. That might make him bargain with Rhodar in good faith—initially at least."

When they reached the street at the end of the alley, Belgarath glanced up once at the evening sky. "We'd better hurry," he said. "I want to get out of the city before they close the gates. I left our horses in a thicket a mile or so outside the walls."

"You went back for them?" Silk sounded a little surprised.

"Of course I did. I don't plan to walk all the way to Morindland." He led them up the street away from the river.

They reached the city gates in fading light just as the guards were preparing to close them for the night. One of the Nadrak soldiers raised his hand as if to bar their way, then apparently changed his mind and motioned them through irritably, muttering curses under his breath. The huge, tar-smeared gate boomed shut behind them, and there was the clinking rattle of heavy chains from inside as the bolts were thrown and locked. Garion glanced up once at the carved face of Torak which brooded down at them from above the gate, then deliberately turned his back.

"Are we likely to be followed?" Silk asked Belgarath as they walked along the dirt highway leading away from the city.

"I wouldn't be very surprised," Belgarath replied. "Drosta knows—or suspects—a great deal about what we're doing. Mallorean Grolims are very subtle, and they can pick the thoughts out of his head without his knowing it. That's probably why they don't bother to follow him when he goes off on his little excursions."

"Shouldn't you take some steps?" Silk suggested as they moved through the gathering twilight.

"We're getting a bit too close to Mallorea to be making unnecessary noise," Belgarath told him. "Zedar can hear me moving around from a long way off, and Torak's only dozing now. I'd rather not take the chance of waking him up with any more loud clatter."

They walked along the highway toward the shadowy line of rank undergrowth at the edge of the open fields surrounding the city. The sound of frogs from the marshy ground near the river was very loud in the twilight.

"Torak isn't really asleep any more then?" Garion asked finally. He had harbored somewhere at the back of his mind the vague hope that they might be able to creep up on the sleeping God and catch him unaware.

"No, not really," his grandfather replied. "The sound of your hand touching the Orb shook the whole world. Not even Torak could sleep through that. He isn't really awake yet, but he's not entirely asleep, either."

"Did it really make all that much noise?" Silk asked curiously.

"They probably heard it on the other side of the universe. I left the horses over there." The old man pointed toward a

shadowy willow grove several hundred yards to the left of the
road.

From behind them there was the rattle of a heavy chain,
startling the frogs into momentary silence.

"They're opening the gate," Silk said. "They wouldn't do
that unless somebody gave them an official reason to."

"Let's hurry," Belgarath said.

The horses stirred and nickered as the three of them pushed
their way through the rustling willows in the rapidly descending
darkness. They led the horses out of the grove, mounted, and
rode back toward the highway.

"They know we're out here somewhere," Belgarath said.
"There's not much point being coy about it."

"Just a second," Silk said. He dismounted and rummaged
through one of the canvas bags tied to their packhorse. He
pulled something out of the bag, then climbed back on his
horse. "Let's go then."

They pushed into a gallop, thudding along the dirt road
under a starry, moonless sky toward the denser shadows where
the forest rose at the edge of the scrubby, burned-off expanse
surrounding the Nadrak capital.

"Can you see them?" Belgarath called to Silk, who was
bringing up the rear and looking back over his shoulder.

"I think so," Silk shouted back. "They're about a mile behind."

"That's too close."

"I'll take care of it as soon as we get into the woods," Silk
replied confidently.

The dark forest loomed closer and closer as they galloped
along the hard-packed road. Garion could smell the trees now.

They plunged into the black shadows under the trees and
felt that slight extra warmth that always lies in a forest. Silk
reined in sharply. "Keep going," he told them, swinging out
of his saddle. "I'll catch up."

Belgarath and Garion rode on, slowing a bit in order to pick
the road out of the darkness. After several minutes, Silk caught
up with them. "Listen," the little man said, pulling his horse
to a stop. His teeth flashed in the shadows as he grinned.

"They're coming," Garion warned urgently as he heard a rumble of hoofs. "Hadn't we better—"

"Listen," Silk whispered sharply.

From behind there were several startled exclamations and the heavy sound of men falling. A horse squealed and ran off somewhere.

Silk laughed wickedly. "I think we can press on," he said gaily. "They'll be delayed for a bit while they round up their horses."

"What did you do?" Garion asked him.

Silk shrugged. "I stretched a rope across the road, about chest-high on a mounted man. It's an old trick, but sometimes old tricks are the best. They'll have to be cautious now, so we should be able to lose them by morning."

"Let's go, then," Belgarath said.

"Where are we headed?" Silk asked as they moved into a canter.

"We'll make directly for the north range," the old man replied. "Too many people know we're here, so let's get to the land of the Morindim as soon as we can."

"If they're really after us, they'll follow us all the way, won't they?" Garion asked, looking back nervously.

"I don't think so," Belgarath told him. "They'll be a long way behind by the time we get there. I don't think they'll risk going into Morind territory just to follow a cold trail."

"Is it *that* dangerous, Grandfather?"

"The Morindim do nasty things to strangers if they catch them."

Garion thought about that. "Won't *we* be strangers too?" he asked. "To the Morindim, I mean?"

"I'll take care of that when we get there."

They galloped on through the remainder of the velvety night, leaving their now-cautious pursuers far behind. The blackness beneath the trees was dotted with the pale, winking glow of fireflies, and crickets chirped interminably. As the first light of morning began to filter through the forest, they reached the edge of another burned-off area, and Belgarath reined in to peer cautiously out at the rank scrub, dotted here and there with charred snags. "We'd better have something to eat," he suggested. "The horses need some rest, and we can catch a bit of sleep before we go on." He looked around in the gradually increasing light. "Let's get away from the road, though." He turned his horse and led them off along the edge of the burn. After several hundred yards, they reached a small clearing that jutted out into the coarse brush. A spring trickled water into a mossy pool at the very edge of the trees, and the grass in the clearing was intensely green. The outer edge of the opening was hemmed in by brambles and a tangle of charred limbs. "This looks like a good place," Belgarath decided.

"Not really," Silk disagreed. He was staring at a crudely squared-off block of stone standing in the center of the clearing. There were ugly black stains running down the sides of the stone.

"For our purposes it is," the old man replied. "The altars of Torak are generally avoided, and we don't particularly want company."

They dismounted at the edge of the trees, and Belgarath began rummaging through one of the packs for bread and dried meat. Garion was in a curiously abstracted mood. He was tired, and his weariness made him a bit light-headed. Quite deliberately, he walked across the springy turf to the blood-stained altar; he stared at it, his eyes meticulously recording details without considering their implication. The blackened stone sat solidly in the center of the clearing, casting no shadow in the pale dawn light. It was an old altar, and had not been used recently. The stains that had sunk into the pores of the rock were black with age, and the bones littering the ground around it were half-sunk in the earth and were covered with a greenish patina of moss. A scurrying spider darted into the vacant eye socket of a mossy skull, seeking refuge in the dark, vaulted emptiness. Many of the bones were broken and showed the marks of the small, sharp teeth of forest scavengers who would feed on anything that was dead. A cheap, tarnished silver brooch lay with its chain tangled about a lumpy vertebra, and not far away a brass buckle, green with verdigris, still clung to a bit of moldering leather.

"Come away from that thing, Garion," Silk told him with a note of revulsion in his voice.

"It sort of helps to look at it," Garion replied quite calmly, still staring at the altar and the bones. "It gives me something to think about beside being afraid." He squared his shoulders, and his great sword shifted on his back. "I don't really think the world needs this sort of thing. Maybe it's time somebody did something about it."

When he turned around, Belgarath was looking at him, his wise old eyes narrowed. "It's a start," the scorcerer observed. "Let's eat and get some sleep."

They took a quick breakfast, picketed their horses, and rolled themselves in their blankets under some bushes at the edge of the clearing. Not even the presence of the Grolim altar nor the peculiar resolve it had stirred in him was enough to keep Garion from falling asleep immediately.

It was almost noon when he awoke, pulled from sleep by a faint whispering sound in his mind. He sat up quickly, looking around to find the source of that disturbance, but neither the forest nor the brush-choked burn seemed to hold any threat. Belgarath stood not far away, looking up at the summer sky where a large, blue-banded hawk was circling.

"What are you doing here?" The old sorcerer did not speak aloud but rather cast the question at the sky with his mind. The hawk spiraled down to the clearing, flared his wings to avoid the altar, and landed on the turf. He looked directly at Belgarath with fierce yellow eyes, then shimmered and seemed to blur. When the shimmering was gone, the misshapen sorcerer Beldin stood in his place. He was still as ragged, dirty, and irritable as he had been the last time Garion had seen him.

"Is this all the farther you've managed to come?" he demanded harshly of Belgarath. "What have you been doing— stopping at every tavern along the way?"

"We ran into a small delay," Belgarath replied calmly.

Beldin grunted with a sour look. "If you keep dawdling along like this, it will take you the rest of the year to get to Cthol Mishrak."

"We'll get there, Beldin. You worry too much."

"Somebody has to. You're being followed, you know."

"How far back are they?"

"Five leagues or so."

Belgarath shrugged. "That's far enough. They'll give up when we get to Morindland."

"What if they don't?"

"Have you been spending time with Polgara lately?" Belgarath asked dryly. "I thought I'd gotten away from all the 'what-ifs.'"

Beldin shrugged, a gesture made grotesque by the hump on his back. "I saw her last week," he reported. "She has some interesting plans for you, you know."

"She came to the Vale?" Belgarath sounded surprised.

"Passed through. She was with the red-haired girl's army."

Garion threw off his blanket. "With *whose* army?" he demanded.

"What's going on down there?" Belgarath asked sharply.

Beldin scratched at his tangled hair. "I never really got the straight of it," he admitted. "All I know is that the Alorns are following that little redheaded Tolnedran. She calls herself the Rivan Queen—whatever that means."

"Ce'Nedra?" Garion was incredulous, though, for some reason, he knew that he shouldn't be.

"I guess she went through Arendia like a pestilence," Beldin continued. "After she passed, there wasn't an able-bodied man left in the kingdom. Then she went on down into Tolnedra and goaded her father into convulsions—I didn't know that he was subject to fits."

"It crops up in the Borune line once in a while," Belgarath said. "It's nothing all that serious, but they try to keep it quiet."

"Anyway," the hunchback went on, "while Ran Borune was still frothing at the mouth, his daughter stole his legions. She's persuaded about half the world to take up arms and follow her." He gave Garion a quizzical look. "You're supposed to marry her, aren't you?"

Garion nodded, not trusting himself to speak.

Beldin grinned suddenly. "You might want to give some thought to running away."

"Ce'Nedra?" Garion blurted again.

"His wits seem a bit scrambled," Beldin observed.

"He's been under a strain, and his nerves aren't too good just now," Belgarath replied. "Are you going back to the Vale?"

Beldin nodded. "The twins and I are going to join Polgara when the campaign starts. She might need some help if the Grolims come at her in force."

"Campaign?" Belgarath exclaimed. "What campaign? I told them just to march up and down and make a lot of noise. I specifically told them *not* to invade."

"They ignored you, it seems. Alorns aren't noted for restraint in such matters. Apparently they got together and decided to take steps. The fat one seems fairly intelligent. He wants to get a Cherek fleet into the Sea of the East to commit a few constructive atrocities on Mallorean shipping. The rest of it seems to be pretty much diversionary."

Belgarath started to swear. "You can't let them out of your sight for a single instant," he raged. "How could Polgara lend herself to this idiocy?"

"The plan does have a certain merit, Belgarath. The more Malloreans they drown now, the fewer we have to fight later."

"We never planned to fight them, Beldin. The Angaraks won't unite unless Torak comes back to weld them together again—*or* unless they're faced with a common enemy. We just talked with Drosta lek Thun, the Nadrak King, and he's so sure that the Murgos and the Malloreans are about to go to war with each other that he wants to ally himself with the west just to get clear of it. When you get back, see if you can talk some sense into Rhodar and Anheg. I've got enough problems already."

"Your problems are only starting, Belgarath. The twins had a visitation a couple days ago."

"A what?"

Beldin shrugged. "What else would you call it? They were working on something—quite unrelated to all this—and the pair of them suddenly went into a trance and began to babble at me. At first they were just repeating that gibberish from the Mrin Codex—you know the place—where the Mrin Prophet's mind broke down and he degenerated into animal noises for a while. Anyway, they went back over that part—only this time it came out coherently."

"What did they say?" Belgarath demanded, his eyes burning.

"Are you sure you want to know?"

"Of course I want to know."

"All right. It went like this: 'Behold, the heart of the stone shall relent, and the beauty that was destroyed shall be restored, and the eye that is not shall be made whole again.'"

Belgarath stared at him. "That's it?" he asked.

"That's it," Beldin told him.

"But what does it mean?" Garion asked.

"Just what it says, Belgarion," Beldin replied. "For some reason the Orb is going to restore Torak."

Garion began to tremble as the full impact of Beldin's words struck him. "Torak's going to win, then," he said numbly.

"It didn't say anything about winning or losing, Belgarion," Beldin corrected him. "All it said was that the Orb is going to undo what it did to Torak when he used it to crack the world. It doesn't say anything about *why*."

"That's always been the trouble with the Prophecy," Belgarath observed. "It can mean any one of a dozen different things."

"Or all of them," Beldin added. "That's what makes it so difficult to understand sometimes. We tend to concentrate on just one thing, but Prophecy includes everything at the same time. I'll work on it and see if I can wring some sense out of it. If I come up with anything, I'll let you know. I'd better be getting back." He leaned slightly forward and curled his arms out in a vaguely winglike gesture. "Watch out for the Morindim," he told Belgarath. "You're a fair sorcerer, but magic's altogether different, and sometimes it gets away from you."

"I think I can handle it if I have to," Belgarath replied tartly.

"Maybe," Beldin said. "If you can manage to stay sober." He shimmered back into the form of the hawk, beat his wings twice, and spiraled up out of the clearing and into the sky.

Garion watched him until he was only a circling speck.

"That was a strange visit," Silk said, rolling out of his blankets. "It looks as if quite a bit's been going on since we left."

"And none of it very good," Belgarath added sourly. "Let's get moving. We're really going to have to hurry now. If Anheg gets his fleet into the Sea of the East and starts sinking Mallorean troop ships, 'Zakath might decide to march north and come across the land bridge. If we don't get there first, it could get very crowded up there." The old man scowled darkly. "I'd like to put my hands on your uncle just about now," he added. "I'd sweat a few pounds off him."

They quickly saddled their horses and rode back along the edge of the sunlit forest toward the road leading north.

Despite the rather lame assurances of the two sorcerers, Garion rode slumped in despair. They were going to lose, and Torak was going to kill him.

"Stop feeling so sorry for yourself," the inner voice told him finally.

"Why did you get me into this?" Garion demanded bitterly.

"We've discussed that before."

"He's going to kill me."

"What gives you that idea?"

"That's what the Prophecy said." Garion stopped abruptly as a thought occurred to him. *"You said it yourself. You're the Prophecy, aren't you?"*

"It's a misleading term—and I didn't say anything about winning or losing."

"Isn't that what it means?"

"No. It means exactly what it says."

"What else could it mean?"

"You're getting more stubborn every day. Stop worrying so much about meanings and just do what you have to do. You almost had it right, back there."

"If all you're going to do is talk in riddles, why bother with it at all? Why go to all the trouble of saying things that nobody's able to understand?"

"Because it's necessary to say it. The word determines the event. The word puts limits on the event and shapes it. Without the word, the event is merely a random happening. That's the whole purpose of what you call prophecy—to separate the significant from the random."

"I don't understand."

"I didn't think you would, but you asked, after all. Now stop worrying about it. It has nothing to do with you."

Garion wanted to protest, but the voice was gone. The conversation, however, had made him feel a little better—not much, but a little. To take his mind off it, he pulled his horse in beside Belgarath's as they reentered the forest on the far side of the burn. "Exactly who are the Morindim, Grandfather?" he asked. "Everybody keeps talking about them as if they were terribly dangerous."

"They are," Belgarath replied, "but you can get through their country if you're careful."

"Are they on Torak's side?"

"The Morindim aren't on anybody's side. They don't even live in the same world with us."

"I don't follow that."

"The Morindim are like the Ulgos used to be—before UL accepted them. There were several groups of Godless Ones. They all wandered off in various directions. The Ulgos went to the west, the Morindim went north. Other groups went south or east and disappeared."

"Why didn't they just stay where they were?"

"They couldn't. There's a kind of compulsion involved in the decisions of the Gods. Anyway, the Ulgos finally found themselves a God. The Morindim didn't. The compulsion to remain separated from other people is still there. They live in that treeless emptiness up there beyond the north range—small nomadic bands, mostly."

"What did you mean when you said that they don't live in the same world with us?"

"The world is a pretty terrible place for a Morind—a demon-haunted place. They worship devils and they live more in dreams than they do in reality. Their society is dominated by the dream-ers and the magicians."

"There aren't really any devils, are there?" Garion asked skeptically.

"Oh, yes. The devils are very real."

"Where do they come from?"

Belgarath shrugged. "I haven't any idea. They do exist, though, and they're completely evil. The Morindim control them by the use of magic."

"Magic? Is that different from what we do?"

"Quite a bit. We're sorcerers—at least that's what we're called. What we do involves the Will and the Word, but that's not the only way to do things."

"I don't quite follow."

"It's not really all that complicated, Garion. There are sev-eral ways to tamper with the normal order of things. Vordai's a witch. What she does involves the use of spirits—usually benign, mischievous sometimes—but not actually wicked. A magician uses devils—evil spirits."

"Isn't that sort of dangerous?"

Belgarath nodded. "*Very* dangerous," he replied. "The ma-gician tries to control the demon with spells—formulas, in-cantations, symbols, mystic diagrams—that sort of thing. As long as he doesn't make any mistakes, the demon is his absolute slave and has to do what he tells it to do. The demon doesn't want to be a slave, so it keeps looking for a way to break the spell."

"What happens if it does?"

"It generally devours the magician on the spot. That happens rather frequently. If you lose your concentration or summon a demon too strong for you, you're in trouble."

"What did Beldin mean when he said that you weren't very good at magic?" Silk asked.

"I've never spent that much time trying to learn about it," the old sorcerer replied. "I have alternatives, after all, and magic is dangerous and not very dependable."

"Don't use it then," Silk suggested.

"I hadn't really planned to. Usually the threat of magic is enough to keep the Morindim at a distance. Actual confrontations are rather rare."

"I can see why."

"After we get through the north range, we'll disguise ourselves. There are a number of markings and symbols that will make the Morindim avoid us."

"That sounds promising."

"Of course we have to get there first," the old man pointed out. "Let's pick up the pace a bit. We've still got a long way to go." And he pushed his horse into a gallop.

Chapter Seven

THEY RODE HARD for the better part of a week, moving steadily northward and avoiding the scattered settlements which dotted the Nadrak forest. Garion noticed that the nights grew steadily shorter; by the time they reached the foothills of the north range, darkness had virtually disappeared. Evening and morning merged into a few hours of luminous twilight as the sun dipped briefly below the horizon before bursting into view once more.

The north range marked the upper edge of the Nadrak forest. It was not so much a mountainous region as it was a string of peaks, a long finger of upthrusting terrain reaching out toward the east from the broad ranges that formed the spine of the continent. As they rode up a scarcely defined trail toward a saddle that stretched between two snowy peaks, the trees around them grew more stunted and finally disappeared entirely. Beyond that point, there would be no more trees. Belgarath stopped at the edge of one of these last groves and cut a half-dozen long saplings.

The wind that came down off the peaks had a bitter chill to it and the arid smell of perpetual winter. When they reached the boulder-strewn summit, Garion looked out for the first time at the immense plain stretching below. The plain, unmarked by trees, was covered with tall grass that bent before the vagrant wind in long, undulating waves. Rivers wandered aimlessly across that emptiness, and a thousand shallow lakes and ponds scattered, blue and glistening under a northern sun, toward the horizon.

"How far does it reach?" Garion asked quietly.

"From here to the polar ice," Belgarath replied. "Several hundred leagues."

"And no one lives out there but the Morindim?"

"Nobody wants to. For most of the year, it's buried in snow and darkness. You can go for six months up here without ever seeing the sun."

They rode down the rocky slope toward the plain and found a low-roofed, shallow cave at the base of the granite cliff that seemed to be the demarcation line between the mountains and the foothills. "We'll stop here for a while," Belgarath told them, reining in his tired mount. "We've got some preparations to make, and the horses need some rest."

They were all kept quite busy for the next several days while Belgarath radically altered their appearances. Silk set crude traps among the maze of rabbit runs twisting through the tall grass, and Garion roamed the foothills in search of certain tuberous roots and a peculiar-smelling white flower. Belgarath sat at the mouth of the cave, fashioning various implements from his saplings. The roots Garion had gathered yielded a dark brown stain, and Belgarath carefully applied it to their skins. "The Morindim are dark-skinned," he explained as he sat painting Silk's arms and back with the stain. "Somewhat darker than Tolnedrans or Nyissans. This will wear off after a few weeks, but it will last long enough to get us through."

After he had stained all their skins into swarthiness, he crushed the odd-smelling flowers to produce a jet black ink. "Silk's hair is the right color already," he said, "and mine will get by, but Garion's just won't do." He diluted some of the ink with water and dyed Garion's sandy hair black. "That's better," he grunted when he had finished, "and there's enough left for the tattoos."

"Tattoos?" Garion asked, startled at the thought.

"The Morindim decorate themselves extensively."

"Will it hurt?"

"We're not really going to tattoo ourselves, Garion," Belgarath told him with a pained look. "They take too long to heal. Besides, I'm afraid your Aunt would go into hysterics if I took you back to her with designs engraved all over you. This ink will last long enough for us to get through Morindland. It will wear off—eventually."

Silk was sitting cross-legged in front of the cave, looking for all the world like a tailor as he sewed fresh rabbit pelts to their clothing.

"Won't they start to smell after a few days?" Garion asked, wrinkling his nose.

"Probably," Silk admitted, "but I don't have time to cure the pelts."

Later, as Belgarath was carefully drawing the tattoos on their faces, he explained the guise they were going to assume. "Garion will be the quester," he said.

"What's that?" Garion asked.

"Don't move your face," Belgarath told him, frowning as he drew lines under Garion's eyes with a raven-feather quill. "The quest is a Morind ritual. It's customary for a young Morind of a certain rank to undertake a quest before he assumes a position of authority in his clan. You'll wear a white fur headband and carry that red spear I fixed up for you. It's ceremonial," he cautioned, "so don't try to stab anybody with it. That's very bad form."

"I'll remember that."

"We'll disguise your sword to look like some sort of relic or something. A magician *might* see past the Orb's suggestion that it's not there—depending on how good he is. One other thing—the quester is absolutely forbidden to speak under any circumstances, so keep your mouth shut. Silk will be your dreamer. He'll wear a white fur band on his left arm. Dreamers

speak in riddles and gibberish for the most part, and they tend
to fall into trances and have fits." He glanced over at Silk. "Do
you think you can handle that?"

"Trust me," Silk replied, grinning.

"Not very likely," Belgarath grunted. "I'll be Garion's magician. I'll carry a staff with a horned skull on it that will make
most Morindim avoid us."

"Most?" Silk asked quickly.

"It's considered bad manners to interfere with a quest, but
it happens now and then." The old man looked critically at
Garion's tattoos. "Good enough," he said and turned to Silk
with his quill.

When it was all done, the three of them were scarcely
recognizable. The markings the old man had carefully drawn
on their arms and faces were not pictures so much as they were
designs. Their faces had been changed into hideous devil masks,
and the exposed parts of their bodies were covered with symbols
etched in black ink. They wore fur-covered trousers and vests
and bone necklaces clattered about their necks. Their stained
arms and shoulders were bared and intricately marked.

Then Belgarath went down into the valley lying just below
the cave, seeking something. It did not take his probing mind
long to find what he needed. As Garion watched with revulsion,
the old man casually violated a grave. He dug up a grinning
human skull and carefully tapped the dirt out of it. "I'll need
some deer horns," he told Garion. "Not too large and fairly
well-matched." He squatted, fierce-looking in his furs and tattoos, and began to scrub at the skull with handfuls of dry sand.

There were weather-bleached horns lying here and there in
the tall grass, since the deer of the region shed their antlers
each winter. Garion gathered a dozen or so and returned to the
cave to find his grandfather boring a pair of holes in the top
of the skull. He critically examined the horns Garion had brought
him, selected a pair of them and screwed them down into the
holes. The grating sound of horn against bone set Garion's
teeth on edge. "What do you think?" Belgarath asked, holding
up the horned skull.

"It's grotesque," Garion shuddered.

"That was the general idea," the old man replied. He attached the skull firmly to the top of a long staff, decorated it with several feathers and then rose to his feet. "Let's pack up and leave," he said.

They rode down through the treeless foothills and out into the bending, waist-high grass as the sun swung down toward the southwestern horizon to dip briefly behind the peaks of the range they had just crossed. The smell of the uncured pelts Silk had sewn to their clothing was not very pleasant, and Garion did his best not to look at the hideously altered skull surmounting Belgarath's staff as they rode.

"We're being watched," Silk mentioned rather casually after an hour or so of riding.

"I was sure we would be," Belgarath replied. "Just keep going."

Their first meeting with the Morindim came just as the sun rose. They had paused on the sloping gravel bank of a meandering stream to water their mounts, and a dozen or so fur-clad riders, their dark faces tattooed into devil masks, cantered up to the opposite bank and stopped. They did not speak, but looked hard at the identifying marks Belgarath had so painstakingly contrived. After a brief, whispered consultation, they turned their horses and rode back away from the stream. Several minutes later, one came galloping back, carrying a bundle wrapped in a fox skin. He paused, dropped the bundle on the bank of the stream, and then rode off again without looking back.

"What was that all about?" Garion asked.

"The bundle's a gift—of sorts," Belgarath answered. "It's an offering to any devils who might be accompanying us. Go pick it up."

"What's in it?"

"A bit of this, a bit of that. I wouldn't open it, if I were you. You're forgetting that you're not supposed to talk."

"There's nobody around," Garion replied, turning his head this way and that, looking for any sign of their being watched.

"Don't be too sure of that," the old man replied. "There could be a hundred of them hiding in the grass. Go pick up the gift and we'll move along. They're polite enough, but they'll be a lot happier when we take our devils out of their territory."

They rode on across the flat, featureless plain with a cloud of flies, drawn by the smell of their untanned fur garments, plaguing them.

Their next meeting, several days later, was less congenial. They had moved into a hilly region where huge, rounded, white boulders rose out of the grass and where shaggy-coated wild oxen with great, sweeping horns grazed. A high overcast had moved in, and the gray sky diffused the light, making the brief twilight that marked the passage of one day into the next an only slightly perceptible darkening. They were riding down a gentle slope toward a large lake, which lay like a sheet of lead under the cloudy sky, when there suddenly arose from the tall grass all around them tattooed and fur-clad warriors holding long spears and short bows that appeared to be made of bone.

Garion reined in sharply and looked at Belgarath for instruction.

"Just look straight at them," his grandfather told him quietly, "and remember that you're not permitted to speak."

"More of them coming," Silk said tersely, jerking his chin toward the crest of a nearby hill where perhaps a dozen Morindim, mounted on paint-decorated ponies, were approaching at a walk.

"Let me do the talking," Belgarath said.

"Gladly."

The man in the lead of the mounted group was burlier than most of his companions, and the black tattooing on his face had been outlined with red and blue, marking him as a man of some significance in his clan and making the devil mask of his features all the more hideous. He carried a large wooden club, painted with strange symbols and inlaid with rows of sharp teeth taken from various animals. The way he carried it indicated that it was more a badge of office than a weapon. He rode without a saddle and with a single bridle strap. He pulled his pony to a stop perhaps thirty yards away. "Why have you come into the lands of the Weasel Clan?" he demanded abruptly. His accent was strange and his eyes were flat with hostility.

Belgarath drew himself up indignantly. "Surely the Headman of the Weasel Clan has seen the quest-mark before," he replied coldly. "We have no interest in the lands of the Weasel Clan, but follow the commands of the Devil-Spirit of the Wolf Clan in the quest he has laid upon us."

"I have not heard of the Wolf Clan," the Headman replied. "Where are their lands?"

"To the west," Belgarath replied. "We have traveled for two waxings and wanings of the Moon-Spirit to reach this place."

The Headman seemed impressed by that.

A Morind with long white braids and with a thin, dirty-looking beard drew his pony in beside that of the Headman. In his right hand he carried a staff surmounted by the skull of a large bird. The gaping beak of the skull had been decorated with teeth, giving it a ferocious appearance. "What is the name of the Devil-Spirit of the Wolf Clan?" he demanded. "I may know him."

"That is doubtful, Magician of the Weasel Clan," Belgarath answered politely. "He seldom goes far from his people. In any case, I cannot speak his name, since he has forbidden it to any but the dreamers."

"Can you say what his aspect is and his attributes?" the white-braided magician asked.

Silk made a long-gurgling sound in the back of his throat, stiffened in his saddle and rolled his eyes gruesomely back in his head until only the whites showed. With a convulsive, jerking motion, he thrust both arms into the air. "Beware the Devil Agrinja, who stalks unseen behind us," he intoned in a hollow, oracular voice. "I have seen his three-eyed face and his hundred-fanged mouth in my dreams. The eye of mortal man may not behold him, but his seven-clawed hands reach out even now to rend apart all who would stand in the path of his chosen quester, the spear-bearer of the Wolf Clan. I have seen him feed in my nightmares. The ravener approaches and he hungers for man-meat. Flee his hunger." He shuddered, dropping his arms and slumping forward in his saddle as if suddenly exhausted.

"You've been here before, I see," Belgarath muttered under his breath. "Try to restrain your creativity, though. Remember that *I* might have to produce what you dream up."

Silk cast him a sidelong wink. His description of the Devil had made a distinct impression on the Morindim. The mounted men looked about nervously, and those standing in the waist-high grass moved involuntarily closer together, grasping their weapons in trembling hands.

Then a thin Morind with a white fur band around his left arm pushed through the cluster of frightened warriors. His right leg ended in a clubfoot, and he lurched grotesquely as he walked. He fixed Silk with a glare of pure hatred, then threw both hands wide, quivering and jerking. His back arched and he toppled over, threshing in the grass in the throes of an apparent seizure. He went completely stiff and then he started to speak. "The Devil-Spirit of the Weasel Clan, dread Horja, speaks to me. He demands to know why the Devil Agrinja sends his quester into the lands of the Weasel Clan. The Devil Horja is too awful to look upon. He has *four* eyes and a hundred and *ten* teeth, and each of his six hands has *eight* claws. He feeds on the bellies of men and he hungers."

"An imitator," Silk sniffed disdainfully, his head still down. "He can't even think up his own dream."

The magician of the Weasel Clan gave the dreamer lying supine in the grass a look of disgust, then turned back to Belgarath. "The Devil-Spirit Horja defies the Devil-Spirit Agrinja," he declared. "He bids him to begone or he will rip out the belly of the quester of Agrinja."

Belgarath swore under his breath.

"What now?" Silk muttered.

"I have to fight him," Belgarath replied sourly. "That's what this was leading up to from the beginning. White-braids there is trying to make a name for himself. He's probably been attacking every magician who crosses his path."

"Can you handle him?"

"We're about to find out." Belgarath slid out of his saddle.

"I warn you to stand aside," he boomed, "lest I loose the hunger of our Devil-Spirit upon you." With the tip of his staff he drew a circle on the ground and a five-pointed star within the circle. Grimly, he stepped into the center of the design.

The white-braided magician of the Weasel Clan sneered and also slid off his pony. Quickly he drew a similar symbol on the ground and stepped into its protection.

"That's it," Silk muttered to Garion. "Once the symbols are drawn, neither one can back down."

Belgarath and the white-braided magician had each begun muttering incantations in a language Garion had never heard, brandishing their skull-surmounted staffs at each other. The dreamer of the Weasel Clan, suddenly realizing that he was in the middle of the impending battle, miraculously recovered from his seizure, scrambled to his feet, and lurched away with a terrified expression.

The Headman, trying to maintain his dignity, carefully backed his pony out of the immediate vicinity of the two muttering old men.

Atop a large, white boulder, twenty yards or so to the left of the two magicians, there was a shimmering disturbance in the air, somewhat like heatwaves rising from a red tile roof on a hot day. The movement caught Garion's eye, and he stared in puzzlement at the strange phenomenon. As he watched, the shimmering became more pronounced, and it seemed that the shattered pieces of a rainbow infused it, flickering, shifting, undulating in waves almost like varihued flames rising from an invisible fire. As Garion watched, fascinated, a second shimmering became apparent, rising above the tall grass off to the right. The second disturbance also began to gather shards of color into itself. As he stared, first at one, then at the other, Garion saw—or imagined that he saw—a shape beginning to emerge in the center of each. The shapes at first were amorphous, shifting, changing, gathering form from the coruscating colors flashing about them in the shimmering air. Then it seemed that the shapes, having reached a certain point, flashed to completion, coalescing quite suddenly with a great rushing together, and two towering forms faced each other, snarling and slavering with mindless hatred. Each stood as high as a house, and their shoulders bulked wide. Their skins were multihued, with waves of color rippling through them.

The one standing in the grass had a third eye glaring balefully from between its other two, and his great arms ended in seven-clawed hands stretched out with a hideously hungry curving. His jutting, muzzlelike mouth gaped wide, filled with row upon row of needlelike teeth as he roared a thunderous howl of hatred and dreadful hunger.

Crouched upon the boulder stood the other. He had a great cluster of shoulders at the top of his trunk, and a nest of long, scaly arms that writhed out in all directions like snakes, each arm terminating in a widespread, many-clawed hand. Two sets of eyes, one atop the other, glared insanely from beneath heavy brow-ridges, and his muzzle, like that of the other figure, sprouted a forest of teeth. He raised that awful face and bellowed, his jaws drooling foam.

But even as the two monsters glared at each other, there seemed to be a kind of writhing struggle going on inside them. Their skins rippled, and large moving lumps appeared in odd places on their chests and sides. Garion had the peculiar feeling that there was something else—something quite different and perhaps even worse—trapped inside each apparition. Growling, the two devils advanced upon each other, but despite their apparent eagerness to fight, they seemed almost driven, whipped toward the struggle. It was as if there was a dreadful reluctance in them, and their grotesque faces jerked this way and that, each snarling first at his opponent and then at the magician who controlled him. That reluctance, Garion perceived, stemmed from something deep inside the nature of each Devil. It was the enslavement, the compulsion to do the bidding of another, that they hated. The chains of spell and incantation in which Belgarath and the white-braided Morind had bound them were an intolerable agony, and there were whimpers of that agony mingled with their snarls.

Belgarath was sweating. Droplets of perspiration trickled down his dark-stained face. The incantations which held the Devil Agrinja locked within the apparition he had created to bind it rippled endlessly from his tongue. The slightest faltering of either the words or the image he had formed in his mind would break his power over the beast he had summoned, and it would turn upon him.

Writhing like things attempting to tear themselves apart from within, Agrinja and Horja closed on each other, grappling, clawing, tearing out chunks of scaly flesh with their awful jaws. The earth shuddered beneath them as they fought.

Too stunned to even be afraid, Garion watched the savage struggle. As he watched, he noted a peculiar difference between the two apparitions. Agrinja was bleeding from his wounds— a strange, dark blood, so deep red as to be almost black. Horja, however, did not bleed. Chunks ripped from his arms and shoulders were like bits of wood. The white-braided magician saw that difference as well, and his eyes grew suddenly afraid. His voice became shrill as he desperately cast incantations at Horja, struggling to keep the Devil under his control. The moving lumps beneath Horja's skin became larger, more agitated. The vast Devil broke free from Agrinja and stood, his chest heaving and a dreadful hope burning in his eyes.

White-braids was screaming now. The incantations tumbled from his mouth, faltering, stumbling. And then one unpronounceable formula tangled his tongue. Desperately he tried it again, and once again it stuck in his teeth.

With a bellow of triumph the Devil Horja straightened and seemed to explode. Bits and fragments of scaly hide flew in all directions as the monster shuddered free of the illusion which had bound him. He had two great arms and an almost human face surmounted by a pair of curving, needle-pointed horns. He had hoofs instead of feet, and his grayish skin dripped slime. He turned slowly and his burning eyes fixed on the gibbering magician.

"Horja!" the white-braided Morind shrieked, "I command you to—" The words faltered as he gaped in horror at the Devil which had suddenly escaped his control. "Horja! I am your master!" But Horja was already stalking toward him, his great hoofs crushing the grass as, step by step, he moved toward his former master.

In wild-eyed panic, the white-braided Morind flinched back, stepping unconsciously and fatally out of the protection of the circle and star drawn upon the ground.

Horja smiled then, a chilling smile, bent and caught the shrieking magician by each ankle, ignoring the blows rained on his head and shoulders by the skull-topped staff. Then the monster stood up, lifting the struggling man to hang upside down by the legs. The huge shoulders surged with an awful power, and, leering hideously, the Devil deliberately and with a cruel slowness tore the magician in two.

The Morindim fled.

Contemptuously the immense Devil hurled the chunks of his former master after them, spattering the grass with blood and worse. Then, with a savage hunting cry, he leaped in pursuit of them.

The three-eyed Agrinja had stood, still locked in a half-crouch, watching the destruction of the white-braided Morind almost with indifference. When it was over, he turned to cast eyes burning with hatred upon Belgarath.

The old sorcerer, drenched with sweat, raised his skull-staff in front of him, his face set with extreme concentration. The interior struggle rippled more intensely within the form of the monster, but gradually Belgarath's will mastered and solidified the shape. Agrinja howled in frustration, clawing at the air until all hint of shifting or changing was gone. Then the dreadful hands dropped, and the monster's head bowed in defeat.

"Begone," Belgarath commanded almost negligently, and Agrinja instantly vanished.

Garion suddenly began to tremble violently. His stomach heaved; he turned, tottered a few feet away, and fell to his knees and began to retch.

"What happened?" Silk demanded in a shaking voice.

"It got away from him," Belgarath replied calmly. "I think it was the blood that did it. When he saw that Agrinja was bleeding and that Horja wasn't, he realized that he'd forgotten something. That shook his confidence, and he lost his concentration. Garion, stop that."

"I can't," Garion groaned, his stomach heaving violently again.

"How long will Horja chase the others?" Silk asked.

"Until the sun goes down," Belgarath told him. "I imagine that the Weasel Clan is in for a bad afternoon."

"Is there any chance that he'll turn around and come after us?"

"He has no reason to. We didn't try to enslave him. As soon as Garion gets his stomach under control again, we can go on. We won't be bothered any more."

Garion stumbled to his feet, weakly wiping his mouth.

"Are you all right?" Belgarath asked him.

"Not really," Garion replied, "but there's nothing left to come up."

"Get a drink of water and try not to think about it."

"Will you have to do that any more?" Silk asked, his eyes a bit wild.

"No." Belgarath pointed. There were several riders along the crest of a hill perhaps a mile away. "The other Morindim in the area watched the whole thing. The word will spread, and nobody will come anywhere near us now. Let's mount up and get going. It's still a long way to the coast."

In bits and pieces, as they rode for the next several days, Garion picked up as much information as he really wanted about the dreadful contest he had witnessed.

"It's the *shape* that's the key to the whole thing," Belgarath concluded. "What the Morindim call Devil-Spirits don't look that much different from humans. You form an illusion drawn out of your imagination and force the spirit into it. As long as you can keep it locked up in that illusion, it has to do what you tell it to. If the illusion falters for any reason, the spirit breaks free and resumes its real form. After that, you have no control over it whatsoever. I have a certain advantage in these matters. Changing back and forth from a man to a wolf has sharpened my imagination a bit."

"Why did Beldin say you were a bad magician then?" Silk asked curiously.

"Beldin's a purist," the old man shrugged. "He feels that it's necessary to get everything into the shape—down to the last scale and toenail. It isn't, really, but he feels that way about it."

"Do you suppose we could talk about something else?" Garion asked.

They reached the coastline a day or so later. The sky had remained overcast, and the Sea of the East lay sullen and rolling under dirty gray clouds. The beach along which they rode was a broad shingle of black, round stones littered with chunks of white, bleached driftwood. Waves rolled foaming up the beach, only to slither back with an endless, mournful sigh. Sea birds hung in the stiff breeze, screaming.

"Which way?" Silk asked.

Belgarath looked around. "North," he replied.

"How far?"

"I'm not positive. It's been a long time, and I can't be sure exactly where we are."

"You're not the best guide in the world, old friend," Silk complained.

"You can't have everything."

They reached the land bridge two days later, and Garion stared at it in dismay. It was not at all what he had expected, but consisted of a series of round, wave-eroded white boulders sticking up out of the dark water and running in an irregular line off toward a dark smudge on the horizon. The wind was blowing out of the north, carrying with it a bitter chill and the smell of polar ice. Patches of white froth stretched from boulder to boulder as the swells ripped themselves to tatters on submerged reefs.

"How are we supposed to cross that?" Silk objected.

"We wait until low tide," Belgarath explained. "The reefs are mostly out of the water then."

"Mostly?"

"We might have to wade a bit from time to time. Let's strip these furs off our clothes before we start. It will give us something to do while we're waiting for the tide to turn, and they're starting to get a bit fragrant."

They took shelter behind a pile of driftwood far up on the beach and removed the stiff, smelly furs from their clothing. Then they dug food out of their packs and ate. Garion noted that the stain that had darkened the skin on his hands had begun to wear thin and that the tattoo-drawings on the faces of his companions had grown noticeably fainter.

It grew darker, and the period of twilight that separated one day from the next seemed longer than it had no more than a week ago.

"Summer's nearly over up here," Belgarath noted, looking out at the boulders gradually emerging from the receding water in the murky twilight.

"How much longer before low tide?" Silk asked.

"Another hour or so."

They waited. The wind pushed at the pile of driftwood erratically and brushed the tall grass along the upper edge of the beach, bending and tossing it.

Finally Belgarath stood up. "Let's go," he said shortly. "We'll lead the horses. The reefs are slippery, so be careful how you set your feet down."

The passage along the reef between the first steppingstones was not all that bad, but once they moved farther out, the wind became a definite factor. They were frequently drenched with stinging spray, and every so often a wave, larger than the others, broke over the top of the reef and swirled about their legs, tugging at them. The water was brutally cold.

"Do you think we'll be able to make it all the way across before the tide comes back in again?" Silk shouted over the noise.

"No," Belgarath shouted back. "We'll have to sit it out on top of one of the larger rocks."

"That sounds unpleasant."

"Not nearly so unpleasant as swimming."

They were perhaps halfway across when it became evident that the tide had turned. Waves more and more frequently broke across the top of the reef, and one particularly large one pulled the legs of Garion's horse out from under him. Garion struggled to get the frightened animal up again, pulling at the reins as

the horse's hoofs scrambled and slid on the slippery rocks of
the reef. "We'd better find a place to stop, Grandfather," he
yelled above the crash of the waves. "We'll be neck-deep in
this before long."

"Two more islands," Belgarath told him. "There's a bigger
one up ahead."

The last stretch of reef was completely submerged, and
Garion flinched as he stepped down into the icy water. The
breaking waves covered the surface with froth, making it impossible to see the bottom. He moved along blindly, probing
the unseen path with numb feet. A large wave swelled and rose
up as far as his armpits, and its powerful surge swept him off
his feet. He clung to the reins of his horse, floundering and
sputtering as he fought to get back up.

And then they were past the worst of it. They moved along
the reef with the water only ankle-deep now; a few moments
later, they climbed up onto the large, white boulder. Garion
let out a long, explosive breath as he reached safety. The wind,
blowing against his wet clothing, chilled him to the bone but
at least they were out of the water.

Later, as they sat huddled together on the leeward side of
the boulder, Garion looked out across the sullen black sea
toward the low, forbidding coastline lying ahead. The beaches,
like those of Morindland behind them, were black gravel, and
the low hills behind them were dark under the scudding gray
cloud. Nowhere was there any sign of life, but there was an
implicit threat in the very shape of the land itself.

"Is that it?" he asked finally in a hushed voice.

Belgarath's face was unreadable as he gazed across the open
water toward the coast ahead. "Yes," he replied. "That's Mallorea."

Part Two

MISHRAK AC THULL

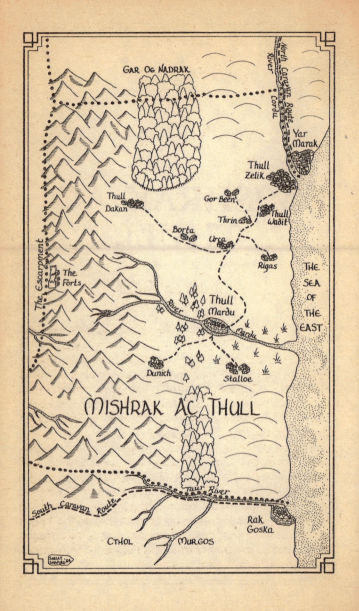

Chapter Eight

THE CROWN HAD been Queen Islena's first mistake. It was heavy and it always gave her a headache. Her decision to wear it had come originally out of a sense of insecurity. The bearded warriors in Anheg's throne room intimidated her, and she felt the need of a visible symbol of her authority. Now she was afraid to appear without it. Each day she put it on with less pleasure and entered the main hall of Anheg's palace with less certainty.

The sad truth was that Queen Islena of Cherek was completely unprepared to rule. Until the day when, dressed in regal crimson velvet and with her gold crown firmly in place, she had marched into the vaulted throne room at Val Alorn to announce that she would rule the kingdom in her husband's absence, Islena's most momentous decisions had involved which gown she would wear and how her hair was to be arranged. Now it seemed that the fate of Cherek hung in the balance each time she was faced with a choice.

The warriors lounging indolently with their ale cups about the huge, open fire pit or wandering aimlessly about on the rush-strewn floor were no help whatsoever. Each time she entered the throne room, all conversation broke off and they rose to watch as she marched to the banner-hung throne, but their faces gave no hint of their true feelings toward her. Irrationally, she concluded that the whole problem had to do with the beards. How could she possibly know what a man was thinking when his face was sunk up to the ears in hair? Only the quick intervention of Lady Merel, the cool blond wife of the Earl of Trellheim, had stopped her from ordering a universal shave.

"You can't, Islena," Merel had told her flatly, removing the quill from the queen's hand, even as she had been in the act of signing the hastily drawn-up proclamation. "They're attached to their beards like little boys attached to a favorite toy. You can't make them cut off their whiskers."

"I'm the Queen."

"Only as long as they permit you to be. They accept you out of respect for Anheg, and that's as far as it goes. If you tamper with their pride, they'll take you off the throne." And that dreadful threat had ended the matter then and there.

Islena found herself relying more and more on Barak's wife, and it was not long before the two of them, one in green and the other in royal crimson, were seldom apart. Even when Islena faltered, Merel's icy stare quelled the hints of disrespect which cropped up from time to time—usually when the ale had been distributed a bit too freely. It was Merel, ultimately, who made the day-to-day decisions which ran the kingdom. When Islena sat upon the throne, Merel, her blond braids coiled about her head to form her own crown, stood to one side in plain view of the hesitant queen. Cherek was ruled by the expressions on her face. A faint smile meant yes; a frown, no; a scarcely perceptible shrug, maybe. It worked out fairly well.

But there was one person who was not intimidated by Merel's cool gaze. Grodeg, the towering, white-bearded High Priest of Belar, inevitably requested private audience with the queen, and once Merel left the council room, Islena was lost.

Despite Anheg's call for a general mobilization, the members of the Bear-cult had not yet left to join the campaign. Their promises to join the fleet later all sounded sincere, but their excuses and delays grew more and more obvious as time went on. Islena knew that Grodeg was behind it all. Nearly every able-bodied man in the kingdom was off with the fleet, which was even now rowing up the broad expanse of the Aldur River to join Anheg in central Algaria. The household guard in the palace at Val Alorn had been reduced to grizzled old men and downy-cheeked boys. Only the Bear-cult remained, and Grodeg pushed his advantage to the limit.

He was polite enough, bowing to the queen when the occasion demanded, and never mentioning her past links with the cult, but his offers to help became more and more insistent; and when Islena faltered at his suggestions concerning this matter or that, he smoothly acted to implement them as if her hesitancy had been acceptance. Little by little, Islena was losing control, and Grodeg, with the armed might of the cult behind him, was taking charge. More and more the cult members infested the palace, giving orders, lounging about the throne room and openly grinning as they watched Islena's attempts to rule.

"You're going to have to do something, Islena," Merel said firmly one evening when the two were alone in the queen's private apartment. She was striding about the carpeted room, her hair gleaming like soft gold in the candlelight, but there was nothing soft in her expression.

"What can I do?" Islena pleaded, wringing her hands. "He's never openly disrespectful, and his decisions always *seem* to be in the best interests of Cherek."

"You need help, Islena," Merel told her.

"Whom can I turn to?" The Queen of Cherek was almost in tears.

The Lady Merel smoothed the front of her green velvet gown. "I think it's time that you wrote to Porenn," she declared.

"What do I say?" Islena begged of her.

Merel pointed at the small table in the corner where parchment and ink lay waiting. "Sit down," she instructed, "and write what I tell you to write."

Count Brador, the Tolnedran ambassador, was definitely growing tiresome, Queen Layla decided. The plump little queen marched purposefully toward the chamber where she customarily gave audiences and where the ambassador awaited her with his satchel full of documents.

The courtiers in the halls bowed as she passed, her crown slightly askew and her heels clicking on the polished oak floors, but Queen Layla uncharacteristically ignored them. This was not the time for polite exchanges or idle chitchat. The Tolnedran had to be dealt with, and she had delayed too long already.

The ambassador was an olive-skinned man with receding hair and a hooked nose. He wore a brown mantle with the gold trim that indicated his relationship to the Borunes. He lounged rather indolently in a large, cushioned chair near the window of the sunny room where he and Queen Layla were to meet. He rose as she entered and bowed with exquisite grace. "Your Highness," he murmured politely.

"My dear Count Brador," Queen Layla gushed at him, putting on her most helpless and scatterbrained expression, "please do sit down. I'm sure we know each other well enough by now to skip all these tedious formalities." She sank into a chair, fanning herself with one hand. "It's turned warm, hasn't it?"

"Summers are lovely here in Sendaria, your Highness," the count replied, settling back in his chair. "I wonder—have you had the chance to think over the proposals I gave you at our last meeting?"

Queen Layla stared at him blankly. "Which proposals were those, Count Brador?" She gave a helpless little giggle. "Please forgive me, but my mind seems to be absolutely gone these days. There are so many details. I wonder how my husband keeps them all straight."

"We were discussing the administration of the port at Camaar, your Highness," the count reminded her gently.

"We were?" The queen gave him a blank look of total incomprehension, secretly delighted at the flicker of annoyance that crossed his face. It was her best ploy. By pretending to have forgotten all previous conversations, she forced him to begin at the beginning every time they met. The count's strategy, she knew, depended upon a gradual build-up to his final proposal, and her pretended forgetfulness neatly defeated that. "Whatever led us into such a tedious subject as that?" she added.

"Surely your Highness recalls," the count protested with just the slightest hint of annoyance. "The Tolnedran merchant vessel, *Star of Tol Horb*, was kept standing at anchor for a week and a half in the harbor before moorage could be found for her. Every day's delay in unloading her was costing a fortune."

"Things are so hectic these days," the queen of Sendaria sighed. "It's the manpower shortage, you understand. Everybody who hasn't gone off to war is busy freighting supplies to the army. I'll send a very stern note to the port authorities about it, though. Was there anything else, Count Brador?"

Brador coughed uncomfortably. "Uh—your Highness has already forwarded just such a note," he reminded her.

"I have?" Queen Layla feigned astonishment. "Wonderful. That takes care of everything then, doesn't it? And you've dropped by to thank me." She smiled girlishly. "How exquisitely courteous of you." She leaned forward to put one hand impulsively on his wrist, quite deliberately knocking the rolled parchment he was holding out of his hand. "How clumsy of me," she exclaimed, bending quickly to pick up the parchment before he could retrieve it. Then she sat back in her chair, tapping the rolled document absently against her cheek as if lost in thought.

"Uh—actually, your Highness, our discussions had moved somewhat beyond your note to the port authorities," Brador told her, nervously eyeing the parchment she had so deftly taken from him. "You may recall that I offered Tolnedran assistance in administering the port. I believe we agreed that such assistance might help to alleviate the manpower shortage your Highness just mentioned."

"What an absolutely marvelous idea," Layla exclaimed. She brought her plump little fist down on the arm of her chair as if in an outburst of enthusiasm. At that prearranged signal, two of her younger children burst into the room, arguing loudly.

"Mother!" Princess Gelda wailed in outrage, "Fernie stole my red ribbon!"

"I did not!" Princess Ferna denied the charge indignantly. "She gave it to me for my blue beads."

"Did not!" Gelda snapped.

"Did so!" Ferna replied.

"Children, children," Layla chided them. "Can't you see that Mother's busy? What will the dear count think of us?"

"But she stole it, Mother!" Gelda protested. "She stole my red ribbon."

"Did not!" Ferna said, spitefully sticking her tongue out at her sister.

Trailing behind them with a look of wide-eyed interest came little Prince Meldig, Queen Layla's youngest child. In one hand the prince held a jam pot, and his face was liberally smeared with the contents. "Oh, that's just impossible," Layla exclaimed, jumping to her feet. "You girls are supposed to be watching him." She bustled over to the jam-decorated prince, crumpled the parchment she was holding and began wiping his face with it. Abruptly she stopped. "Oh dear," she said as if suddenly realizing what she was doing. "Was this important, Count Brador?" she asked the Tolnedran, holding out the rumpled, sticky document.

Brador's shoulders, however, had slumped in defeat. "No, your Highness," he replied in a voice filled with resignation, "not really. The royal house of Sendaria has me quite outnumbered, it appears." He rose to his feet. "Perhaps another time," he murmured, bowing. "With your Highness's permission," he said, preparing to leave.

"You mustn't forget this, Count Brador," Layla said, pressing the parchment into his cringing hands.

The count's face had a faintly martyred expression as he withdrew. Queen Layla turned back to her children, who were grinning impishly at her. She began to scold them in a loud voice until she was certain the count was well out of earshot, then she knelt, embraced them all and began to laugh.

"Did we do it right, Mother?" Princess Gelda asked.

"You were absolutely perfect," Queen Layla replied, still laughing.

Sadi the eunuch had grown careless, lulled somewhat by the air of polite civility that had pervaded the palace at Sthiss Tor for the past year, and one of his associates, seizing upon his unwariness, had taken the opportunity to poison him. Sadi definitely did not appreciate being poisoned. The antidotes all tasted vile, and the aftereffects left him weak and light-headed. Thus it was that he viewed the appearance of the mail-shirted emissary of King Taur Urgas with thinly veiled irritation.

"Taur Urgas, King of the Murgos, greets Sadi, chief servant of Immortal Salmissra," the Murgo declaimed with a deep bow as he entered the cool, dimly lighted study from which Sadi conducted most of the nation's affairs.

"The servant of the Serpent Queen returns the greetings of the right arm of the Dragon-God of Angarak." Sadi mouthed the formula phrases almost indifferently. "Do you suppose we could get to the point? I'm feeling a bit indisposed at the moment."

"I was very pleased at your recovery," the ambassador lied, his scarred face carefully expressionless. "Has the poisoner been apprehended yet?" He drew up a chair and sat down at the polished table Sadi used for a desk.

"Naturally," Sadi replied, absently rubbing his hand over his shaved scalp.

"And executed?"

"Why would we want to do that? The man's a professional poisoner. He was only doing his job."

The Murgo looked a bit startled.

"We look upon a good poisoner as a national asset," Sadi

told him. "If we start killing them every time they poison somebody, very soon there won't be any of them left, and you never know when *I* might want somebody poisoned."

The Murgo ambassador shook his head incredulously. "You people have an amazing amount of tolerance, Sadi," he said in his harshly accented voice. "What about his employer?"

"That's another matter," Sadi replied. "His employer is currently entertaining the leeches at the bottom of the river. Is your visit official, or did you merely stop by to inquire after my health?"

"A bit of each, Excellency."

"You Murgos are an economical race," Sadi observed dryly. "What does Taur Urgas want this time?"

"The Alorns are preparing to invade Mishrak ac Thull, your Excellency."

"So I've heard. What's that got to do with Nyissa?"

"Nyissans have no reason to be fond of Alorns."

"Nor any to be fond of Murgos, either," Sadi pointed out.

"It was Aloria that invaded Nyissa following the death of the Rivan King," the Murgo reminded him, "and it was Cthol Murgos that provided the market for Nyissa's primary export."

"My dear fellow, please get to the point," Sadi said, rubbing his scalp wearily. "I'm not going to operate on the basis of long-past insults or long-forgotten favors. The slave trade is no longer significant, and the scars left by the Alorn invasion disappeared centuries ago. What does Taur Urgas want?"

"My king wishes to avoid bloodshed," the Murgo stated. "The Tolnedran legions form a significant part of the armies massing in Algaria. If a threat—just a threat, mind you—of unfriendly activity suddenly appeared on his unprotected southern frontier, Ran Borune would recall those legions. Their loss would persuade the Alorns to abandon this adventure."

"You want *me* to invade Tolnedra?" Sadi demanded incredulously.

"Naturally not, Lord Sadi. His Majesty merely wishes your permission to move certain forces through your territory to pose the threat on Tolnedra's southern border. No blood need be shed at all."

"Except Nyissan blood, once the Murgo army withdraws. The legions would swarm down across the River of the Woods like angry hornets."

"Taur Urgas would be more than willing to leave garrisons behind to guarantee the integrity of Nyissan territory."

"I'm sure he would," Sadi observed dryly. "Advise your king that his proposal is quite unacceptable at this particular time."

"The King of Cthol Murgos is a powerful man," the Murgo said firmly, "and he remembers those who thwart him even more keenly than he remembers his friends."

"Taur Urgas is a madman," Sadi told him bluntly. "He wants to avoid trouble with the Alorns so that he can concentrate on 'Zakath. Despite his insanity, however, he's *not* so foolish as to send an army into Nyissa uninvited. An army must eat, and Nyissa's a bad place to forage for food—as history has demonstrated. The most tempting fruit has bitter juice."

"A Murgo army carries its own food," the ambassador replied stiffly.

"Good for them. But where do they plan to find drinking water? I don't believe we're getting anywhere with this. I'll convey your proposal to her Majesty. She, of course, will make the final decision. I suspect, however, that you'll need to offer something much more attractive than a permanent Murgo occupation to persuade her to consider the matter favorably. Was that all?"

The Murgo rose to his feet, his scarred face angry. He bowed coldly to Sadi and withdrew without further conversation.

Sadi thought about it for a while. He could gain a great deal of advantage at a minimal cost if he played this right. A few carefully worded dispatches to King Rhodar in Algaria would put Nyissa among the friends of the west. If Rhodar's army should happen to win, Nyissa would benefit. If, on the other hand, it appeared that the west was about to lose, the proposal of Taur Urgas could be accepted. In either case, Nyissa would be on the winning side. The whole notion appealed to Sadi enormously. He stood up, his iridescent silk robe rustling, and went to a nearby cabinet. He took out a crystal decanter containing a dark blue liquid and carefully measured some of the thick syrup into a small glass and drank it. Almost immediately a euphoric calm came over him as his favorite drug took effect. A moment or two later, he felt that he was ready to face his queen. He was even smiling as he walked from his study into the dim corridor leading to the throne room.

As always, Salmissra's chamber was dimly lighted by oil lamps hanging on long silver chains from the shadowy ceiling. The chorus of eunuchs still knelt adoringly in the queen's presence, but they no longer sang her praises. Noise of any kind irritated Salmissra now, and it was wise not to irritate her. The Serpent Queen still occupied the divanlike throne beneath the towering statue of Issa. She dozed interminably, stirring her mottled coils with the seething dry hiss of scale rubbing against scale. But even in restless doze, her tongue flickered nervously. Sadi approached the throne, perfunctorily prostrated himself on the polished stone floor, and waited. His scent on the air would announce him to the hooded serpent who was his queen.

"Yes, Sadi?" she whispered finally, her voice a dusty hiss.

"The Murgos wish an alliance, my Queen," Sadi informed her. "Taur Urgas wants to threaten the Tolnedrans from the south to force Ran Borune to withdraw his legions from the Thullish border."

"Interesting," she replied indifferently. Her dead eyes bored into him and her coils rustled. "What do you think?"

"Neutrality costs nothing, Divine Salmissra," Sadi replied. "Alliance with either side would be premature."

Salmissra turned, her mottled hood flaring as she regarded her reflection in the mirror beside her throne. The crown still rested on her head, as polished and glistening as her scales. Her tongue flickered, and her eyes, flat as glass, looked at the mirror. "Do what you think best, Sadi," she told him in an uncaring tone.

"I'll deal with the matter, my Queen," Sadi said, putting his face to the floor in preparation to leave.

"I have no need of Torak now," she mused, still staring at the mirror. "Polgara saw to that."

"Yes, my Queen," Sadi agreed in a neutral voice, beginning to rise.

She turned to look at him. "Stay a while, Sadi. I'm lonely."

Sadi sank immediately back to the polished floor.

"I have such strange dreams sometimes, Sadi," she hissed. "Such very strange dreams. I seem to remember things—things that happened when my blood was warm and I was a woman. Strange thoughts come to me in my dreams, and strange hungers." She looked directly at him, her hood flaring again as her pointed face stretched out toward him. "Was I really like that, Sadi? It all seems like something seen through smoke."

"It was a difficult time, my Queen," Sadi replied candidly. "For all of us."

"Polgara was right, you know," she continued in that expiring whisper. "The potions enflamed me. I think it's better this way—no passions, no hungers, no fears." She turned back to her mirror. "You may go now, Sadi."

He rose and started toward the door.

"Oh, Sadi."

"Yes, my Queen?"

"If I caused you trouble before, I'm sorry."

He stared at her.

"Not very much, of course—but just a little." Then she returned to her reflection.

Sadi was trembling as he closed the door behind him. Sometime later, he sent for Issus. The shabby, one-eyed hireling entered the chief eunuch's study with a certain hesitancy, and his face was a bit apprehensive.

"Come in, Issus," Sadi told him calmly.

"I hope you aren't holding any grudges, Sadi," Issus said nervously, looking about to be sure they were alone. "There was nothing personal in it, you know."

"It's all right, Issus," Sadi assured him. "You were only doing what you were paid to do."

"How did you manage to detect it?" Issus asked with a certain professional curiosity. "Most men are too far gone for the antidote to work before they realize they've been poisoned."

"Your concoction leaves just the faintest aftertaste of lemon," Sadi replied. "I've been trained to recognize it."

"Ah," Issus said. "I'll have to work on that. Otherwise it's a very good poison."

"An excellent poison, Issus," Sadi agreed. "That brings us to the reason I sent for you. There's a man I think I can dispense with."

Issus' single eye brightened, and he rubbed his hands together. "The usual fee?"

"Naturally."

"Who is he?"

"The Murgo ambassador."

Issus' face clouded for a moment. "He'll be difficult to get to." He scratched at his stubbled scalp.

"You'll find a way. I have the utmost confidence in you."

"I'm the best," Issus agreed with no trace of false modesty.

"The ambassador's pressing me in certain negotiations that I need to delay," Sadi continued. "His sudden demise should interrupt things a bit."

"You don't really have to explain, Sadi," Issus told him. "I don't need to know why you want him killed."

"But you do need to know *how*. For various reasons, I'd like for this to look very natural. Could you arrange for him— and perhaps a few others in his household—to come down with some kind of fever? Something suitably virulent?"

Issus frowned. "That's tricky. Something like that can get out of hand. You might end up infecting an entire neighborhood, and there would be very few survivors."

Sadi shrugged. "One sometimes must make sacrifices. Can you do it?"

Issus nodded gravely.

"Do it then, and I'll compose a letter expressing my regrets to King Taur Urgas."

Queen Silar sat at her loom in the great hall of the Algar Stronghold, humming softly to herself as her fingers passed the shuttle back and forth with a drowsy, clicking sound. Sun-

light streamed down from the narrow windows set high up in
the wall, filling the huge, narrow room with a diffused golden
light. King Cho-Hag and Hettar were away from the Stronghold, preparing a huge encampment some few leagues out from
the base of the eastern escarpment for the army of Alorns,
Arends, Sendars, and Tolnedrans approaching from the west.
Although he was still within the borders of the kingdom, Cho-
Hag had formally transferred authority to his wife, extracting
a pledge of support from all of the assembled Clan-Chiefs.

The Queen of Algaria was a silent woman, and her calm
face seldom betrayed her emotions. She had spent her entire
life in the background, often so unobtrusively that people did
not even realize that she was present. She had, however, kept
her eyes and her ears open. Her crippled husband, moreover,
had confided in her. His quiet, dark-haired queen knew exactly
what was going on.

Elvar, Archpriest of Algaria, stood, white-robed and much
puffed-up with his own importance, reading to her the set of
carefully prepared proclamations which would effectively
transfer all power to him. His tone was condescending as he
explained them to her.

"Is that all?" she asked when he had finished.

"It's really for the best, your Highness," he told her loftily.
"All the world knows that women are unsuited to rule. Shall
I send for pen and ink?"

"Not just yet, Elvar," she replied calmly, her hands busy
at her loom.

"But—"

"You know, I just had the oddest thought," she said, looking
directly at him. "You're the Archpriest of Belar here in Algaria,
but you never go out of the Stronghold. Isn't that a bit peculiar?"

"My duties, your Highness, compell me—"

"Isn't your first duty to the people—and to the children of
Belar? We've been terribly selfish keeping you here when your
heart must be yearning to be out among the clans, overseeing
the religious instruction of the children."

He stared at her, his mouth suddenly agape.

"And all the other priests as well," she continued. "They all seem to be concentrated here at the Stronghold, pressed into administrative duties. A priest is too valuable a man for such tasks. This situation must be corrected immediately."

"But—"

"No, Elvar. My duty as queen is absolutely clear. The children of Algaria must come first. I release you from all your duties here at the Sronghold so that you may return to your chosen vocation." She smiled suddenly. "I'll even draw up an itinerary for you myself," she said brightly. She thought a moment. "The times are troubled," she added, "so perhaps I'd better provide you with an escort—several trustworthy men from my own clan who can be depended upon to make sure that you aren't interrupted in your travels or distracted from your preaching by any disturbing messages from abroad." She looked at him again. "That will be all, Elvar. You'd probably better go pack. It will be a number of seasons before you return, I imagine."

The Archpriest of Belar was making strangled noises.

"Oh, one other thing." The queen carefully chose another skein of yarn and held it up to the sunlight. "It's been years since anyone made a survey of the herds. As long as you're going to be out there anyway, I think I'd like an accurate count of all the calves and colts in Algaria. It will give you something to occupy your mind. Send me a report from time to time, won't you?" She returned to her weaving. "You're dismissed, Elvar," she said placidly, not even bothering to look up as the Archpriest, shaking with rage, tottered away to make preparations for his roving imprisonment.

Lord Morin, High Chamberlain to his Imperial Majesty, Ran Borune XXIII, sighed as he entered the Emperor's private garden. Another tirade was undoubtedly in the offing, and Morin had already heard it all a dozen times at least. The Emperor had an extraordinary capacity for repeating himself sometimes.

Ran Borune, however, was in an odd mood. The bald, beak-nosed little Emperor sat pensively in his chair beneath a shady arbor, listening to the trilling of his canary. "He's never spoken again, did you know that, Morin?" the Emperor said as his chamberlain approached across the close-clipped grass. "Just that one time when Polgara was here." He looked at the little golden bird again, his eyes sad. Then he sighed. "I think I came out second best in that bargain. Polgara gave me a canary and took Ce'Nedra in exchange." He looked around at his sun-drenched garden and the cool marble walls surrounding it. "Is it just my imagination, Morin, or does the palace seem sort of cold and empty now?" He lapsed once more into moody silence, staring with unseeing eyes at a bed of crimson roses.

Then there was an odd sound, and Lord Morin looked sharply at the Emperor, half afraid that his ruler was about to go into another seizure. But there was no evidence of that. Instead, Morin perceived that Ran Borune was chuckling. "Did you see how she tricked me, Morin?" The Emperor laughed. "She deliberately goaded me into that fit. What a son she would have made! She could have been the greatest Emperor in Tolnedra's history." Ran Borune was laughing openly now, his secret delight at Ce'Nedra's cleverness suddenly emerging.

"She *is* your daughter after all, your Majesty," Lord Morin observed.

"To think that she could raise an army of that size when she's barely sixteen," the Emperor marveled. "What a splendid child!" He seemed quite suddenly to have recovered from the gloomy peevishness that had dogged him since his return to Tol Honeth. His laughter trailed away after several moments, and his bright little eyes narrowed shrewdly. "Those legions she stole from me are likely to become fractious without professional leadership," he mused.

"I'd say that's Ce'Nedra's problem, your Majesty," Morin replied. "Or Polgara's."

"Well—" The Emperor scratched one ear. "I don't know, Morin. The situation out there isn't too clear." He looked at his chamberlain. "Are you acquainted with General Varana?"

"The Duke of Anadile? Of course, your Majesty. A thoroughly professional sort of fellow—solid, unassuming, extremely intelligent."

"He's an old friend of the family," Ran Borune confided. "Ce'Nedra knows him and she would listen to his advice. Why don't you go to him, Morin, and suggest that he might want to take a leave of absence—perhaps go to Algaria and have a look at things?"

"I'm certain that he'd be overjoyed at the idea of a vacation," Lord Morin agreed. "Garrison life in the summertime can be very tedious."

"It's just a suggestion," the Emperor stressed. "His presence in the war zone would have to be strictly unofficial."

"Naturally, your Majesty."

"And if he just *happened* to make a few suggestions—or even provide a bit of leadership, we certainly wouldn't have any knowledge of it, would we? After all, what a private citizen does with his own time is *his* business, right?"

"Absolutely, your Majesty."

The Emperor grinned broadly. "And we'll all stick to that story, won't we, Morin?"

"Like glue, your Majesty," Morin replied gravely.

The crown prince of Drasnia burped noisily in his mother's ear, sighed, and promptly fell asleep on her shoulder. Queen Porenn smiled at him, tucked him back in his cradle, and turned again to the stringy-appearing man in nondescript clothing who sprawled in a nearby chair. The emaciated man was known only by the peculiar name "Javelin." Javelin was the chief of the Drasnian intelligence service and one of Porenn's closest advisers.

"Anyway," he continued his report, "the Tolnedran girl's army is about two days' march from the Stronghold. The engineers are moving along ahead of schedule with the hoists on top of the escarpment, and the Chereks are preparing to begin the portage from the east bank of the Aldur."

"Everything seems to be going according to plan, then," the queen said, resuming her seat at the polished table near the window.

"There's a bit of trouble in Arendia," Javelin noted. "The usual ambushes and bickerings—nothing really serious. Queen

Layla's got the Tolnedran, Bravor, so completely off-balance that he might as well not even be in Sendaria." He scratched at his long, pointed jaw. "There's peculiar information coming out of Sthiss Tor. The Murgos are trying to negotiate something, but their emissaries keep dying. We'll try to get somebody closer to Sadi to find out exactly what's going on. Let's see—what else? Oh, the Honeths have finally united behind one candidate—a pompous, arrogant jackass who's offended just about everybody in Tol Honeth. They'll try to buy the crown for him, but he'd be hopelessly incompetent as emperor. Even with all their money, it's going to be difficult for them to put him on the throne. I guess that's about all, your Highness."

"I've had a letter from Islena in Val Alorn," Queen Porenn told him.

"Yes, your Highness," Javelin replied urbanely, "I know."

"Javelin, have you been reading my mail again?" she demanded with a sudden flash of irritation.

"Just trying to stay current with what's going on in the world, Porenn."

"I've told you to stop that."

"You didn't really expect me to do it, did you?" He seemed actually surprised.

She laughed. "You're impossible."

"Of course I am. I'm supposed to be."

"Can we get any help to Islena?"

"I'll put some people on it," he assured her. "We can probably work through Merel, the wife of the Earl of Trellheim. She's starting to show some signs of maturity and she's close to Islena."

"I think we'd better have a close look at our own intelligence service, too," Porenn suggested. "Let's pin down everyone who might have any connections with the Bear-cult. The time might come when we'll have to take steps."

Javelin nodded his agreement.

There was a light tapping at the door.

"Yes?" Porenn answered.

The door opened and a servant thrust his head into the room.

"Excuse me, your Highness," he said, "but there's a Nadrak merchant here—a man named Yarblek. He says he wants to discuss the salmon run." The servant looked perplexed.

Queen Porenn straightened in her chair. "Send him in," she ordered, "at once."

Chapter Nine

THE SPEECHES WERE over. The orations that had caused Princess Ce'Nedra such agony had done their work, and she found herself less and less in the center of things. At first the days opened before her full of glorious freedom. The dreadful anxiety that had filled her at the prospect of addressing vast crowds of men two or three times a day was gone now. Her nervous exhaustion disappeared, and she no longer awoke in the middle of the night trembling and terrified. For almost an entire week she reveled in it, luxuriated in it. Then, of course, she became dreadfully bored.

The army she had gathered in Arendia and northern Tolnedra moved like a great sea in the foothills of Ulgoland. The Mimbrate knights, their armor glittering in the bright sunlight and their long, streaming, many-colored pennons snapping in the breeze, moved at the forefront of the host, and behind them, spreading out across the rolling green hills, marched the solid mass of Ce'Nedra's infantry, Sendars, Asturians, Rivans, and a few Chereks. And there, solidly in the center, forming the very core, marched the gleaming ranks of the legions of Imperial Tolnedra, their crimson standards aloft and the white plumes on their helmets waving in time to their measured steps. It was very stirring for the first few days to ride at the head of the enormous force, moving at her command toward the east, but the novelty of it all soon wore thin.

Princess Ce'Nedra's gradual drift away from the center of command was largely her own fault. The decisions now had to do more often than not with logistics—tedious little details concerning bivouac areas and field-kitchens—and Ce'Nedra found discussions of such matters tiresome. Those details, however, dictated the snail's pace of her army.

Quite suddenly, to everyone's astonishment, King Fulrach of Sendaria became the absolute commander of the host. It was he who decided how far they would march each day, when they would rest and where they would set up each night's encampment. His authority derived directly from the fact that the supply wagons were his. Quite early during the march down through northern Arendia, the dumpy-looking Sendarian monarch had taken one look at the rather sketchy plans the Alorn kings had drawn up for feeding the troops, had shaken his head in disapproval, and then had taken charge of that aspect of the campaign himself. Sendaria was a land of farms, and her storehouses bulged. Moreover, at certain seasons, every road and lane in Sendaria crawled with wagons. With an almost casual efficiency, King Fulrach issued a few orders, and soon whole caravans of heavily laden wagons moved down through Arendia to Tolnedra and then turned eastward to follow the army. The pace of the army was dictated by those creaking supply wagons.

They were only a few days into the Ulgo foothills when the full weight of King Fulrach's authority became clear.

"Fulrach," King Rhodar of Drasnia objected when the King of the Sendars called a halt for yet another rest period, "if we don't move any faster than this, it will take us all summer to get to the eastern escarpment."

"You're exaggerating, Rhodar," King Fulrach replied mildly. "We're making pretty good time. The supply wagons are heavy, and the wagon horses have to be rested every hour."

"This is impossible," Rhodar declared. "I'm going to pick up the pace."

"That's up to you, of course." The brown-bearded Sendar shrugged, coolly eyeing Rhodar's vast paunch. "But if you exhaust my wagon horses today, you won't eat tomorrow."

And that ended that.

The going in the steep passes of Ulgoland was even slower. Ce'Nedra entered that land of thick forests and rocky crags with apprehension. She vividly remembered the flight with Grul the Eldrak and the attacks of the Algroths and the Hrulgin that had so terrified her that previous winter. There were few meetings with the monsters that lurked in the Ulgo mountains, however. The army was so large that even the fiercest creatures avoided it. Mandorallen, the Baron of Vo Mandor, rather regretfully reported only brief sightings.

"Mayhap if I were to ride a day's march in advance of our main force, I might find opportunity to engage some of the more frolicsome beasts," he mused aloud one evening, staring thoughtfully into the fire.

"You never get enough, do you?" Barak asked him pointedly.

"Never mind, Mandorallen," Polgara told the great knight. "The creatures aren't hurting us, and the Gorim of Ulgo would be happier if we didn't bother them."

Mandorallen sighed.

"Is he always like that?" King Anheg asked Barak curiously.

"You have absolutely no idea," Barak replied.

The slow march through Ulgoland, regardless of how much it chafed Rhodar, Brand, and Anheg, did, however, conserve the strength of the army, and they came down onto the plains of Algaria in surprisingly good shape.

"We'll go on to the Algarian Stronghold," King Rhodar decided as the army poured down out of the last pass and fanned out across the rolling grasslands. "We need to regroup a bit, and I don't see any point in moving to the base of the escarpment until the engineers are ready for us. Besides, I'd prefer not to announce the size of our army to any Thull who happens to glance down from the top of the cliff."

And so, in easy stages, the army marched across Algaria,

trampling a mile-wide swath through the tall grass. Vast herds of cattle paused briefly in their grazing to watch with mild-eyed astonishment as the horde marched by, then returned to their feeding under the protective watch of mounted Algar clansmen.

The encampment that was set up around the towering Stronghold in south central Algaria stretched for miles, and the watch fires at night seemed almost a reflection of the stars. Once she was comfortably quartered in the Stronghold, Princess Ce'Nedra found herself even more removed from the day-to-day command of her troops. Her hours seemed filled with tedium. This is not to say that she did not receive reports. A rigorous schedule of training was instituted, in part because large portions of the army were not professional soldiers, but primarily to avoid the idleness that led to discipline problems. Each morning, Colonel Brendig, the sober-faced Sendarian baronet who seemed utterly devoid of humor, reported the progress of the previous day's training with excruciating thoroughness, along with all sorts of other tedious little details—most of which Ce'Nedra found extremely distasteful.

One morning after Brendig had respectfully withdrawn, Ce'Nedra finally exploded. "If he mentions the word 'sanitation' one more time, I think I'll scream," she declared to Adara and Polgara. The princess was pacing up and down, flinging her arms in the air in exasperation.

"It *is* fairly important in an army of this size, Ce'Nedra," Adara calmly pointed out.

"But does he have to *talk* about it all the time? It's a disgusting subject."

Polgara, who had been patiently teaching the little blond waif, Errand, how to lace up his boots, looked up, assessed Ce'Nedra's mood in a single glance, and then made a suggestion. "Why don't you young ladies take some horses and go for a ride? A bit of fresh air and exercise seems definitely to be in order."

It took only a short while for them to find the blond Mimbrate girl, Ariana. They knew exactly where to look. It took a bit longer, however, to wrench her away from her rapt contemplation of Lelldorin of Wildantor. Lelldorin, with the aid of his cousin Torasin, was struggling to teach a group of Arendish serfs the basics of archery. Torasin, a fiery young Asturian patriot, had joined the army late. There had been, Ce'Nedra gathered, some unpleasantness between two young men, but the prospect of war and glory had finally been too much for Torasin to resist. He had overtaken the army in the western foothills of Ulgoland, mounted on a horse half-dead from hard riding. His reconciliation with Lelldorin had been emotional, and now the two were closer than ever. Ariana, however, watched only Lelldorin. Her eyes glowed as she gazed at him with an adoration so totally mindless that it was frightening.

The three girls, dressed in soft leather Algar riding clothes, cantered out through the encampment in bright midmorning sunlight, followed inevitably by Olban, youngest son of the Rivan Warder, and a detachment of guards. Ce'Nedra did not know exactly what to make of Olban. Since a hidden Murgo had made an attempt on her life in the Arendish forest, the young Rivan had appointed himself the chief of her personal bodyguards, and absolutely nothing could move him to abandon that duty. For some reason, he seemed almost grateful for the opportunity to serve, and Ce'Nedra was glumly certain that only physical force could make him stop.

It was a warm, cloudless day, and the blue sky stretched over the incredible expanse of the Algarian plain, where tall grass bent before a vagrant breeze. Once they were out of sight of the encampment, Ce'Nedra's spirits rose enormously. She rode the white horse King Cho-Hag had given her, a patient, even-tempered animal she had named Noble. Noble was probably not a good name for him, since he was a lazy horse. A great part of his placidity arose from the fact that his new owner was so tiny that she had virtually no weight. Moreover, in an excess of affection, Ce'Nedra babied him outrageously, slipping apples and bits of sweets to him whenever possible. As a result of his light exercise and rich diet, Noble was developing a noticeable portliness.

In the company of her two friends, and trailed by the watchful young Olban, the princess, mounted on her stout white horse, rode out across the grassland, exulting in the sense of freedom their ride brought to her.

They reined in at the base of a long, sloping hill to rest their mounts. Noble, puffing like a bellows, cast a reproachful look over his shoulder at his tiny mistress, but she heartlessly ignored his unspoken complaint. "It's an absolutely wonderful day for a ride," she exclaimed enthusiastically.

Ariana sighed.

Ce'Nedra laughed at her. "Oh, come now, it's not as if Lelldorin were going someplace, Ariana, and it's good for men to miss us a little once in a while."

Ariana smiled rather wanly, then sighed again.

"Perhaps it's not as good for us to miss them, however," Adara murmured without any trace of a smile.

"What *is* that lovely fragrance?" Ce'Nedra asked suddenly.

Adara lifted her porcelain face to sniff at the light breeze, then suddenly looked around as if trying to pinpoint their exact location. "Come with me," she said with an uncharacteristic note of command in her voice, and she led them around the base of the hill to the far side. About halfway up the grassy slope there was a patch of low, dark green bushes covered with pale lavender flowers. There had been that morning a hatch of blue butterflies, and the winged creatures hovered in an ecstatic cloud over the flowers. Without pausing, Adara pressed her mount up the slope and swung down from her saddle. There with a low cry she knelt almost reverently, gathering the bushes in her arms as if embracing them.

When Ce'Nedra drew closer, she was amazed to see tears welling up in her gentle friend's gray eyes, although Adara was actually smiling. "Whatever is wrong, Adara?" she asked.

"They're *my* flowers," Adara replied in a vibrant voice. "I didn't realize that they'd grow and spread this way."

"What are you talking about?"

"Garion created this flower last winter—just for me. There was only one—just one. I saw it come into existence right there in his hand. I'd forgotten it until just now. Look how far it's spread in just one season."

Ce'Nedra felt a sudden pang of jealousy. Garion had never

created a flower for *her*. She bent and pulled one of the lavendar blooms from a bush, tugging perhaps just a bit harder than necessary. "It's lopsided," she sniffed, looking at the flower critically. Then she bit her lip, wishing she hadn't said that.

Adara gave her a quick look of protest.

"I'm only teasing, Adara," Ce'Nedra said quickly with a false little laugh. In spite of herself, still wanting to find something else wrong with the flower, she bent her face to the small, crooked blossom in her hand. Its fragrance seemed to erase all of her cares and to lift her spirits tremendously.

Ariana had also dismounted, and she too was breathing in the gentle odor of the flowers, although there was a slight frown on her face. "Might I gather some few of thy blossoms, Lady Adara?" she inquired. "Methinks they have some strange property concealed within their blushing petals that may be of some interest to lady Polgara—some healing agent too subtle for my limited familiarity with unguents and aromatic herbs to discern."

Rather predictably, Ce'Nedra, having gone one way, suddenly reversed herself. "Marvelous!" she exclaimed, clapping her hands with delight. "Wouldn't it be wonderful if your flower turned out to be a great medicine, Adara? Some miraculous cure? We could call it 'Adara's rose,' and sick men would bless your name forever."

"It doesn't exactly look like a rose, Ce'Nedra," Adara pointed out.

"Nonsense," Ce'Nedra brushed the distinction aside. "I'm supposed to be a queen, after all, so if I say it's a rose, then it's a rose, and that's that. We'll take the flowers back to Lady Polgara at once." She turned back to her tubby horse, who was lazily regarding the flowers as if wondering whether or not to eat a few of them. "Come, Noble," the princess said to him with extravagant overstatement. "We'll gallop back to the Stronghold."

Noble winced visibly at the word "gallop."

Polgara examined the flowers carefully, but, to the disappointment of the princess and her friends, she would not commit herself immediately concerning their medicinal value. A bit subdued, the little princess returned quietly to her quarters and her duties.

Colonel Brendig was awaiting her. Upon reflection, Ce'Nedra concluded that Colonel Brendig was by far the most practical man she had ever met. No detail was too small for him. In a lesser man, such concern with little things might have been passed off as mere fussiness, but the colonel's belief that big things were made up of little things gave his patient attention to detail a certain dignity. He seemed to be everywhere in the camp; in his wake, tent-ropes were tightened, cluttered heaps of equipment were arranged into neat stacks, and casually open doublets were quickly buttoned up.

"I hope that her Majesty found her ride refreshing," the colonel said politely, bowing as Ce'Nedra entered the room.

"Thank you, Colonel Brendig," the princess replied. "My majesty did." She was in a whimsical frame of mind, and it was always a delight to tease this sober-faced Sendar.

A brief smile touched Brendig's lips, and then he immediately got down to the business of the midday report. "I'm pleased to advise your majesty that the Drasnian engineers have nearly completed the hoists atop the escarpment," he reported. "All that remains is the rigging of the counterweights which will help to lift the Cherek warships."

"That's nice," Ce'Nedra said with the vacant, empty-headed smile she knew drove him absolutely wild.

Brendig's jaw tightened slightly, but his face betrayed no other sign of his momentary flash of irritation. "The Chereks are beginning to remove the masts and rigging from their ships in preparation for the portage," he continued, "and the fortified postions up on top of the escarpment are several days ahead of schedule."

"How wonderful!" Ce'Nedra exclaimed, clapping her hands with a great show of girlish delight.

"Your Majesty, *please*," Brendig complained.

"I'm sorry, Colonel Brendig," Ce'Nedra apologized, affectionately patting his hand. "For some reason you bring out the very worst in me. Don't you *ever* smile?"

He looked at her with an absolutely straight face. "I am smiling, your Majesty," he said. "Oh—you have a visitor from Tolnedra."

"A visitor? Who?"

"A General Varana, the Duke of Anadile."

"Varana? Here? What on earth is he doing in Algaria? Is he alone?"

"There are a number of other Tolnedran gentlemen with him," Brendig replied. "They aren't in uniform, but they have the general bearing of military men. They *say* that they're here as private observers. General Varana expressed a desire to pay his respects whenever it might be convenient."

"Of course, Colonel Brendig," Ce'Nedra said with an enthusiasm that was no longer feigned. "Please send for him at once."

Ce'Nedra had known General Varana since her earliest childhood. He was a stocky man with graying, curly hair and a stiff left knee that gave him a noticeable limp. He was blessed with that wry, understated sense of humor so characteristic of the Anadilian family. Of all the noble houses of Tolnedra, the Borunes were most comfortable with the Anadiles. Both families were southern, for one thing, and the Anadiles usually sided with the Borunes in disputes with the powerful families of the north. Although Anadile was only a duchy, there had never been any hint of subservience in the family's alliances with the Grand Dukes of the House of Borune. Indeed, Anadilian dukes, more often than not, poked gentle fun at their more powerful neighbors. Serious historians and statesmen had long considered it a misfortune for the Empire that the talented House of Anadile had not enough wealth to make a serious bid for the Imperial Throne.

When General Varana politely limped into the room where Ce'Nedra impatiently awaited him, there was a faint smile hovering on his lips and a quizzical lift to one of his eyebrows. "Your Majesty," he greeted her with a bow.

"Uncle Varana," the princess exclaimed, flying to embrace him. Varana was not, in fact, her uncle, but she had always thought of him as such.

"What have you gone and done now, my little Ce'Nedra?" He laughed, enfolding her in his thick-muscled arms. "You're turning the world upside-down, you know. What's a Borune doing in the middle of Algaria with an Alorn army at her back?"

"I'm going to invade Mishrak ac Thull," she declared impishly.

"Really? Whatever for? Did King Gethell of Thulldom insult the House of Borune in some way? I hadn't heard about it."

"It's an Alorn matter," Ce'Nedra replied airily.

"Oh, I see. That explains it, I suppose. Alorns don't need reasons for the things they do."

"You're laughing at me," she accused him.

"Of course I am, Ce'Nedra. The Anadiles have been laughing at the Borunes for thousands of years."

She pouted. "It's *very* serious, Uncle Varana."

"Naturally it is," he agreed, gently touching her out-thrust lower lip with one thick finger, "but that's no reason not to laugh about it."

"You're impossible," Ce'Nedra said helplessly, laughing in spite of herself. "What are you doing here?"

"Observing," he told her. "Generals do that a lot. You've got the only war that's going on just now, so several of us thought we'd drop by and have a look. Morin suggested it."

"My father's chamberlain?"

"I think that's his function, yes."

"Morin wouldn't do that—not on his own."

"Really? What astonishing news."

Ce'Nedra frowned, nibbling absently at a lock of her hair. Varana reached out and took the lock out from between her teeth. "Morin doesn't do anything unless my father tells him to," Ce'Nedra mused, once again lifting the curl to her lips.

Varana took the lock out of her fingers again.

"Don't do that," she told him.

"Why not? That's the way I broke you of sucking your thumb."

"This is different. I'm thinking."

"Think with your mouth closed."

"This was my father's idea, wasn't it?"

"I wouldn't presume to say I knew the Emperor's mind," he replied.

"Well, I would. What's that old fox up to?"

"That's hardly respectful, child."

"You say you're here to observe?"

He nodded.

"And perhaps make a few suggestions?"

He shrugged. "If anyone cares to listen. I'm not here officially, you understand. Imperial policy forbids that. Your claim to the Rivan throne is not formally recognized in Tol Honeth."

She cast a sidelong glance at him through her thick eyelashes. "These suggestions you might make—if you happened to be near a Tolnedran legion that seemed to need a bit of direction, is it at all possible that one of these suggestions might be 'forward march?'"

"That situation might arise, yes," he admitted gravely.

"And you have a number of other officers of the general staff with you?"

"I think several of them *do*, in fact, serve occasionally on that body." His eyes were twinkling with suppressed mirth.

Ce'Nedra lifted the lock again, and General Varana took it away from her once more.

"How would you like to meet King Rhodar of Drasnia?" she asked him.

"I'd be honored to meet his Majesty."

"Why don't we go see him, then?"

"Why don't we?"

"Oh, I love you, Uncle." She laughed, throwing her arms about him again.

They found King Rhodar in conference with the other leaders of the army in a large airy chamber King Cho-Hag had set aside for their use. There was no longer any pretence of formality among the leaders of the army, and most of them sprawled in comfortable horsehide chairs, watching as the crimson-robed Rhodar measured off distances with a piece of string on a large map that covered one entire wall. "It doesn't really seem all that far to me," he was saying to King Cho-Hag.

"That's because your map is flat, Rhodar," Cho-Hag replied. "The country's very hilly through there. Believe me, it will take three days."

King Rhodar made an indelicate sound of disgust. "I guess we'll have to give up the idea, then. I'd like to burn out those forts, but I'm not going to start ordering suicide missions. Three days' ride is just too far."

"Your Majesty," Ce'Nedra said politely.

"Yes, child?" Rhodar was still frowning at the map.

"I'd like for you to meet someone."

King Rhodar turned.

"Your Majesty," Ce'Nedra said formally, "may I present his Grace, the Duke of Anadile? General Varana, his Majesty, King Rhodar of Drasnia."

The two men bowed politely to each other, their eyes probing, assessing.

"The general's reputation precedes him," King Rhodar noted.

"But his Majesty's skill as a military man has been kept a secret," Varana replied.

"Do you think that satisfies the demands of courtesy?" Rhodar asked.

"If not, we can both lie a little bit later on about how excruciatingly polite we were to each other," Varana suggested.

King Rhodar flashed him a quick grin. "All right, what's Tolnedra's leading tactician doing in Algaria?"

"Observing, your Majesty."

"You're going to stick to that story?"

"Naturally. For political reasons, Tolnedra must maintain a neutral posture in this affair. I'm certain that Drasnian intelligence has briefed your Majesty on the realities of the situation. The five spies you have in the Imperial palace are thoroughly professional."

"Six, actually," King Rhodar noted in passing.

General Varana raised one eyebrow. "I suppose we should have known," he said.

"It changes from time to time." Rhodar shrugged. "You know our strategic situation?"

"I've been filled in, yes."

"What's your assessment—as an observer?"

"You're in trouble."

"Thanks," Rhodar said dryly.

"The numbers dictate that you take a defensive posture."

Rhodar shook his head. "That might work if all we had to worry about was Taur Urgas and the Southern Murgos, but 'Zakath is landing more troops at Thull Zelik every day. If we fortify and try to sit tight, and he decides to move against us, he'll be able to bury us in Malloreans by autumn. The key to the whole situation is putting Anheg's fleet into the Sea of the East to stop those troop ships. We're going to have to gamble a bit in order to pull that off."

Varana studied the map. "If you're going to go down the River Mardu, you'll have to neutralize the Thullish capital," he said, pointing at Thull Mardu. "It's an island—like Tol Honeth—and it's right in the middle of the river. You'll never get a fleet past it as long as a hostile force holds it. You'll have to take the city."

"That had already occured to us," King Anheg said from where he sprawled in his chair with his ever-present ale cup in his hand.

"You know Anheg?" Rhodar asked the general.

Varana nodded. "By reputation," he replied. He bowed to King Anheg. "Your Majesty," he said.

"General," Anheg responded, inclining his head.

"If Thull Mardu is heavily defended, it will cost you a third of your army to take it," Varana continued.

"We're going to lure the garrison out," Rhodar told him.

"How?"

"That's going to be up to Korodullin and me," King Cho-Hag said quietly. "Once we get to the top of the escarpment, the Mimbrate knights are going to move out and crush every city and town in the uplands, and my clansmen will strike down into the farming regions to burn every standing crop."

"They'll realize that's only a diversion, your Majesty," Varana pointed out.

"Naturally," Brand agreed in his rumbling voice, "but a diversion from what? We don't think they'll fully realize that

Thull Mardu is our main objective. We'll try our best to make our depredations as general as possible. The loss of those towns and crops might be acceptable at first, but it won't be long before they'll have to take steps to protect them."

"And you think they'll pull the garrison out of Thull Mardu to meet you?"

"That's the idea," King Rhodar replied.

Varana shook his head. "They'll bring Murgos up from Rak Goska and Malloreans from Thull Zelik. Then instead of a quick raid on Thull Mardu, you'll have a general war on your hands."

"That's what *you'd* do, General Varana," King Rhodar disagreed, "but you aren't 'Zakath or Taur Urgas. Our strategy's based on our assessment of those two men. Neither of them will commit his forces unless he's convinced that we pose a major threat. Each of them wants to save as much of his army as possible. In their view, we're only an incidental annoyance—and an excuse to put an army into the field. For them, the real war starts when they attack each other. Each of them will hold back, and King Gethell of the Thulls will have to meet us on his own with only token support from the Murgos and the Malloreans. If we move fast enough, we'll have Anheg's fleet into the Sea of the East and all our troops pulled back to the escarpment before they realize what we're up to."

"And then?"

"And then Taur Urgas will stay in Rak Goska as if his foot were nailed to the floor." King Anheg chuckled. "I'll be in the Sea of the East drowning Malloreans by the shipload, and he'll be cheering me on every step of the way."

"And 'Zakath won't dare risk those troops he already has at Thull Zelik by moving against us," Brand added. "If he loses too many men, Taur Urgas will have the upper hand."

General Varana considered that. "A three-way deadlock, then," he mused. "Three armies in the same region, and not one of them willing to move."

"The very best kind of war." King Rhodar grinned. "Nobody gets hurt."

"Tactically, your only problem is gauging the severity of

your raids before you attack Thull Mandu," Varana noted. "They'll have to be serious enough to pull the garrison out of the city, but not so serious as to alarm 'Zakath or Taur Urgas. That's a very fine line to walk, gentlemen."

Rhodar nodded. "That's why we're so delighted to have Tolnedra's foremost tactician here to advise us," he said, bowing floridly.

"Please, your Majesty," General Varana interposed, lifting one hand. "*Suggest*, not advise. An observer can only suggest. The term advice implies partisanship that is not in line with the Empire's position of strict neutrality."

"Ah," King Rhodar said. He turned to King Cho-Hag. "We must make arrangements for the comfort of the Imperial suggester and his staff," he declared with a broad grin.

Ce'Nedra watched with secret delight as these two brilliant men began what was obviously going to be a firm friendship. "I'll leave you gentlemen to your entertainments," she told them. "Military discussions give me a headache, so I'll rely on you not to get me in trouble." She curtsied to them with a winsome little smile and withdrew.

Two days later, Relg arrived from Ulgoland with the contingent of his leaf-mailed countrymen sent by the Gorim. Taiba, who had hovered silently in the background since the army had arrived at the Stronghold, joined Ce'Nedra and Lady Polgara to greet the Ulgos as the wagons which carried them creaked up the hill toward the main gate. The beautiful Marag woman wore a plain, even severe, linen dress, but her violet eyes were glowing. Relg, his cowled leaf-mail shirt covering his head and shoulders like lizard skin, climbed down from the lead wagon and only perfunctorily answered the greetings of Barak and Mandorallen. His large eyes searched the group gathered at the gate until they found Taiba, and then a kind of tension seemed to go out of him. Without speaking, he walked toward her. Their meeting was silent, and they did not touch, though Taiba's hand moved involuntarily toward him several times. They stood in the golden sunlight with their eyes lost in each other's faces, drawing about them a profound kind of privacy that absolutely ignored the presence of others. Taiba's eyes remained constantly on Relg's face, but there was in them nothing of that vacant, placid adoration that filled Ariana's eyes when she looked at Lelldorin. There was rather a question—even a challenge. Relg's answering look was the troubled gaze of a man torn between two overpowering compulsions. Ce'Nedra watched them for a few moments, but was finally forced to avert her eyes.

The Ulgos were quartered in dim, cavernous rooms built into the foundations of the Stronghold where Relg could lead his countrymen through the painful process of adjusting their eyes to the light of day and training them to ignore the unreasoning panic which assailed all Ulgos when they were exposed to the open sky.

That evening another smaller contingent arrived from the south. Three men, two in white robes and one in filthy rags, appeared at the gate demanding entrance. The Algars at the gate admitted them immediately, and one guard was sent to Lady Polgara's candlelit apartment to inform her of their arrival.

"You'd better bring them here," she advised the poor man, who was ashen-faced and trembling. "They haven't been in the company of other men for a very long time, and crowds might make them nervous."

"At once, Lady Polgara," the shaking Algar said, bowing. He hesitated for a moment. "Would he *really* do that to me?" he blurted.

"Would who do what to you?"

"The ugly one. He said that he was going to—" The man stopped, suddenly realizing to whom he was speaking. His face turned red. "I don't think I should repeat what he said, Lady Polgara—but it was an awful thing to threaten a man with."

"Oh," she said. "I believe I know what you mean. It's one of his favorite expressions. I think you're safe. He only says that to get people's attention. I'm not even sure you *can* do it to somebody and keep him alive at the same time."

"I'll bring them at once, Lady Polgara."

The sorceress turned to look at Ce'Nedra, Adara, and Ariana, who had joined her for supper. "Ladies," she said gravely, "we're about to have guests. Two of them are the sweetest men in the world, but the third is a bit uncontrolled in his use of language. If you're at all sensitive about such things, you'd better leave."

Ce'Nedra, remembering her encounter with the three in the Vale of Aldur, rose immediately.

"Not you, Ce'Nedra," Polgara told her. "You'll have to stay, I'm afraid."

Ce'Nedra swallowed hard. "I really would leave, if I were you," she advised her friends.

"Is he *that* bad?" Adara asked. "I've heard men swear before."

"Not like this one," Ce'Nedra warned.

"You've managed to make me very curious." Adara smiled. "I think I'll stay."

"Don't say I didn't warn you," Ce'Nedra murmured.

Beltira and Belkira were as saintly as Ce'Nedra remembered them, but the misshapen Beldin was even uglier and nastier. Ariana fled before he had even finished greeting Lady Polagra. Adara turned deathly pale, but bravely kept her seat. Then the hideous little man turned to greet Ce'Nedra with a few raucous questions that made the princess blush to the roots of her hair. Adara prudently withdrew at that point.

"What's wrong with your wenches, Pol?" Beldin asked innocently, scratching at his matted hair. "They seemed a little vaporish."

"They're well-bred ladies, Uncle," Polgara replied. "Certain expressions are offensive to their ears."

"Is *that* all?" He laughed coarsely. "This redheaded one seems a bit less delicate."

"Your remarks offend me as much as they offend my companions, Master Beldin," Ce'Nedra retorted stiffly, "but I don't think I'll be routed by the foul mouthings of an ill-bred hunchback."

"Not bad," he complimented her, sprawling uncouthly in a chair, "but you've got to learn to relax. An insult's got a certain rhythm and flow to it that you haven't quite picked up yet."

"She's very young, Uncle," Polgara reminded him.

Beldin leered at the princess. "Isn't she, though?"

"Stop that," Polgara told him.

"We've come—"

"—to join your expedition," the twins said. "Beldin feels—"

"—that you might encounter Grolims, and—"

"—need our help."

"Isn't that pathetic?" Beldin demanded. "They still haven't learned to talk straight." He looked at Polgara. "Is this all the army you've got?"

"The Chereks will be joining us at the river," she replied.

"You should have talked faster," he told Ce'Nedra. "You haven't got nearly enough men. Southern Murgos proliferate like maggots in dead meat, and Malloreans spawn like blow-flies."

"We'll explain our strategy to you in good time, Uncle," Polgara promised him. "We are *not* going to meet the armies of Angarak head on. What we're doing here is only diversionary."

He grinned a hideous little grin. "I'd have given a lot to see your face when you found out that Belgarath had slipped away from you," he said.

"I wouldn't dwell on that, Master Beldin," Ce'Nedra advised. "Lady Polgara was not pleased by Belgarath's decision, and it might not be prudent to raise it again."

"I've seen Pol's little tantrums before." He shrugged. "Why don't you send somebody out for a pig or a sheep, Pol? I'm hungry."

"It's customary to cook it first, Uncle."

He looked puzzled. "What for?" he asked.

Chapter Ten

THREE DAYS LATER the army began to move out from the Algar Stronghold toward the temporary encampment the Algars had erected on the east bank of the Aldur River. The troops of each nation moved in separate broad columns, trampling a vast track through the knee-high grass. In the center column the legions of Tolnedra, standards raised, marched with parade-ground perfection. The appearance of the legions had improved noticeably since the arrival of General Varana and his staff. The mutiny on the plains near Tol Vordue had given Ce'Nedra a large body of men, but no senior officers, and once the danger of surprise inspections was past, a certain laxity had set in. General Varana had not mentioned the rust spots on the breastplates nor the generally unshaven condition of the troops. His expression of mild disapproval had seemed to be enough. The hard-bitten sergeants who now commanded the legions had taken one look at his face and had immediately taken steps. The rust spots vanished, and shaving regularly once again became popular. There were, to be sure, a few contusions here and there on some freshly shaved faces, mute evidence that the heavy-fisted sergeants had found it necessary to vigorously persuade their troops that the holiday was over.

To one side of the legions rode the glittering Mimbrate knights, their varicolored pennons snapping in the breeze from the up-raised forest of their lances. Their faces shone with enthusiasm and little else. Ce'Nedra privately suspected that a large part of their fearsome reputation stemmed from that abysmal lack of anything remotely resembling thought. With only a little encouragement, a force of Mimbrates would cheerfully mount an assault on winter or a changing tide.

On the other flank of the marching legions came the green- and brown-clad bowmen of Asturia. The placement was quite deliberate. The Asturians were no more blessed with intelligence than their Mimbrate cousins, and it was generally considered prudent to interpose other troops between the two Arendish forces to avoid unpleasantness.

Beyond the Asturians marched the grim-faced Rivans, all in gray, and accompanying them were the few Chereks who were not with the fleet, which even now was in the process of being prepared for the portage to the base of the escarpment. Flanking the Mimbrates marched the Sendarian militiamen in their homemade uniforms, and at the rear of the host, the creaking lines of King Fulrach's supply wagons stretched back to the horizon. The Algar clans, however, did not ride in orderly columns, but rather in little groups and clusters as they drove herds of spare horses and half-wild cattle along on the extreme flanks of the host.

Ce'Nedra, in her armor and mounted on her white horse, rode in the company of General Varana. She was trying, without much success, to explain her cause to him.

"My dear child," the general said finally, "I'm a Tolnedran and a soldier. Neither of those conditions encourages me to accept any kind of mysticism. My primary concerns at this moment have to do with feeding this multitude. Your supply lines stretch all the way back across the mountains and then up through Arendia. That's a very long way, Ce'Nedra."

"King Fulrach's taken care of that, Uncle," she told him

rather smugly. "All the time we've been marching, his Sendars have been freighting supplies along the Great North Road to Aldurford and then barging them upriver to the camp. There are whole acres of supply dumps waiting for us."

General Varana nodded approvingly. "It appears that Sendars make perfect quartermasters," he observed. "Is he bringing weapons as well?"

"I think they said something about that," Ce'Nedra replied. "Arrows, spare lances for the knights, that sort of thing. They seemed to know what they were doing, so I didn't ask too many questions."

"That's foolish, Ce'Nedra," Varana said bluntly. "When you're running an army, you should know every detail."

"I'm not running the army, Uncle," she pointed out. "I'm leading it. King Rhodar's running it."

"And what will you do if something happens to him?"

Ce'Nedra suddenly went cold.

"You *are* going to war, Ce'Nedra, and people *do* get killed and injured in wars. You'd better start taking an interest in what's going on around you, my little princess. Going off to war with your head wrapped in a pillow isn't going to improve your chances of success, you know." He gave her a very direct look. "Don't chew your fingernails, Ce'Nedra," he added. "It makes your hands unsightly."

The encampment at the river was vast, and in the very center stood King Fulrach's main supply dump, a virtual city of tents and neatly stacked equipment. A long string of flat-bottomed barges were moored to the riverbank, patiently waiting to be unloaded.

"Your people have been busy," King Rhodar observed to the dumpy-looking Sendarian monarch as they rode along a narrow alleyway between mountainous heaps of canvas-covered produce and stacks of stoutly boxed equipment. "How did you know what to have them bring?"

"I took notes while we were coming down through Arendia," King Fulrach replied. "It wasn't too hard to see what we were going to need—boots, arrows, spare swords, and the like. At present, about all we're bringing in is food. The Algar herds will provide fresh meat, but men get sick on a steady diet of nothing but meat."

"You've already got enough food here to feed the army for a year," King Anheg noted.

Fulrach shook his head. "Forty-five days," he corrected meticulously. "I want thirty days' worth here and two weeks' worth in the forts the Drasnians are building up on top of the escarpment. That's our margin of safety. As long as the barges replenish our food supplies daily, we'll always have that much on hand. Once you decide what your goals are, the rest is just simple mathematics."

"How do you know how much a man's going to eat in one day?" Rhodar asked, eyeing the high-piled foodstuffs. "Some days I'm hungrier than others."

Fulrach shrugged. "It averages out. Some eat more, some eat less; but in the end, it all comes out about the same."

"Fulrach, sometimes you're so practical, you almost make me sick," Anheg said.

"Somebody has to be."

"Don't you Sendars have any sense of adventure? Don't you *ever* do something without planning it all out in advance?"

"Not if we can help it," the King of Sendaria replied mildly.

Near the center of the supply-dump a number of large pavilions had been erected for the use of the leaders of the army and their supporting staff. About midafternoon, after she had bathed and changed clothes, Princess Ce'Nedra went over to the main tent to see what was happening.

"They're anchored about a mile downriver," Barak was reporting to his cousin. "They've been here for about four days now. Greldik's more or less in charge."

"Greldik?" Anheg looked surprised. "He doesn't have any official position."

"He knows the river." Barak shrugged. "Over the years he's sailed just about any place where there's water and a chance to make some profit. He tells me that the sailors have been drinking pretty steadily since they anchored. They know what's coming."

Anheg chuckled. "We'd better not disappoint them, then. Rhodar, how much longer will it be before your engineers are ready to start lifting my ships up the escarpment?"

"A week or so," King Rhodar replied, looking up from his midafternoon snack.

"It will be close enough," Anheg concluded. He turned back to Barak. "Tell Greldik that we'll start the portage tomorrow morning—before the sailors have time to sober up."

Ce'Nedra had not fully understood the meaning of the word "portage" until she arrived the following morning at the riverbank to find the sweating Chereks hauling their ships out of the water and manhandling them along by main strength on wooden rollers. She was appalled at the amount of effort required to move a ship even a few inches.

She was not alone in that. Durnik the smith took one shocked look at the procedure and immediately went looking for King Anheg. "Excuse me, your Honor," he said respectfully, "but isn't this bad for the boats—as well as the men?"

"Ships," Anheg corrected. "They're called ships. A boat is something else."

"Whatever you call them—won't banging them along over those logs spring their seams?"

Anheg shrugged. "They all leak quite a bit anyway," he replied. "And it's always been done this way."

Durnik quickly saw the futility of trying to talk to the King of Cherek. He went instead to Barak, who was rather glumly considering the huge ship his crew had rowed upriver to meet him. "She looks very impressive when she's afloat," the big red-bearded man was saying to his friend, Captain Greldik, "but I think she'll be even more impressive when we have to pick her up and carry her."

"You're the one who wanted the biggest warship afloat," Greldik reminded him with a broad smirk. "You'll have to buy enough ale to float that whale of yours before your crew's drunk enough to try to portage her—not to mention the fact that it's customary for a captain to join in when the time comes to portage."

"Stupid custom," Barak growled sourly.

"I'd say that you're in for a bad week, Barak." Greldik's grin grew broader.

Durnik took the two seamen aside and began talking earnestly with them, drawing diagrams on the sandy riverbank with a stick. The more he talked, the more interested they became.

What emerged from their discussions a day later were a pair of low-slung cradles with a dozen wheels on each side. As the rest of the Chereks jeered, the two ships were carefully slid out of the water onto the cradles and firmly lashed in place. The jeering faded noticeably, however, when the crews of the two ships began trundling their craft across the plain. Hettar, who happened to ride by, watched for a few moments with a puzzled frown. "Why are you pulling them by hand," he asked, "when you're in the middle of the largest herd of horses in the world?"

Barak's eyes went very wide, and then an almost reverent grin dawned on his face.

The jeers that had risen as Barak's and Greldik's ships had been maneuvered onto their wheeled carriages turned rather quickly into angry mutterings as the carriages, pulled by teams of Algar horses, rolled effortlessly toward the escarpment past men straining with every ounce of strength to move their ships a few inches at a time. To leave it all to artistry, Barak and Greldik ordered their men to lounge indolently on the decks of their ships, drinking ale and playing dice.

King Anheg stared very hard at his impudently grinning cousin as the big ship rolled past. His expression was profoundly offended. "That's going *too* far!" he exploded, jerking off his dented crown and throwing it down on the ground.

King Rhodar put on a perfectly straight face. "I'd be the first to admit that it's probably not nearly as good as moving them by hand, Anheg. I'm sure there are some rather profound philosophical reasons for all that sweating and grunting and cursing, but it *is* faster, wouldn't you say? And we really ought to move right along with this."

"It's unnatural," Anheg growled, still glaring at the two

ships, which were already several hundred yards away.

Rhodar shrugged. "Anything's unnatural the first time you try it."

"I'll think about it," Anheg said darkly.

"I wouldn't think for too long," Rhodar suggested. "Your popularity as a monarch is going to go downhill with every mile—and Barak's the sort of man who'll parade that contraption of his back and forth in front of your sailors every step of the way to the escarpment."

"He *would* do that, wouldn't he?"

"I think you can count on it."

King Anheg sighed bitterly. "Go fetch that unwholesomely clever Sendarian blacksmith," he sourly instructed one of his men. "Let's get this over with."

Later that day the leaders of the army gathered again in the main tent for a strategy meeting. "Our biggest problem now is to conceal the size of our forces," King Rhodar told them all. "Instead of marching everybody to the escarpment all at once and then milling around at the base of the cliff, it might be better to move the troops in small contingents and have them go directly up to the forts on top as soon as they arrive."

"Will such a piecemeal approach not unduly delay our progress?" King Korodullin asked.

"Not all that much," Rhodar replied. "We'll move your knights and Cho-Hag's clansmen up first so you can start burning cities and crops. That will give the Thulls something to think about beside how many infantry regiments we're bringing up. We don't want them to start counting noses."

"Couldn't we build false campfires and so on to make it appear that we have more men?" Lelldorin suggested brightly.

"The whole idea is to make our army appear smaller, not bigger," Brand explained gently in his deep voice. "We don't want to alarm Taur Urgas or 'Zakath sufficiently to make them commit their forces. It will be an easy campaign if all we have to deal with are King Gethell's Thulls. If the Murgos and the Malloreans intervene, we'll be in for a serious fight."

"And that's the one thing we definitely want to avoid," King Rhodar added.

"Oh," Lelldorin said, a bit abashed, "I didn't think of that." A slow flush rose in his cheeks.

"Lelldorin," Ce'Nedra said, hoping to help him cover his embarrassment, "I think I'd like to go out and visit with the troops for a bit. Would you accompany me?"

"Of course, your Majesty," the young Asturian agreed, quickly rising to his feet.

"That's not a bad idea," Rhodar agreed. "Encourage them a bit, Ce'Nedra. They've walked a long way, and their spirits may be sagging."

Lelldorin's cousin Torasin, dressed in his customary black doublet and hose, also rose to his feet. "I'll go along, if I may," he said. He grinned rather impudently at King Korodullin. "Asturians are good plotters, but rather poor strategists, so I probably wouldn't be able to add much to the discussions."

The King of Arendia smiled at the young man's remark. "Thou art pert, young Torasin, but methinks thou art not so fervent an enemy of the crown of Arendia as thou dost pretend."

Torasin bowed extravagantly, still grinning. Once they were outside the tent, he turned to Lelldorin. "I could almost learn to like that man—if it weren't for all those thees and thous," he declared.

"It's not so bad—once you get used to it," Lelldorin replied.

Torasin laughed. "If I had someone as pretty as Lady Ariana for a friend, she could thee me and thou me all she wanted," he said. He looked archly at Ce'Nedra. "Which troops did you wish to encourage, your Majesty?" he bantered.

"Let's visit your Asturian countrymen," she decided. "I don't think I'd care to take you two into the Mimbrate camp—unless your swords had been taken away from you and your mouths had been bricked up."

"Don't you trust us?" Lelldorin asked.

"I *know* you," she replied with a little toss of her head. "Where are the Asturians encamped?"

"That way," Torasin answered, pointing toward the south end of the supply dump.

Smells of cooking were carried by the breeze from the Sendarian field kitchens, and those smells reminded the princess of something. Instead of randomly circulating among the Asturian tents, she found herself quite deliberately searching for some specific people.

She found Lammer and Detton, the two serfs who had joined her army on the outskirts of Vo Wacune, finishing their afternoon meal in front of a patched tent. They both looked better fed than they had when she had first seen them, and they were no longer dressed in rags. When they saw her approaching, they scrambled awkwardly to their feet.

"Well, my friends," she asked, trying to put them at ease, "how do you find army life?"

"We don't have anything to complain about, your Ladyship," Detton replied respectfully.

"Except for all the walking," Lammer added. "I hadn't realized that the world was this big."

"They gave us boots," Detton told her, holding up one foot so that she could see his boot. "They were a bit stiff at first, but the blisters have all healed now."

"Are you getting enough to eat?" Ce'Nedra asked them.

"Plenty," Lammer said. "The Sendars even cook it for us. Did you know that there aren't any serfs in the kingdom of the Sendars, my Lady? Isn't that astonishing? It gives a man something to think about."

"It does indeed," Detton agreed. "They grow all that food, and everybody always has plenty to eat and clothes to wear and a house to sleep in, and there's not a single serf in the whole kingdom."

"I see that they've given you equipment, too," the princess said, noting that the two now wore conical leather helmets and stiff leather vests.

Lammer nodded and pulled off his helmet. "It's got steel plates in it to keep a man from getting his brains knocked out," he told her. "They lined us all up as soon as we got here and gave every man a helmet and these hard leather tunics."

"They gave each of us a spear and a dagger, too," Detton said.

"Have they showed you how to use them?" Ce'Nedra asked.

"Not yet, your Ladyship," Detton replied. "We've been concentrating on learning how to shoot arrows."

Ce'Nedra turned to her two companions. "Could you see that somebody takes care of that?" she said. "I want to be sure that everybody knows how to defend himself, at least."

"We'll see to it, your Majesty," Lelldorin answered.

Not far away, a young serf was seated cross-legged in front of another tent. He lifted a handmade flute to his lips and began to play. Ce'Nedra had heard some of the finest musicians in the world performing at the palace in Tol Honeth, but the serf boy's flute caught at her heart and brought tears to her eyes. His melody soared toward the azure sky like an unfettered lark.

"How exquisite," she exclaimed.

Lammer nodded. "I don't know much about music," he said, "but the boy seems to play well. It's a shame he's not right in the head."

Ce'Nedra looked at him sharply. "What do you mean?"

"He comes from a village in the southern part of the forest of Arendia. I'm told it's a very poor village and that the lord of the region is very harsh with his serfs. The boy's an orphan, and he was put to watching the cows when he was young. One time one of the cows strayed, and the boy was beaten half to death. He can't talk any more."

"Do you know his name?"

"Nobody seems to know it," Detton replied. "We take turns looking out for him—making sure he's fed and has a place to sleep. There's not much else you can do for him."

A small sound came from Lelldorin, and Ce'Nedra was startled to see tears streaming openly down the earnest young man's face.

The boy continued his playing, his melody heartbreakingly true, and his eyes sought out Ce'Nedra's and met them with a kind of grave recognition.

They did not stay much longer. The princess knew that her rank and position made the two serfs uncomfortble. She had made sure that they were all right and that her promise to them was being kept, and that was all that really mattered.

As Ce'Nedra, Lelldorin, and Torasin walked toward the camp of the Sendars, they suddenly heard the sound of squabbling on the other side of a large tent.

"I'll pile it any place I want to," one man was saying belligerently.

"You're blocking the street," another man replied.

"Street?" the first snorted. "What are you talking about? This isn't a town. There aren't any streets."

"Friend," the second man explained with exaggerated patience, "we have to bring the wagons through here to get to the main supply dump. Now please move your equipment so I can get through. I still have a lot to do today."

"I'm not going to take orders from a Sendarian teamster who's found an easy way to avoid fighting. I'm a soldier."

"Really?" the Sendar replied dryly. "How much fighting have you seen?"

"I'll fight when the time comes."

"It may come quicker than you'd expected if you don't get your gear out of my way. If I have to get down off this wagon to move it myself, it's likely to make me irritable."

"I'm all weak with fright," the soldier retorted sarcastically.

"Are you going to move it?"

"No."

"I tried to warn you, friend," the teamster said in a resigned tone.

"If you touch my gear, I'll break your head."

"No. You'll *try* to break my head."

There was a sudden sound of scuffling and several heavy blows.

"Now get up and move your gear like I told you to," the teamster said. "I don't have all day to stand around and argue with you."

"You hit me when I wasn't looking," the soldier complained.

"Do you want to watch the next one coming?"

"All right, don't get excited. I'm moving it."

"I'm glad we understand each other."

"Does that sort of thing happen very often?" Ce'Nedra asked quietly.

Torasin, grinning broadly, nodded. "Some of your troops feel the need to bluster, your Majesty," he replied, "and the Sendarian wagonneers usually don't have the time to listen. Fistfights and street-brawling are second nature to those fellows, so their squabbles with the soldiers almost always end up the same way. It's very educational, really."

"Men!" Ce'Nedra said.

In the camp of the Sendars they met Durnik. With him there was an oddly matched pair of young men.

"A couple of old friends," Durnik said as he introduced them. "Just arrived on the supply barges. I think you've met Rundorig, Princess. He was at Faldor's farm when we visited there last winter."

Ce'Nedra did in fact remember Rundorig. The tall, hulking young man, she recalled, was the one who was going to marry Garion's childhood sweetheart, Zubrette. She greeted him warmly and gently reminded him that they had met before. Rundorig's Arendish background made his mind move rather slowly. His companion, however, was anything but slow. Durnik introduce him as Doroon, another of Garion's boyhood friends. Doroon was a small, wiry young man with a protruding Adam's apple and slightly bulging eyes. After a few moments of shyness, his tongue began to run away with him. It was a bit hard to follow Doroon. His mind flitted from idea to idea, and his mouth raced along breathlessly, trying to keep up.

"It was sort of rough going up in the mountains, your Ladyship," he replied in answer to her question about their trip from Sendaria, "what with how steep the road was and all. You'd think that as long as the Tolnedrans were building a highway, they'd have picked leveler ground—but they seem to be fascinated by straight lines—only that's not always the easiest way. I wonder why they're like that." The fact that Ce'Nedra herself was Tolnedran seemed not to have registered on Doroon.

"You came along the Great North Road?" she asked him.

"Yes—until we got to a place called Aldurford. That's a funny kind of name, isn't it? Although it makes sense if you stop and think about it. But that was after we got out of the mountains where the Murgos attacked us. You've never *seen* such a fight."

"Murgos?" Ce'Nedra asked him sharply, trying to pin down his skittering thoughts.

He nodded eagerly. "The man who was in charge of the wagons—he's a great big fellow from Muros, I think he said—wasn't it Muros he said he came from, Rundorig? Or maybe it was Camaar—for some reason I always get the two mixed up. What was I talking about?"

"The Murgos," Durnik supplied helpfully.

"Oh, yes. Anyway, the man in charge of the wagons said that there had been a lot of Murgos in Sendaria before the war. They pretended that they were merchants, but they weren't—they were spies. When the war started, they all went up into the mountains, and now they come out of the woods and try to ambush our supply wagons—but we were ready for them, weren't we Rundorig? Rundorig hit one of the Murgos with a big stick when the Murgo rode past our wagon—knocked him clear off his horse. Whack! Just like that! Knocked him clear off his horse. I'll bet *he* ws surprised." Doroon laughed a short little laugh, and then his tongue raced off again, describing in jerky, helter-skelter detail the trip from Sendaria.

Princess Ce'Nedra was strangely touched by her meeting with Garion's two old friends. She felt, moreover, a tremendous burden of responsibility as she realized that she had reached into almost every life in the west with her campaign. She had separated husbands from their wives and fathers from their children; and she had carried simple men, who had never been further than the next village, a thousand leagues and more to fight in a war they probably did not even begin to understand.

The next morning the leaders of the army rode the few remaining leagues to the installations at the base of the escarpment. As they topped a rise, Ce'Nedra reined Noble in sharply and gaped in openmouthed astonishment as she saw the eastern escarpment for the first time. It was impossible!

Nothing could be so vast! The great black cliff reared itself above them like an enormous wave of rock, frozen and forever marking the boundary between east and west, and seemingly blocking any possibility of ever passing in either direction. It immediately stood as a kind of stark symbol of the division between the two parts of the world—a division that could no more be resolved than that enormous cliff could be leveled.

As they rode closer, Ce'Nedra noted a great deal of bustling activity both at the foot of the escarpment and along its upper rim. Great hawsers stretched down from overhead, and Ce'Nedra saw elaborately intertwined pulleys along the foot of the huge cliffs.

"Why are the pulleys at the bottom?" King Anheg demanded suspiciously.

King Rhodar shrugged. "How should I know? I'm not an engineer."

"All right, if you're going to be that way about it, I'm not going to let your people touch a single one of my ships until somebody tells me why the pulleys are down here instead of up there."

King Rhodar sighed and beckoned to an engineer who was meticulously greasing a huge pulley block. "Have you got a sketch of the rigging handy?" the portly monarch asked the grease-spattered workman.

The engineer nodded, pulled a rolled sheet of grimy parchment out from under his tunic, and handed it to his king. Rhodar glanced at it and handed it to Anheg.

Anheg stared at the complex drawing, struggling to trace out which line went where, and more importantly why it went there. "I can't read this," he complained.

"Neither can I," Rhodar told him pleasantly, "but you wanted to know why the pulleys are down here instead of up there. The drawing tells you why."

"But I can't read it."

"That's not my fault."

Not far away a cheer went up as a boulder half the size of a house and entwined in a nest of ropes rose majestically up the face of the cliff to the accompaniment of a vast creaking of hawsers.

"You'll have to admit that that's impressive, Anheg," Rhodar said. "Particularly when you note that the entire rock is being lifted by those eight horses over there—with the help of that counterweight, of course." He pointed at another block of stone which was just as majestically coming down from the top of the escarpment.

Anheg squinted at the two rocks. "Durnik," he said over his shoulder, "do you understand how all those work?"

"Yes, King Anheg," the smith replied. "You see, the counterweight off-balances the—"

"Don't explain it to me, please," Anheg said. "As long as somebody I know and trust understands, that's all that's really important."

Later that same day, the first Cherek ship was lifted to the top of the escarpment. King Anheg watched the procedure for a moment or two, then winced and turned his back. "It's unnatural," he muttered to Barak.

"You've taken to using that expression a great deal lately," Barak noted.

Anheg scowled at his cousin.

"I just mentioned it, that's all," Barak said innocently.

"I don't like changes, Barak. They make me nervous."

"The world moves on, Anheg. Things change every day."

"That doesn't necessarily mean that I have to like it," the King of Cherek growled. "I think I'll go to my tent for a drink or two."

"Want some company," Barak offered.

"I thought you wanted to stand around and watch the world change."

"It can do that without my supervision."

"And probably will," Anheg added moodily. "All right, let's go. I don't want to watch this anymore." And the two of them went off in search of something to drink.

Chapter Eleven

MAYASERANA, QUEEN OF Arendia, was in a pensive mood. She sat at her embroidery in the large, sunny nursery high in the palace at Vo Mimbre. Her infant son, the crown prince of Arendia, cooed and gurgled in his cradle as he played with the string of brightly colored beads that had been the ostensible gift of the crown prince of Drasnia. Mayaserana had never met Queen Porenn, but the shared experience of motherhood made her feel very close to the reputedly exquisite little blonde on her far northern throne.

Seated in a chair not far from the queen sat Nerina, Baroness of Vo Ebor. Each lady wore velvet, the queen in deep purple, and the Baroness in pale blue, and each wore the high, conical white headdress so admired by the Mimbrate nobility. At the far end of the nursery, an elderly lutanist softly played a mournful air in a minor key.

The Baroness Nerina appeared to be even more melancholy than her queen. The circles beneath her eyes had grown deeper and deeper in the weeks since the departure of the Mimbrate knights, and she seldom smiled. Finally she sighed and laid aside her embroidery.

"The sadness of thy heart doth resound in thy sighing, Nerina," the queen said gently. "Think not so of dangers and separation, lest thy spirits fail thee utterly."

"Instruct me in the art of banishing care, Highness," Nerina replied, "for I am in sore need of such teaching. My heart is bowed beneath a burden of concern, and try though I might to control them, my thoughts, like unruly children, return ever to the dreadful peril of my absent lord and our dearest friend."

"Be comforted in the knowledge that thy burden is shared by every lady in all of Mimbre, Nerina."

Nerina sighed again. "My care, however, lies in more mournful certainty. Other ladies, their affections firm-fixed on one beloved, can dare to hope that he might return from dreadful war unscathed; but I, who love two, can find no reason for such optimism. I must needs lose one at the least, and the prospect doth crush my soul."

There was a quiet dignity in Nerina's open acceptance of the implications of the two loves that had become so entwined in her heart that they could no longer be separated. Mayaserana, in one of those brief flashes of insight which so sharply illuminated understanding, perceived that Nerina's divided heart lay at the very core of the tragedy that had lifted her, her husband, and Sir Mandorallen into the realms of sad legend. If Nerina could but love one more than the other, the tragedy would end, but so perfectly balanced was her love for her husband with her love for Sir Mandorallen that she had reached a point of absolute stasis, forever frozen between the two of them.

The queen sighed. Nerina's divided heart seemed somehow a symbol of divided Arendia, but, though the gentle heart of the suffering baroness might never be made one, Mayaserana was resolved to make a last effort to heal the breach between Mimbre and Asturia. To that end, she had summoned to the palace a deputation of the more stable leaders of the rebellious north, and her summons had appeared over a title she rarely used, Duchess of Asturia. At her instruction, the Asturians were even now drawing up a list of their grievances for her consideration.

Later on that same sunny afternoon, Mayaserana sat alone on the double throne of Arendia, painfully aware of the vacancy beside her.

The leader and spokesman of the group of Asturian noblemen was a Count Reldegen, a tall, thin man with iron gray hair and beard, who walked with the aid of a stout cane. Reldegen wore a rich green doublet and black hose, and, like the rest of the deputation, his sword was belted at his side. The fact that the Asturians came armed into the queen's presence had stirred some angry muttering, but Mayaserana had refused to listen to urgings that their weapons be taken from them.

"My Lord Reldegen," the queen greeted the Asturian as he limped toward the throne.

"Your Grace," he replied with a bow.

"Your *Majesty*," a Mimbrate courtier corrected him in a shocked voice.

"Her Grace summoned us as the Duchess of Asturia," Reldegen informed the courtier coolly. "That title commands more respect from us than other, more recent embellishments."

"Gentlemen, please," the queen said firmly. "Prithee, let us not commence hostilities anew. Our purpose here is to examine the possibilities of peace. I entreat thee, my Lord Reldegen, speak to the purpose. Unburden thyself of the causes of that rancor which hath so hardened the heart of Asturia. Speak freely, my Lord, and with no fear of reprisal for thy words." She looked quite sternly at her advisers. "It is our command that no man be taken to task for what is spoken here."

The Mimbrates glowered at the Asturians, and the Asturians scowled back.

"Your Grace," Reldegen began, "our chief complaint lies, I think, in the simple fact that our Mimbrate overlords refuse to recognize our titles. A title's an empty thing, really, but it implies a responsibility which has been denied to us. Most of us here are indifferent to the privileges of rank, but we keenly feel the frustration of being refused the chance to discharge our obligations. Our most talented men are compelled to waste their lives in idleness, and might I point out, your Grace, that the loss of that talent injures Arendia even more than it injures us."

"Well spoken, my Lord," the queen murmured.

"Might I respond, your Majesty," the aged, white-bearded Baron of Vo Serin inquired.

"Certainly, my Lord," Mayaserana replied. "Let us all be free and open with one another."

"The titles of the Asturian gentlemen are theirs for the asking," the baron declared. "For five centuries the crown hath awaited but the required oath of fealty to bestow them. No title may be granted or recognized until its owner swears allegiance to the crown."

"Unfortunately, my Lord," Reldegen said, "we are unable to so swear. The oaths of our ancestors to the Duke of Asturia are still in force, and we are still bound by them."

"The Asturian Duke of whom thou speakest died five hundred years ago," the old baron reminded him.

"But his line did not die with him," Reldegen pointed out. "Her Grace is his direct descendant, and our pledges of loyalty are still in force."

The queen stared first at one and then at the other. "I pray thee," she said, "correct me if my perception is awry. Is the import of what hath been revealed here that Arendia hath been divided for half a millennium by an ancient *formality*?"

Reldegen pursed his lips thoughtfully. "There's a bit more to it than that, your Grace, but that does seem to be the core of the problem."

"Five hundred years of strife and bloodshed over a *technicality*?"

Count Reldegen struggled with it. He started to speak several times, but broke off each time with a look of helpless perplexity. In the end he began to laugh. "It *is* sort of Arendish, isn't it?" he asked rather whimsically.

The old Baron of Vo Serin gave him a quick look, then he too began to chuckle. "I pray thee, my Lord Reldegen, lock

this discovery in thy heart lest we all become the subject of
general mirth. Let us not confirm the suspicion that abject
stupidity is our most prevailing trait."

"Why was this absurdity not discovered previously?" Mayaserana demanded.

Count Reldegen shrugged sadly. "I suppose because Asturians and Mimbrates don't talk to each other, your Grace. We
were always too eager to get to the fighting."

"Very well," the queen said crisply, "what is required to
rectify this sorry confusion?"

Count Reldegen looked at the Baron. "A proclamation perhaps?" he suggested.

The old man nodded thoughtfully. "Her Majesty could release thee from thy previous oath. It hath not been common
practice, but there are precedents."

"And then we all swear fealty to her as Queen of Arendia?"

"That would seem to satisfy all the demands of honor and
propriety, yes."

"But I'm the same person, am I not?" the queen objected.

"Technically thou art not, your Majesty," the baron explained. "The Duchess of Asturia and the Queen of Arendia
are separate entities. Thou art indeed two persons in one body."

"This is most confusing, gentlemen," Mayaserana observed.

"That's probably why no one noticed it before, your Grace,"
Reldegen told her. "Both you and your husband have two titles
and two separate formal identities." He smiled briefly. "I'm
surprised that there was room on the throne for such a crowd."
His face grew serious. "It won't be a cure-all, your Grace,"
he added. "The divisions between Mimbre and Asturia are so
deep-seated that they'll take generations to erase."

"And wilt thou also swear fealty to my husband?" the queen
asked.

"As the King of Arendia, yes; as the Duke of Mimbre,
never."

"That will do for a start, my Lord. Let us see then to this
proclamation. Let us with ink and parchment bandage our poor
Arendia's most gaping wound."

"Beautifully put, your Grace," Reldegen said admiringly.

* * *

Ran Borune XXIII had spent almost his entire life inside the Imperial compound at Tol Honeth. His infrequent trips to the major cities of Tolnedra had, for the most part been made inside closed carriages. It was entirely probable that Ran Borune had never walked a continuous mile in his life, and a man who has not walked a mile has no real conception of what a mile is. From the very outset, his advisers despaired of ever making him understand the concept of distance.

The suggestion that ultimately resolved the difficulty came from a rather surprising source. A sometime tutor named Jeebers—a man who had narrowly escaped imprisonment or worse the previous summer—put forth the suggestion diffidently. Master Jeebers now did everything diffidently. His near brush with Imperial displeasure had forever extinguished the pompous self-importance that had previously marred his character. A number of his acquaintances were surprised to discover that they even liked the balding, skinny man now.

Master Jeebers had pointed out that if the Emperor could only see things in exact scale, he might then understand Like so many good ideas that had surfaced from time to time in Tolnedra, this one immediately got out of hand. An entire acre of the Imperial grounds was converted into a scale replica of the border region of eastern Algaria and the opposing stretches of Mishrak ac Thull. To give it all perspective, a number of inch-high human figures were cast in lead to aid the Emperor in conceptualizing the field of operations.

The Emperor immediately announced that he'd really like to have more of the lead figures to aid his understanding of the masses of men involved, and a new industry was born in Tol Honeth. Overnight lead became astonishingly scarce.

In order that he might better see the field, the Emperor mounted each morning to the top of a thirty-foot-high tower that had hastily been erected for that purpose. There, with the aid of a great-voiced sergeant of the Imperial guard, the Emperor deployed his leaden regiments of infantry and cavalry in precise accordance with the latest dispatches from Algaria.

The general staff very nearly resigned their commissions en

masse. They were, for the most part, men of advanced middle age, and joining the Emperor atop his tower each morning involved some strenuous climbing. They all tried at various times to explain to the beak-nosed little man that they could see just as well from the ground, but Ran Borune would have none of it.

"Morin, he's killing us," one portly general complained bitterly to the Emperor's chamberlain. "I'd rather go off to war than climb that ladder four times a day."

"Move the Drasnian pikemen four paces to the left!" the sergeant bellowed from the top of the tower, and a dozen men on the ground began redeploying the tiny lead figures.

"We all must serve in the capacity our Emperor choses for us," Lord Morin replied philosophically.

"I don't see *you* climbing the ladder," the general accused.

"Our Emperor has chosen another capacity for me," Morin said rather smugly.

That evening the weary little Emperor sought his bed. "It's very exciting, Morin," he murmured drowsily, holding the velvet-lined case that contained the solid gold figures representing Ce'Nedra and Rhodar and the rest of the army's leaders close to his chest, "but it's very tiring, too."

"Yes, your Majesty."

"There always seems to be so much that I still have to do."

"That's the nature of command, your Majesty," Morin observed.

But the Emperor had already dropped off.

Lord Morin removed the case from the Emperor's hands and carefully pulled the covers up around the sleeping man's shoulders. "Sleep, Ran Borune," he said very gently. "You can play with your little toy soldiers again tomorrow."

Sadi the eunuch had quietly left the palace at Sthiss Tor by a secret doorway that opened behind the slaves' quarters onto a shabby back street that twisted and turned in the general direction of the harbor. He had quite deliberately waited for the cover of the afternoon rainstorm and had dressed himself in the shabby clothing of a dockworker. Accompanying him was the one-eyed assassin, Issus, who also wore nondescript clothing. Sadi's security precautions were routine, but his choice of Issus as his companion was not. Issus was not a member of the palace guard nor of Sadi's personal retinue, but Sadi was not concerned on this afternoon's outing with appearances or proprieties. Issus was by and large uncorrupted by palace politics and had a reputation for unswerving loyalty to whomever was paying him at the moment.

The two passed down the rainswept street to a certain disreputable establishment frequented by lower-class workers, and went through a rather noisy taproom to the maze of cubicles at the back, where other entertainments were provided. At the end of a foul-smelling hallway, a lean, hard-eyed woman, whose arms were covered from wrist to elbow with cheap, gaudy bracelets, pointed wordlessly at a scarred door, then turned abruptly and disappeared through another doorway.

Behind the door lay a filthy room with only a bed for furniture. On the bed were two sets of clothing that smelled of tar and salt water, and sitting on the floor were two large tankards of lukewarm ale. Wordlessly, Sadi and Issus changed clothes. From beneath the soiled pillow, Issus pulled a pair of wigs and two sets of false whiskers.

"How can they drink this?" Sadi demanded, sniffing at one of the tankards and wrinkling his nose.

Issus shrugged. "Alorns have peculiar tastes. You don't have to drink it all, Sadi. Splash most of it on your clothes. Drasnian sailors spill a lot of ale when they're out in search of amusement. How do I look?"

Sadi gave him a quick glance. "Ridiculous," he replied. "Hair and a beard don't really suit you, Issus."

Issus laughed. "And they look particularly out of place on *you*." He shrugged and carefully poured ale down the front of his tar-spattered tunic. "I suppose we look enough like Drasnians to get by, and we certainly smell like Drasnians. Hook your beard on a little tighter, and let's get moving before it stops raining."

"Are we going out the back?"

Issus shook his head. "If we're being followed, the back

will be watched. We'll leave the way ordinary Drasnian sailors leave."

"And how is that?"

"I've made arrangements to have us thrown out."

Sadi had never been thrown out of any place before, and he found the experience not particularly amusing. The two burly ruffians who unceremoniously pitched him into the street were a bit rough about it, and Sadi picked up several scrapes and abrasions in the process.

Issus staggered to his feet and stood bawling curses at the closed door, then lurched over and pulled Sadi up out of the mud. Together they reeled in apparent drunkenness down the street toward the Drasnian enclave. Sadi noted that there had been two men in a doorway across the street when he and Issus had been ejected and that the two did not move to follow.

Once they entered the Drasnian enclave, Issus led the way rather quickly to the house of Droblek, the Drasnian port authority. They were admitted immediately and conveyed at once to a dimly lighted but comfortable room where the enormously fat Droblek sat sweating. With him was Count Melgon, the aristocratic ambassador from Tolnedra.

"Novel attire for the chief eunuch of Salmissra's household," Count Melgon observed as Sadi pulled off his wig and false beard.

"Just a bit of deception, my Lord Ambassador," Sadi replied. "I didn't particularly want this meeting to become general knowledge."

"Can he be trusted?" Droblek asked bluntly, pointing at Issus.

Sadi's expression became whimsical. "*Can* you be trusted, Issus?" he asked.

"You've paid me for up to the end of the month." Issus shrugged. "After that, we'll see. I might get a better offer."

"You see?" Sadi said to the two seated men. "Issus can be trusted until the end of the month—at least as much as anybody in Sthiss Tor can be trusted. One thing I've noticed about Issus—he's a simple, uncomplicated man. Once you buy him, he stays bought. I think it's referred to as professional ethics."

Droblek grunted sourly. "Do you suppose we could get to the point? Why did you go to so much trouble to arrange this meeting? Why didn't you just summon us to the palace?"

"My dear Droblek," Sadi murmured, "you know the kind of intrigue that infests the palace. I'd prefer that what passes between us remain more or less confidential. The matter itself is rather uncomplicated. I've been approached by the emissary of Taur Urgas."

The two regarded him with no show of surprise.

"I gather that you already knew."

"We're hardly children, Sadi," Count Melgon told him.

"I am at present in negotiations with the new ambassador from Rak Goska," Sadi mentioned.

"Isn't that the third one so far this summer?" Melgon asked.

Sadi nodded. "The Murgos seem to be particularly susceptible to certain fevers which abound in the swamps."

"We've noticed that," Droblek said dryly. "What is your prognosis for the present emissary's continued good health?"

"I don't imagine he's any more immune than his countrymen. He's already beginning to feel unwell."

"Maybe he'll be lucky and recover," Droblek suggested.

"Not very likely," Issus said with an ugly laugh.

"The tendency of Murgo ambassadors to die unexpectedly has succeeded in keeping the negotiations moving very slowly," Sadi continued. "I'd like for you gentlemen to inform King Rhodar and Ran Borune that these delays will probably continue."

"Why?" Droblek asked.

"I want them to understand and appreciate my efforts in their present campaign against the Angarak kingdoms."

"Tolnedra has no involvement in that campaign," Melgon asserted quickly.

"Of course not." Sadi smiled.

"Just how far are you willing to go, Sadi?" Doblek asked curiously.

"That depends almost entirely upon who's winning at any given moment," Sadi replied urbanely. "If the Rivan Queen's campaign in the east begins to run into difficulties, I suspect that the pestilence will subside and the Murgo emissaries will stop dying so conveniently. I'd almost have to make an accommodation with Taur Urgas at that point."

"Don't you find that just a bit contemptible, Sadi?" Droblek asked acidly.

Sadi shrugged. "We're a contemptible sort of people, Droblek," he admitted, "but we survive. That's no mean accomplishment for a weak nation lying between two major powers. Tell Rhodar and Ran Borune that I'll stall the Murgos off for as long as things continue to go in their favor. I want them both to be aware of their obligation to me."

"And will you advise them when your position is about to change?" Melgon asked.

"Of course not," Sadi replied. "I'm corrupt, Melgon. I'm not stupid."

"You're not much of an ally, Sadi," Droblek told him.

"I never pretended to be. I'm looking out for myself. At the moment, my interests and yours happen to coincide, that's all. I *do*, however, expect to be remembered for my assistance."

"You're trying to play it both ways, Sadi," Droblek accused him bluntly.

"I know." Sadi smiled. "Disgusting, isn't it?"

Queen Islena of Cherek was in an absolute panic. This time Merel had gone too far. The advice they had received from Porenn had *seemed* quite sound—had indeed raised the possibility of a brilliant stroke which would disarm Grodeg and the Bear-cult once and for all. The imagined prospect of the helpless rage into which this would plummet the towering ecclesiast was almost a satisfaction in itself. Like so many people, Queen Islena took such pleasure in an imagined triumph the the real thing became almost too much trouble. The victories of the imagination involved no risks, and a confrontation with an enemy always ended satisfactorily when both sides of the conversation came from one's own daydreams. Left to her own devices, Islena would probably have been content to let it go at that.

Merel, however, was less easily satisfied. The plan devised

by the little queen of Drasnia had been quite sound, but it suffered from one flaw—they did not have enough men to bring it off. Merel, however, had located an ally with certain resources and had brought him into the queen's inner circle. A group of men in Cherek had not accompanied Anheg and the fleet to Algaria largely because they were not the sort of men who made good sailors. At Merel's stern-faced insistence, the Queen of Cherek suddenly developed an overpowering enthusiasm for hunting. It was in the forest, safe from prying ears, that the details of the coup were worked out.

"When you kill a snake, you cut off its head," Torvik the huntsman had pointed out as he, Merel, and Islena sat in a forest glade while Torvik's men roved through the woods harvesting enough game to make it appear that Islena had spent her day in a frenzy of slaughter. "You don't accomplish all that much by snipping pieces off its tail an inch or so at a time," the broad-shouldered huntsman continued. "The Bearcult isn't really that concentrated in one place. With a little luck, we can gather up all the important members presently in Val Alorn in one sweep. That should irritate our snake enough to make him stick his neck out. Then we'll simply chop off his head."

Torvik's use of such terminology had made the queen wince. She had not been entirely sure that the blunt, grizzled forester had been speaking figuratively.

And now it had been done. Torvik and his huntsmen had moved quietly through the dark streets of Val Alorn for the entire night, gathering up the sleeping members of the Bearcult, marching them in groups to the harbor and then locking them in the holds of waiting ships. Because of their years of experience, the hunters had been very thorough in rounding up their quarry. By morning, the only members of the Bear-cult left in the city were the High Priest of Belar and the dozen or so underpriests lodged in the temple.

Queen Islena sat, pale and trembling, on the throne of Cherek. She wore her purple gown and her gold crown. In her hand she held a scepter. The scepter had a comforting weight to it and could possibly be used as a weapon in an emergency. The queen was positive that an emergency was about to descend on her.

"This is all your fault, Merel," she bitterly accused her blond friend. "If you'd just left things alone, we wouldn't be in this mess."

"We'd be a worse one," Merel replied coldly. "Pull yourself together, Islena. It's done now, and you can't undo it."

"Grodeg terrifies me," Islena blurted.

"He won't be armed. He won't be able to hurt you."

"I'm only a woman," Islena quailed. "He'll roar at me in that awful voice of his, and I'll go absolutely to pieces."

"Stop being such a coward, Islena," Merel snapped. "Your timidity's brought Cherek right to the edge of disaster. Every time Grodeg's raised his voice to you, you've given him anything he wanted—just because you're afraid of harsh talk. Are you a child? Does noise frighten you that much?"

"You forget yourself, Merel," Islena flared suddenly. "I *am* queen, after all."

"Then by all the Gods, *be* queen! Stop behaving like a silly, frightened serving girl. Sit up straight on your throne as if you had some iron in your backbone—and pinch your cheeks. You're as pale as a bedsheet." Merel's face hardened. "Listen to me, Islena," she said. "If you give even one hint that you're starting to weaken, I'll have Torvik run his spear into Grodeg right here in the throne room."

"You wouldn't!" Islena gasped. "You *can't* kill a priest."

"He's a man—just like any other man," Merel declared harshly. "If you stick a spear in his belly, he'll die."

"Not even Anheg would dare to do that."

"I'm not Anheg."

"You'll be cursed!"

"I'm not afraid of curses."

Torvik came into the throne room, a broad-bladed boarspear held negligently in one big hand. "He's coming," he announced laconically.

"Oh, dear," Islena quavered.

"Stop that!" Merel snapped.

Grodeg was livid with rage as he strode into the throne room. His white robe was rumpled as if he had thrown it on hastily, and his white hair and beard were uncombed. "I will speak with the queen alone!" he thundered as he approached across the rush-strewn floor.

"That is the queen's decision to make, not yours, my Lord High Priest," Merel advised him in a flinty voice.

"Does the wife of the Earl of Trellheim speak for the throne?" Grodeg demanded of Islena.

Islena faltered, then saw Torvik standing directly behind the tall priest. The boarspear in his hand was no longer so negligently grasped. "Calm yourself, revered Grodeg," the queen said, quite suddenly convinced that the life of the infuriated priest hinged not only on her words but even on her tone of voice. At the tiniest quaver, Merel would give the signal, and Torvik would sink that broad, sharp blade into Grodeg's back with about as much emotion as he showed about swatting a fly.

"I want to see you alone," Grodeg repeated stubbornly.

"No."

"No?" he roared incredulously.

"You heard me, Grodeg," she told him. "And stop shouting at me. My hearing is quite good."

He gaped at her, then quickly recovered. "Why have all my friends been arrested?" he demanded.

"They were not arrested, my Lord High Priest," the queen replied. "They have all volunteered to join my husband's fleet."

"Ridiculous!" he snorted.

"I think you'd better choose your words a bit more carefully, Grodeg," Merel told him. "The queen's patience with your impertinence is wearing thin."

"Impertinence?" he exclaimed. "How *dare* you speak that way to me?" He drew himself up and fixed a stern eye on the queen. "I insist upon a private audience," he told her in a thunderous voice.

The voice which had always cowed her before quite suddenly irritated Islena. She was trying to save this idiot's life,

and he kept shouting at her. "My Lord Grodeg," she said with
an unaccustomed hint of steel in her voice, "if you bellow at
me one more time, I'll have you muzzled."

His eyes widened in amazement.

"We have nothing to discuss in private, my Lord," the queen
continued. "All that remains is for you to receive your instructions—which you will follow to the letter. It is our decree that
you will proceed directly to the harbor, where you will board
the ship which is waiting to transport you to Algaria. There
you will join the forces of Cherek in the campaign against the
Angaraks."

"I refuse!" Grodeg retorted.

"Think carefully, my Lord Grodeg," Merel purred. "The
queen has given you a royal command. Refusal could be considered treason."

"I am the High Priest of Belar," Grodeg ground out between
clenched teeth, obviously having great difficulty in modulating
his voice. "You wouldn't dare ship me off like some peasant
conscript."

"I wonder if the High Priest of Belar might like to make a
small wager on that," Torvik said with deceptive mildness. He
set the butt of his spear on the floor, took a stone from the
pouch at his belt and began to hone the already razor-sharp
blade. The steely sound had an obviously chilling effect on
Grodeg.

"You will go to the harbor now, Grodeg," Islena told him,
"and you will get on that ship. If you do not, you will go to
the dungeon, where you will keep the rats company until my
husband returns. Those are your choices; join Anheg or join
the rats. Decide quickly. You're starting to bore me, and quite
frankly, I'm sick of the sight of you."

Queen Porenn of Drasnia was in the nursery, ostensibly
feeding her infant son. Out of respect for the queen's person,
she was unspied upon while she was nursing. Porenn, however,
was not alone. Javelin, the bone-thin chief of Drasnian intelligence, was with her. For the sake of appearance, Javelin was
dressed in a serving maid's gown and cap, and he looked

surprisingly feminine in the disguise he wore with no apparent trace of self-consciousness.

"Are there really that many cultists in the intelligence service?" the queen asked, a little dismayed.

Javelin sat with his back politely turned. "I'm afraid so, your Highness. We should have been more alert, but we had other things on our minds."

Porenn thought about it for a moment, unconsciously rocking her suckling baby. "Islena's moving already, isn't she?" she asked.

"That's the word I received this morning," Javelin replied. "Grodeg's on his way to the mouth of the Aldur River already, and the queen's men are moving out into the countryside, rounding up every member of the cult as they go."

"Will it in any way hamper our operations to jerk that many people out of Boktor?"

"We can manage, your Highness," Javelin assured her. "We might have to speed up the graduation of the current class at the academy and finish their training on the job, but we'll manage."

"Very well then, Javelin," Porenn decided. "Ship them all out. Get every cult member out of Boktor, and separate them. I want them sent to the most miserable duty posts you can devise, and I don't want any of them within fifty leagues of any other one. There will be no excuses, no sudden illnesses, and no resignations. Give each of them something to do, and then *make* him do it. I want every Bear-cultist who's crept into the intelligence service out of Boktor by nightfall."

"It will be my pleasure, Porenn," Javelin said. "Oh, incidentally, that Nadrak merchant, Yarblek is back from Yar Nadrak, and he wants to talk to you about the salmon runs again. He seems to have this obsessive interest in fish."

Chapter Twelve

THE RAISING OF the Cherek fleet to the top of the eastern escarpment took a full two weeks, and King Rhodar chafed visibly at the pace of the operation.

"You knew this was going to take time, Rhodar," Ce'Nedra said to him as he fumed and sweated, pacing back and forth with frequent dark looks at the towering cliff face. "Why are you so upset?"

"Because the ships are right out in the open, Ce'Nedra," he replied testily. "There's no way to hide them or disguise them while they're being raised. Those ships are the key to our whole campaign, and if somebody on the other side starts putting a few things together, we might have to meet all of Angarak instead of just the Thulls."

"You worry too much," she told him. "Cho-Hag and Korodullin are burning everything in sight up there. 'Zakath and Taur Urgas have other things to think about beside what we're hauling up the cliff."

"It must be wonderful to be so unconcerned about things," he said sarcastically.

"Be nice, Rhodar," she said.

General Varana, still scrupulously dressed in his Tolnedran mantle, limped toward them with that studiously diffident expression that indicated he was about to make another suggestion.

"Varana," King Rhodar burst out irritably, "why don't you put on your uniform?"

"Because I'm not really officially here, your Majesty," the general replied calmly. "Tolnedra *is* neutral in this affair, you'll recall."

"That's a fiction, and we all know it."

"A necessary one, however. The Emperor is still holding diplomatic channels open to Taur Urgas and 'Zakath. Those discussions would deteriorate if someone saw a Tolnedran general swaggering around in full uniform." He paused briefly. "Would a small suggestion offend your Majesty?" he asked.

"That all depends on the suggestion," Rhodar retorted. Then he made a face and apologized. "I'm sorry, Varana. This delay's making me bad-tempered. What did you have in mind?"

"I think you might want to give some thought to moving your command operations up to the top about now. You'll want things running smoothly by the time the bulk of your infantry arrives, and it usually takes a couple of days to iron out the wrinkles when you set things up."

King Rhodar stared at a Cherek ship being hoisted ponderously up the cliff face. "I'm not going to ride up on one of those, Varana," he declared flatly.

"It's absolutely safe, your Majesty," Varana assured him. "I've made the trip myself several times. Even Lady Polgara went up that way just this morning."

"Polgara could fly down if something went wrong," Rhodar said. "I don't have her advantages. Can you imagine the size of the hole I'd make in the ground if I fell that far?"

"The alternative is extremely strenuous, your Majesty. There are several ravines running down from the top. They've been leveled out a bit so that the horses can go up, but they're still *very* steep."

"A little sweating won't hurt me."

Varana shrugged. "As your Majesty wishes."

"I'll keep you company, Rhodar," Ce'Nedra offered brightly. He gave her a suspicious look.

"I don't really trust machines either," she confessed. "I'll go change clothes, and then we can start."

"You want to do it *today*?" His voice was plaintive.

"Why put it off?"

"I can think of a dozen reasons."

The term "very steep" turned out to be a gross understatement. "Precipitous" might have been more accurate. The incline made riding horses out of the question, but ropes had been strung along the steeper stretches to aid in the climb. Ce'Nedra, dressed in one of her short Dryad tunics, scampered hand over hand up the ropes with the agility of a squirrel. King Rhodar's pace, however, was much slower.

"Please stop groaning, Rhodar," she told him after they had climbed for an hour or so. "You sound like a sick cow."

"That's hardly fair, Ce'Nedra," he wheezed, stopping to mop his streaming face.

"I never promised to be fair," she retorted with an impish grin. "Come along, we still have a long way to go." And she flitted up another fifty yards or so.

"Don't you think you're a little underdressed?" he puffed disapprovingly, staring up at her. "Proper ladies don't show off so much leg."

"What's wrong with my legs?"

"They're bare—that's what's wrong with them."

"Don't be such a prig. I'm comfortable. That's all that matters. Are you coming or not?"

Rhodar groaned again. "Isn't it almost time for lunch?"

"We just had lunch."

"Did we? I'd forgotten already."

"You always seem to forget your last meal—usually before the crumbs have been brushed away."

"That's the nature of a fat man, Ce'Nedra." He sighed.

"The last meal is history. It's the next one that's important."
He stared mournfully up the brutal trail ahead and groaned
again.

"This was all your idea," she heartlessly reminded him.

The sun was low in the west when they reached the top.
As King Rhodar collapsed, Princess Ce'Nedra looked around
curiously. The fortifications which had been erected along the
top of the escarpment were extensive and quite imposing. The
walls were of earth and stone and were perhaps thirty feet high.
Through an open gate the princess saw a series of other, lower
walls, each fronted by a ditch bristling with sharpened stakes
and thorny brambles. At various points along the main wall
rose imposing blockhouses, and within the walls were neat
rows of huts for the soldiers.

The forts swarmed with men, and their various activities
raised an almost perpetual cloud of dust. A party of Algar
clansmen, smoke-stained and mounted on spent-looking horses,
rode slowly in through the gate; and a few moments later, a
contingent of gleaming Mimbrate knights, pennons snapping
from their lances and the great hoofs of their chargers clattering
on the stony ground, rode out in search of yet another town to
destroy.

The huge hoists at the edge of the escarpment creaked and
groaned under the weight of the Cherek ships being raised from
the plain below; some distance away, within the fortified walls,
the growing fleet sat awaiting the final portage to the headwaters
of the upper River Mardu, some fifty leagues distant.

Polgara, accompanied by Durnik and the towering Barak,
approached to greet the princess and the prostrate King of
Drasnia.

"How was the climb?" Barak inquired.

"Ghastly," Rhodar wheezed. "Does anybody have anything
to eat? I think I've melted off about ten pounds."

"It doesn't show," Barak told him.

"That sort of exertion isn't really good for you, Rhodar,"
Polgara told the gasping monarch. "Why were you so stubborn
about it?"

"Because I have an absolute horror of heights," Rhodar

replied. "I'd climb ten times as far to avoid being hauled up that cliff by those contraptions. The idea of all that empty air under me makes my flesh creep."

Barak grinned. "That's a lot of creeping."

"Will somebody *please* give me something to eat?" Rhodar asked in an anguished tone of voice.

"A bit of cold chicken?" Durnik offered solicitously, handing him a well-browned chicken leg.

"Where did you ever find a chicken?" Rhodar exclaimed, eagerly seizing the leg.

"The Thulls brought some with them," Durnik told him.

"Thulls?" Ce'Nedra gasped. "What are Thulls doing here?"

"Surrendering," Durnik replied. "Whole villages of them have been showing up for the past week or so. They walk up to the edge of the ditches along the front of the fortification and sit down and wait to be captured. They're very patient about it. Sometimes it's a day or so before anybody has the time to go out and capture them, but they don't seem to mind."

"Why do they want to be captured?" Ce'Nedra asked him.

"There aren't any Grolims here," Durnik explained. "No altars to Torak and no sacrificial knives. The Thulls seem to feel that getting away from that sort of thing is worth the inconvenience of being captured. We take them in and put them to work on the fortifications. They're good workers, if you give them the proper supervision."

"Is that entirely safe?" Rhodar asked around a mouthful of chicken. "There might be spies among them."

Durnik nodded. "We know," he said, "but the spies are usually Grolims. A Thull doesn't have the mental equipment to be a spy, so the Grolims have to do it themselves."

Rhodar lowered his chicken leg in astonishment. "You're letting Grolims inside the fortifications?" he demanded.

"It's nothing all that serious," Durnik told him. "The Thulls know who the Grolims are, and we let them deal with the problem. They usually take them a mile or so along the escarpment and then throw them off. At first they wanted to do it right here, but some of their elders pointed out that it might not be polite to drop Golims down on top of the men working below, so they take them some place where they won't bother anybody when they fall. A very considerate people, the Thulls. One could almost get to like them."

"You've sunburned your nose, Ce'Nedra," Polgara told the little princess. "Didn't you think of wearing a hat?"

"Hats give me a headache." Ce'Nedra shrugged. "A little sunburn won't hurt me."

"You have an appearance to maintain, dear," Polgara pointed out. "You're not going to look very queenly with your nose peeling."

"It's nothing to worry about, Lady Polgara. You can fix it, can't you? You know—" Ce'Nedra made a little gesture with her hand that was meant to look magical.

Polgara gave her a long, chilly look.

King Anheg of Cherek, accompanied by the broad-shoul-dered Rivan Warder, approached them. "Did you have a nice climb?" he asked Rhodar pleasantly.

"How would you like a punch in the nose?" Rhodar asked him.

King Anheg laughed coarsely. "My," he said, "aren't we grumpy today? I've just had some news from home that ought to brighten your disposition a bit."

"Dispatches?" Rhodar groaned, hauling himself wearily to his feet.

Anheg nodded. "They sent them up from down below while you were getting your exercise. You're not going to believe what's been going on back there."

"Try me."

"You absolutely won't believe it."

"Anheg, spit it out."

"We're about to get some reinforcements. Islena and Porenn have been very busy these last few weeks."

Polgara looked at him sharply.

"Do you know something?" Anheg said, holding out a folded dispatch. "I wasn't even aware of the fact that Islena knew how to read and write, and now I get this."

"Don't be cryptic, Anheg," Polgara told him. "What have the ladies been up to?"

"I gather that after we left, the Bear-cult began to make itself a bit obnoxious. Grodeg apparently felt that with the men out of the way, he could take over. He started throwing his weight around in Val Alorn, and cult members began to surface in the headquarters of Drasnian intelligence in Boktor. It looks as if they've been making preparations for something for years. Anyway, Porenn and Islena began passing information back and forth, and when they realized how close Grodeg was to getting his hands on real power in the two kingdoms, they took steps. Porenn ordered all the cult members out of Boktor— sent them to the most miserable duty posts she could think of—and Islena rounded up the Bear-cult in Val Alorn—every last one of them—and shipped them out to join the army."

"They did *what*?" Rhodar gasped.

"Isn't it amazing?" A slow grin spread across Anheg's coarse face. "The beauty of the whole thing is that Islena could get away with it, while I couldn't. Women aren't supposed to be aware of the subtleties involved in arresting priests and noblemen—the need for evidence against them and so on—so what would be gross impropriety on my part will be laughed off as ignorance on hers. I'll have to apologize to Grodeg, of course, but it will be after the fact. The cult will be here, and they'll have no honest reason to go back home."

Rhodar's answering grin was every bit as wicked as Anheg's. "How did Grodeg take it?"

"He was absolutely livid. I guess Islena faced him down personally. She gave him the choice of joining us or going to the dungeon."

"You can't put the High Priest of Belar in a dungeon," Rhodar exclaimed.

"Islena didn't know that, and Grodeg *knew* that she didn't. She'd have had him chained to the wall in the deepest hole she could find before anybody had gotten around to telling her that it was illegal. Can't you just see my Islena delivering that kind of ultimatum to the old windbag?" There was a note of fierce pride in Anheg's voice.

King Rhodar's face grew very sly. "There's bound to be

some rather hot fighting in this campaign sooner or later," he noted.

Anheg nodded.

"The Bear-cult prides itself on its fighting ability, doesn't it?"

Anheg nodded again, grinning.

"They'd be perfect for spearheading any attacks, wouldn't they?"

Anheg's grin grew positively vicious.

"I imagine that their casualties will be heavy," the King of Drasnia suggested.

"It's in a good cause, after all," Anheg replied piously.

"If you two have quite finished gloating, I think it's time I got the princess in out of the sun," Polgara told the two grinning monarchs.

The fortified positions atop the escarpment bustled with activity for the next several days. Even as the last of the Cherek ships were raised up the cliffs, the Algars and Mimbrates extended their depredations out into the Thullish countryside. "There aren't any crops standing for fifty leagues in any direction," Hettar reported back. "We'll have to go out farther to find anything else to burn."

"You find many Murgos?" Barak asked the hawk-faced man.

"A few." Hettar shrugged. "Not enough to make it interesting, but we run across one every now and then."

"How's Mandorallen doing?"

"I haven't seen him for a few days," Hettar replied. "There's a lot of smoke coming from the direction he went, though, so I imagine he's keeping busy."

"What's the country like out there?" King Anheg asked.

"Not bad, once you get past the uplands. The part of Thulldom along the escarpment here is pretty forbidding."

"What do you mean by forbidding? I've got to haul ships through that country."

"Rock, sand, a few thornbushes and no water," Hettar replied. "And it's hotter than the backdoor of a furnace."

"Thanks," Anheg said.

"You wanted to know," Hettar told him. "Excuse me. I need a fresh horse and some more torches."

"You're going out again?" Barak asked him.

"It's something to do."

Once the last of the ships had been raised, the Drasnian hoists began lifting tons of food and equipment that soon swelled King Fulrach's supply dumps within the forts to overflowing. The Thullish prisoners proved to be an invaluable asset, carrying whatever burden they were told to carry without complaint or hesitation. Their coarse features shone with such simpleminded gratitude and eagerness to please that Ce'Nedra found it impossible to hate them, even though they were technically the enemy. Slowly, bit by bit, the princess discovered the facts that made the lives of the Thullish people such an unrelieved horror. There was not a family among them that had not lost several members to the knives of the Grolims—husbands, wives, children, and parents had all been selected for sacrifice, and the thought uppermost in every Thull's life was to avoid the same fate at any cost. The perpetual terror had erased every hint of human affection from the Thull's makeup. He lived in dreadful isolation, without love, without companionship, without any feeling but constant anxiety and dread. The reputedly insatiable appetite of Thullish women had nothing whatsoever to do with morals or lack of them. It was a simple matter of survival. To escape the knife, a Thullish woman was forced to remain perpetually pregnant. She was not driven by lust, but by fear, and her fear dehumanized her entirely.

"How can they live that way?" the princess burst out to Lady Polgara as the two of them returned to their makeshift quarters in the stout blockhouse which had been erected inside the walls for the use of the leaders of the army. "Why don't they rebel and drive the Grolims out?"

"And just who's supposed to lead a rebellion, Ce'Nedra?" Polgara asked her calmly. "The Thulls know that there are Grolims who can pick the thoughts from a man's mind as easily as you'd pick fruit in an orchard. If a Thull even considered organizing some kind of resistance, he'd be the next one dragged to the altar."

"But their lives are so *horrible*," Ce'Nedra objected.

"Perhaps we can change that," Polgara said. "In a way what we're trying to do is not only for the benefit of the west, but for the Angaraks as well. If we win, they'll be liberated from the Grolims. They might not thank us at first, but in time they might learn to appreciate it."

"Why shouldn't they thank us?"

"Because if we win, dear, it will be because we've killed their God. That's a very hard thing to thank someone for."

"But Torak is a monster."

"He's still their God," Polgara replied. "The loss of one's God is a very subtle and terrible injury. Ask the Ulgos what it's like to live without one. It's been five thousand years since UL became their God, and they still remember what it was like before he accepted them."

"We *are* going to win, aren't we?" Ce'Nedra asked suddenly, all her fears flooding to the surface.

"I don't know, Ce'Nedra," Polgara answered quietly. "No one does—not me, not Beldin, not my father, not even Aldur. All we can do is try."

"What will happen if we lose?" the princess asked in a tiny, frightened voice.

"We'll be enslaved in exactly the same way the Thulls are," Polgara replied quietly. "Torak will become King and God over the entire world. The other Gods will be banished forever, and the Grolims will be unleashed upon us all."

"I won't live in that kind of world," Ce'Nedra declared.

"None of us would care to."

"Did you ever meet Torak?" the princess asked suddenly.

Polgara nodded. "Once or twice—the last time was at Vo Mimbre just before his duel with Brand."

"What's he really like?"

"He's a God. The force of his mind is overwhelming. When he speaks to you, you must listen to him—and when he commands, you *must* obey him."

"Not *you*, certainly."

"I don't think you understand, dear." Polgara's face was grave, and her glorious eyes were as distant as the moon. Without seeming to think about it, she reached out, picked up Errand and sat him on her lap. The child smiled at her and, as he so often did, he reached out and touched the white lock at her brow. "There's a compulsion in Torak's voice that's almost impossible to resist," she continued. "You *know* that he's twisted and evil, but when he speaks to you, your will to resist crumbles, and you're suddenly very weak and afraid."

"Surely *you* weren't afraid."

"You still don't understand. Of course I was afraid. We all were—even my father. Pray that you never meet Torak. He's not some petty Grolim like Chamdar or a scheming old wizard like Ctuchik. He's a God. He's hideously maimed, and at some point he was thwarted. Something he needed—something so profound that no human could even conceive of it—was denied to him, and that refusal or rejection drove him mad. His madness is not like the madness of Taur Urgas, who, in spite of everything is still human. Torak's madness is the madness of a God—a being who can *make* his diseased imaginings come to pass. Only the Orb can truly withstand him. I could perhaps resist him for a time, but if he lays the full force of his will upon me, ultimately I'll have to give him what he wants—and what he wants from me is too dreadful to think about."

"I don't exactly follow you, Lady Polgara."

Garion's Aunt looked gravely at the tiny girl. "Perhaps you don't at that," she said. "It has to do with a part of the past that the Tolnedran Historical Society chooses to ignore. Sit down, Ce'Nedra, and I'll try to explain."

The princess sat on a rude bench in their rough chamber. Polgara's mood was unusual—very quiet, even pensive. She placed her arms about Errand and held him close, nestling her cheek against his blond curls as if taking comfort from the contact with this small boy. "There are two Prophecies, Ce'Nedra," she explained in her rich voice, "but the time is coming when there will only be one. Everything that is or was or is yet to be will become a part of whichever Prophecy prevails. Every man, every woman, every child has two possible destinies. For some, the differences are not all that great, but in my case, they're rather profound."

"I don't quite understand."

"In the Prophecy which we serve—the one that has brought us here—I am Polgara the sorceress, daughter to Belgarath and guardian to Belgarion."

"And in the other?"

"In the other, I am the bride of Torak."

Ce'Nedra gasped.

"And now you see why I was afraid," Polgara continued. "I've been terrified of Torak since my father first explained this to me when I was no older than you are now. I'm not so much afraid for myself, but more because I know that if I falter—if Torak's will overpowers mine—then the Prophecy we serve will fail. Torak will not only win me, but all of mankind as well. At Vo Mimbre, he called to me, and I felt— very briefly—the awful compulsion to run to him. But I defied him. I've never done anything in my life that was so hard to do. It was *my* defiance, however, that drove him into the duel with Brand, and only in that duel could the power of the Orb be released against him. My father gambled everything on the strength of my will. The old wolf is a great gambler sometimes."

"Then if—" Ce'Nedra could not say it.

"If Garion loses?" Polgara said it so calmly that it was quite obvious that she had considered the possibility many times before. "Then Torak will come to claim his bride, and there will be no power on earth sufficient to stop him."

"I would sooner die," the princess blurted.

"So would I, Ce'Nedra, but that option may not be open to me. Torak's will is so much stronger than mine that he may be able to take from me the ability or even the desire to will myself out of existence. If it should happen, it may very well be that I'll be deliriously happy to be his chosen and beloved— but deep inside, I think that a part of me will be screaming and will continue to scream in horror down through all the endless centuries to the very end of days."

It was too horrible to think about. Unable to restrain herself, the princess threw herself on her knees, clasped her arms about Polgara and Errand, and burst into tears.

"Now, now, there's no need to cry, Ce'Nedra," Polgara told her gently, smoothing the sobbing girl's hair with her hand. "Garion has still not reached the City of Endless Night, and Torak is still asleep. There's a little time left. And who knows? We might even win."

Chapter Thirteen

ONCE THE CHEREK fleet had been raised, the pace of activities within the fortifications began to quicken. King Rhodar's infantry units began to arrive from the encampment at the Aldur River to make the tortuous climb up the narrow ravines to the top of the escarpment; lines of wagons from the main supply dumps freighted food and equipment to the base of the cliff where the great hoists waited to lift the supplies up the mile-high basalt face; and the Mimbrate and Algar raiding parties moved out, usually before dawn, in their now far-flung search for as yet unravaged towns and crops. The depredations of the raiders, their short, savage sieges of poorly fortified Thullish towns and villages, and the mile-wide swaths of fire that they cut through fields of ripe grain had finally swung the sluggish Thulls into poorly organized attempts at resistance. The Thulls, however, inevitably raced to the last point of Mimbrate attack and arrived hours or even days too late, to discover only smoking ruins, dead soldiers, and terrified and dispossessed townsmen, or, when they attempted to intercept the

swiftly moving Algars, they normally found only acre upon
acre of blackened earth. The raiders had moved on, and the
desperate attempts of the Thulls to catch up with them were
entirely futile.

The notion of attacking the forts from which the raiders
operated did not occur to the Thulls, or if it did, it was quickly
dismissed. The Thulls were not emotionally suited to attacking
heavily defended fortifications. They much preferred dashing
about, chasing fires, and complaining bitterly to their Murgo
and Mallorean allies about the lack of support they were re-
ceiving. The Malloreans of Emperor 'Zakath steadfastly refused to emerge from their staging areas around Thull Zelik.
The Murgos of Taur Urgas, however, did make a few sorties
in southern Thulldom, in part as a gesture toward the notion
of Angarak unity—but more, King Rhodar surmised, as a part
of their overall maneuvering for position. Murgo scouts were
even occasionally discovered in the vicinity of the forts themselves. In order to sweep the area clear of these prying Murgo
eyes, patrols went out every day from the forts to range through
the arid hills. The parched, rocky valleys near the forts were
randomly searched by Drasnian pikemen and platoons of legionnaires. Algar clansmen, supposedly resting from their long-
range raids, amused themselves with an impromptu game they
called "Murgo hunting." They made a great show of their
frequent excursions and piously insisted that they were sacri-
ficing their rest time out of a sense of responsibility for the
security of the forts. They did not, of course, fool anybody
with their protestations.

"The area *does* need to be patroled, Rhodar," King Cho-
Hag insisted. "My children are performing a necessary duty,
after all."

"Duty?" Rhodar snorted. "Put an Algar on a horse and show
him a hill he hasn't seen the backside of yet, and he'll always
find an excuse to go take a look."

"You wrong us," Cho-Hag replied with a look of hurt innocence.

"I *know* you."

Ce'Nedra and her two closest companions had watched the

periodic departure of the lighthearted Algar horsemen with increasingly sour expressions. Though Ariana was perhaps more sedentary in her habits and was accustomed, as all Mimbrate ladies were, to waiting quite patiently while the men were out playing, Adara, Garion's Algar cousin, felt her confinement most keenly. Like all Algars, she felt a deep-seated need to have the wind in her face and the thunder of hoofs in her ears. She grew petulant after a time and sighed often.

"And what shall we do today, ladies?" Ce'Nedra asked the two of them brightly one morning after breakfast. "How shall we amuse ourselves until lunchtime?" She said it rather extravagantly, since she already had plans for the day.

"There is always embroidery," Ariana suggested. "It doth pleasantly occupy the fingers and eyes while leaving the mind and lips free for conversation."

Adara sighed deeply.

"Or maybe we might go and observe my lord as he instructs his serfs in their warlike preparations." Ariana usually found some excuse to watch Lelldorin for at least half of each day.

"I'm not sure that I'm up to watching a group of men murder hay bales with arrows again today," Adara said a bit waspishly.

Ce'Nedra moved quickly to head off any incipient bickering. "We could make an inspection tour," she suggested archly.

"Ce'Nedra, we've looked at every blockhouse and every hut within the walls a dozen times already," Adara said with some asperity, "and if I have some polite old sergeant explain the workings of a catapult to me one more time, I think I'll scream."

"We have not, however, inspected the outer fortifications, have we?" the princess asked slyly. "Wouldn't you say that's part of our duty too?"

Adara looked at her quickly, and then a slow smile appeared on her face. "Absolutely," she agreed. "I'm surprised that we hadn't thought of that before. We've been most neglectful, haven't we?"

Ariana's face took on a worried frown. "King Rhodar, I fear, would be most strenuous in his objections to such a plan."

"Rhodar isn't here," Ce'Nedra pointed out. "He's off with

King Fulrach taking an inventory of the supply dumps."

"Lady Polgara would most certainly not approve," Ariana suggested, though her tone indicated that she was weakening.

"Lady Polgara is conferring with Beldin the sorcerer," Adara mentioned, her eyes dancing mischievously.

Ce'Nedra smirked. "That rather leaves us to our own devices, doesn't it, ladies?"

"We shall be soundly scolded upon our return," Ariana said.

"And we will all be very contrite, won't we?" Ce'Nedra giggled.

A quarter of an hour later, the princess and her two friends, dressed in soft black leather Algar riding clothes, passed at a canter out through the central gate of the vast fort. They were accompanied by Olban, the youngest son of the Rivan Warder. Olban had not liked the idea, but Ce'Nedra had given him no time to object and definitely no time to send a message to anyone who could step in and stop the whole excursion. Olban looked worried, but, as always, he accompanied the little Rivan Queen without question.

The stake-studded trenches in front of the walls were very interesting, but one trench looked much like another, and it took a rare mind indeed to find much pleasure in the finer points of excavation.

"Very nice," Ce'Nedra said brightly to a Drasnian pikeman standing guard atop a high mound of dirt. "Splendid ditches— and all those excellently sharp stakes." She looked out at the arid landscape before the fortifications. "Where did you ever find all the wood for them?"

"The Sendars brought it in, your Majesty," he replied, "from someplace up north, I think. We had the Thulls cut and sharpen the stakes for us. They're quite good stake-makers—if you tell them what you want."

"Didn't a mounted patrol go out this way about a half an hour ago?" Ce'Nedra asked him.

"Yes, your Majesty. Lord Hettar of Algaria and some of his men. They went off that way." The guard pointed toward the south.

"Ah," Ce'Nedra said. "If anyone should ask, tell them that we're going out to join him. We should return in a few hours."

The guard looked a bit dubious about that, but Ce'Nedra moved quickly to head off any objections. "Lord Hettar promised to wait for us just beyond the south end of the fortifications," she told him. She turned to her companions. "We really mustn't keep him waiting too long. You ladies took absolutely *too* much time changing clothes." She smiled winsomely at the guard. "You know how it is," she said. "The riding habit must be just so, and the hair absolutely *has* to be brushed one last time. Sometimes it takes forever. Come along, ladies. We must hurry, or Lord Hettar will be vexed with us." With a brainless little giggle, the princess wheeled Noble and rode south at a gallop.

"Ce'*Nedra*," Ariana exclaimed in a shocked voice once they were out of earshot, "you *lied* to him."

"Of course."

"But that's dreadful."

"Not nearly as dreadful as spending another day embroidering daisies on a stupid petticoat," the princess replied.

They left the fortifications and crossed a low, burned-brown string of hills. The broad valley beyond was enormous. Dun brown and treeless mountains reared up fully twenty miles away at the valley's far end. They cantered down into that vast emptiness, feeling dwarfed into insignificance by the colossal landscape. Their horses seemed no more than ants crawling toward the indifferent mountains.

"I hadn't realized it was so big," Ce'Nedra murmured, shading her eyes to gaze at the distant hilltops.

The floor of the valley was as flat as a tabletop, and it was only sparsely sprinkled with low, thorny bushes. The ground was scattered with round, fist-sized rocks, and the dust spurted, yellow and powdery, from each step of their horses' hoofs. Although it was scarcely midmorning, the sun was already a furnace, and shimmering heatwaves rippled the valley floor ahead, making the dusty, gray-green bushes seem to dance in the windless air.

It grew hotter. There was no trace of moisture anywhere, and the sweat dried almost instantly on the flanks of their panting horses.

"I think we should give some thought to going back," Adara said, reining in her mount. "There's no way we can reach those hills at the end of the valley."

"She's right, your Majesty," Olban told the princess. "We've already come too far."

Ce'Nedra pulled Noble to a stop, and the white horse drooped his head as if on the verge of absolute exhaustion. "Oh, quit feeling sorry for yourself," she chided him irritably. This was not going at all as she had expected. She looked around. "I wonder if we could find some shade somewhere," she said. Her lips were dry, and the sun seemed to hammer down on her unprotected head.

"The terrain doth not suggest such comfort, princess," Ariana said, looking around at the flat emptiness of the rock-strewn valley floor.

"Did anyone think to bring any water?" Ce'Nedra asked, dabbing at her forehead with a kerchief.

No one had.

"Maybe we *should* go back," she decided, looking about rather regretfully. "There's nothing to see out here, anyway."

"Riders coming," Adara said sharply, pointing toward a mounted group of men emerging from an indented gulley that lay like a fold on the flanks of a rounded hill a mile or so away.

"Murgos?" Olban demanded with a sharp intake of his breath. His hand went immediately to his sword.

Adara raised her hand to shade her eyes and stared at the approaching horsemen intently. "No," she replied. "They're Algars. I can tell by the way they ride."

"I hope they have some water with them," Ce'Nedra said.

The dozen or so Algar riders rode directly toward them with a great cloud of yellow dust rising behind them. Adara suddenly gasped, and her face went very pale.

"What is it?" Ce'Nedra asked her.

"Lord Hettar is with them," Adara said in a choked voice.

"How can you possibly recognize anybody at that distance?"

Adara bit her lip, but did not reply.

Hettar's face was fierce and unforgiving as he reined in his sweating horse. "What are you doing out here?" he demanded bluntly. His hawk-face and black scalp lock gave him a wild, even frightening appearance.

"We thought we'd go riding, Lord Hettar," Ce'Nedra replied brightly, trying to outface him.

Hettar ignored that. "Have you lost your mind, Olban?" he harshly asked the young Rivan. "Why did you permit the ladies to leave the forts?"

"I do not tell her Majesty what to do," Olban answered stiffly, his face red.

"Oh, come now, Hettar," Ce'Nedra protested. "What's the harm in our taking a little ride?"

"We killed three Murgos not a mile from here just yesterday," Hettar told her. "If you want exercise, run around the inside of the forts for a few hours. Don't just ride out unprotected in hostile territory. You've acted very foolishly, Ce'Nedra. We'll go back now." His face was grim as a winter sea, and his tone left no room for discussion.

"We had just made the same decision, my Lord," Adara murmured, her eyes downcast.

Hettar looked sternly at the condition of their horses. "You're an Algar, Lady Adara," he said pointedly. "Didn't it occur to you to bring water for your mounts? Surely you know better than to take a horse out in this kind of heat without any precautions at all."

Adara's pale face grew stricken.

Hettar shook his head in disgust. "Water their horses," he curtly told one of his men, "and then we'll escort them back. Your excursion is over, ladies."

Adara's face was flaming with a look of almost unbearable shame. She twisted this way and that in her saddle, trying to avoid Hettar's stern, unforgiving stare. No sooner had her horse been watered than she jerked her reins and dug her heels into his flanks. Her startled mount scrambled his hoofs in the gravel and leaped away, running back the way they had come across the rock-littered valley floor.

Hettar swore and drove his mount after her.

"Whatever is she doing?" Ce'Nedra exclaimed.

"Lord Hettar's rebuke hath stung our gentle companion beyond her endurance," Ariana observed. "His good opinion is dearer to her than her life itself."

"Hettar?" Ce'Nedra was stunned.

"Hath not thine eye informed thee how it doth stand with our dear friend?" Ariana asked in mild surprise. "Thou art strangely unobservant, Princess."

"Hettar?" Ce'Nedra repeated. "I had no idea."

"Mayhap it is because I am Mimbrate," Ariana concluded. "The ladies of my people are most sensitive to the signs of gentle affection in others."

It took perhaps a hundred yards for Hettar to overtake Adara's plunging horse. He seized her reins in one fist and jerked her roughly to a stop, speaking sharply to her, demanding to know what she was doing. Adara twisted this way and that in her saddle, trying to keep him from seeing her face as he continued to chide her.

Then a flicker of movement no more than twenty feet from the two of them caught Ce'Nedra's eye. Astonishingly, a mail-shirted Murgo rose up out of the sand between two scrubby bushes, shaking off the sheet of brown-splotched canvas beneath which he had lain concealed. As he rose, his short bow was already drawn.

"Hettar!" Ce'Nedra screamed as the Murgo raised his bow.

Hettar's back was to the Murgo, but Adara saw the man aiming his arrow at the Algar's unprotected back. With a desperate move, she ripped her reins from Hettar's grip and drove her horse into his. His mount lurched back, stumbled and fell, throwing the unprepared man to the ground even as Adara, flailing her horse's flanks with the ends of her reins, plunged directly at the Murgo.

With only the faintest flicker of annoyance, the Murgo released his arrow at the charging girl.

Even at that distance, Ce'Nedra could hear the distinct sound the arrow made when it struck Adara. It was a sound she would remember with horror for the remainder of her life. Adara

doubled sharply, her free hand clutching at the arrow buried
low in her chest, but her plunging gallop did not falter nor
change as she rode the Murgo down. He tumbled and rolled
beneath the churning hoofs of her horse, then lurched again to
his feet as soon as she had passed over him, his hand jerking
at his sheathed sword. But Hettar was already upon him, sabre
flashing in the glaring sunlight. The Murgo screamed once as
he fell.

Hettar, his dripping sabre still in his hand, turned angrily
to Adara. "What a stupid thing," he roared at her, but his shout
cut off suddenly. Her horse had come to a stop a few yards
beyond the Murgo, and she drooped in her saddle, her dark
hair falling like a veil across her pale face and both of her
hands pressed to her chest. Then, slowly, she toppled from her
saddle.

With a strangled cry, Hettar dropped his sabre and ran to
her.

"Adara!" the princess wailed, her hands going to her face
in horror even as Hettar gently turned the stricken girl over.
The arrow, still standing out of her lower chest, throbbed with
the rhythm of her faltering heartbeat.

When the rest of them reached the pair, Hettar was holding
Adara in his arms, staring into her pale face with a stricken
look. "You little fool," he was murmuring in a broken voice.
"You little fool."

Ariana slid from her saddle even before her horse stopped
moving and ran to Hettar's side. "Do not move her, my Lord,"
she told him sharply. "The arrow hath pierced her lung, and
shouldst thou move her, its keen edge will gash out her life."

"Take it out," Hettar said from between clenched teeth.

"Nay, my Lord. To pull the arrow now will do more damage
than to leave it."

"I can't bear to see it sticking out of her like that," he almost
sobbed.

"Then don't look, my Lord," Ariana said bluntly, kneeling
beside Adara and placing a cool, professional hand on the
wounded girl's throat.

"She's not dead, is she?" Hettar almost begged.

Ariana shook her head. "Gravely wounded, but her life doth still pulse within her. Instruct thy men to improvise a litter at once, my Lord. We must convey our dear friend to the fortress and Lady Polgara's ministrations immediately, lest her life drain away."

"Can't *you* do something?" he croaked.

"Not here in this sun-blasted desolation, my Lord. I have neither instruments nor medications, and the wound may be past my skill. The Lady Polgara is her only hope. The litter, my Lord. Quickly!"

Polgara's face was somber, and her eyes as hard as flint when she emerged from Adara's sickroom late that afternoon.

"How is she?" Hettar demanded. He had been pacing up and down in the main corridor of the blockhouse for hours, stopping every so often to strike savagely at the crudely built stone walls with his impotent fists.

"Somewhat improved," Polgara replied. "The crisis is past, but she's still terribly weak. She's asking for you."

"She *will* recover, won't she?" Hettar's question had a note of fear in it.

"Probably—if there aren't any complications. She's young, and the wound looked more serious than it actually was. I gave her something that will make her very talkative, but don't stay too long. She needs rest." Polgara's eyes moved to Ce'Nedra's tear-streaked face. "Come to my room after you've seen her, your Majesty," she said firmly. "You and I have something to discuss."

Adara's porcelain face was framed by the tumbled mass of her dark brown hair spreading across the pillow. She was very pale, but, though her eyes had a slightly unfocused look about them, they were very bright. Ariana sat quietly at the bedside.

"How do you feel, Adara?" Ce'Nedra asked in the quiet but cheerful voice one always assumes with the sick.

Adara gave her a wan little smile.

"Are you in any pain?"

"No," Adara's voice had a little dying fall to it. "No pain, but I feel very light-headed and strange."

"Why did you do that, Adara?" Hettar asked very directly. "You didn't have to ride right at the Murgo like that."

"You spend too much time with horses, my Lord Sha-dar," Adara told him with a faint smile. "You've forgotten how to understand the feelings of your own kind."

"What's that supposed to mean?" He sounded puzzled.

"Exactly what it says, my Lord Hettar. If a mare looked admiringly at a stallion, you'd know how things stood immediately, wouldn't you? But when it comes to people, you simply can't see at all, can you?" She coughed weakly.

"Are you all right?" he asked sharply.

"I'm surprisingly well—considering the fact that I'm dying."

"What are you talking about? You're not dying."

She smiled slightly. "Please don't," she told him. "I know what an arrow in the chest means. That's why I wanted to see you. I wanted to look at your face once more. I've been watching your face for such a long time now."

"You're tired," he said brusquely. "You'll feel better after you've slept."

"I'll sleep, all right," she said ruefully, "but I doubt that I'll feel anything afterward. The sleep I'm gong to is the sleep one doesn't wake up from."

"Nonsense."

"Of course it is, but it's true nonetheless." She sighed. "Well, dear Hettar, you've finally escaped me, haven't you? I gave you a good chase, though. I even asked Garion to see if he could use sorcery on you."

"Garion?"

She nodded slightly. "You see how desperate I was? He said he couldn't, though." She made a little face. "What good is sorcery if you can't use it to make someone fall in love?"

"Love?" he repeated in a startled voice.

"What did you think we were talking about, Lord Hettar? The weather?" She smiled fondly at him. "Sometimes you can be impossibly dense."

He stared at her in amazement.

"Don't be alarmed, my Lord. In a little while, I'll stop chasing you, and you'll be free."

"We'll talk about that when you're better," he told her gravely.

"I'm not going to get better. Haven't you been listening? I'm dying, Hettar."

"No," he said, "as a matter of fact, you're not dying. Polgara assured us that you're going to be all right."

Adara looked quickly at Ariana.

"Thine injury is not mortal, dear friend," Ariana confirmed gently. "Truly, thou art not dying."

Adara closed her eyes. "How inconvenient," she murmured, a faint blush coming to her cheeks. She opened her eyes again. "I apologize, Hettar. I wouldn't have said any of this if I'd known that my meddling physicians were going to save my life. As soon as I'm up and about, I'll return to my own clan. I won't bother you again with my foolish outbursts."

Hettar looked down at her, his hard-angled face expressionless. "I don't think I'd like that," he told her, gently taking her hand. "There are things you and I need to talk about. This isn't the time or the place, but don't go trying to make yourself unaccessible."

"You're just being kind." She sighed.

"No. Practical. You've given me something to think about beside killing Murgos. It's probably going to take me a while to get used to the idea, but after I've thought it over, we'll definitely need to talk."

She bit her lip and tried to hide her face. "What a stupid mess I've made of things," she said. "If I were somebody else, I'd laugh at me. It would really be better if we didn't see each other again."

"No," he said firmly, still holding her hand, "it wouldn't. And don't try to hide from me, because I'll find you—even if I have to have every horse in Algaria go looking for you."

She gave him a startled look.

"I *am* a Sha-dar, remember? Horses do what I tell them to."

"That's not fair," she objected.

He gave her a quizzical little smile. "And trying to have Garion use sorcery on me *was*?" he asked her.

"Oh, dear!" She blushed.

"She must rest now," Ariana told them. "Thou canst speak with her further on the morrow."

When they were back out in the hallway, Ce'Nedra turned on the tall man. "You might have said something a bit more encouraging," she scolded him.

"It would have been premature," he replied. "We're a rather reserved people, Princess. We don't say things just to be talking. Adara understands the situation." Hettar seemed as fierce as ever, his sharp-angled face hard, and his manelike scalp lock flowing over one leather-armored shoulder. His eyes, however, had softened slightly, and there was a faintly puzzled crease between his brows. "Didn't Polgara want to see you?" he asked. It was polite, but it was a dismissal nonetheless.

Ce'Nedra stalked away, muttering to herself about the lack of consideration that seemed to infect the male half of the population.

Lady Polgara sat quietly in her room, waiting. "Well?" she said when the princess entered. "Would you care to explain?"

"Explain what?"

"The reason for the idiocy that almost cost Adara her life."

"Surely you don't think it was *my* fault," Ce'Nedra protested.

"Whose fault was it, then? What were you doing out there?"

"We just went for a little ride. It's so boring being cooped up all the time."

"Boring. What a fascinating reason to kill your friends."

Ce'Nedra gaped at her, her face suddenly very pale.

"Why do you think we built these fortifications to begin with, Ce'Nedra? It was to provide us with some measure of protection."

"I didn't know there were Murgos out there," the princess wailed.

"Did you bother to find out?"

The entire implication of what she had done quite suddenly came crashing in on Ce'Nedra. She began to tremble violently, and her shaking hand went to her mouth. It *was* her fault! No matter how she might twist and turn and try to evade the responsibility, her foolishness had nearly killed one of her dearest friends. Adara had almost paid with her life for a bit of childish thoughtlessness. Ce'Nedra buried her face in her hands in a sudden storm of weeping.

Polgara let her cry for several moments, giving her ample time to accept her guilt; and when she finally spoke, there was no hint of forgiveness in her voice. "Tears won't wash out blood, Ce'Nedra," she said. "I thought I could at least begin to trust your judgment, but it appears that I was wrong. You may leave now. I don't believe I have anything more to say to you this evening."

Sobbing, the princess fled.

Chapter Fourteen

"Is this place all like this?" King Anheg asked as the army trudged through one of the flat, gravel-strewn valleys with the bare, sun-baked mountains around it dancing in the shimmering heat. "I haven't seen a tree since we left the forts."

"The country changes about twenty leagues out, your Majesty," Hettar replied quietly, lounging in his saddle as they rode in the blazing sunlight. "We start to hit trees when we begin coming down out of the uplands. They're a kind of low, scraggly spruce, but they break up the monotony a bit."

The column behind them stretched out for miles, dwarfed into a thin line by the enormous emptiness and marked more by the cloud of yellow dust raised by thousands of feet than by the presence of men and horses. The Cherek ships, covered with canvas, jolted along over the rocky ground on their low, wheeled cradles, and the dust hung over them in the stifling heat like a gritty blanket.

"I'd pay a lot for a breeze right now," Anheg said wistfully, wiping his face.

"Just leave things the way they are, Anheg," Barak advised him. "It wouldn't take much to start a dust storm."

"How much farther is it to the river?" King Rhodar asked plaintively, looking at the unchanging landscape. The heat was having a brutal effect on the corpulent monarch. His face was beet red, and he was soaked and dripping with sweat.

"Still about forty leagues," Hettar replied.

General Varana, mounted on a roan stallion, cantered back from the vanguard of the column. The general wore a short leather kilt and a plain breastplate and helmet bearing no marks of his rank. "The Mimbrate knights just flushed out another pocket of Murgos," he reported.

"How many?" King Rhodar asked.

"Twenty or so. Three or four got away, but the Algars are chasing them."

"Shouldn't our patrols be farther out?" King Anheg fretted, mopping his face again. "Those ships don't look *that* much like wagons. I'd rather not have to fight my way down the River Mardu—if we ever get there."

"I've got people moving around out there, Anheg," King Cho-Hag assured him.

"Has anyone run across any Malloreans yet?" Anheg asked.

"Not so far," Cho-Hag replied. "All we've seen so far are Thulls and Murgos."

"It looks as if 'Zakath is holding firm at Thull Zelik," Varana added.

"I wish I knew more about him," Rhodar said.

"The Emperor's emissaries report that he's a very civilized man," Varana said. "Cultured, urbane, very polite."

"I'm sure there's another side to him," Rhodar disagreed. "The Nadraks are terrified of him, and it takes a lot to frighten a Nadrak."

"As long as he stays at Thull Zelik, I don't care what kind of man he is," Anheg declared.

Colonel Brendig rode forward from the toiling column of infantry and wagons stretched out behind them. "King Fulrach asks that we halt the column for a rest period," he reported.

"*Again?*" Anheg demanded irritably.

"We've marched for two hours, your Majesty," Brendig pointed out. "Marching in all this heat and dust is very exhausting for infantry. The men won't be much good in a fight if they're all wrung out from walking."

"Halt the column, Colonel," Polgara told the Sendarian baronet. "We can rely on Fulrach's judgment in these matters." She turned to the King of Cherek. "Stop being so peevish, Anheg," she chided him.

"I'm being broiled alive, Polgara," he complained.

"Try walking for a few miles," she told him sweetly. "That may give you some insight into how the infantry feels."

Anheg scowled, but remained silent.

Princess Ce'Nedra pulled in her sweating mount as the column halted. The princess had spoken very little since Adara had been wounded. The dreadful sense of her responsibility for her friend's nearly fatal injury had sobered her enormously, and she had retreated into a kind of shell that was totally unnatural for her. She removed the loose-woven straw hat that a captive Thull had made for her back at the fort and squinted at the blistering sky.

"Put the hat back on, Ce'Nedra," Lady Polgara told her. "I don't want you getting sunstroke."

Ce'Nedra obediently put her hat back on. "He's coming back," she reported, pointing at a speck in the sky high above them.

"Will you excuse me?" General Varana said, turning his horse to leave.

"You're being absurd, Varana," King Rhodar told the Tolnedran. "Why do you insist on refusing to admit he can do things you don't want to believe in?"

"It's a matter of principle, your Majesty," the general replied. "Tolnedrans do not believe in sorcery. I am a Tolnedran, therefore I do not admit that it exists." He hesitated. "I must concede, however, that his information is surprisingly accurate—however he gets it."

A large, blue-banded hawk fell suddenly out of the broiling

air like a stone, flared his wings at the last moment, and settled on the ground directly in front of them.

General Varana resolutely turned his back and stared with apparently deep interest at a featureless hill some five miles distant.

The hawk began to shimmer and change even as he folded his wings. "Are you stopping *again*?" Beldin demanded irascibly.

"We have to rest the troops, Uncle," Polgara replied.

"This isn't a Sunday stroll, Pol," Beldin retorted. He began to scratch one armpit, befouling the air around him with a string of rancid curses.

"What's the matter?" Polgara asked mildly.

"Lice," he grunted.

"How did you get lice?"

"I visited some other birds to ask if they'd seen anything. I think I picked them up in a vulture's nest."

"What could possibly possess you to go consorting with vultures?"

"Vultures aren't that bad, Pol. They perform a necessary function, and the chicks do have a certain charm. The she-vulture had been picking at a dead horse about twenty leagues south of here. After she told me about it, I went down to take a look. There's a Murgo column coming this way."

"How many?" General Varana asked quickly, his back still turned to them.

"A thousand or so," Beldin shrugged. "They're pushing hard. They'll probably intercept you tomorrow morning."

"A thousand Murgos aren't that much to worry about," King Rhodar said, frowning. "Not to an army of this size. But what's the point of throwing a thousand men away? What does Taur Urgas hope to accomplish?" He turned to Hettar. "Do you suppose you could ride ahead and ask Korodullin and the Baron of Vo Mandor to join us. I think we ought to have a conference."

Hettar nodded and loped his horse ahead toward the gleaming ranks of the Mimbrate knights at the head of the column.

"Were there any Grolims with the Murgos, Uncle?" Polgara asked the filthy hunchback.

"Not unless they were well-hidden," he replied. "I didn't probe too much, though. I didn't want to give myself away."

General Varana abruptly abandoned his careful study of the hills around them and turned his horse about to join them. "My first guess would be that the Murgo column is a token gesture from Taur Urgas. He probably wants to get on the good side of King Gethell; and since the Malloreans won't leave Thull Zelik, he can pick up some advantage by committing a few troops to aid in the defense of the Thullish towns and villages we've been destroying."

"That makes sense, Rhodar," Anheg agreed.

"Maybe," Rhodar said dubiously. "Taur Urgas doesn't think like a rational man, though."

King Korodullin, flanked by Mandorallen and the Baron of Vo Ebor, thundered back to join them. Their armor flashed in the sun, and all three were flushed and miserable-looking in their steel casings.

"How can you stand all that?" Rhodar asked.

"Custom, your Majesty," Korodullin replied. "The armor doth inflict some discomfort, but we have learned to endure it."

General Varana quickly sketched in the situation for them.

Mandorallen shrugged. "It is of no moment. I will take some few dozen men and smash this threat from the south."

Barak looked at King Anheg. "You see what I mean about him?" he said. "Now you can understand why I was so nervous all the time we were chasing across Cthol Murgos."

King Fulrach had ridden forward to join the conference, and he cleared his throat diffidently. "Might I make a suggestion?" he asked.

"We eagerly await the practical wisdom of the King of the Sendars," Korodullin replied with extravagant courtesy.

"The Murgo column doesn't really pose much of a threat, does it?" Fulrach inquired.

"Not really, your Majesty," Varana replied. "At least, now

that we know that they're out there. We think that they're some kind of minor relief column sent to placate the Thulls. Their presence in our vicinity is probably entirely accidental."

"I don't want them getting close enough to recognize my ships, though," Anheg declared firmly.

"We'll take care of that, Anheg," Rhodar told him.

"Any one of the elements of our army might easily overcome so slight a threat," Fulrach continued, "but mightn't it be better—from a morale standpoint—to give the victory to the entire army?"

"I don't quite follow you, Fulrach," Anheg said.

"Instead of letting Sir Mandorallen annihilate these thousand Murgos all by himself, why not select a contingent from each part of the army to deal with them? Not only will that give us some experience in tactical coordination, but it'll give all the men a sense of pride. An easy victory now will stiffen their backs when we run into more difficult times later."

"Fulrach, sometimes you positively amaze me," Rhodar declared. "I think the whole trouble is that you don't *look* that clever."

The contingents that were to turn south to meet the approaching Murgos were selected by lot, once again at the suggestion of King Fulrach. "That way there'll be no suspicion in the army that this is some kind of elite force," he noted.

While the rest of the column pushed on toward the headwaters of the River Mardu, the miniature army under the command of Barak, Hettar, and Mandorallen veered to the south to intercept the enemy spearhead.

"They'll be all right, won't they?" Ce'Nedra nervously asked Polgara as she watched them growing smaller and smaller as they rode off across the arid valley toward the solid line of mountains to the south.

"I'm certain they will, dear," Polgara replied confidently.

The princess, however, did not sleep that night. For the first time, members of her army were committed to a real battle, and she tossed and turned the entire night, imagining all manner of disasters.

About midmorning of the following day, however, the special force returned. There were a few bandages here and there and perhaps a dozen empty saddles, but the look of victory shone on every face.

"Very nice little fight," Barak reported. The huge man was grinning broadly. "We caught them just before sundown. They never knew what hit them."

General Varana, who had accompanied the force to observe, was a bit more precise as he described the engagement to the assembled kings. "The general tactics did work pretty much as we'd planned," he said. "The Asturian archers swept the column with an arrow storm to begin with, and then the infantry units moved into position at the top of a long slope. We interspersed legionnaires, Drasnian pikemen, Sendars and the Arendish serf units evenly along the entire front with the archers behind them to continue harassing the enemy with arrows. As we expected, the Murgos charged. As soon as they'd committed themselves, the Chereks and Rivans moved into position behind them, and the Algars began slashing their flanks. When the Murgo assault began to falter, the Mimbrate knights made their charge."

"It was absolutely splendid!" Lelldorin exclaimed, his eyes very bright. There was a bandage around the young Asturian's upper arm, but he seemed to have forgotten that it was there as he gesticulated wildly. "Just at the point when the Murgos were completely confused, there was a sound like thunder, and the knights came curving around the side of a hill with their lances advanced and their pennons streaming. They bore down on the Murgos—a wave of solid steel—and the hoofs of their horses shook the earth. And then at the last moment, they all lowered their lances. It was like watching a wave break. And then they hit the Murgos with a great crash, and they didn't even slow down. They rode through them as if they weren't even there! They absolutely crushed them, and then we all ran in to finish up. It was glorious!"

"He's as bad as Mandorallen, isn't he?" Barak observed to Hettar.

"I think it's in their blood," Hettar replied sagely.

"Did any of them get away?" Anheg asked.

Barak gave his cousin an evil grin. "After it got dark, we could hear a few of them trying to crawl away. That's when Relg and his Ulgos went out to tidy up. Don't worry, Anheg. Nobody's going to report back to Taur Urgas."

"He *is* likely to be waiting for news, isn't he?" Anheg grinned.

"I hope he's patient, then," Barak replied, "because he'll be waiting for a long time."

Ariana, her face somber, took Lelldorin to task very firmly for his lack of discretion, even as she tended his wound. Her words far surpassed a simple scolding. She grew eloquent, and her lengthy, involuted sentences gave her remonstrance a depth and scope that reduced her young man very nearly to tears. His wound, admittedly minor, became a symbol of his careless lack of regard for her. Her expression grew martyred, and his grew anguished. Ce'Nedra observed how neatly Ariana twisted each of the young man's lame excuses into an even greater personal injury, and filed this excellent technique away in a compartment of her complex little mind for future use. True, Garion was somewhat brighter than Lelldorin, but the tactic would probably work on him too, if she practiced a little.

Taiba's meeting with Relg, on the other hand, involved no words. The beautiful Marag woman who had emerged from the slave pens beneath Rak Cthol only to enter a slavery even more profound, flew to the Ulgo fanatic's side upon his return. With a low cry, she unthinkingly embraced him. Relg flinched away from her, but the almost automatic, "Don't touch me," seemed to die on his lips, and his eyes went very wide as she clung to him. Then Taiba remembered his aversion and help-lessly let her arms drop, but her violet eyes glowed as they drank in his pale, large-eyed face. Then slowly, almost as if he were putting his arm into a fire, Relg reached out and took her hand. A brief look of incredulity crossed her face, followed almost immediately by a slow blush. They looked into each other's eyes for a moment, then walked off together, hand in hand. Taiba's eyes were demurely downcast, but there hovered about her rich, sensual mouth a tiny little smile of triumph.

The victory over the Murgo column raised the spirits of the army tremendously. The heat and dust no longer seemed to sap their energy as it had during the first few days of the march, and a growing sense of camaraderie grew between the diversified units as they pushed steadily eastward.

It took them four more days of steady marching to reach the headwaters of the River Mardu and another day to push on down along the tumbling flow to a spot where the ships could safely be launched. Hettar and his Algar patrols ranged far ahead and reported that there remained only one more stretch of rapids about ten leagues ahead before the river settled into tranquility on the Thullish plain.

"We can portage around the rapids," King Anheg declared. "Let's get these ships into the water. We've lost enough time already."

There was a rather high earthbank at that point, but the army attacked it vigorously with shovels and mattocks, and it was soon reduced to a sloping ramp. One by one the ships were rolled down the ramp into the water.

"We'll need a while to raise the masts," Anheg said.

"Leave that until later," Rhodar told him.

Anheg looked at him sharply.

"You're not going to be able to use your sails anyway, Anheg, and the masts stick up too high. The stupidest Thull in the world will know what's going on if he sees a forest of ship masts coming down the river toward him."

It was evening by the time the ships had all been launched and Polgara led the princess, Ariana and Taiba on board Barak's ship. A breeze coming upriver gently rippled the surface of the water and set the ship to rocking slowly. Beyond the watchfires, the Thullish grassland stretched as if forever beneath a purpling sky where, one by one, the stars were emerging.

"How far is it to Thull Mardu?" Ce'Nedra asked Barak.

The big man pulled at his beard, squinting downriver. "One day to the rapids," he replied, "then one day to make the portage around them. Then about two days after that."

"Four days," she said in a small voice.

He nodded.

"I wish it was over," she sighed.

"All in good time, Ce'Nedra," he told her. "All in good time."

Chapter Fifteen

THE SHIPS WERE horribly crowded, even though scarcely half the army could squeeze aboard them. The Algar clansmen and the Mimbrate knights patrolled the banks as the Chereks rowed downriver toward the rapids, and those infantry elements that could not be carried by the ships rode in close files on the spare horses of the cavalry.

The Thullish grasslands on either side of the river were gently rolling, long hillsides covered with deep, sun-browned grass. Just back from the river there were sparse clusters of the twisted, sprucelike trees that had dotted the lower foothills, and near the water itself rose thickets of willow and creeping brambles. The sky remained clear, and it was still hot, though the river added enough moisture to the air to alleviate the parched aridity that had plagued men and horses alike in the vast, stony uplands. It was an alien landscape for all of them, and the cavalry patrolling the banks rode warily with their hands close to their weapons.

And then they rounded a wide bend and saw the white, tumbling water of the rapids ahead. Barak swung the tiller of his big ship over and beached her. "Looks like it's time to get out and walk," he grunted.

A dispute had arisen near the bow of the ship. The brown-bearded King Fulrach was loudly protesting the decision to leave his supply wagons behind at the rapids. "I didn't bring them all this way just to leave them sitting here," he declared with uncharacteristic heat.

"They take too long to get anyplace," Anheg told him. "We're in a hurry, Fulrach. I've got to get my ships past Thull Mardu before the Murgos or the Malloreans wake up to what we're doing."

"You didn't object to having them along when you got hungry or thirsty in the uplands," Fulrach told him angrily.

"That was then. This is now. I've got to take care of my ships."

"And *I'm* going to take care of my wagons."

"They'll be all right, Fulrach," Rhodar said placatingly. "We *do* have to hurry, and your wagons can't move fast enough to keep up."

"If somebody comes along and burns them, you're going to get very hungry before we get back to the forts, Rhodar."

"We'll leave men to guard them, Fulrach. Be reasonable. You worry too much."

"Somebody's got to. You Alorns seem to forget that the fighting's only half of it."

"Stop acting like an old woman, Fulrach," Anheg said bluntly.

Fulrach's face grew very cold. "I don't know that I care for that last remark, Anheg," he said stiffly. Then he turned on his heel and stalked away.

"What's got into him?" the King of Cherek asked innocently.

"Anheg, if you don't learn how to keep your mouth shut, we might have to muzzle you," Rhodar told him.

"I thought we came here to fight Angaraks," Brand said mildly. "Have the rules been changed?"

The irritable bickering among her friends worried Ce'Nedra, and she went to Polgara with her concern.

"It's nothing all that important, dear," the lady replied as she scrubbed Errand's neck. "The upcoming battle's got them a bit edgy, that's all."

"But they're men," Ce'Nedra protested, "trained warriors."

"What does that have to do with it?" Polgara asked, reaching for a towel.

The princess couldn't think of an answer.

The portage at the rapids went smoothly, and the ships reentered the river below the tumbling stretch of seething white-water by late afternoon. Ce'Nedra by now was virtually ill as a result of the almost unbearable tension. All the months she had spent in raising the army and marching eastward were about to come to a final culmination. Within two days, they would hurl themselves at the walls of Thull Mardu. Was it the right time? Was it, in fact, really necessary? Couldn't they just portage around the city and avoid the battle entirely? Although the Alorn kings had assured her that the city *had* to be neutralized, Ce'Nedra's doubts grew with each mile. What if this was a mistake? The princess worried and fretted and worried some more as she stood at the prow of Barak's ship, staring at the broad river winding through the Thullish grasslands.

Finally, just at evening of the second day after the portage, Hettar galloped back and reined in his horse on the north bank of the river. He motioned with his arm, and Barak swung his tiller over, angling the big ship in closer to the bank.

"The city's about two leagues ahead," the tall Algar called across the intervening space. "If you get too much closer, they'll see you from the walls."

"This is close enough, then," Rhodar decided. "Pass the word to anchor the ships. We'll wait here until dark."

Barak nodded and made a quick gesture to a waiting sailor. The man quickly raised a tall pole with a bit of bright red bunting nailed to its tip, and the fleet behind them slowed in answer to the signal. There was a creaking of windlasses as the anchors settled to the bottom, and the ships rocked and swung sluggishly in the current.

"I still don't like this part," Anheg growled morosely. "Too many things can go wrong in the dark."

"They'll go wrong for them, too," Brand told him.

"We've been over it a dozen times, Anheg," Rhodar said. "We all agreed that its the best plan."

"It's never been done before," Anheg said.

"That's the whole point, isn't it?" Varana suggested. "The people inside the city won't expect it."

"Are you *sure* your men will be able to see where they're going?" Anheg demanded of Relg.

The zealot nodded. He was wearing his cowled leaf-mail shirt and was carefully testing the edge of his hook-pointed knife. "What you think of as darkness is normal light for us," he replied.

Anheg scowled at the purpling sky overhead. "I *hate* being the first one to try something new," he announced.

They waited as evening settled on the plain. From the thickets at the river's edge, birds clucked sleepily, and the frogs began their evening symphony. Slowly out of the gathering darkness, the cavalry units began to group up along the banks. The Mimbrate knights on their great chargers massed into ranks, and the Algar clansmen spread like a dark sea beyond them. Commanding the south bank were Cho-Hag and Korodullin. The north was led by Hettar and Mandorallen.

Slowly it grew darker.

A young Mimbrate knight who had been injured during the attack on the Murgo column stood leaning against the rail, looking pensively out into the twilight. The knight had dark, curly hair and the snowy complexion of a young girl. His shoulders were broad, his neck columnar, and his eyes had an open innocence in them. His expression, however, was faintly melancholy.

The waiting had become unbearable, and Ce'Nedra *had* to talk to someone. She leaned on the rail beside the young man. "Why so sad, Sir Knight?" she asked him quietly.

"Because I am forbidden to take part in this night's adventure by reason of this slight injury, your Majesty," he replied, touching his splinted arm. He seemed unsurprised by her presence or by the fact that she had spoken to him.

"Do you hate the Angaraks so much that missing the chance to kill them causes you pain?" Ce'Nedra's question was gently mocking.

"Nay, my Lady," he answered. "I have no malice in me for any man, whatever his race. What I lament is being denied the chance to try my skills in the contest."

"Contest? Is that how you think of it?"

"Assuredly, your Majesty. In what other light should it be considered? I hold no personal rancor toward the men of Angarak, and it is improper to hate thine opponent in a test of arms. Some few men have fallen beneath my lance or my sword at diverse tourneys, but I have never hated any of them. Much to the contrary, I have had some affection for them as we strove with one another."

"But you were trying to cripple them." Ce'Nedra was startled at the young man's casual attitude.

"It is a part of the contest, your Majesty. A true test of arms may not be decided save by the injury or death of one of the combatants."

"What's your name, Sir Knight?" she asked him.

"I am Sir Beridel," he replied, "son of Sir Andorig, Baron of Vo Enderig."

"The man with the apple tree?"

"The very same, your Majesty." The young man seemed pleased that she had heard of his father and the strange duty Belgarath had imposed on him. "My father now rides at the right hand of King Korodullin. I would ride with them this night but for this stroke of ill fortune." He looked sadly at his broken arm.

"There will be other nights, Sir Beridel," she assured him, "and other contests."

"Truly, your Majesty," he agreed. His face brightened momentarily, but then he sighed and went back to his somber brooding.

Ce'Nedra drifted away, leaving him to his thoughts.

"You can't really talk to them, you know," a rough voice said to her from the shadows. It was Beldin, the ugly hunchback.

"He doesn't seem to be afraid of anything," Ce'Nedra said a bit nervously. The foul-mouthed sorcerer always made her nervous.

"He's a Mimbrate Arend," Beldin snorted. "He doesn't have enough brains to be afraid."

"Are all the men in the army like him?"

"No. Most of them *are* afraid, but they'll go through with the attack anyway—for a variety of reasons."

"And you?" she could not help asking. "Are you afraid too?"

"My fears are a bit more exotic," he said dryly.

"Such as?"

"We've been at this for a very long time—Belgarath, Pol, the twins and I—and I'm more concerned about something going wrong than I am about my own personal safety."

"How do you mean, wrong?"

"The Prophecy is very complex—and it doesn't say everything. The two possible outcomes of all this are still absolutely balanced as far as I can tell. Something very, very slight could tip that balance one way or the other. It could be something that I've overlooked. That's what I'm afraid of."

"All we can do is the best we can."

"That might not be enough."

"What else can we do?"

"I don't know—and that's what worries me."

"Why worry about something if you can't do anything about it?"

"Now you're starting to sound like Belgarath. He tends to shrug things off and trust to his luck sometimes. I like things a little neater." He stared off into the darkness. "Stay close to Pol tonight, little girl," he said after a moment. "Don't get separated from her. It might take you someplace you hadn't planned to go, but you're supposed to stay with her, no matter what."

"What does that mean?"

"I don't *know* what it means," he retorted irritably. "All I know is that you and she and the blacksmith and that stray child you picked up are supposed to stay together. Something unexpected is going to happen."

"You mean a disaster? We must warn the others."

"We don't *know* that it's a disaster," he replied. "That's the whole problem. It might be necessary, and if it is, we don't want to tamper with it. I think we've about run this discussion into the ground. Go find Polgara and stay with her."

"Yes, Beldin," Ce'Nedra said meekly.

As the stars began to come out, the anchors were raised and the Cherek fleet began to slip quietly downriver toward Thull Mardu. Though they were still some miles above the city, commands were issued in hoarse whispers, and the men all took great care to avoid making noise as they shifted their weapons and equipment, tightening belts, giving their armor quick, last-minute checks and settling their helmets more firmly on their heads.

Amidships, Relg was leading his Ulgos in a quiet religious service, muttering the harsh gutturals of the Ulgo tongue in a scarcely audible murmur. Their pale faces had been smeared with soot, and they looked like so many shadows as they knelt in prayer to their strange God.

"They're the key to the whole thing," Rhodar observed quietly to Polgara as he watched the devotions of the Ulgos. "Are you sure that Relg is all right for this? Sometimes he seems a bit unstable."

"He'll be fine," Polgara replied. "The Ulgos have even more reason to hate Torak than you Alorns do."

The drifting ships slowly rounded a wide bend in the river, and there, a half-mile downstream, stood the walled city of Thull Mardu, rising from its island in the middle of the river. There were a few torches atop the walls, and a faint glow rising from within. Barak turned and, shielding it with his body, he briefly uncovered a muffled lantern, letting out a single flicker of light. The anchors sank very slowly through the dark waters toward the riverbottom; with a very faint creak of ropes, the ships slowed, then stopped.

Somewhere inside the city a dog began to bark excitedly.

Then a door banged open, and the barking cut off suddenly with a yelp of pain.

"I don't have much use for a man who kicks his own dog," Barak muttered.

Relg and his men moved very quietly to the rail and began to clamber down ropes into the small boats waiting below.

Ce'Nedra watched breathlessly, straining with her eyes to see in the darkness. The very faint starlight briefly showed her several shadows drifting down toward the city. Then the shadows were gone. Behind them there was a faint splash of an oar, followed by an angrily hissed admonition. The princess turned and saw a moving tide of small boats coming downriver from the anchored fleet. The spearhead of the assault slid silently by, following Relg and his Ulgos toward the fortified island city of the Thulls.

"Are you sure there are enough of them?" Anheg whispered to Rhodar.

The rotund King of Drasnia nodded. "All they have to do is secure a landing place for us and hold the gate once the Ulgos get it open," he murmured. "There's enough of them for that."

A faint night breeze rippled the surface of the river, setting the ship to rocking. Unable to bear the suspense any longer, Ce'Nedra lifted her fingertips to the amulet Garion had given her so many months before. As always, a buzz of conversation filled her ears.

"Yaga, tor gohek vilta." It was Relg's harsh voice, speaking in a whisper. "Ka tak. Veed!"

"Well?" Polgara asked, one eyebrow slightly raised.

"I can't tell what they're saying," Ce'Nedra replied helplessly. "They're talking in Ulgo."

A strangled groan quite suddenly seemed to come from the amulet itself and then was quickly and horribly cut off.

"I-I think they just killed somebody," Ce'Nedra said in a quavering voice.

"It's started then," Anheg said with a certain grim satisfaction.

Ce'Nedra pulled her fingertips from the amulet. She could

no longer bear to listen to the sound of men dying in the dark.
They waited.

Then someone screamed, a scream filled with a terrible
agony.

"That's it!" Barak declared. "That's the signal! Pull the
anchor!" he shouted to his men.

Very suddenly beneath the high, dark walls of Thull Mardu,
two separate fires flared up, and shadowy figures could be seen
moving about them. At the same moment, there was a clanking
rattle of heavy chains inside the city and a creaking groan as
a broad gate swung ponderously down to form a bridge across
the narrow north channel of the river.

"Man your oars!" Barak roared to his crew. He swung his
tiller hard over, steering toward the rapidly lowering bridge.

More torches appeared along the tops of the walls, and there
were shouts of alarm. Somewhere an iron bell began to clang
a note of desperate urgency.

"It worked!" Anheg exclaimed, gleefully pounding Rhodar
on the back. "It actually worked!"

"Of course it worked," Rhodar replied, his voice also ju-
bilant. "Don't pound on me so hard, Anheg. I bruise easily."

All need for silence was gone now, and a great roar went
up from the massed fleet following in Barak's wake. Torches
flared, and the faces of the troops lining the rails were bathed
in their ruddy glow.

A great splash suddenly erupted from the river twenty yards
to the right of Barak's ship, showering everyone on deck with
a deluge of water.

"Catapult!" Barak shouted, pointing at the walls looming
ahead. Like a huge, preying insect, the heavy-beamed frame
of the siege-engine balanced atop the wall, its long throwing
arm already cocking back to cast another boulder at the approaching fleet. Then the arm stopped as a storm of arrows
swept the top of the wall clean. A crowd of Drasnians, easily
identifiable by the long pikes they carried, overran the position.

"Watch out, down there," one of them roared into the confusion at the base of the wall, and the siege engine ponderously
toppled outward and fell with a crash onto the rocks below.

There was a thunder of hoofs across the now-lowered bridge, and the Mimbrate knights crashed into the city.

"As soon as we tie up to the bridge, I want you and the princess and the other ladies to go to the north bank," King Rhodar said tersely to Polgara. "Get back out of harm's way. This will probably take the rest of the night, and there's no point in exposing any of you to any accidents."

"Very well, Rhodar," Polgara agreed. "And don't *you* do anything foolish, either. You're a rather large target, you know."

"I'll be all right, Polgara—but I'm not going to miss this." He laughed then, a strangely boyish laugh. "I haven't had so much fun in years," he declared.

Polgara gave him a quick look. "Men!" she said in a tone that said everything.

A guard of Mimbrate knights escorted the ladies and Errand perhaps a thousand yards upstream to an indented cove on the north bank of the stream, well away from the press of the horsemen rushing toward the beleaguered city. The cove had a gently sloping sand beach and was protected on three sides by steep, grass-covered banks. Durnik the smith and Olban quickly raised a tent for them, built a small fire, and then climbed up the bank to watch the attack.

"It's going according to plan," Durnik reported from his vantage point. "The Cherek ships are lining up side by side across the south channel. As soon as they get the planking in place, the troops on the other side will be able to cross."

"Can you tell if the men inside have taken the south gate yet?" Olban demanded, peering toward the city.

"I can't tell for sure," Durnik replied. "There's fighting going on in that part of the city, though."

"I'd give anything to be there," Olban lamented.

"You stay right where you are, young man," Polgara told him firmly. "You appointed yourself bodyguard to the Rivan Queen, and you're not going to go running off just because things are more interesting someplace else."

"Yes, Lady Polgara," the young Rivan answered, suddenly abashed. "It's just—"

"Just what?"

"I wish I knew what was happening, that's all. My father and my brothers are in the middle of the fighting, and I have to stand here and watch."

A sudden great belch of flame shot up from inside the walls to illuminate the river with sooty red light.

Polgara sighed. "Why do they always have to burn things?" she asked sadly.

"It adds to the confusion, I suppose," Durnik replied.

"Perhaps," Polgara said, "but I've seen this happen too many times before. It's always the same. There always has to be a fire. I don't believe I care to watch any more of this." She turned her back on the burning city and walked slowly away from the riverbank.

The night was interminable. Toward dawn, as the stars began to fade from the paling sky, the Princess Ce'Nedra, drawn with fatigue, stood atop a grassy bank near the cove, watching with a kind of sick fascination as the city of Thull Mardu died. Entire districts seemed to be in flames, and great fountains of orange sparks belched toward the sky as roofs caved in and buildings collapsed. What had seemed so stirring, so glorious in her anticipation had turned out to be something quite different in reality, and she was sick at what she had done. She still, nonetheless, brought her fingertips up to touch the amulet at her throat. She *had* to know what was happening. No matter how horrible the events were in the city, not knowing what was happening was even worse.

"Sort of a nice little fight," she heard King Anheg say. The King of Cherek seemed to be someplace very high—atop the walls of the city perhaps.

"Pretty routine," Barak, Earl of Trellheim, replied. "The Murgo garrison fought pretty well, but the Thulls kept falling all over themselves trying to surrender."

"What did you do with all of them?" King Cho-Hag asked.

"We herded them into the central square," Barak answered. "They've been amusing themselves by killing the Grolims we flushed out of the temple."

Anheg suddenly chuckled, an evil sort of sound. "How's Grodeg?" he asked.

"It looks like he's going to live," Barak said.

"That's a shame. When I saw that axe sticking out of his back, I thought somebody's solved one of my problems for me."

"It was too low," Barak said rather mournfully. "It broke his spine, but it didn't hit anything else significant. He won't be walking any more, but he's still breathing."

"You can't depend on a Murgo to do anything right," Anheg said in disgust.

"They *did* thin out the Bear-cult pretty thoroughly," Barak noted cheerfully. "I don't think there are more than two dozen of them left. They fought pretty well, though."

"That's what they were here for. How long do you think it will be before daylight?"

"Half an hour, maybe."

"Where's Rhodar?"

"He and Fulrach are sacking the warehouses," King Cho-Hag replied. "The Murgos had some supply dumps here. Fulrach wants to confiscate them."

"He would," Anheg said. "Maybe we'd better send somebody for them. It's getting on toward the time when we'll want to think about pulling out of here. As soon as it gets light, all this smoke's going to announce what we've done to anyone within twenty leagues. It's about time to start the fleet moving, and it's a long march back to the forts on top of the escarpment."

"How long will it take you to get to the Sea of the East?" Cho-Hag asked.

"A couple days," Anheg told him. "You can move a ship pretty fast when you've got the current behind you. It will take your army a week at least to get back to the forts, won't it?"

"Probably," Cho-Hag said. "The infantry can't move all that fast. There's Brendig! I'll send him to fetch Rhodar." He shouted down to the Sendar. "Colonel Brendig, see if you can find Rhodar. Ask him to join us."

"What's that?" Barak asked suddenly.

"What's what?" Anheg demanded.

"I thought I saw something out there—way to the south—where you can just start to make out that hilltop."

"I don't see anything."

"It was just a flicker—something moving."

"Probably a Murgo scout creeping in for a look." Anheg laughed shortly. "I don't imagine we'll be able to keep what happened here a secret for very long."

"There it is again," Barak said.

"I saw it that time, too," King Cho-Hag agreed.

There was a long silence as the sky imperceptibly grew lighter. Ce'Nedra held her breath.

"Belar!" Anheg swore in a stunned voice. "They stretch for miles!"

"Lelldorin!" Barak shouted down from the wall. "Brendig's gone to get Rhodar. Go find them and tell them to get up here at once. The plain to the south is covered with Murgos."

Chapter Sixteen

"LADY POLGARA!" CE'NEDRA cried, jerking back the flap of the tent. "Lady Polgara!"

"What is it, Ce'Nedra?" Polgara's voice came from the darkness inside the tent.

"Barak and Anheg are up on the walls of the city," the princess said in a frightened voice. "They just saw a Murgo army coming up from the south."

Polgara came quickly out into the firelight, holding the sleepy Errand by the hand. "Where's Beldin?" she demanded.

"I haven't seen him since early last night."

Polgara raised her face and closed her eyes. A moment or so later there was a rushing sound of wings, and the large hawk settled to the sand not far from their flickering fire.

Beldin was swearing sulfurously even as he shimmered and blurred back into his natural shape.

"How did they slip past you, Uncle?" Polgara asked him.

"There are Grolims with them," he growled, still sizzling the air around him with oaths. "The Grolims could feel me watching, so the troops moved only at night, and the Grolims shielded them."

"Where did they hide in the daytime?"

"In the Thullish villages, apparently. There are dozens of communities out there. It never occurred to me to pay all that much attention to them." He began to swear again, berating himself savagely for having missed the movement of the Murgo army.

"There's no point in swearing about it, Uncle," Polgara told him coolly. "It's done, now."

"Unfortunately there's a bit more, Pol," the sorcerer told her. "There's another army at least as big coming in from the north—Malloreans, Nadraks, and Thulls. We're caught right between them."

"How long have we got before they reach us?" Polgara asked.

Beldin shrugged. "Not long. The Murgos have some rough ground to cross—probably about an hour. The Malloreans will be here in quite a bit less."

Polgara began to curse fervently under her breath. "Go to Rhodar," she told the hunchback. "Tell him that we have to release Anheg's fleet immediately—before the Angaraks can bring up catapults and destroy the ships where they're anchored."

The deformed man nodded and stooped slightly, curving his arms out like wings even as he began to waver and change.

"Olban," Polgara called to the young Rivan, "go find Sir Mandorallen and Lord Hettar. Send them to me at once. Hurry."

Olban gave her one startled look, then ran for his horse.

Durnik the smith came sliding down the grassy bank onto their little beach. His face was grave. "You and the ladies must leave at once, Mistress Pol," he told her. "There's going to be fighting here, and the middle of a battle's no place for any of you."

"I'm not going anywhere, Durnik," she replied with a trace of irritation. "I started all this, and I'm going to see it through."

Ariana had gone back into the tent as soon as the situation became clear to her. She now emerged again, carrying the stout canvas bag in which she kept her medical supplies. "Have I thy permission to leave, Lady Polgara?" she asked with a certain cool professionalism. "In battle men are injured, and I must go make preparations for their care. This spot is somewhat too remote and confined to receive the wounded."

Polgara gave her a quick look. "All right," she agreed. "Just be careful not to get too close to the fighting."

Taiba pulled on her cloak. "I'll go with you," she told Ariana. "I don't know that much about it, but you can teach me as we go along."

"Go help them get set up, Durnik," Polgara told the smith. "Then come back here."

Durnik nodded gravely and helped the two women up the steep bank.

Mandorallen thundered up on his charger with Hettar at his side.

"You know what's happened?" Polgara demanded.

Mandorallen nodded.

"Is there any possibility of withdrawing before the enemy forces arrive?"

"Nay, my Lady Polgara," the great knight replied. "They are too close. Moreover, our purpose has ever been to gain passage for the ships of Cherek into the Sea of the East. We must buy them time to sail beyond the reach of the siege engines of the Angaraks."

"I didn't want this," Polgara said angrily and she began to mutter curses again.

Brand, the gray-cloaked Rivan Warder, accompanied by General Varana, rode up to join Mandorallen and Hettar at the top of the steep bank. The four of them dismounted and slid down the bank to the sand. "We've begun evacuating the city," the big Rivan said in his deep voice, "and most of the fleet is pulling anchor. We're holding just enough ships to maintain the bridges across the south channel."

"Is there any possibility of putting the entire army on one bank or the other?" Polgara asked him.

He shook his head. "There isn't time, Polgara."

"We're going to be divided by the river," she pointed out,

"and neither force is going to be strong enough to meet the Angaraks coming against it."

"A tactical necessity, my dear Lady Polgara," General Varana told her. "We have to hold both banks until the fleet is clear."

"I think Rhodar misjudged the Angarak intentions," Brand said. "He was so sure that Taur Urgas and 'Zakath would both want to avoid taking casualties that he didn't consider this possibility."

General Varana clasped his muscular hands behind his back and limped back and forth along the little beach, his face creased with thought. "I think I begin to understand the meaning of that Murgo column we destroyed in the uplands," he said.

"Your Grace?" Mandorallen asked, puzzled.

"It was a test of our commitment," Varana explained. "The Angaraks needed to know when we were making our major move. One of the basic rules of war is not to become involved in serious conflicts if what you're doing is merely diversionary. That column was bait. Unfortunately, we took it."

"You mean we shouldn't have attacked the column?" Hettar asked him.

Varana made a rueful face. "Apparently not. It gave away our intentions—let them know that *this* expedition was *not* a diversion. I underestimated Taur Urgas. He threw away a thousand men just to find out what we were up to."

"What now?" Hettar asked.

"We get ready to fight," Varana said. "I wish we had better terrain for it, but I suppose we'll have to make do with what we have."

Hettar looked out across the river, his hawk-face hungry. "I wonder if I've got time to make it over to the south bank," he mused.

"One side or the other," Brand said, looking puzzled. "What's the difference?"

"The Murgos are over there," Hettar replied. "I don't really have anything against Malloreans."

"This isn't a personal fight, Lord Hettar," Varana pointed out.

"It is with me," Hettar said grimly.

"We must needs see to the safety of Lady Polgara and the princess," Mandorallen said. "Mayhap an escort should be provided to convey them back to the forts atop the escarpment."

Brand shook his head. "The region is likely to be patrolled heavily," he disagreed. "It wouldn't be safe."

"He's right, Mandorallen," Polgara told the knight. "Besides, you need every man you've got right here." She looked off toward the northeast. "Then, too, there's that." She pointed toward a heavy cloudbank that had begun to stain the sky just above the horizon. The clouds were an inky black, seething and rolling and illuminated from within by fitful flickers of lightning.

"A storm?" General Varana asked, looking a bit surprised.

"Not at this time of year—and certainly not from that direction," Polgara replied. "The Grolims are up to something, and that's going to be *my* fight. Deploy your forces, gentlemen. If there's going to be a battle, let's be ready for it."

"The ships are moving," Durnik reported as he and Olban came back to the sheltered little cove, "and the troops are leaving the city."

King Rhodar rode up. His broad face was streaked with soot and perspiration. "Anheg's leaving," he said, swinging down from his saddle with a grunt.

"Where's Fulrach?" Brand asked.

"He's taking the bulk of the troops across to the south bank."

"Isn't that going to leave us a little undermanned on this side?" General Varana inquired politely.

"That bridge is too narrow," Rhodar told him. "It would take hours to bring enough men across to make any difference. Brendig's already got a crew undermining the supports so that we can bring the bridge down before the Angaraks get here."

"What for?" Ce'Nedra asked him.

"Thull Mardu's too good a vantage point, your Highness," General Varana explained. "We don't want any Angaraks on the island if we can help it." He looked at King Rhodar. "Have you given any thought to tactics?" he asked.

"We want to give Anheg a half a day, if possible," Rhodar

replied. "The ground along the river gets marshy about twenty leagues downstream, and the Angaraks won't be able to get close enough to pester him, once he gets that far. Let's form up a conventional infantry line—pikemen, the legions, Sendars, and so on. We'll put the archers in support and use the Algars to slash at the flanks. I want to hold the Mimbrate knights in reserve until the Malloreans mass up for their first charge."

"That's not a winning tactic, if your Majesty will forgive my saying so," General Varana said.

"We aren't here to win, Varana," Rhodar told him. "We're here to delay the Angaraks for about six hours and then withdraw. I'm not going to waste lives trying to win a battle I haven't any chance of winning." He turned to Hettar. "I want you to send a force of your clansmen on a sweep downriver. Tell them to uproot any Malloreans they find emplaced along the riverbank. The significance of the fleet still may have escaped 'Zakath and Taur Urgas. Angaraks aren't good sailors, so they probably don't realize what Anheg can do, once he gets into the Seas of the East."

"Excuse me, your Majesty," Varana objected, "but all of your strategy—even the fleet—is merely a delaying action."

"That's the whole point, Varana," Rhodar told him bluntly. "All of this is really rather insignificant. What's really important is going to happen in Mallorea when Belgarion reaches Cthol Mishrak. We'd better move, gentlemen. The Malloreans will be here before long, and we want to be ready for them."

The cloudbank Polgara had pointed out was sweeping toward them with an alarming speed, a seething darkness of rolling purple, stalking forward on crooked legs of lightning. A hot wind seemed to flee out ahead of it, flattening the grass and whipping the manes and tails of the horses wildly. As King Rhodar and the others moved out to meet the approaching Mallorean army, Polgara, her face pale and her hair tossing behind her in the wind, climbed the grassy bank with Ce'Nedra and Durnik behind her and stood watching the approach of the cloud. "Take the child, Ce'Nedra," she said quite calmly. "Don't let go of him, no matter what happens."

"Yes, Lady Polgara," Ce'Nedra said, holding out her arms to Errand. The child came to her immediately, his serious little face unafraid. She picked him up and held him close, her cheek against his.

"Errand?" he said, pointing at the approaching storm.

Then, among the ranks of their army, shadowy figures rose up out of the ground. The figures wore black robes and polished steel masks and carried cruel-pointed short spears. Without pausing to even think, a mounted young Mimbrate knight swept his broadsword from its scabbard and swung the whistling blade at one of the steel-masked figures. His sword passed through the figure with no effect. As he struck, however, a sizzling bolt of lightning struck him, seeming to attach itself to the point of his helmet. He stiffened convulsively as the lightning, like a writhing snake of intense light, clung to the tip of his steel helm. Smoke boiled out of the slits of his visor as he roasted inside his armor. His horse lurched forward onto its knees while the ghastly, flickering light engulfed them both. Then the lightning was gone, and horse and man collapsed, stone dead.

Polgara hissed and then raised her voice. She did not seem to be speaking that loudly, but the effect of her words reached the farthest edges of the army. "Do not touch the shadows," she warned. "They're Grolim illusions and can't hurt you unless you touch them. They're here to draw the lightning to you, so stay clear of them."

"But, Mistress Pol," Durnik protested, "the troops won't be able to hold ranks if they have to keep dodging the shadows."

"I'll take care of the shadows," she replied grimly. She raised both arms above her head, her fists clenched. A look of dreadful concentration filled her face, and then she spoke a single word, opening her hands as she did so. The grass, which had been bending toward them in the hot wind preceding the storm, suddenly flattened in the opposite direction as the force of Polgara's will rippled outward. As that force passed over each shadowy Grolim illusion, the figures seemed to flinch, then shrivel, and then with silent detonations, each shadow exploded into shards and fragments of darkness.

Polgara was gasping as the last of the shadows on the farthest edge of the army vanished, and she would have collapsed had Durnik not jumped to her side to support her. "Are you all right?" he asked worriedly.

"Just give me a moment," she said, wilting against him. "That took a great deal of effort." She smiled at him, a wan little smile, and then her head drooped wearily.

"Won't they come back?" Ce'Nedra demanded. "What I mean is, it didn't actually hurt the real Grolims, did it? Just their shadows."

Polgara laughed weakly. "Oh, it hurt them, all right," she replied. "Those Grolims don't *have* shadows any more. Not one of them will ever cast a shadow again."

"Not ever?" the princess gasped.

"Not ever."

Then Beldin joined them, swooping in with the wind tearing at his feathers. "We've got work to do, Polgara," he growled even as he shimmered into his natural shape. "We're going to have to break up this storm they're bringing in from the west. I talked with the twins. They'll work on the southern side of it, and you and I'll take this side."

She looked at him inquiringly.

"Their army's going to be advancing right behind the storm," he explained. "There's no point in trying to hold it back now. It's got too much momentum. What we want to do is break open the rear edge of it and let it spill back over the Angaraks."

"How many Grolims are working on the storm, Uncle?" she asked him.

"Who knows?" He shrugged. "But it's taking every bit of effort they can muster just to keep it under control. If the four of us hit the back side all at once, the pressures in the storm itself will do the rest."

"Why not just let it pass over?" Durnik asked. "Our troops aren't children. They won't fall apart just because of a little squall."

"This isn't just a little squall, blacksmith," Beldin said acidly. Something large and white thudded to the ground a few feet away. "If you get four or five of those hailstones on top of the head, you won't care *how* the battle turns out."

"They're as big as hens' eggs," Durnik said in astonishment.

"And they'll probably get bigger." Beldin turned back to Polgara. "Give me your hand," he told her. "I'll pass the signal to Beltira, and we'll all strike at the same time. Get ready."

More of the hailstones thudded into the springy turf, and one particularly large one shattered into a thousand fragments as it crashed down on a large rock with stunning force. From the direction of the army came an intermittent banging as the hailstones bounced off the armor of the Mimbrate knights or clanged down on the hastily raised shields of the infantry.

And then, mixed with the hail, the rain squalls struck—seething sheets of water driven before the wind like raging waves. It was impossible to see, and almost impossible to breathe. Olban jumped forward with his shield raised to protect Ce'Nedra and Errand. He winced once as a large hailstone struck his shoulder, but his shield arm did not waver.

"It's breaking, Pol!" Beldin shouted. "Let's push it once more. Let them eat their own storm for a while."

Polgara's face twisted into an agony of concentration, and then she half-slumped as she and Beldin unleashed their combined wills at the rolling sky. The sound of it was beyond belief as the vast forces collided. The sky ripped suddenly apart and lightning staggered and lurched through the smoking air. Great, incandescent bolts crashed into each other high above, showering the earth beneath with fireballs. Men fell, charred instantly into black, steaming husks in the driving downpour, but the casualties were not only among the men of the west.

The vast storm with its intolerable pressures recoiled as the combined wills of Polgara and Beldin on the north bank and the twins on the south bank ripped open the back edge of it, and the advancing Malloreans received that recoil full in the teeth. A curtain of lightning swept back across their close-packed ranks like an enormous, blinding broom, littering the earth with their smoking dead. As the fabric of Grolim sorcery which had driven the stormfront toward the river ripped apart, the gale winds suddenly reversed and flowed back, shrieking and howling, confounding the advancing Angaraks with rain and hail.

From out of the center of the dreadful cloud overhead, swirling fingers of murky black twitched and reached down toward the earth with hideous roaring sounds. With a last, almost convulsive jerk, one of those huge, swirling funnels touched the earth in the midst of the red-clad Malloreans. Debris sprayed up and out from the point of the dreadful vortex as, with ponderous immensity, it cut an erratic course two hundred yards wide directly through the enemy ranks. Men and horses were ripped to pieces by the insane winds within the swirling column of cloud, and bits of armor and shreds of red tunics—and worse—showered down on the stunned and terrified Malloreans on either side of the swath of absolute destruction moving inexorably through their midst.

"Beautiful!" Beldin exulted, hopping up and down in a grotesque display of glee.

There was the sudden sound of a great horn, and the close-packed ranks of Drasnian pikemen and Tolnedran legionnaires facing the faltering ranks of the Malloreans opened. From behind them, his armor streaming water, Mandorallen led the charge of the Mimbrate knights. Full upon the confused and demoralized Malloreans they fell, and the sound of the impact as they struck was a terrible, rending crash, punctuated by screams. Rank upon rank was crushed beneath the charge, and the terrified Malloreans wavered and then broke and fled. Even as they ran, the clans of Algar swept in among them from the flanks, their sabres flashing in the rain.

At a second blast of Mandorallen's horn, the charging Mimbrates reined in, wheeled and galloped back, leaving a vast wreckage behind them.

The rain slackened fitfully, little more than errantly passing showers now, and patches of blue appeared among the racing clouds overhead. The Grolim storm had broken and dispersed back across the plains of Mishrak ac Thull.

Ce'Nedra looked toward the south bank and saw that the storm there had also dispersed and that the forces under the command of King Cho-Hag and King Korodullin were assaulting the front ranks of the demoralized Murgo army. Then the princess looked sharply at the south channel of the river.

The last bridges of Cherek ships had broken loose during the violent storm, and there was now only open water on that side of the island. The last troops remaining in the city were streaming across the bridge over the north channel. A tall Sendarian lad was among the last to cross. As soon as he reached the bank, he came immediately upriver. As he drew nearer, Ce'Nedra recognized him. It was Rundorig, Garion's boyhood friend from Faldor's farm, and he was openly weeping.

"Goodman Durnik," he sobbed as he reached them, "Doroon's dead."

"What did you say?" Lady Polgara demanded, raising her tired face suddenly.

"Doroon, Mistress Pol," Rundorig wept. "He drowned. We were crossing over to the south bank when the storm broke the ropes holding the ships. Doroon fell into the river, and he didn't know how to swim. I tried to save him, but he went under before I could reach him." The tall young man buried his face in his hands.

Polgara's face went absolutely white, and her eyes filled with sudden tears. "Take care of him, Durnik," she told the smith, then turned and walked away, her head bowed in her grief.

"I tried, Durnik," Rundorig blurted, still sobbing. "I really tried to reach him—but there were too many people in my way. I couldn't get to him in time. I saw him go under, and there was nothing I could do."

Durnik's face was very grave as he put his arm about the weeping boy's shoulders. The smith's eyes were also filled, and he said nothing.

Ce'Nedra, however, could not weep. She had reached out her hand and plucked these unwarlike young men from their homes and dragged them halfway across the world, and now one of Garion's oldest friends had died in the chill waters of the River Mardu. His death was on her head, but she could not weep. A terrible fury suddenly filled her. She turned to Olban. "Kill them!" she hissed from between clenched teeth.

"My Queen?" Olban gaped at her.

"Go!" she commanded. "Take your sword and go. Kill as many Angaraks as you can—for me, Olban. Kill them for me!" And then she could weep.

Olban looked first at the sobbing little princess and then at the milling ranks of the Malloreans, still reeling from the savagery of the Mimbrate assault. His face grew exultant as he drew his sword. "As my Queen commands!" he shouted and ran to his horse.

Even as the decimated front ranks of the Malloreans fled, hurried by the sabre-wielding Algars, greater and greater numbers of their countrymen reached the field, and soon the low hills to the north were covered with them. Their red tunics made it look almost as if the earth itself were bleeding. It was not the Malloreans, however, who mounted the next attack. Instead, thick-bodied Thulls in mud-colored smocks marched reluctantly into position. Directly behind the Thulls, mounted Malloreans urged them on with whips.

"Basic Mallorean strategy," Beldin growled. "'Zakath wants to let the Thulls do most of the dying. He'll try to save his own troops for the campaign against Taur Urgas."

Ce'Nedra raised her tear-streaked face. "What do we do now?" she asked the misshapen sorcerer.

"We kill Thulls," he said bluntly. "A charge or two by the Mimbrates ought to break their spirits. Thulls don't make very good soldiers, and they'll run away as soon as we give them the chance."

Even as the sluggish forces of Mishrak ac Thull flowed like a mudslide downhill toward the solid line of pikemen and legionnaires, the Asturian archers just to the rear of the infantry raised their bows and filled the air with a solid, arching sheet of yard-long arrows. The Thulls quailed as rank after rank melted under the withering storm of arrows. The shouts of the Malloreans at the rear became more desperate, and the crack of their whips filled the air.

And then Mandorallen's horn sounded, the ranks of infantry opened, and the armored knights of Mimbre charged again. The Thulls took one look at the steel-clad men and horses crashing toward them and immediately bolted. The Mallorean whip-men were swarmed under and trampled in the panic-stricken flight of the Thull army.

"So much for the Thulls." Beldin grunted with satisfaction as he watched the rout. He grinned an evil grin. "I imagine that 'Zakath will speak firmly to King Gethell about this."

Mandorallen's knights thundered back to their positions behind the infantry, and the two armies glared at each other across a field littered with Angarak dead.

Ce'Nedra began to shiver as a sudden chill swept the battlefield. Although the sun had broken through the ragged clouds as the Grolim storm rapidly dispersed, there was no warmth to it. Even though all trace of wind had died, it grew colder. Then from the ground and from the dark surface of the river, tendrils of fog began to rise.

Beldin hissed. "Polgara," he snapped to the grieving sorceress, "I need you."

"Leave me alone, Uncle," she replied in a voice still choked with sorrow.

"You can cry later," he told her harshly. "The Grolims are drawing the heat out of the air. If we don't stir up a wind, the fog's going to get so thick you'll be able to walk on it."

She turned, and her face was very cold. "You don't respect anything, do you?" she said flatly.

"Not much," he admitted, "but that's beside the point. If the Grolims can build up a good fog bank, we'll have the whole stinking Mallorean army on top of us before we can even see them coming. Let's go, Pol. People get killed; it happens. You can get sentimental about it later." He held out his gnarled, lumpy hand to her.

The tendrils of fog had begun to thicken, lying in little pockets now. The littered battlefield in front of the infantry lines seemed to waver, and then disappeared entirely as the fog congealed into a solid wall of white.

"Wind, Pol," Beldin said, taking hold of her hand. "As much wind as you can raise."

The struggle which ensued then was a silent one. Polgara

and Beldin, their hands joined together, gathered in their wills and then reached out with them, probing, searching for some weakness in the mass of dead-calm air that imprisoned the thickening fog along the banks of the river. Fitful little gusts of breeze swirled the eddying fog, then died as quickly as they had arisen.

"Harder, Pol," Beldin urged. His ugly face streamed with rivulets of sweat as he struggled with the vast inertness of unmoving air.

"It's not going to work this way, Uncle," she declared, pulling her hand free. Her face showed her own strain. "There's nothing to get hold of. What are the twins doing?"

"The Hierarchs of Rak Cthol are riding with Taur Urgas," the hunchback replied. "The twins have their hands full dealing with them. They won't be able to help."

Polgara straightened then, steeling herself. "We're trying to work too close," she said. "Every time we start a little local breeze, a dozen Grolims jump in and smother it."

"All right," Beldin agreed.

"We'll have to reach out farther," she continued. "Start the air moving somewhere out beyond their range so that by the time it gets here, it has so much momentum that they can't stop it."

Beldin's eyes narrowed. "That's dangerous, Pol," he told her. "Even if we *can* do it, it's going to exhaust the both of us. If they throw anything else at us, neither of us will have any strength left to fight them."

"It's a gamble, Uncle," she admitted, "but the Grolims are stubborn. They'll try to protect this fog bank even after all chance of maintaining it has gone. They'll get tired, too. Maybe too tired to try anything else."

"I don't like maybes."

"Have you got a better idea?"

"Not right now, no."

"All right, then."

They joined hands again.

It took, it seemed to the princess, an eternity. With her heart in her throat she stared at the two of them as they stood with their hands joined and their eyes closed—reaching out with their minds toward the hot, barren uplands to the west, trying with all their strength to pull that heated air down into the broad valley of the River Mardu. All around her, Ce'Nedra seemed to feel the oppressive chill of Grolim thought lying heavily on the stagnant air, holding it, resisting all effort to dissipate the choking fog.

Polgara was breathing in short gasps, her chest heaving and her face twisted with an inhuman striving. Beldin, his knotted shoulders hunched forward, struggled like a man attempting to lift a mountain.

And then Ce'Nedra caught the faintest scent of dust and dry, sun-parched grass. It was only momentary, and she thought a first that she had imagined it. Then it came again, stronger this time, and the fog eddied sluggishly. But once more that faint scent died, and with it the breath of air that had carried it.

Polgara groaned then, an almost strangled sound, and the fog began to swirl. The wet grass at Ce'Nedra's feet, drenched with droplets of mist, bent slightly, and the dusty smell of the Thullish uplands grew stronger.

It seemed that the blanket of concentration that had held the fog motionless became more desperate as the Grolims fought to stop the quickening breeze pouring down the valley from the acrid stretches to the west. The blanket began to tatter and to fall apart as the weaker of the Grolims, pushed beyond their capacity, collapsed in exhaustion.

The breeze grew stronger, became a hot wind that rippled the surface of the river. The grass bent before it, and the fog began to seethe like some vast living thing, writhing at the touch of the arid wind.

Ce'Nedra could see the still-burning city of Thull Mardu now, and the infantry lines drawn up on the plain beside the river.

The hot, dusty wind blew stronger, and the fog, as insub-stantial as the thought that had raised it from the earth, dissolved, and the morning sun broke through to bathe the field in golden light.

"Polgara!" Durnik cried in sudden alarm.

Ce'Nedra whirled in time to see Polgara, her face drained deathly white, slowly toppling to the earth.

Chapter Seventeen

LELLDORIN OF WILDANTOR had been nervously pacing back and forth along the ranks of his bowmen, stopping often to listen for any sound coming out of the fog from the field lying in front of the massed infantry. "Can you hear anything?" he asked urgently of a Tolnedran legionnaire standing nearby.

The Tolnedran shook his head.

That same whisper came out of the fog from a dozen different places.

"Can you hear anything?"

"Can *you* hear anything?"

"What are they doing?"

Somewhere to the front, there was a faint clink.

"There!" everyone cried almost in unison.

"Not yet!" Lelldorin snapped to one of his countrymen who was raising his bow. "It could be just a wounded Thull out there. Save your arrows."

"Is that a breeze?" a Drasnian pikeman asked. "Please, Belar, let it be a breeze."

Lelldorin stared into the fog, nervously fingering his bow-string.

Then he felt a faint touch of air on his cheek.

"A breeze," someone exulted.

"A breeze." The phrase raced through the massed army.

Then the faint breath of air died, and the fog settled again, seeming thicker than ever.

Someone groaned bitterly.

The fog stirred then and began to eddy sluggishly. It *was* a breeze!

Lelldorin held his breath.

The fog began to move, flowing gray over the ground like water.

"There's something moving out there!" a Tolnedran barked. "Get ready!"

The flowing fog moved faster, thinning, melting in the hot, dusty breeze blowing down the valley. Lelldorin strained his eyes to the front. There were moving shapes out there, no more than seventy paces from the infantry.

Then, as if all its stubborn resistance had broken at once, the fog shimmered and dissolved, and the sun broke through. The entire field before them was filled with Malloreans. Their stealthy forward pace froze momentarily as they flinched in the sudden light of the sun.

"Now!" Lelldorin shouted, raising his bow. Behind him, his archers with one universal motion followed his action, and the sudden release of a thousand bowstrings all at once was like some vast, thrumming note. A whistling sheet of arrows soared over the heads of the solidly standing infantry, seemed to hang motionless in the air for a moment, then hurtled into the close-packed Mallorean ranks.

The creeping attack of the Malloreans did not waver or falter; it simply dissolved. With a vast, sighing groan, entire regiments fell in their tracks under the Asturian arrow storm.

Lelldorin's hand flickered to the forest of arrows thrust

point-first into the turf at his feet. He smoothly nocked another shaft, drew and released. And then again—and again. The sheet of arrows overhead was like some great slithering bridge arching over the infantry and riddling the Malloreans as it fell among them.

The storm of Asturian arrows crept inexorably across the field, and the Mallorean dead piled up in windrows as if some enormous scythe had passed through their ranks.

And then Sir Mandorallen's brazen horn sounded its mighty challenge, the ranks of archers and infantry opened, and the earth shook beneath the thunder of the charge of the Mimbrate knights.

Demoralized by the arrow storm and the sight of that inexorable charge descending upon them, the Malloreans broke and fled.

Laughing delightedly, Lelldorin's cousin Torasin lowered his bow to jeer at the backs of the routed Angaraks. "We did it, Lelldorin!" he shouted, still laughing. "We broke their backs!" He was half-turned now, not facing the littered field. His bow was in his hands; his dark hair was thrown back; and his face reflected his exultant delight. Lelldorin would always remember him so.

"Tor! Look out!" Lelldorin shouted, but it was too late. The Mallorean answer to the Asturian arrow storm was a storm of their own. From a hundred catapults concealed behind the low hills to the north, a great cloud of rocks hurtled into the air and crashed down into the close-packed ranks along the riverbank. A stone perhaps somewhat larger than a man's head struck Torasin full in the chest, smashing him to the ground.

"Tor!" Lelldorin's cry was anguished as he ran to his stricken cousin. Torasin's eyes were closed, and blood was flowing from his nose. His chest was crushed.

"Help me!" Lelldorin cried to a group of serfs standing nearby. The serfs obediently moved to assist him, but their eyes, speaking louder than any words, said that Torasin was already dead.

* * *

Barak's face was bleak as he stood at the tiller of his big ship. His oarsmen stroked to the beat of a muffled drum, and the ship raced downriver.

King Anheg of Cherek lounged against the rail. He had pulled off his helmet so that the cool river air could blow the stink of smoke out of his hair. His coarse-featured face was as grim as his cousin's. "What do you think their chances are?" he asked.

"Not very good," Barak replied bluntly. "We never counted on the Murgos and Malloreans hitting us at Thull Mardu. The army's split in two by the river, and both halves of it are outnumbered. They're going to have a bad time of it, I'm afraid." He glanced over his shoulder at the half-dozen small, narrow-beamed boats trailing in the wake of his big ship. "Close it up!" he bellowed at the men in the smaller boats.

"Malloreans ahead! On the north bank!" the lookout at the mast shouted. "About a half a mile!"

"Wet down the decks," Barak ordered.

The sailors tossed buckets on long ropes over the side, hauled up water, and soaked the wooden decks.

"Signal the ships behind us," Anheg told the bearded sailor standing in the very stern of the ship. The sailor nodded, turned and lifted a large flag attached to a long pole. He began to wave it vigorously at the ships strung out behind them.

"Be careful with that fire!" Barak shouted to the men clustered around a raised platform filled with gravel and covered with glowing coals. "If you set us ablaze, you'll all have to swim to the Sea of the East."

Just to the front of the platform stood three heavy-limbed catapults, cocked and ready.

King Anheg squinted ahead at the Malloreans gathered around a dozen or so siege engines standing solidly on the north bank. "Better send in your arrow-boats now," he suggested.

Barak grunted and waved his arm in a broad chopping motion to the six narrow boats in his wake. In answer, the lean little boats leaped ahead, cutting through the water. Mounted at the prow of each arrow-boat stood a long-armed catapult armed with a loosely packed bundle of arrows. Aided by the current, the narrow little boats sped past, their oars bending.

"Load the engines!" Barak roared to the men around the gravel-based fire. "And don't slop any of that tar on my decks."

With long iron hooks, the sailors lifted three large earthenware pots out of the coals. The pots contained a seething mixture of tar, pitch, and naptha. They were quickly dipped in tar barrels and then hastily wrapped in naptha-soaked rags. Then they were placed in the baskets of the waiting engines.

As the arrow-boats, speeding like greyhounds, swept in close to shore where the Malloreans struggled to aim their catapults, the arrow-bundles were suddenly hurled high into the air by the lashing arms of the Cherek engines. The arrows rose swiftly, then slowed at the top of their arching flight, separating and spreading out as they flew. Then, in a deadly rain, they fell upon the red-tunicked Malloreans.

Barak's ship, trailing just behind the arrow-boats, ran in close to the brush-covered riverbank, and the red-bearded man stood with both of his big hands on the tiller, staring intently at his catapult master, a gray-bearded old sailor with arms like oak stumps. The catapult master was squinting at a line of notches chipped into the railing in front of his engines. Over his head he held a long white baton and he indicated direction by pointing it either to the right or the left. Barak moved his tiller delicately in response to the movements of the baton. Then the baton cut sharply straight down, and Barak locked his tiller in an iron grip. The rags wrapped around the pots leaped into flame as they were touched by waiting torches.

"Shoot!" the catapult master barked. With a thudding crash, the beams lashed forward, hurling the flaming pots and their deadly contents in a high arch toward the struggling Malloreans and their siege engines. The pots burst open upon impact, spraying fire in front of them. The Mallorean catapults were engulfed in flame.

"Good shooting," Anheg noted professionally.

"Child's play," Barak shrugged. "A shoreline emplacement isn't much of a challenge, really." He glanced back. The arrow-boats of Greldik's ship were sweeping in to rake the Malloreans with more arrows, and the catapults on his bearded friend's decks were cocked and loaded. "Malloreans don't appear to be any brighter than Murgos. Didn't it ever occur to them that we might shoot back?"

"It's an Angarak failing," Anheg replied. "It shows up in all their writings. Torak never encouraged creative thinking."

Barak gave his cousin a speculative look. "You know what I think, Anheg? I think that all that fuss you raised back at Riva—about Ce'Nedra leading the army, I mean—I think that it wasn't entirely sincere. You're too intelligent to be so stubborn about something that wasn't that important."

Anheg winked broadly.

"No wonder they call you Anheg the sly," Barak chuckled. "What was it all about?"

"It pulled Brand's teeth." The King of Cherek grinned. "He's the one who could have stopped Ce'Nedra cold if I'd given him the chance. Rivans are very conservative, Barak. I sided with Brand and did all the talking. Then when I gave in, he didn't have any ground left to stand on."

"You were very convincing. I thought for a while that your reason had slipped."

"Thank you," the Cherek King replied with a mock bow. "When you've got a face like mine, it's easy for people to think the worst about you. I've found that useful from time to time. Here come the Algars." He pointed at the hills just behind the burning Mallorean siege engines. A great crowd of horsemen came surging over the hilltops to sweep down like a wolfpack upon the confounded Malloreans.

Anheg sighed then. "I'd like to know what's happening to them back there at Thull Mardu," he said. "I don't suppose we'll ever find out, though."

"Not very likely," Barak agreed. "We'll all get sunk eventually, once we get out into the Sea of the East."

"We'll take a lot of Malloreans with us, though, won't we, Barak?"

Barak's reply was an evil grin.

"I don't really care much for the notion of drowning," Anheg said, making a face.

"Maybe you'll get lucky and catch an arrow in the belly."

"Thanks," Anheg said sourly.

An hour or so later, after three more Angarak positions on the riverbanks had been destroyed, the land along the River Mardu turned marshy, flattening out into a sea of reeds and bending cattails. At Anheg's orders, a raft piled high with firewood was moored to a dead snag and set afire. Once the blaze was going well, buckets of greenish crystals were hurled into the flames. A thick pillar of green smoke began to climb into the blue sky.

"I hope Rhodar can see that." The King of Cherek frowned.

"If he can't, the Algars will," Barak replied. "They'll get word back to him."

"I just hope he's got enough time left to make his retreat."

"Me too," Barak said. "But as you say, we'll probably never know."

King Cho-Hag, Chief of the Clan-Chiefs of Algaria, sat his horse beside King Korodullin of Arendia. The fog was nearly gone now, and only a filmy haze remained. Not far away, the twin sorcerers, Beltira and Belkira, exhausted by their efforts, sat side by side on the ground, their heads bowed and their chests heaving. Cho-Hag shuddered inwardly at the thought of what might have happened if the two saintly old men had not been there. The hideous illusions of the Grolims that had risen from the earth just before the storm had struck terror into the hearts of the bravest warriors. Then the storm, its intensity deafening, had smashed down on the army, and after that had come the choking fog. The two sweet-faced sorcerers, however, had met and overcome each Grolim attack with calm determination. Now the Murgos were coming, and it was time for steel instead of sorcery.

"I'd let them get a little closer," Cho-Hag advised in his quiet voice as he and Korodullin watched the veritable sea of Murgos advancing against the emplaced ranks of Drasnian pikemen and Tolnedran legionnaires.

"Art thou sure of thy strategy, Cho-Hag?" the young Arendish King asked with a worried frown. "It hath ever been the custom of the knights of Mimbre to meet an attack head-on. Thy proposal to charge the flanks puzzles me."

"It will kill more Murgos, Korodullin," Cho-Hag replied, shifting his weak legs in their stirrups. "When your knights charge in from either flank, you'll cut off whole regiments of the enemy. Then we can grind the ones who've been cut off up against the infantry."

"It is passing strange to me to work thus with foot troops," Korodullin confessed. "I have a vast ignorance of unmounted combat."

"You aren't alone, my friend," Cho-Hag told him. "It's as alien to me as it is to you. It would be unfair of us, though, not to let the foot troops have a *few* Murgos, wouldn't it? They *did* walk a long way, after all."

The King of Arendia considered that gravely. He was quite obviously incapable of anything remotely resembling humor. "I had not considered that," he confessed. "'Twould be selfish in the extreme of us to deny them *some* part in the battle, I must agree. How many Murgos dost thou think would be their fair portion?"

"Oh, I don't know," Cho-Hag replied with a straight face. "A few thousand or so, I imagine. We wouldn't want to appear stingy—but it doesn't do to be over generous, either."

Korodullin sighed. "It is a difficult line to walk, King Cho-Hag—this fine division between parsimony and foolish prodigality."

"One of the prices of kingship, Korodullin."

"Very true, Cho-Hag, very true." The young King of Arendia sighed again and bent all his concentration to the problem of how many of the advancing Murgos he could really afford to give away. "Thinkest thou that two Murgos apiece might content those who fight afoot?" he asked rather hesitantly.

"Sounds fair to me."

Korodullin smiled then with happy relief. "Then that is what we shall allot them," he declared. "I have not divided up Murgos before, but it is not nearly so difficult as I had imagined."

King Cho-Hag began to laugh.

* * *

Lady Ariana put her arms about Lelldorin's shaking shoulders and drew him gently away from the pallet upon which his cousin's body lay.

"Can't you do *something*, Ariana?" he pleaded, tears streaming down his face. "Perhaps a bandage of some sort—and a poultice."

"He is beyond my art, my Lord," Ariana replied gently, "and I share thy sorrow at his death."

"Don't say that word, Ariana. Torasin *can't* be dead."

"I'm sorry, my Lord," she said simply. "He is gone, and none of my remedies or skill can bring him back."

"Polgara can do it," Lelldorin declared suddenly, an impossible hope leaping into his eyes. "Send for Polgara."

"I have no one to send, my Lord," Ariana told him, looking around the makeshift tent where she and Taiba and a few others were caring for the wounded. "The injured men here command all our attention and care."

"I'll go then," Lelldorin declared, his eyes still streaming tears. He spun and dashed from the tent.

Ariana sighed mournfully and drew a blanket over Torasin's pale face. Then she turned back to the wounded men who were being carried in a steady stream into her tent.

"Don't bother yourself with him, my Lady," a lean-faced Arendish serf told her as she bent over the body of the man's companion.

Ariana looked at the thin serf inquiringly.

"He's dead," the serf explained. "He took a Mallorean arrow right through the chest." He looked down at the dead man's face. "Poor Detton," he sighed. "He died in my arms. Do you know what his last words were?"

Ariana shook her head.

"He said, 'At least I had a good breakfast.' And then he died."

"Why didst thou bring him here, since thou didst know he was already dead?" Ariana asked him gently.

The lean, bitter-faced serf shrugged. "I didn't want to leave him just lying in a muddy ditch like a dead dog," he replied.

"In his whole life, nobody ever treated him as if he mattered at all. He was my friend, and I didn't want to leave him there like a pile of garbage." He laughed a short, bitter laugh. "I don't suppose it matters very much to him, but at least there's a little bit of dignity here." He awkwardly patted the dead man's shoulder. "Sorry, Detton," he said, "but I guess I'd better go back to the fighting."

"What is thy name, friend?" Ariana asked.

"I'm called Lammer, my Lady."

"Is the need for thee in the battle urgent?"

"I doubt it, my Lady. I've been shooting arrows at the Malloreans. I'm not very good at it, but it's what I'm supposed to do."

"My need for thee is greater, then," she declared. "I have many wounded here and few hands to help with their care. Despite thy surly exterior, I sense a great compassion in thee. Wilt thou help me?"

He regarded her for a moment. "What do you want me to do?" he said.

"Taiba is boiling cloth for bandages over that fire there," she replied. "See to the fire first, then thou wilt find a cart just outside with blankets in it. Bring in the blankets, good Lammer. After that I will have other tasks for thee."

"All right," Lammer replied laconically, moving toward the fire.

"What can we do for her?" the Princess Ce'Nedra demanded of the misshapen Beldin. The princess was staring intently into Polgara's pale, unconscious face as the sorceress lay exhausted in the arms of Durnik the smith.

"Let her sleep," Beldin grunted. "She'll be all right in a day or so."

"What's the matter with her?" Durnik asked in a worried voice.

"She's exhausted," Beldin snapped. "Isn't that obvious?"

"Just from raising a breeze? I've seen her do things that looked a lot harder."

"You don't have the faintest idea of what you're talking

about, blacksmith," Beldin growled. The hunchbacked sorcerer was himself pale and shaking. "When you start tampering with the weather, you're putting your hands on the most powerful forces in the world. I'd rather try to stop a tide or uproot a mountain than stir up a breeze in dead air."

"The Grolims brought in that storm," Durnik said.

"The air was already moving. Dead-calm air is altogether different. Do you have the remotest idea of how much air you've got to move to stir even the faintest breath of air? Do you know what kind of pressures are involved—how much all that air *weighs*?"

"Air doesn't weigh anything," Ce'Nedra protested.

"Really?" Beldin replied with heavy sarcasm. "I'm so glad you told me. Would the two of you shut up and let me get my breath?"

"But how is it that she collapsed and you didn't?" Ce'Nedra protested.

"I'm stronger than she is," Beldin replied, "and more vicious. Pol throws her whole heart into things when she gets excited. She always did. She pushed beyond her strength, and it exhausted her." The twisted little man straightened, shook himself like a dog coming out of water and looked around, his face bleak. "I've got work to do," he said. "I *think* we've pretty much worn out the Mallorean Grolims, but I'd better keep an eye on them, just to be safe. You two stay here with Pol— and keep an eye on that child." He pointed at Errand, who stood on the sandy beach with his small face very serious.

Then Beldin crouched, shimmering already into the form of a hawk, and launched himself into the air almost before his feathers were fully formed.

Ce'Nedra stared after him as he spiraled upward over the battlefield and then turned her attention back to the unconscious Polgara.

The charge of Korodullin's Mimbrate knights came at the last possible moment. Like two great scythes, the armored men on their massive chargers sliced in at a thundering gallop from the flanks with their lances leveled and cut through the horde of Murgos rushing toward the waiting pikemen and legion-naires. The results were devastating. The air was filled with screams and the sounds of steel striking steel with stunning impact. In the wake of the charge lay a path of slaughtered Murgos, a trail of human wreckage a hundred yards wide.

King Cho-Hag, sitting on his horse on a hilltop some distance to the west, nodded his approval as he watched the carnage. "Good," he said finally. He looked around at the eager faces of the Algar clansmen clustered around him. "All right, my children," he said calmly, "let's go cut up the Murgo reserves." And he led them at a gallop as they poured down off the hill, smoothly swung around the outer flanks of the tightly packed assault forces and then slashed into the unprepared Murgo units bringing up the rear.

The slash-and-run tactics of the clans of the Algars left heaps of sabred dead in their wake as they darted in and out of the milling confusion of terrified Murgos. King Cho-Hag himself led several charges, and his skill with the sabre, which was legendary in Algaria, filled his followers with an awed pride as they watched his whiplike blows raining down on Murgo heads and shoulders. The whole thrust of Algar strategy was based on speed—a sudden dash on a fast horse and a series of lightninglike sabre slashes, and then out before the enemy could gather his wits. King Cho-Hag's sabre arm was the fastest in Algaria.

"My King!" one of his men shouted, pointing toward the center of several close-packed Murgo regiments milling about in a shallow valley a few hundred yards away. "There's the black banner!"

King Cho-Hag's eyes suddenly gleamed as a wild hope surged through him. "Bring my banner to the front!" he roared, and the clansman who carried the burgundy-and-white banner of the Chief of the Clan-Chiefs galloped forward with the standard streaming above his head. "Let's go, my children!" Cho-Hag shouted and drove his horse directly at the Murgos in the valley. With sabre raised, the crippled King of the Algars led his men down into the Murgo horde. His warriors slashed to the right and to the left, but Cho-Hag plunged directly at the center, his eyes fixed on the black banner of Taur Urgas, King of the Murgos.

And then, in the midst of the household guard, Cho-Hag saw the blood-red mail of Taur Urgas himself. Cho-Hag raised his bloody sabre and shouted a ringing challenge. "Stand and fight, you Murgo dog!" he roared.

Startled by that shout, Taur Urgas wheeled his horse to stare incredulously at the charging King of Algaria. His eyes suddenly bulged with the fervid light of insanity, and his lips, foam-flacked, drew back in a snarl of hatred. "Let him come!" he grated. "Clear the way for him!"

The startled members of his personal guard stared at him.

"Make way for the King of Algaria!" Taur Urgas shrieked. "He is mine!" And the Murgo troops melted out of Cho-Hag's path.

The Algar King reined in his horse. "And so it's finally come, Taur Urgas," he said coldly.

"It has indeed, Cho-Hag," Taur Urgas replied. "I've waited for this moment for years."

"If I'd known you were waiting, I'd have come sooner."

"Today is your last day, Cho-Hag." The Murgo King's eyes were completely mad now, and foam drooled from the corners of his mouth.

"Do you plan to fight with threats and hollow words, Taur Urgas? Or have you forgotten how to draw your sword?"

With an insane shriek, Taur Urgas ripped his broad-bladed sword from its scabbard and drove his black horse toward the Algar King. "Die!" he howled, slashing at the air even as he charged. "Die, Cho-Hag!"

It was not a duel, for there were proprieties in a duel. The two kings hacked at each other with an elemental brutality, thousands of years of pent-up hatred boiling in their blood. Taur Urgas, totally mad now, sobbed and gibbered as he swung his heavy sword at his enemy. Cho-Hag, cold as ice and with an arm as fast as the flickering tongue of a snake, slid the crushing Murgo blows aside, catching them on his sliding sabre and flicking his blade like a whip, its edge biting again and again into the shoulders and face of the King of the Murgos.

The two armies, stunned by the savagery of the encounter, recoiled and gave the mounted kings room for their deadly struggle.

Frothing obscenities, Taur Urgas hacked insanely at the elusive form of his foe, but Cho-Hag, colder yet, feinted and parried and flicked his whistling sabre at the Murgo's bleeding face.

Finally, driven past even what few traces of reason were left to him, Taur Urgas hurled his horse directly at Cho-Hag with a wild animal scream. Standing in his stirrups, he grasped his sword hilt in both hands, raising it like an axe to smash his enemy forever. But Cho-Hag danced his horse to one side and thrust with all his strength, even as Taur Urgas began his massive blow. With a steely rasp, his sabre ran through the Murgo's blood-red mail and through the tensed body, to emerge dripping from his back.

Unaware in his madness that he had just received a mortal wound, Taur Urgas raised his sword again, but the strength drained from his arms and the sword fell from his grasp. With stunned disbelief, he gaped at the sabre emerging from his chest, and a bloody froth burst from his mouth. He lifted his hands like claws as if to tear away the face of his enemy, but Cho-Hag contemptuously slapped his hands away, even as he pulled his slender, curved blade out of the Murgo's body with a slithering whistle.

"And so it ends, Taur Urgas," he declared in an icy voice.

"No!" Taur Urgas croaked, trying to pull a heavy dagger from his belt.

Cho-Hag watched his feeble efforts coldly. Dark blood suddenly spurted from the open mouth of the Murgo King, and he toppled weakly from his saddle. Struggling, coughing blood, Taur Urgas lurched to his feet, gurgling curses at the man who had just killed him.

"Good fight, though," Cho-Hag told him with a bleak smile, and then he turned to ride away.

Taur Urgas fell, clawing at the turf in impotent rage. "Come back and fight," he sobbed. "Come back."

Cho-Hag glanced over his shoulder. "Sorry, your Majesty,"

he replied, "but I have pressing business elsewhere. I'm sure you understand." And with that he began to ride away.

"Come back!" Taur Urgas wailed, belching blood and curses and digging his fingers into the earth. "Come back!" Then he collapsed facedown in the bloody grass. "Come back and fight, Cho-Hag!" he gasped weakly.

The last that Cho-Hag saw of him, the dying King of Cthol Murgos was biting at the sod and clawing at the earth with trembling fingers.

A vast moan shuddered through the tight-packed regiments of the Murgos, and a sudden cheer rose from the ranks of the Algars as Cho-Hag, victorious, rode back to join the army.

"They're coming again," General Varana announced with cool professionalism as he watched the waves of oncoming Malloreans.

"Where *is* that signal?" Rhodar demanded, staring intently downriver. "What's Anheg doing down there?"

The front ranks of the Mallorean assault struck with a resounding crash. The Drasnian pikemen began to thrust with their long, wide-bladed spears, wreaking havoc among the red-garbed attackers, and the legions raised their shields in the interlocked position that presented a solid wall against which the Malloreans beat futilely. Upon a sharp, barked command, the legionnaires turned their shields slightly and each man thrust his lance out through the opening between his shield and the next. The Tolnedran lances were not as long as the Drasnian pikes, but they were long enough. A huge, shuddering cry went through the front ranks of the Malloreans, and they fell in heaps beneath the feet of the men behind.

"Are they going to break through?" Rhodar puffed. Even though he was not directly involved in the fighting, the Drasnian King began to pant at each Mallorean charge.

Varana carefully assessed the strength of the assault. "No," he concluded, "not this time. Have you worked out how you're going to make your withdrawal? It's a little difficult to pull back when your troops are engaged."

"That's why I'm saving the Mimbrates," Rhodar replied.

"They're resting their horses now for one last charge. As soon as we get the signal from Anheg, Mandorallen and his men will shove the Malloreans back, and the rest of us will run like rabbits."

"The charge will only hold them back for so long," Varana advised, "and then they'll come after you again."

"We'll form up again upriver a ways," Rhodar said.

"It's going to take a long time to get back to the escarpment if you're going to have to stop and fight every half-mile or so," Varana told him.

"I know that," Rhodar snapped peevishly. "Have you got any better ideas?"

"No," Varana replied. "I was just pointing it out, that's all."

"Where *is* that signal?" Rhodar demanded again.

On a quiet hillside some distance from the struggle taking place on the north bank, the simpleminded serf boy from the Arendish forest was playing his flute. His melody was mournful, but even in its sadness, it soared to the sky. The boy did not understand the fighting and he had wandered away unnoticed. Now he sat alone on the grassy hillside in the warm, midmorning sunlight with his entire soul pouring out of his flute.

The Mallorean soldier who was creeping up behind him with drawn sword had no ear for music. He did not know— or care—that the song the boy played was the most beautiful song any man had ever heard.

The song ended very suddenly, never to begin again.

The stream of casualties being carried to Ariana's makeshift hospital grew heavier, and the overtaxed Mimbrate girl was soon forced into making some cruel decisions. Only those men with some chance of survival could be treated. The mortally hurt were quickly given a drink of a bitter-tasting potion of herbs that would ease their pain and then were left to die. Each such decision wrung Ariana's heart, and she worked with tears standing in her eyes.

And then Brand, the Rivan Warder, entered the tent with a

stricken face. The big Rivan's mail shirt was blood-spattered, and there were savage sword cuts along the edge of his broad, round shield. Behind him, three of his sons bore the limp, bleeding form of their younger brother, Olban.

"Can you see to him?" Brand asked Ariana hoarsely.

A single glance, however, told the blond girl that the wound in Olban's chest was mortal. "I can make him comfortable," she replied a bit evasively. She quickly knelt beside the bleeding young man, lifted his head, and held a cup to his lips.

"Father," Olban said weakly after he had drunk, "I have something I have to tell you."

"Time enough for that later," Brand told him gruffly, "after you're better."

"I'm not going to get better, father," Olban said in a voice scarcely more than a whisper.

"Nonsense," Brand told him, but there was no conviction in his voice.

"There's not much time, father," Olban said, coughing weakly. "Please listen."

"Very well, Olban," the Warder said, leaning forward to catch his son's words.

"At Riva—after Belgarion came—I was humiliated because you had been deposed. I couldn't bear it, father." Olban coughed again, and a bloody froth came to his lips.

"You should have known me better than that, Olban," Brand said gently.

"I do—now." Olban sighed. "But I was young and proud, and Belgarion—a nobody from Sendaria—had pushed you from your rightful place."

"It wasn't my place to begin with, Olban," Brand told him. "It was his. Belgarion's the Rivan King. That has nothing to do with position or place. It's a duty—and it's his, not mine."

"I hated him," Olban whispered. "I began to follow him every place. Wherever he went, I wasn't far behind him."

"What for?" Brand asked.

"At first I didn't know. Then one day he came out of the throne room wearing his robe and crown. He seemed so puffed-up with his own importance—as if he really *was* a king instead of just a common Sendarian scullion. Then I knew what I had to do. I took my dagger and I threw it at his back."

Brand's face suddenly froze.

"For a long time after that, I tried to avoid him," Olban continued. "I knew that what I had done was wrong—even as the dagger left my fingers. I thought that if I stayed away from him, he'd never find out that I was the one who'd tried to kill him. But he has powers, father. He has ways of knowing things no man could possibly know. He sought me out one day and gave me back the dagger I'd thrown at him and he told me that I should never tell anyone what I'd done. He did that for you, father—to keep my disgrace from you."

Grim-faced, Brand rose to his feet. "Come," he said to his other three sons. "We have fighting to do—and no time to waste on traitors." Quite deliberately he turned his back on his dying son.

"I tried to repay his mercy, father," Olban pleaded. "I pledged my life to protecting his queen. Doesn't that count for anything?"

Brand's face was stony, and he kept his back turned in grim silence.

"Belgarion forgave me, father. Can't you find it in your heart to forgive me too?"

"No," Brand said harshly, "I cannot."

"Please, father," Olban begged. "Don't you have one tear for me?"

"Not one," Brand told him, but Ariana saw that his words were a lie. The grim, gray-clad man's eyes were full, but his face remained granitelike. Without another word, he strode from the tent.

Wordlessly, each of Olban's brothers clasped his hand in turn, and then they left to follow their father.

Olban wept quietly for a time, but then his growing weakness and the drug Ariana had given him drained away his grief. He lay, half-dozing on his pallet for a time, then struggled to raise himself and beckoned to the Mimbrate girl. She knelt beside him, supporting him with one arm about his shoulders and her head bent to catch his faltering words. "Please," he whispered. "Please tell her Majesty what I said to my father—and tell her how sorry I was." And then his head fell forward against Ariana, and he quietly died in her arms.

Ariana had no time to mourn, for precisely then three Sendars carried Colonel Brendig into her tent. The colonel's left arm was mangled beyond all hope of repair.

"We were bringing down the bridge that crosses to the city," one of the Sendars reported tersely. "There was a support that wouldn't give way, so the colonel went down himself to chop it away. When it finally broke, the timbers of the bridge fell on him."

Ariana gravely examined Brendig's shattered arm. "I fear there is no recourse, my Lord," she told him. "The arm will have to come off, lest it mortify and carry thy life away with it."

Brendig nodded soberly. "That's about what I'd expected," he replied. "I suppose we'd better get on with it, then."

"There!" King Rhodar shouted, pointing downriver. "The smoke—it's green! That's the signal. We can start the retreat now."

General Varana, however was staring at the riverbank upstream. "It's too late, I'm afraid, your Majesty," he said quietly. "A column of Malloreans and Nadraks have just reached the river to the west of us. It very much looks as if we've been cut off."

Chapter Eighteen

THE NEWS OF the death of Taur Urgas spread through the Murgo army in a vast groan, and the heart went out of the black-robed troops. Taur Urgas had been feared by his men, but his savage madness had lent them all a peculiar sense that they were invincible. They had felt somehow that nothing could stand in his path, and that they, as the instruments of his brutal will, shared in some measure his apparent invulnerability. But with his death, each Murgo became aware with a sudden cold touch of fear that he also could die, and the assault on the armies of the west along the south bank faltered.

King Cho-Hag watched the crumbling of the Murgo resolve with a certain grim satisfaction, then rode down to the lines of infantry and the milling Mimbrate knights to confer with the other leaders. King Fulrach strode forward from the ranks of his Sendars. The dumpy, brown-bearded monarch looked almost comical in his burnished breastplate, but his sword showed signs of recent use, and his helmet was dented in a couple of places, mute evidence that the King of Sendaria had participated in the fight.

"Have you seen Anheg's signal yet?" Fulrach demanded as he approached.

Cho-Hag shook his head. "It should come any time now, though," he replied. "We'd better make some plans. Have you seen Korodullin?"

"The physicians are working on him," Fulrach said.

"Is he hurt?" Cho-Hag was startled.

"I don't think it's too serious. He went to help his friend, the Baron of Vo Ebor, and a Murgo hit him in the head with a mace. His helmet absorbed most of the blow. He's bleeding out of the ears a bit, but the physicians say he'll receover. The baron's in worse shape, though."

"Who's in charge of the Mimbrates, then?"

"Sir Andorig. He's a good man in a fight, but his understanding is a bit limited."

Cho-Hag laughed shortly. "You've just described most of Arendia, my friend. They're *all* good in a fight, and they *all* have limited understanding." Carefully he dismounted, holding onto his saddle as his weak legs nearly buckled. "We can make our decisions without Andorig's help, I think." He looked at the retreating Murgos. "As soon as we see Anheg's signal, I think we're going to want to get out of here in a hurry. The Murgos are demoralized right now, but they'll probably stiffen up again as soon as the shock wears off."

Fulrach nodded. "Did you really kill Taur Urgas in a duel?" he asked.

Cho-Hag nodded. "It wasn't really all that much of a duel. He was raving when he came at me and didn't even try to defend himself. When Anheg signals, we'll have the Mimbrates charge the Murgo front. The Murgos will probably break and run. I'll follow after them with my clansmen to hurry them along. That should give you and your foot troops time to start upriver. Andorig and I'll keep the Murgos off your back until you get clear. How does that sound?"

King Fulrach nodded. "It sounds workable," he agreed. "Do you think they'll try to follow us?"

Cho-Hag grinned. "I'll encourage them not to," he replied. "Have you got any idea of what's going on across the river?"

"It's hard to say, but things don't look very good."

"Can you think of any way we can send them help?"

"Not on short notice," Fulrach answered.

"Neither can I," Cho-Hag said. He began to pull himself back up into his saddle. "I'll go give Andorig his instructions. Keep your eyes open for Anheg's signal."

"Belgarath!" Ce'Nedra called out silently, her hand tightly clasped about the amulet at her throat. "Belgarath, can you hear me?" She was standing several yards away from where Durnik was trying to make the unconscious Polgara as comfortable as possible. The princess had her eyes tightly closed and she was putting every ounce of concentration into casting her thought to the sky, reaching out with all her heart toward the ancient sorcerer.

"Ce'Nedra?" The old man's voice was as clear as if he were standing beside her. "What are you doing? Where's Polgara?"

"Oh, Belgarath!" The princess almost sobbed with relief. "Help us. Lady Polgara's unconscious, and the Malloreans are attacking again. We're being slaughtered, Belgarath. Help us."

"Slow down," he commanded brusquely. "What happened to Pol? Where are you?"

"We're at Thull Mardu," Ce'Nedra replied. "We had to take the city so that the Cherek fleet could go on down the river. The Malloreans and the Murgos crept up on us. They've been attacking since early this morning."

Belgarath started to swear. "What's wrong with Pol?" he demanded harshly.

"The Grolims brought in an awful storm, and then there was fog. Lady Polgara and Beldin made the wind blow, and then she just collapsed. Beldin said that she exhausted herself and that we have to let her sleep."

"Where's Beldin?"

"He said that he had to keep an eye on the Grolims. Can you help us?"

"Ce'Nedra, I'm a thousand leagues away from you. Garion, Silk, and I are in Mallorea—practically on Torak's doorstep. If I so much as raise my hand, it will wake him, and Garion's not ready to meet him yet."

"We're doomed, then," Ce'Nedra wailed.

"Stop that," he snapped. "This isn't the time for hysterics. You're going to have to wake Polgara."

"We've tried—and Beldin says that we've got to let her rest."

"She can rest later," Belgarath retorted. "Is that bag she always carries somewhere about—the one she keeps all those herbs in?"

"I—I think so. Durnik was carrying it a little while ago."

"Durnik's with you? Good. Now listen, and listen carefully. Get the bag and open it. What you want will be in a silk pouch. Don't open any jars or bottles. She keeps her poisons in those. In one of the silk bags you'll find a yellow-colored powder. It has a very acrid odor to it. Put a spoonful or so of that powder into a pot of boiling water. Put the pot beside Pol's head and cover her face with a cloak so she has to breathe the fumes."

"What will that do?"

"It will wake her up."

"Are you sure?"

"Don't argue with me, Ce'Nedra. She'll wake up, believe me. Those fumes would wake up a dead stick. As soon as she's awake, she'll know what to do."

Ce'Nedra hesitated. "Is Garion there?" she blurted finally.

"He's asleep. We had a rough time last night."

"When he wakes up, tell him that I love him." She said it very fast, as if afraid that if she thought about it at all, she wouldn't be able to say it.

"Why confuse him?" the old man asked her.

"Belgarath!" Ce'Nedra's voice was stricken.

"I was teasing. I'll tell him. Now get to work—and don't do this any more. I'm trying to sneak up on Torak, and it's a little hard to sneak when you're shouting at somebody a thousand leagues away."

"We aren't shouting."

"Oh yes we are—it's a special kind of shouting, but it's shouting all the same. Now take your hand off that amulet and get to work." And then his voice was gone.

Durnik, of course, would never understand, so Ce'Nedra did what was necessary by herself. She rummaged around until she found a small pot. She filled it with water and set it on the small fire the smith had built the night before. Then she opened Polgara's herb bag. The blond child, Errand, stood at her side, watching her curiously.

"What are you doing, Princess?" Durnik asked, still hovering anxiously over the sleeping Polgara.

"I'm fixing something to make her rest easier," Ce'Nedra lied.

"Are you sure you know what you're doing? Some of those are very dangerous."

"I know which one I'm looking for," she replied. "Trust me, Durnik."

The powder she finally located was so acrid that it made her eyes water. She carefully measured out a bit of it and dumped it into the pot. The steaming fumes were awful, and the princess kept her face averted as she carried the pot to where Polgara lay. She set the pot beside the lady's pale, sleeping face and then laid a cloak across her. "Give me a stick," the princess said to the smith.

Durnik, his face dubious, handed her a broken-off arrow.

Ce'Nedra carefully propped up the cloak, making a small tent over the pot and Polgara's face.

"What now?" Durnik asked.

"Now we wait," Ce'Nedra told him.

Then, coming from the direction of the battle, a group of Sendarian soldiers, evidently wounded, appeared at the top of the grassy bank surrounding the secluded little beach. Their jerkins all had bloodstains on them, and several of the men wore bandages. Unlike most of the wounded who had already passed that morning, however, these men still carried their weapons.

Under the tented cloak, Polgara began to cough.

"What have you done?" Durnik cried, snatching the cloak away.

"It was necessary," Ce'Nedra replied. "I talked with Belgarath. He told me that I had to wake her up—and how to do it."

"You'll hurt her," Durnik accused. With sudden, uncharacteristic anger, he kicked the fuming pot, sending it rolling down the beach toward the water's edge.

Polgara's eyelids were fluttering as she continued to cough. When she opened her eyes, however, her look was blank, uncomprehending.

"Can you spare us some water?" one of the wounded Sendars asked as the group of men approached.

"There's a whole river right there," Ce'Nedra replied absently, pointing even as she intently stared into Polgara's eyes.

Durnik, however, gave the men a startled look, then suddenly reached for his sword.

But the men in Sendarian jerkins had jumped down from the bank and were already upon them. It took three of them to disarm the powerful smith and to hold his arms.

"You're not Sendars," Durnik exclaimed, struggling with his captors.

"How clever of you to notice," one of them replied in an accent so guttural that it was almost unintelligible. Another of them drew his sword and stood over the dazed Polgara. "Stop fighting, friend," he told Durnik with an ugly smirk, "or I'll kill this woman."

"Who are you?" Ce'Nedra demanded indignantly. "What do you think you're doing?"

"Actually, we're members of the Imperial Elite Guard," the man with the sword answered urbanely. "And we're here, your Highness, to extend to you the invitation of his Imperial Majesty 'Zakath, Emperor of Mallorea. His Majesty requests the honor of your presence in his pavilion." His face hardened, and he looked at his men. "Bring them," he ordered. "Let's get out of here before someone comes along and starts asking questions."

* * *

"They're digging in," Hettar reported to King Rhodar, gesturing toward the west and their now-blocked escape route. "They've already got a trenchline running from the river for about a half a mile."

"Is there any chance of going around them?" Rhodar asked.

Hettar shook his head. "That whole flank's seething with Nadraks."

"We'll have to go through them, then," the King of Drasnia decided.

"I can't very well attack trenches with cavalry," Hettar pointed out.

"We'll storm them with the infantry units," Rhodar declared. "We'll have a certain advantage. The Asturian bows have a longer range than the short ones the Malloreans use. We'll move the archers to the front as we advance. They can rake the trenches and then harass the Mallorean archers behind the lines. The pikemen will go in first." The sweating fat man looked at General Varana. "Can your legionnaires clear the trenches once we open a hole for you?"

Varana nodded. "We train extensively for trench fighting," he replied confidently. "We'll clear the trenches."

"We'll bring the wounded with the main force," Rhodar said. "Somebody locate Polgara and the princess. It's time to leave."

"What task hast thou for Lord Hettar and me," Mandorallen inquired. The great knight's armor showed a number of dents, but he spoke as calmly as if he had not spent the entire morning involved in heavy fighting.

"I want you and your knights to hold the rear," Rhodar told him. "Keep that army out there off my back." He turned to Hettar. "And I want you and your clansmen to go to work on the Nadraks. I don't want them to come swarming in while we're working in the trenches."

"It's a desperate move, King Rhodar," General Varana said seriously. "Attacking even hasty fortifications is always costly, and you're going to do it with another army coming at you from the rear. If your attack is beaten back, you'll be caught between two superior forces. They'll grind you to dogmeat right on the spot."

"I know," Rhodar admitted glumly, "but our only hope of escape is breaking through those lines that have us blocked off. We've *got* to get back upriver. Tell your men that we *have* to take those trenches on the first charge. Otherwise, we're all going to die right here. All right, gentlemen, good luck."

Once again Mandorallen led his steel-clad knights in their fearsome charge, and once again the attacking Malloreans recoiled, driven back by the dreadful shock as the mounted men of Mimbre struck their front ranks. This time, however, the pikemen and legionnaires, as soon as they were disengaged from the enemy, turned sharply to the left and, at a jingling trot, abandoned their positions to follow the Sendars and Asturians who were already withdrawing from the field toward the west.

The delaying action of the Mimbrate knights was costly. Riderless horses galloped wildly about the battlefield, quite frequently adding to the havoc by trampling through the Mallorean ranks. Here and there among the red tunics that carpeted the field lay the single gleaming form of a fallen knight. Again and again the Mimbrates hurled themselves against the advancing red tide, slowing the Malloreans, but not quite able to stop them.

"It's going to be tight, your Majesty," General Varana advised as he and King Rhodar rode toward the hastily drawn lines blocking their escape. "Even if we break through, the bulk of the Mallorean forces are going to be hot on our heels."

"You've got a great talent for the obvious, General," Rhodar replied. "As soon as we get through, we'll put the archers at the rear and let the Malloreans march through a rain of arrows. That will hold them back."

"Until the archers run out of arrows," Varana added.

"After we break through, I'll send the Algars on ahead. Fulrach's got whole wagonloads of arrows at the rapids."

"Which is two days march ahead."

"Do you always look at the dark side of things?"

"Just trying to anticipate, your Majesty."

"Would you mind anticipating someplace else?"

The Algars had moved out to the right flank of the retreating army and were gathering in their characteristic small bands, preparing to charge the Nadraks drawn up on the hills above the river. Hettar, his scalp lock streaming, moved forward at a steady lope, his sabre drawn and his eyes like flint. The Nadraks appeared at first to be awaiting his charge, but then, amazingly, they turned away and rode rapidly toward the river.

From the midst of that sudden surge, a half-dozen men riding under the Nadrak banner swerved out toward the advancing Algars. One of the riders was waving a short stick with a white rag tied to it. The group reined in sharply about a hundred yards in front of Hettar's horse.

"I've got to talk to Rhodar," one of the Nadraks bellowed in a shrill voice. He was a tall, emaciated man with a pock-marked face and a scraggly beard, but on his head he wore a crown.

"Is this some trick?" Hettar shouted back.

"Of course it is, you jackass," the scrawny man replied. "But it's not on you this time. Get me to Rhodar at once."

"Keep an eye on them," Hettar told a nearby Clan-Chief, pointing at the Nadrak forces now streaming toward the Mallorean trenches lying in the path of the retreating army. "I'll take this maniac to see King Rhodar." He turned and led the group of Nadrak warriors toward the advancing infantry.

"Rhodar!" the thin man wearing the crown shrieked as they approached the Drasnian King. "Don't you ever answer your mail?"

"What are you doing, Drosta?" King Rhodar shouted back.

"I'm changing sides, Rhodar," King Drosta lek Thun replied with an almost hysterical laugh. "I'm joining forces with you. I've been in touch with your queen for weeks. Didn't you get her messages?"

"I thought you were playing games."

"Naturally I'm playing games." The Nadrak King giggled.

"I've always got something up my sleeve. Right now my army's opening an escape route for you. You *do* want to escape, don't you?"

"Of course I do."

"So do I. My troops will butcher the Malloreans in those trenches, and then we can all make a run for it."

"I don't trust you, Drosta," Rhodar said bluntly.

"Rhodar," Drosta said in mock chagrin, "how can you say that to an old friend?" He giggled again, his voice shrill and nervous.

"I want to know why you're changing sides in the middle of a battle—particularly when your side's winning."

"Rhodar, my kingdom's awash with Malloreans. If I don't help you to defeat them, 'Zakath will simply absorb Gar og Nadrak. It's much too long and involved to talk about now. Will you accept my aid?"

"I'll take all the help I can get."

"Good. Maybe later we can get drunk together and talk things over, but for right now, let's get out of here before 'Zakath hears about this and comes after me personally." The King of Gar og Nadrak laughed again, the same shrill, almost hysterical laugh as before. "I did it, Rhodar," he exulted. "I actually betrayed 'Zakath of Mallorea and got away with it."

"You haven't gotten away with it yet, Drosta," Rhodar told him dryly.

"I will if we run fast enough, Rhodar, and right now I *really* feel like running."

'Zakath, dread Emperor of boundless Mallorea, was a man of medium height with glossy black hair and a pale, olive-tinged complexion. His features were regular, even handsome, but his eyes were haunted by a profound melancholy. He appeared to be about thirty-five years old, and he wore a plain linen robe with no ornament or decoration upon it to indicate his exalted rank.

His pavilion stood in the center of the camp of the Malloreans, a vast sea of tents standing on the plains of Mishrak ac Thull. The earthen floor of the pavilion was covered with priceless Mallorean carpets, and the polished tables and chairs were inlaid with gold and with mother of pearl. Candles filled the pavilion with glowing light. Somewhere nearby, a small group of musicians played subdued melodies set in a minor key.

The Emperor's only companion was a half-grown cat, a common, mackeral-striped tabby with that gangling, long-legged awkwardness of the adolescent feline. While 'Zakath watched with a sort of sad-eyed amusement, the young cat stalked a scrap of balled-up parchment, her feet noiseless on the carpet and her face set in a look of intent concentration.

As Princess Ce'Nedra and her companions were escorted into the pavilion, 'Zakath, seated on a low, cushioned divan, held up his hand for silence, his eyes still fixed on the cat. "She hunts," the Emperor murmured in a dead voice.

The cat crept nearer to her intended prey, crouched and shifted her hind feet nervously, her bottom twitching from side to side and her tail lashing. Then she leaped at the parchment. The ball crackled as she pounced on it, and, startled, she jumped high into the air. She batted the ball experimentally with one paw; suddenly finding a new game, she bounded it across the floor with a series of soft-pawed jabs, scampering after it with awkward enthusiasm.

'Zakath smiled sadly. "A young cat," he said, "with much yet to learn." He rose gracefully to his feet and bowed to Ce'Nedra. "Your Imperial Highness," he greeted her formally. His voice was resonant, but there was that peculiar deadness in it.

"Your Imperial Majesty," Ce'Nedra replied, inclining her head in response.

"Please, Goodman," 'Zakath said to Durnik, who was supporting the still-dazed Polgara, "let the lady rest here." He indicated the divan. "I'll send for my physicians, and they will see to her indisposition."

"Your Majesty is too kind." Ce'Nedra mouthed the ritual phrase, but her eyes were searching 'Zakath's face for some hint of his real intentions. "One is surprised to meet such courtesy—under the circumstances."

He smiled again, rather whimsically. "And, of course, all

Malloreans are supposed to be raving fanatics—like Murgos. Courtesy is out of character, right?"

"We have very little information about Mallorea and its people," the princess responded. "I was not certain what to expect."

"That's surprising," the Emperor observed. "I have a great deal of information about your father and your Alorn friends."

"Your Majesty has the aid of Grolims in gathering intelligence," Ce'Nedra said, "while we must rely on ordinary men."

"The Grolims are overrated, Princess. Their first loyalty is to Torak; their second to their own hierarchy. They tell me only what they want to tell me—although periodically I manage to have a bit of additional information extracted from one of them. It helps to keep the rest of them honest."

An attendant entered the pavilion, fell to his knees, and pressed his face to the carpet.

"Yes?" 'Zakath inquired.

"Your Imperial Majesty asked that the King of Thulldom be brought here," the attendant replied.

"Ah, yes. I'd nearly forgotten. Please excuse me for a moment, Princess Ce'Nedra—a small matter requiring my attention. Please, you and your friends make yourselves comfortable." He looked critically at Ce'Nedra's armor. "After we've dined, I'll have the women of my household see to more suitable clothing for you and for Lady Polgara. Does the child require anything?" He looked curiously at Errand, who was intently watching the cat.

"He'll be all right, your Majesty," Ce'Nedra replied. Her mind was working very rapidly. This urbane, polished gentleman might be easier to deal with than she had anticipated.

"Bring in the King of the Thulls," 'Zakath ordered, his hand wearily shading his eyes.

"At once, your Imperial Majesty," the attendant said, scrambling to his feet and backing out of the pavilion, bent in a deep bow.

Gethell, the King of Mishrak ac Thull, was a thick-bodied man with lank, mud-colored hair. His face was a pasty white as he was led in, and he was trembling violently. "Y-Your

Imperial Majesty," he stammered in a croaking voice.

"You forgot to bow, Gethell," 'Zakath reminded him gently. One of the Mallorean guards doubled his fist and drove it into Gethell's stomach. The Thull monarch doubled over.

"Much better," 'Zakath said approvingly. "I've asked you here in regard to some distressing news I received from the battlefield, Gethell. My commanders report that your troops did not behave well during the engagement at Thull Mardu. I am no soldier, but it seems to me that your men might have stood at least *one* charge by the Mimbrate knights before they ran away. I'm informed however, that they did not. Have you any explanation for that?"

Gethell began to babble incoherently.

"I thought not," 'Zakath told him. "It's been my experience that the failure of people to do what's expected of them is the result of poor leadership. It appears that you've not taken the trouble to encourage your men to be brave. That was a serious oversight on your part, Gethell."

"Forgive me, dread 'Zakath," the King of the Thulls wailed, falling to his knees in terror.

"But of course I forgive you, my dear fellow," 'Zakath told him. "How absurd of you to think that I wouldn't. A reprimand of some sort *is* in order, though, don't you think?"

"I freely accept full responsibility," Gethell declared, still on his knees.

"Splendid, Gethell. Absolutely splendid. I'm so glad that this interview is going so well. We've managed to avoid all kinds of unpleasantness." He turned to the attendant. "Would you be so good as to take King Gethell out and have him flogged?" he asked.

"At once, your Imperial Majesty."

Gethell's eyes started from his head as the two soldiers dragged him to his feet.

"Now," 'Zakath mused. "What do we do with him after we've flogged him?" He thought a moment. "Ah, I know. Is there any stout timber in the vicinity?"

"It's all open grassland, your Imperial Majesty."

"What a pity." 'Zakath sighed. "I was going to have you

crucified, Gethell, but I suppose I'll have to forgo that. Perhaps an extra fifty lashes will serve as well."

Gethell began to blubber.

"Oh, come now, my dear fellow, that just won't do. You *are* a king, after all, and you absolutely *must* provide a good example for your men. Run along now. I have guests. One hopes that the sight of your public flogging will give your troops greater incentive to do better. They'll reason that if I'd do that to *you*, then what I'll do to *them* will be infinitely worse. When you recover, encourage them in that belief, because the next time this happens, I'll have made arrangements to have the necessary timber on hand. Take him away," he said to his men without so much as a glance over his shoulder.

"Forgive me for the interruption, your Highness," he apologized. "These little administrative details consume so much of one's time."

The King of the Thulls was dragged sobbing from the pavilion.

"I've ordered a small supper for you and your friends, Princess Ce'Nedra," 'Zakath continued. "All the finest delicacies. Then I'll make arrangements for the absolute comfort of you and your companions."

"I hope that this won't offend your Imperial Majesty," Ce'Nedra began bravely, "but one is curious about your plans in regard to our future."

"Please set your mind at rest, your Highness," 'Zakath replied in his dead-sounding voice. "Word has reached me that the madman, Taur Urgas, is dead. I will never be able to repay you for that service, and I bear you absolutely no ill will whatsoever." He glanced toward one corner of his tent where his cat, purring ecstatically, was lying on her back in Errand's lap with all four paws in the air. The smiling child was gently stroking her furry belly. "How charming," 'Zakath murmured in an oddly melancholy voice.

Then the Emperor of boundless Mallorea rose and approached the divan where Durnik supported Lady Polgara. "My Queen," he said, bowing to her with profound respect. "Your beauty quite transcends all reports."

Polgara opened her eyes and gave him a level gaze. A wild hope leaped in Ce'Nedra's heart. Polgara was conscious.

"You are courteous, my Lord," Polgara told him in a weak voice.

"You *are* my queen, Polgara," 'Zakath told her, "and I can now understand my God's ages-old longing for you." He sighed then as his apparently habitual melancholy descended upon him once again.

"What are you going to do with us?" Durnik asked, his arms still holding Polgara protectively.

'Zakath sighed again. "The God of my people is not a good or kindly God," he told the smith. "If the arranging of things had been left to me, all might have been different. I was not consulted, however. I am Angarak, and I must bow to the will of Torak. The sleep of the Dragon-God grows fitful, and I must obey his commands. Though it wounds me deeply, I must turn you and your companions over to the Grolims. They will deliver you up to Zedar, disciple of Torak in Cthol Mishrak, City of Night, where *he* will decide your fate."

Part Three

MALLOREA

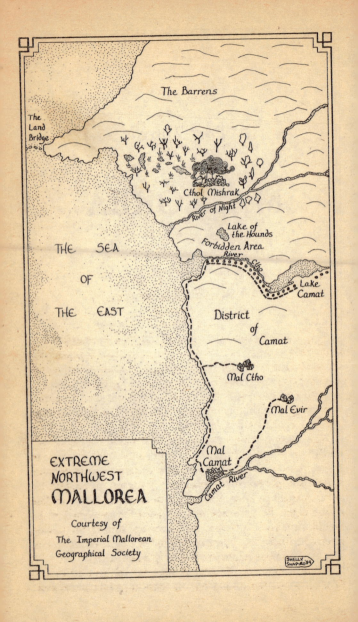

The Barrens

The Land Bridge

Cthol Mishrak

River of Night

Lake of the Hounds

Forbidden Area River

THE SEA

OF

THE EAST

Cuo

Lake Camat

District

of

Camat

Mal Ctho

Mal Evir

Mal Camat

Camat River

EXTREME
NORTHWEST
MALLOREA

Courtesy of
The Imperial Mallorean
Geographical Society

SHELLY SHAPIRO 89

Chapter Nineteen

THEY REMAINED FOR nearly a week in the Imperial compound as the personal guests of the Emperor 'Zakath, who for some strange reason seemed to take a melancholy pleasure in their company. Quarters were provided for them within the labyrinth of silken tents and pavilions that sheltered 'Zakath's household staff, and their every comfort received the personal attention of the Emperor himself.

The strange, sad-eyed man puzzled Princess Ce'Nedra. Although he was the absolute soul of courtesy, the memory of his interview with King Gethell frightened her. His ruthlessness was all the more chilling because he never lost his temper. He never seemed to sleep either, and when, often in the middle of the night, he felt some obscure need for conversation, he would send for Ce'Nedra. He never apologized for having interrupted her rest. It apparently did not even occur to him that his summons might in some way inconvenience her.

"Where did King Rhodar receive his military training?" 'Zakath asked her during one of these midnight interviews.

"None of my information about him even hints about any such talent." The Emperor was seated deep in the purple cushions of a soft chair with golden candlelight playing over his face and his cat dozing in his lap.

"I really couldn't say, your Majesty," Ce'Nedra replied, toying absently with the sleeve of the pale silk gown that had been provided for her soon after her arrival. "I only met Rhodar last winter."

"Very peculiar," 'Zakath mused. "We had always assumed that he was just a foolish old man doting on his young wife. We had never even considered him a possible threat. We concentrated our attentions on Brand and Anheg. Brand is too self-effacing to be a good leader, and Anheg seemed too erratic to give us much concern. Then Rhodar appeared out of nowhere to take charge of things. The Alorns are an enigma, aren't they? How can a sensible Tolnedran girl stand them?"

She smiled briefly. "They have a certain charm, your Majesty," she told him rather pertly.

"Where is Belgarion?" The question came without any warning.

"We don't know, your Majesty," Ce'Nedra answered evasively. "Lady Polgara was furious when he slipped away."

"In the company of Belgarath and Kheldar," the Emperor added. "We heard of the search for them. Tell me, Princess, does he by any chance have Cthrag Yaska with him?"

"Cthrag Yaska?"

"The burning stone—what you in the west call the Orb of Aldur."

"I'm not at liberty to discuss that, your Majesty," she told him rather primly, "and I'm sure you're too courteous to try to wring the information out of me."

"Princess," he said reprovingly.

"I'm sorry, your Majesty," she apologized and gave him that quick, little girl smile that was always her weapon of last resort.

'Zakath smiled gently. "You're a devious young woman, Ce'Nedra," he said.

"Yes, your Majesty," she acknowledged. "What prompted you and Taur Urgas to bury your enmity and unite against us?" Ce'Nedra wanted to demonstrate that she too could ask surprise questions.

"There was no unity in our attack, Princess," he replied. "I was merely responding to Taur Urgas."

"I don't understand."

"So long as he remained at Rak Goska, I was perfectly content to stay at Thull Zelik; but as soon as he began to march north, I had to respond. The land of the Thulls is of too much strategic importance to allow it to be occupied by a hostile force."

"And what now, 'Zakath?" Ce'Nedra asked him impudently. "Taur Urgas is dead. Where will you turn now in search of an enemy?"

He smiled a wintry smile. "How little you understand us, Ce'Nedra. Taur Urgas was only the symbol of Murgo fanaticism. Ctuchik is dead, and Taur Urgas is dead, but Murgodom lives on—even as Mallorea will live on when I am gone. Our enmity goes back for eons. At last, however, a Mallorean Emperor is in a position to crush Cthol Murgos once and for all and make himself undisputed overking of Angarak."

"It's all for power, then?"

"What else is there?" he asked sadly. "When I was very young, I thought that there might be something else—but events proved that I was wrong." A brief look of pain crossed his face, and he sighed. "In time you will discover that same truth. Your Belgarion will grow colder as the years pass and the chill satisfaction of power comes more and more to possess him. When it is complete, and only his love of power remains, then he and I will move against each other as inevitably as two great tides. I will not attack him until his education is complete. There is no satisfaction in destroying a man who does not fully comprehend reality. When all of his illusions are gone and only his love of power remains, then he will be a fit opponent." His face had grown bleak. He looked at her, his eyes as dead and cold as ice. "I think I've kept you from your rest too long,

Princess," he said. "Go to bed and dream of love and other absurdities. The dreams will die all too soon, so enjoy them while you can."

Early the next morning, Ce'Nedra entered the pavilion where Polgara rested, recuperating from the struggle with the Grolims at Thull Mardu. She was alert, but still dreadfully weak.

"He's every bit as insane as Taur Urgas was," Ce'Nedra reported. "He's so obsessed with the idea of becoming overking of Angarak that he isn't even paying any attention to what we've been doing."

"That may change once Anheg starts sinking his troop ships," Polgara replied. "There's nothing we can do at the moment, so just keep listening to him and be polite."

"Do you think we should try to escape?"

"No."

Ce'Nedra looked at her, a bit startled.

"What's happening is supposed to happen. There's some reason that the four of us—you, Durnik, Errand, and I—are supposed to go to Mallorea. Let's not tamper with it."

"You knew this was going to happen?"

Polgara gave her a weary smile. "I knew that's where we were going. I didn't know how, exactly. 'Zakath isn't interfering in any way, so don't aggravate him."

Ce'Nedra sighed in resignation. "Whatever you say, Lady Polgara," she said.

It was early afternoon of that same day when the first reports of King Anheg's activities in the Sea of the East reached the Emperor 'Zakath. Ce'Nedra, who was present when the dispatches were delivered, felt a secret sense of satisfaction as the icy man showed the first hint of irritation she had seen in him.

"Are you certain of this?" he demanded of the trembling messenger, holding up the parchment.

"I only carried the dispatch, dread Lord." The messenger quailed, cringing back from his Emperor's anger.

"Were you at Thull Zelik when the ships arrived?"

"There was only one ship, dread Lord."

"One ship out of fifty?" 'Zakath's tone was incredulous. "Weren't there others—perhaps coming along the coast?"

"The sailors said there weren't, your Imperial Majesty."

"What kind of barbarian is this Anheg of Cherek?" 'Zakath exclaimed to Ce'Nedra. "Each of those ships carried two hundred men."

"King Anheg is an Alorn, your Majesty," Ce'Nedra replied coolly. "They're an unpredictable people."

With a great deal of effort, 'Zakath regained his composure. "I see," he said after a moment's reflection. "This was your plan from the beginning, wasn't it, Princess? The entire attack on Thull Mardu was a subterfuge."

"Not entirely, your Majesty. I was assured that the city had to be neutralized to permit the passage of the fleet."

"But why is he drowning *my* soldiers? I bear the Alorns no malice."

"Torak does—or so I'm told—and it is Torak who will command the combined armies of Angarak. We cannot allow your forces to land on this continent, your Majesty. We cannot give Torak that advantage."

"Torak is asleep—and he's likely to remain so for a number of years yet."

"Our information indicates that it will not be nearly so long. Belgarath himself is convinced that the time is near at hand."

His eyes narrowed slightly. "I must hand you all over to the Grolims, then," he said. "I'd hoped to wait until Polgara had regained her strength before subjecting her to the journey; but if what you say is true, there is little time to waste. Advise your friends to make their preparations, Princess. You will depart for Thull Zelik tomorrow morning."

"As your Majesty wishes," Ce'Nedra replied, a chill going down her spine as she bowed her head in acquiescence.

"I am a secular man, Princess," he said by way of explanation. "I bow to the altar of Torak when the occasion demands it, but I make no pretence at excessive piety. I will not involve myself in a religious dispute between Belgarath and Zedar, and I most certainly will not stand between Torak and Aldur when they confront each other. I would strongly advise you to follow the same course."

"That decision is not mine to make, your Majesty. My part

in this was decided for me long before I was born."

He looked amused. "The Prophecy, you mean? We Angaraks have one also, Princess, and I don't imagine yours is any more reliable than ours. Prophecy is no more than a trick of the priesthood to maintain its grip on the gullible."

"Then you believe in nothing, my Lord?"

"I believe in my own power. Nothing else makes any sense."

The Grolims who escorted them in easy stages northward across the summer-browned plains of Mishrak ac Thull toward Thull Zelik were coldly proper. Ce'Nedra could not be sure if their behavior was the result of warnings from the Emperor of Mallorea or their fear of Polgara. The stifling heat was past now, and the air smelled faintly of the dusty end of summer. The Thullish plain was dotted with villages, random collections of thatch-roofed cottages and dirt streets. The villagers watched, sullen and afraid, as the priests of Torak rode through the little towns, their faces cold and aloof.

The plain to the west of Thull Zelik was covered with the red tents of the vast staging area that had been erected for the Mallorean army. With the exception of caretaker detachments, however, the huge camp was empty. The troops already in Mishrak ac Thull were with 'Zakath near Thull Mardu, and the steady stream of new arrivals had been quite suddenly cut off.

Thull Zelik itself was like any port town in the world, smelling of salt water, fish, tar, and rotting seaweed. The gray stone buildings were low and squat, almost like the Thulls themselves, and the cobblestoned streets all sloped down to the harbor, which lay in the curve of a broad estuary and faced a somewhat similar harbor on the other side.

"What city is that?" Ce'Nedra curiously asked one of the Grolims as she looked across the dirty water toward the far shore.

"Yar Marak," the black-robed priest answered curtly.

"Ah," she said, remembering now her tedious geography lessons. The two cities, one Thullish, the other Nadrak, faced each other across the estuary at the mouth of the River Cordu, and the boundary between Mishrak ac Thull and Gar og Nadrak ran down the precise center of the river.

"When the Emperor returns from Thull Mardu, I imagine he'll take steps to eradicate that place over there," one of the other Grolims added. "He was not pleased with the behavior of King Drosta on the battlefield, and some chastisement seems in order."

They proceeded directly down a cobbled avenue to the harbor, where but a few ships were moored to the wharves.

"My crew absolutely refuses to put to sea," the Mallorean captain of the ship upon which they were to embark reported to the Grolims. "The Chereks out there are like a pack of wolves, burning and sinking everything afloat."

"The Cherek fleet is farther south," the priest in charge of the detachment of Grolims declared.

"The Cherek fleet is everywhere, revered priest," the captain disagreed. "Two days ago they burned four coastal towns two hundred leagues to the south of here, and yesterday they sank a dozen ships a hundred leagues to the north. You wouldn't believe how fast they can move. They don't even take the time to loot the towns they burn." He shuddered. "They're not men! They're a natural disaster."

"We will set sail within the hour," the Grolim insisted.

"Not unless your priests know how to man oars and handle the rigging," the captain told him. "My men are terrified. They won't sail."

"We'll convince them," the Grolim said darkly. He gave a few orders to his under-priests. An altar was quickly erected on the high stern deck, and a brazier filled with glowing coals was placed to one side of it.

The leader of the Grolims took his place at the altar and began chanting in a deep, hollow voice, his arms raised to the sky. In his right hand he held a gleaming knife. At random, his cohorts selected a sailor and dragged him, screaming and struggling, to the stern deck. As Ce'Nedra watched with horror, he was bent backward across the altar and butchered with an almost casual efficiency. The Grolim who had wielded the knife lifted the dead man's dripping heart. "Behold our offering, Dragon-God of Angarak!" he cried in a great voice, then turned and deposited the heart in the smoking brazier. The heart steamed and sizzled horribly for a moment, then began to blacken and shrivel as the fire consumed it. From the bow of the ship a gong clanged in iron celebration of the sacrifice.

The Grolim at the altar, his bloody hands dripping, turned to confront the ashen-faced sailors crowded amidships. "Our ceremonies will continue until the ship sails," he told them. "Who will be the next to give his heart to our beloved God?"

The ship set sail immediately.

Ce'Nedra, sick with revulsion, turned her face away. She looked at Polgara, whose eyes burned with hatred and who seemed in the grip of an overpowering interior struggle. Ce'Nedra knew her, and she knew that it was only by a tremendous effort of her will that Polgara was able to keep herself from unleashing a terrible retribution on the blood-stained Grolim at the altar. Beside her, protected in the clasp of one of her arms, stood Errand. On the child's face was an expression Ce'Nedra had never seen there before. His look was sad, compassionate, and at the same time filled with a kind of iron-hard resolution, as if, had he but the power, he would destroy every altar to Torak in all the world.

"You will go belowdecks now," one of their Grolim captors told them. "It will be a matter of some days before we reach the shores of boundless Mallorea."

They sailed north, hugging the Nadrak coastline, fearfully ready to run for any beach that offered itself, should Cherek ships appear on the horizon. At a certain point, the Mallorean captain peered about at the empty sea, swallowed hard, and swung his tiller over for the quick, terrified dash across open water to the east.

Once, a day or more out from the Nadrak coast, they saw a dreadful column of thick black smoke rising far to the south, and a day or so farther on they sailed through a sea littered with charred debris where bodies, pale and bloated, bobbed in the dark waves of the eastern sea. The frightened sailors pulled their oars with all their strength, not even needing the encouragement of whips to row faster.

Then, one murky morning when the sky behind them threatened rain squalls and the air was oppressively heavy with the advancing storm, a low, dark smudge appeared on the horizon ahead of them, and the sailors doubled their efforts, rushing desperately toward the safety of the Mallorean coast ahead.

The beach upon which the small boats from their ship landed them was a sloping shingle of dark, salt-crusted gravel where the waves made a strange, mournful sighing as they receded. Awaiting them some distance up from the water's edge sat a mounted party of Grolims, their black robes belted at the waist with crimson sashes.

"Archpriests," Polgara noted coldly. "We're to be escorted with some ceremony, I take it."

The Grolim who had commanded their escort went quickly up the gravel stand toward the waiting group and prostrated himself before them, speaking with a hushed reverence. One of the Archpriests, an aged man with a deeply lined face and sunken eyes, dismounted rather stiffly and came down to where Ce'Nedra and her friends had just stepped from the small boat.

"My Queen," he said to Polgara, bowing respectfully. "I am Urtag, Archpriest of the district of Camat. I am here with my brethren to escort you to the City of Night."

"I'm disappointed not to find Zedar waiting," the sorceress replied coldly. "I trust he's not indisposed."

Urtag gave her a quick look of irritation. "Do not rail against your foreordained fate, Queen of Angarak," he advised her.

"I have two fates awaiting me, Urtag," she said. "Which one I will follow has not yet been decided."

"I do not have any doubts about the matter," he declared.

"That's probably because you've never dared to look at the alternatives," she replied. "Shall we go, Urtag? A windy beach is hardly the place for philosophical discussion."

The Grolim Archpriests had brought horses with them, and the party was soon mounted and riding away from the sea across a line of low, wooded hills in a generally northeasterly direc-

tion. The trees bordering the upper edge of the gravel beach
had been dark-boughed spruces, but once they topped the first
rise they entered a vast forest of white-barked aspens. To
Ce'Nedra's eyes, the stark, white trunks looked almost corpse-
like, and the entire forest had a gloomy, unhealthy quality about
it.

"Mistress Pol," Durnik said in a voice that was scarcely
more than a whisper, "shouldn't we be working on some kind
of plan?"

"For what, Durnik?" she asked him.

"For our escape, of course."

"But we don't want to escape, Durnik."

"We don't?"

"The Grolims are taking us to the place we want to go."

"Why do we want to go to this Cthol Mishrak of theirs?"

"We have something to do there."

"From everything I've heard it's a bad sort of place," he
told her. "Are you sure you haven't made some mistake?"

She reached out and laid her hand on his arm. "Dear Durnik,"
she said, "you'll just have to trust me."

"Of course, Mistress Pol," he replied immediately. "But
shouldn't I know what to expect? If I should have to take steps
to protect you, I ought to be prepared."

"I'd tell you if I knew, Durnik," she said, "but I don't know
what we should expect. All I know is that the four of us are
supposed to go to Cthol Mishrak. What's going to happen there
needs us in order for it to be complete. Each of us has something
to do there."

"Even me?"

"Especially you, Durnik. At first I didn't understand who
you really are. That's why I tried to keep you from coming
along. But now I *do* understand. You have to be there because
you're going to do the one thing that's going to turn the entire
outcome one way or the other."

"What is it?"

"We don't know."

His eyes grew wide. "What if I do it wrong?" he asked in
a worried voice.

"I don't think you can," she reassured him. "From everything I understand, what you're going to do will flow very naturally out of who and what you are." She gave him a brief, wry little smile. "You won't be able to do it wrong, Durnik— any more than you'd be able to lie or cheat or steal. It's built into you to do it right, so don't worry about it."

"That's all very well for you to say, Mistress Pol," he replied, "but if you don't mind, I *will* worry about it just a bit—privately, of course."

She laughed then, a light, fond little laugh. "You dear, dear man," she said impulsively taking his hand. "Whatever would we do without you?"

Durnik blushed and tried to look away, but her glorious eyes held his, and he blushed even more.

After they had passed through the forest of aspen, they entered a strangely desolate landscape. White boulders stuck up out of tangled weeds like tombstones in a long-abandoned graveyard, and dead trees thrust their crooked limbs at the overcast sky like pleading fingers. The horizon ahead was covered with a bank of darker cloud, a cloud so intensely black that it seemed almost purple. Oddly, Ce'Nedra noted, the cloudbank did not seem to be moving at all. There was no sign anywhere of any human habitation, and the route they followed was not even marked by a trail.

"Does no one live there?" the princess asked Polgara.

"Cthol Mishrak is deserted except for a few Grolims," the sorceress replied. "Torak smashed the city and drove its people out the day my father and King Cherek and his sons stole the Orb back from the iron tower."

"When was that?"

"A very long time ago, Ce'Nedra. As nearly as we've been able to determine, it was precisely on the same day that Beldaran and I were born—and the day our mother died. It's a bit hard to say for sure. We were a bit casual about keeping track of time in those days."

"If your mother had died and Belgarath was here, who took care of you?"

"Beldin, of course." Polgara smiled. "He wasn't a very good

mother, but he did the best he could until Father returned."

"Is that why you're so fond of him?"

"One of the reasons, yes."

The ominous cloudbank still did not move. It stretched across the sky as stationary as a range of mountains; as they rode toward it, it loomed higher and higher.

"That's a very strange cloud," Durnik noted, looking speculatively at the thick curtain of purple ahead. "The storm is coming in behind us, but that cloud doesn't seem to be moving at all."

"It doesn't move, Durnik," Polgara told him. "It never has moved. When the Angaraks built Cthol Mishrak, Torak put that cloud there to hide the city. It's been there ever since."

"How long is that?"

"About five thousand years."

"The sun never shines there?"

"Never."

The Grolim Archpriests had begun to look about with a certain apprehension, and finally Urtag called a halt. "We must make ourselves known," he declared. "We don't want the watchers to mistake us for intruders."

The other Archpriests nodded nervously, and then all removed polished steel masks from beneath their robes and carefully covered their faces with them. Then each of them untied a thick torch from his saddle and ignited it with a brief, mumbled incantation. The torches burned with a peculiarly green-tinged flame and gave off a reeking, sulfurous smoke.

"I wonder what would happen if I were to blow out your torches," Polgara suggested with a hint of a mischievous smile. "I could, you know."

Urtag gave her a worried look. "This is no time for foolishness, my Lady," he warned her. "The watchers are very savage with intruders. Our lives depend on those torches. Please don't do anything to bring down a disaster on us all."

She laughed lightly and let it go at that.

As they rode in beneath the cloud, it grew steadily darker. It was not precisely the clean darkness of night, but was rather a kind of dirty murkiness, a deep shade hovering in the air. They crested a rise and saw before them a cloud-enshrouded basin, and in its center, half-obscured by the pervasive gloom, stood the ravaged City of Night. The vegetation around them had shrunk to a few sparse weeds and an unhealthy-looking, stunted grass, pale and sick for want of sun. The boulders thrusting up out of the earth were splotched with a sort of leprous lichen that ate into the rock itself, and nodules of a white fungus lumped in grotesque profusion, spreading out across the dank soil as if the ground itself were diseased.

With a slow, careful pace, their sputtering torches held above their heads, the Grolim Archpriests led the way down into the gloomy basin and across the unwholesome plain toward the shattered walls of Cthol Mishrak.

As they entered the city, the princess saw furtive hints of movement among the tumbled stones. Shadowy forms scurried from place to place among the ruins, and the sound of their movements was the clicking scrape made by creatures whose feet were clawed. Some of the shapes were upright, others were not. Ce'Nedra grew cold and afraid. The watchers of Cthol Mishrak were neither beast nor human, and they seemed to exude a kind of indiscriminate malice toward all other living things. More than anything, she was afraid that one of them might suddenly turn and confront her with a face that might rip away her sanity by its hideousness.

As they passed down a broken street, Urtag began to intone an ancient prayer to Torak, his voice hollow and shaking. The dank air grew colder, and the diseaselike lichen ate at the tumbled stones of the ruined houses. Mold seemed to cling to everything, and the pale fungus grew in grotesque lumps in corners and crannies. The smell of decay was everywhere, a damp, rotten stench, and slimy pools of stagnant water lay among the ruins.

In the center of the city stood the rusted stump of a vast iron tower, the broken-off girders which had supported it thicker than a man's waist. Just to the south of the stump lay a broad, rusted trail of total destruction where the tower had fallen, crushing everything beneath it. Over the eons, the iron had rusted down into a sort of damp red mud that outlined the enormous dimensions of the fallen structure.

The stump had eroded down, the years rounding off the broken edges. The rust mingled in places with a kind of thick black ooze that ran down the faces of the iron plates like gobbets of clotted blood.

Urtag, trembling visibly now, dismounted before a vast, arched portal and led them through a half-open iron door. The echoing chamber they entered was as large as the Imperial throne room in Tol Honeth. Wordlessly, his torch held high over his head, Urtag led them across the pitted floor to another iron-arched doorway and then down a flight of clanging iron steps that reached into the darkness beneath. At the bottom of the stairs, perhaps fifty feet below the wreckage above, stood another door of black iron, studded with great, round rivet-heads. Hesitantly, Urtag rapped his knuckles on the door, and the sound of his rapping echoed hollowly in the chamber beyond.

"Who comes to disturb the slumber of the Dragon-God of Angarak?" a muffled voice demanded from behind the door.

"I am Urtag, the Archpriest of Camat." The Grolim's voice was frightened. "As commanded, I bring the prisoners to the Disciple of Torak."

There was a moment of silence, and then the rattling sound of an immense chain, followed by the grating of an enormous bolt. Then slowly, creakingly, the door opened.

Ce'Nedra gasped. Standing in the doorway was Belgarath! It was a moment before her startled eyes began to sort out the subtle differences that informed her that the white-haired man before her was not indeed the old sorcerer, but rather someone who looked so much like him that they could easily pass for brothers. Subtle though the differences were, they were none-theless profound. In the eyes of the man in the doorway there was a haunted look—a look compounded of grief and horror and a dreadful self-loathing, all overlaid with the helpless ador-ation of a man who has given himself utterly to a dreadful master.

"Welcome to the tomb of the one-eyed God, Polgara," he greeted the sorceress.

"It's been a long time, Belzedar," she replied in an oddly neutral voice.

"I've given up the right to that name," he told her, and his tone was faintly regretful.

"It was your decision, Zedar."

He shrugged. "Perhaps," he said. "Perhaps not. Maybe what I'm doing is also necessary." He pushed the door open wider. "Come inside, if you will. This crypt is habitable—if only barely." He looked directly at Urtag then. "You have performed a service, Urtag, Archpriest of Torak, and a service should not be unrewarded. Come." And he turned and led them back into the vaulted chamber beyond. The walls were of stone, massive blocks set without mortar, and bolted to the topmost tier were great iron arches supporting the ceiling and the immense ruin above. The great chill of masses of cold stone and iron was held off by large, glowing braziers set in each corner. In the center of the room stood a table and several chairs, and along one wall lay a cluster of loosely rolled pallets and a neat stack of gray woolen blankets. On the table stood a pair of large candles, their flame unwinking and steady in the dead air of the tomb.

Zedar paused briefly at the table to pick up one of the candles, then led them across the flagstone floor to an arched alcove set in the far wall. "Your reward, Urtag," he said to the Grolim. "Come and behold the face of your God." He lifted the candle.

Lying upon its back on a stone bier within the alcove lay a huge figure, robed and cowled in black. The face was concealed by a polished steel mask. The eyes of the mask were closed.

Urtag took one terrified look, then prostrated himself on the floor.

There was a deep, rasping sigh, and the recumbent figure in the alcove moved slightly. As Ce'Nedra stared in horrified fascination, the vast, steel-covered face turned restlessly toward them. For a moment the polished left eyelid opened. Behind that eyelid burned the dreadful fire of the eye that was not.

The steel face moved as if it were flesh, twisting into an expression of contempt at the priest groveling on the flagstones, and a hollow murmuring came from behind the polished lips.

Urtag started violently and raised his suddenly stricken face, listening to the hollow muttering which he alone in the dim crypt could hear clearly. The hollow voice continued, murmuring in Urtag's ears. The Archpriest's face drained as he listened, and a look of unspeakable horror slowly twisted his features. The hollow muttering droned on. The words were indistinct, but the inflections were not. Desperately, Ce'Nedra covered her ears.

Finally Urtag screamed and scrambled to his feet. His face had gone absolutely white, and his eyes were starting from their sockets. Gibbering insanely, Urtag fled, and the sound of his screams echoed back down the iron stairway as he ran in terror from the ruined tower.

Chapter Twenty

THE WHISPERING HAD begun almost as soon Belgarath, Silk, and Garion reached the coast of Mallorea. It was indistinct at first, little more than a sibilant breath sounding perpetually in Garion's ears, but in the days that followed as they moved steadily south, occasional words began to emerge. The words were the sort to be reckoned with—home, mother, love, and death—words upon which attention immediately fastened.

Unlike the land of the Morindim which they had left behind, northern-most Mallorea was a land of rolling hills covered with a tough-stemmed, dark green grass. Occasional nameless rivers wound among those hills, roiling and turbulent beneath a lead gray sky. They had not seen the sun for what seemed weeks. A sort of dry overcast had moved in off the Sea of the East, and a stiff breeze, chill and smelling of the polar ice, pressed continually at their backs as they moved south.

Belgarath now rode with extreme caution. There was no sign of that half-doze that was his custom in more civilized

291

parts of the world, and Garion could feel the subtle push of the old man's mind as he probed ahead for any hidden dangers. So delicate was the sorcerer's searching that it seemed only a slowly expiring breath, light, tentative, concealed artfully in the sound of the breeze passing through the tall grass.

Silk also rode warily, pausing frequently to listen, and seeming on occasion to sniff at the air. Often he would even go so far as to dismount and put his ear to the turf, to see if he might pick up the muffled tread of unseen horses approaching.

"Nervous work," the little man said as he remounted after one such pause.

"Better to be a little overcautious than to blunder into something," Belgarath replied. "Did you hear anything?"

"I think I heard a worm crawling around down there," Silk answered brightly. "He didn't say anything, though. You know how, worms are."

"Do you mind?"

"You did ask, Belgarath."

"Oh, shut up!"

"You heard him ask, didn't you, Garion?"

"That is probably the most offensive habit I've ever encountered in anyone," Belgarath told the little thief.

"I know," Silk answered. "That's why I do it. Infuriating, isn't it? How far do we have to go before we come to woods again?"

"Several more days. We're still a goodly distance north of the tree line. Winter's too long and summer too short for trees to grow up here."

"Boring sort of place, isn't it?" Silk observed, looking around at the endless grass and the rounded hills that all looked the same.

"Under the circumstances, I can stand a little boredom. The alternatives aren't all that pleasant."

"I can accept that."

They rode on, their horses wading through the knee-high, gray-green grass.

The whispering inside Garion's head began again. "Hear me, Child of Light." That sentence emerged quite clearly from the rest of the unintelligible sibilance. There was a dreadfully compelling quality in that single statement. Garion concentrated, trying to hear more.

"*I wouldn't do that,*" the familiar dry voice told him.

"*What?*"

"*Don't do what he tells you to do.*"

"*Who is it?*"

"*Torak, of course. Who did you think it was?*"

"*He's awake?*"

"*Not yet. Not fully at any rate—but then he's never been entirely asleep either.*"

"*What's he trying to do?*"

"*He's trying to talk you out of killing him.*"

"*He's not afraid of me, is he?*"

"*Of course he's afraid. He doesn't know what's going to happen any more than you do, and he's just as frightened of you as you are of him.*"

That immediately made Garion feel better. "*What should I do about the way he keeps whispering to me?*"

"*There's not much you can do. Just don't get into the habit of obeying his orders, that's all.*"

They camped that evening as they usually did in a well-sheltered hollow between two hills and, as usual, they built no fire to give away their location.

"I'm getting a bit tired of cold suppers," Silk complained, biting down hard on a piece of dried meat. "This beef's like a strip of old leather."

"The exercise is good for your jaws," Belgarath told him.

"You can be a very unpleasant old man when you set your mind to it, do you know that?"

"The nights are getting longer, aren't they?" Garion said to head off any further wrangling.

"The summer's winding down," Belgarath told him. "It will be autumn up here in another few weeks, and winter will be right on its heels."

"I wonder where we'll be when winter comes," Garion said rather plaintively.

"I wouldn't do that," Silk advised. "Thinking about it isn't going to help, and it's only going to make you nervous."

"Nervouser," Garion corrected. "I'm already nervous."

"Is there such a word as 'nervouser?'" Silk asked Belgarath curiously.

"There is now," Belgarath replied. "Garion just invented it."

"I wish I could invent a word," Silk said admiringly to Garion, his ferretlike little eyes gleaming mischievously.

"Please don't poke fun at me, Silk. I'm having enough trouble as it is."

"Let's get some sleep," Belgarath suggested. "This conversation isn't going anywhere, and we've got a long way to ride tomorrow."

That night the whispering invaded Garion's sleep, and it seemed to convey its meaning in images rather than words. There was an offer of friendship—of a hand outstretched in love. The loneliness that had haunted his boyhood from the moment he had discovered that he was an orphan seemed to fade, to pass somehow behind him with that offer, and he found himself rather desperately wanting to run toward that hand reaching toward him.

Then, very clearly, he saw two figures standing side by side. The figure of the man was very tall and very powerful, and the figure of the woman was so familiar that the very sight of her caught at Garion's heart. The tall, powerful man seemed to be a stranger, and yet was not. His face went far beyond mere human handsomeness. It was quite the most beautiful face Garion had ever seen. The woman, of course, was not a stranger. The white lock at the brow and the glorious eyes were the most familiar things in Garion's life. Side by side, the beautiful stranger and Aunt Pol reached out their arms to him.

"You will be our son," the whispering voice told him. "Our beloved son. I will be your father, and Polgara your mother. This will be no imaginary thing, Child of Light, for I can make all things happen. Polgara will really be your mother, and all of her love will be yours alone; and I, your father, will love and cherish you both. Will you turn away from us and face again the bitter loneliness of the orphan child? Does that chill emptiness compare with the warmth of loving parents? Come to us, Belgarion, and accept our love."

Garion jerked himself out of sleep, sitting bolt upright, trembling and sweating. *"I need help,"* he cried out silently, reaching into the vaults of his mind to find that other, nameless presence.

"What's your problem now?" the dry voice asked him.

"He's cheating," Garion declared, outraged.

"Cheating? Did somebody come along and make up a set of rules while I wasn't watching?"

"You know what I mean. He's offering to make Aunt Pol my mother if I'll do what he says."

"He's lying. He can't alter the past. Ignore him."

"How can I? He keeps reaching into my mind and putting his hand on the most sensitive spots."

"Think about Ce'Nedra. That'll confuse him."

"Ce'Nedra?"

"Every time he tries to tempt you with Polgara, think about your flighty little princess. Remember exactly how she looked when you peeked at her while she was bathing that time back in the Wood of the Dryads."

"I did not peek!"

"Really? How is it that you remember every single detail so vividly, then?"

Garion blushed. He had forgotten that his daydreams were not entirely private.

"Just concentrate on Ce'Nedra. It will probably irritate Torak almost as much as it does me." The voice paused. *"Is that all you can really think about?"* it asked then.

Garion did not try to answer that.

They pushed on southward under the dirty overcast and two days later they reached the first trees, scattered sparsely at the edge of the grassland where great herds of antlered creatures grazed as placidly and unafraid as cattle. As the three of them rode south, the scattered clumps of trees became thicker, and soon spread into a forest of dark-boughed evergreens.

The whispering blandishments of Torak continued, but Garion countered them with thoughts of his red-haired little princess. He could sense the irritation of his enemy each time he intruded these daydreams upon the carefully orchestrated images Torak kept trying to instill in his imagination. Torak wanted him to think of his loneliness and fear and of the possibility of becoming a part of a loving family, but the intrusion of Ce'Nedra into the picture confused and baffled the God. Garion soon perceived that Torak's understanding of men was severely limited. Concerned more with elementals, with those towering compulsions and ambitions which had inflamed him for the endless eons, Torak could not cope with the scattered complexities and conflicting desires that motivated most men. Garion seized on his advantage to thwart the insidious and compelling whispers with which Torak tried to lure him from his purpose.

The whole business was somehow peculiarly familiar. This had happened before—not perhaps in exactly the same way, but very similarly. He sorted through his memories, trying to pin down this strange sense of repetition. It was the sight of a twisted tree stump, lightning-blasted and charred, that suddenly brought it all flooding back in on him. The stump, when seen from a certain angle, bore a vague resemblance to a man on horseback, a dark rider who seemed to watch them as they rode by. Because the sky was overcast, the stump cast no shadow, and the image clicked into place. Throughout his childhood, hovering always on the edge of his vision, Garion had seen the strange, menacing shape of a dark-cloaked rider on a black horse, shadowless even in the brightest sunlight. That had been Asharak the Murgo, of course, the Grolim whom Garion had destroyed in his first open act as a sorcerer. But had it? There had existed between Garion and that dark figure which had so haunted his childhood a strange bond. They had been enemies; Garion had always known that; but in their enmity there had always been a curious closeness, something that seemed to pull them together. Garion quite deliberately began to examine a startling possibility. Suppose that the dark rider had *not* in fact been Asharak—or if it had been, suppose that Asharak had somehow been suffused by another, more powerful awareness.

The more he thought about it, the more convinced Garion became that he had stumbled inadvertantly across the truth of the matter. Torak had demonstrated that, even though his body slept, his awareness could still move about the world, twisting events to his own purposes. Asharak had been involved, certainly, but the dominating force had always been the consciousness of Torak. The Dark God had stood watch over him since infancy. The fear he had sensed in that dark shape that had hovered always on the edge of his boyhood had not been Asharak's fear, but Torak's. Torak had known who he was from the beginning, had known that one day Garion would take up the sword of the Rivan King and come to the meeting that had been ordained since before the world was made.

Acting upon a sudden impulse, Garion put his left hand inside his tunic and took hold of his amulet. Twisting slightly, he reached up and laid the marked palm of his right hand on the Orb, which stood on the pommel of the great sword strapped across his back.

"*I know you now,*" he declared silently, hurling the thought at the murky sky. "*You might as well give up trying to win me over to your side, because I'm not going to change my mind. Aunt Pol is not your wife, and I'm not your son. You'd better stop trying to play games with my thoughts and get ready, because I'm coming to kill you.*"

The Orb beneath his hand flared with a sudden exultation as Garion threw his challenge into the Dark God's teeth, and the sword at Garion's back suddenly burst into a blue flame that flickered through the sheath enclosing it.

There was a moment of deadly silence, and then what had been a whisper suddenly became a vast roar. "*Come, then, Belgarion, Child of Light,*" Torak hurled back the challenge. "*I await thee in the City of Night. Bring all thy will and all thy courage with thee, for I am ready for our meeting.*"

"What in the name of the seven Gods do you think you're doing?" Belgarath almost screamed at Garion, his face mottled with angry astonishment.

"Torak's been whispering at me for almost a week now," Garion explained calmly, taking his hand from the Orb. "He's been offering me all kinds of things if I'd give up this whole idea. I got tired of it, so I told him to stop."

Belgarath spluttered indignantly, waving his hands at Garion.

"He knows I'm coming, Grandfather," Garion said, trying to placate the infuriated old man. "He's known who I was since the day I was born. He's been watching me all this time. We're not going to be able to take him by surprise, so why try? I wanted to let him know that I was on to him. Maybe it's time for *him* to start worrying and being afraid just a little bit, too."

Silk was staring at Garion. "He's an Alorn, all right," he observed finally.

"He's an idiot!" Belgarath snapped angrily. He turned back to Garion. "Did it ever occur to you that there might be something out here to worry about besides Torak?" he demanded.

Garion blinked.

"Cthol Mishrak is *not* unguarded, you young blockhead. You've just succeeded in announcing our presence to every Grolim within a hundred leagues."

"I didn't think of that," Garion mumbled.

"I didn't think you'd thought. Sometimes I don't think you know *how* to think."

Silk looked around apprehensively. "Now what do we do?" he asked.

"We'd better get out of here—as fast as our horses can carry us," Belgarath said. He glared at Garion. "Are you sure you don't have a trumpet somewhere under your clothes?" he asked with heavy sarcasm. "Maybe you'd like to blow a few fanfares as we go along." He shook his head in disgust and then gathered up his reins. "Let's ride," he said.

Chapter Twenty-One

THE ASPENS WERE stark white and motionless under the dead sky, and they rose, straight and slender, like the bars of an interminable cage. Belgarath led them at a walk, carefully weaving his way through the endless stretches of this vast, silent forest.

"How much farther?" Silk asked the old man tensely.

"Not much more than a day, now," Belgarath replied. "The clouds ahead are getting thicker."

"You say the cloudbank never moves?"

"Never. It's been stationary since Torak put it there."

"What if a wind came along? Wouldn't that move it?"

Belgarath shook his head. "The normal rules have been suspended in that region. For all I know, the cloud might not actually be cloud. It might be something else."

"Like what?"

"An illusion of some kind, perhaps. The Gods are very good at illusions."

"Are they looking for us? The Grolims, I mean."

Belgarath nodded.

"Are you taking steps to keep them from finding us?"

"Naturally." The old man looked at him. "Why this sudden urge for conversation? You've been talking steadily for the last hour."

"I'm a little edgy," Silk admitted. "This is unfamiliar territory, and that always makes me nervous. I'm much more comfortable when I've got my escape routes worked out in advance."

"Are you always ready to run?"

"In my profession you have to be. What was that?"

Garion heard it too. Faintly, somewhere far off behind them, there was a deep-toned baying—one animal at first, but soon joined by several others. "Wolves?" he suggested.

Belgarath's face had grown bleak. "No," he replied, "not wolves." He shook his reins, and his nervous horse began to trot, the sound of its hoofs muffled by the rotting loam lying thick beneath the aspens.

"What is it then, Grandfather?" Garion asked, also pushing his horse into a trot.

"Torak's Hounds," Belgarath replied tersely.

"Dogs?"

"Not really. They're Grolims—rather specialized ones. When the Angaraks built the city, Torak decided that he needed something to guard the surrounding countryside. Certain Grolims volunteered to take on nonhuman shapes. The change was permanent."

"I've dealt with watchdogs before," Silk said confidently.

"Not like these. Let's see if we can outrun them." Belgarath didn't sound very hopeful.

They pushed their horses into a gallop, weaving in and out among the tree trunks. The limbs slapped against their faces as they rode, and Garion raised his arm to ward them off as the three of them plunged on.

They crested a low ridge and galloped down the far side. The baying behind them seemed to be closer now.

Then Silk's horse stumbled, and the little man was almost thrown from his saddle. "This isn't working, Belgarath," he said as the old man and Garion reined in. "This ground's too treacherous for us to keep this pace."

Belgarath held up his hand and listened for a moment. The deep-toned baying was definitely closer. "They're outrunning us anyway," the old man agreed.

"You'd better think of something," Silk said, looking back nervously.

"I'm working on it." Belgarath raised his face to sniff at the air. "Let's keep going. I just got a whiff of stagnant water. The area's dotted with swampy places. We might be able to hide our scent if we can get into a big enough patch of water."

They moved on down the slope toward the bottom of the valley. The odor of standing water grew steadily stronger as they rode.

"Just ahead." Garion pointed toward a patch of brown water intermittently visible among the white tree trunks.

The swamp was quite extensive, a broad patch of reeking, oily water trapped in the bottom of a thickly grown basin. Dead trees thrust up out of the water, their leafless branches seeming almost like clawed hands reaching up in mute supplication to the indifferent sky.

Silk wrinkled his nose. "It stinks bad enough to hide our scent from almost anything," he said.

"We'll see," Belgarath replied. "This would probably throw off an ordinary dog, but don't forget that the Hounds are really Grolims. They have the ability to reason, so they won't be relying on scent alone."

They pushed their reluctant horses into the murky water and began to splash along, changing direction frequently, weaving in and out among the dead tree trunks. Their horses' hoofs stirred up rotting vegetation from the bottom, filling the air with an even more powerful stench.

The sound of the baying Hounds drew closer, filled now with an excitement and a terrible hunger.

"I think they've hit the edge of the swamp," Silk said, cocking his head to listen.

There was a momentary bafflement in the baying behind them.

"Grandfather!" Garion cried, reining in sharply.

Directly before them, knee-deep in the brown water stood a slavering black dog-shape. It was enormous—fully as large as a horse, and its eyes actually burned with a malevolent green fire. Its front shoulders and chest were massive, and the fangs protruding from its mouth were at least a foot long, curving down cruelly and dripping foam.

"We have you now," it growled, seeming almost to chew on the words as it twisted its muzzle into speech. The voice issuing from its mouth was a rasping, tearing sound.

Silk's hand instantly flashed toward one of his hidden daggers.

"Never mind," Belgarath told him. "It's only a projection—a shadow."

"It can do that?" Silk's tone was startled.

"I told you that they're Grolims."

"We hunger," the fiery-eyed Hound rumbled. "I will return soon with my pack-mates, and we will feed on man-meat." Then the shape flickered and vanished.

"They know where we are now." Silk's voice was alarmed. "You'd better do something, Belgarath. Can't you use sorcery?"

"That would just pinpoint our location. There are other things out there as well as the Hounds."

"I'd say we'll have to chance it. Let's worry about one thing at a time. Did you see those teeth?"

"They're coming," Garion said tensely. From far back in the swamp, he could clearly hear the sound of splashing.

"Do something, Belgarath!"

The sky overhead had grown darker, and the air seemed suddenly oppressively heavy. From far off there was an angry mutter of thunder. A vast sigh seemed to pass through the forest.

"Keep going," Belgarath said, and they splashed off through the slimy brown water toward the far side of the swamp. The aspen trees on the solid ground ahead of them quite suddenly turned the silvery undersides of their leaves upward, and it was almost as if a great, pale wave had shuddered through the forest.

The Hounds were very close now, and their baying was triumphant as they plunged through the oily, reeking swamp.

And then there was a brilliant blue-white flash, and a shattering clap of thunder. The sky ripped open above them. With a sound nearly as loud as the thunder, they were engulfed in a sudden deluge. The wind howled, ripping away the aspen leaves in great sheets and whirling them through the air. The rain drove horizontally before the sudden gale, churning the swamp to froth and obliterating everything more than a few feet away.

"Did you do this?" Silk shouted at Belgarath.

But Belgarath's stunned face clearly said that the storm was as much a surprise to him as to Silk. They both turned to look at Garion. "Did you do it?" Belgarath demanded.

"He didn't. I did." The voice which came from Garion's mouth was not his. "I've labored too long at this to be thwarted by a pack of dogs."

"I didn't hear a thing," Belgarath marveled, wiping at his streaming face. "Not even a whisper."

"You were listening at the wrong time," the voice of Garion's inner companion replied. "I set it in motion early last spring. It's just now getting here."

"You knew we'd need it?"

"Obviously. Turn east. The Hounds won't be able to track you in all this. Swing around and come at the city from the east side. There are fewer watchers on that flank."

The downpour continued, punctuated by ripping claps of thunder and flashes of lightning.

"How long will the rain last?" Belgarath shouted over the noise.

"Long enough. It's been building in the Sea of the East for a week. It hit the coast this morning. Turn east."

"Can we talk as we ride?" Belgarath asked. "I have a great many questions."

"This is hardly the time for discussion, Belgarath. You have to hurry. The others arrived at Cthol Mishrak this morning, just ahead of the storm. Everything's ready there, so move."

"It's going to be *tonight?*"

"It will, if you get there in time. Torak's almost awake now. I think you'd better be there when he opens his eyes."

Belgarath wiped his streaming face again, and his eyes had a worried look. "Let's go," he said sharply and he led them splashing off through the driving rain to solid ground.

The rain continued for several hours, driven before a screaming wind. Sodden, miserable, and half-blinded by flying leaves and twigs, the three of them cantered toward the east. The baying of the Hounds trapped in the swamp faded behind them, taking on a baffled, frustrated note as the thunderous deluge obliterated all scents from the swamp and the forest.

When night fell, they had reached a low range of hills far to the east, and the rain had subsided into a steady, unpleasant drizzle, punctuated by periodic squalls of chilly, gusting wind and erratic downpours that swept in randomly off the Sea of the East.

"Are you sure you know the way?" Silk asked Belgarath.

"I can find it," Belgarath said grimly. "Cthol Mishrak's got a peculiar smell to it."

The rain slackened into a few scattered droplets pattering on the leaves overhead and died out entirely by the time they reached the edge of the wood. The smell of which Belgarath had spoken was not a sharp reek, but rather was a muted, dank compound of odors. Damp rust seemed to be a major part of it, although the reek of stagnant water was also present, and the musty scent of fungus. The overall effect was one of decay. When they reached the last of the trees, Belgarath reined in. "Well, there it is," he said in a quiet voice.

The basin before them was faintly illuminated by a kind of pale, sickly radiance that seemed to emanate from the ground itself, and in the center of that large depression reared the jagged, broken remains of the city.

"What's that strange light?" Garion whispered tensely.

Belgarath grunted. "Phosphorescence. It comes from the fungus that grows everywhere out there. The sun never shines on Cthol Mishrak, so it's a natural breeding ground for unwholesome things that grow in the dark. We'll leave the horses here." He dismounted.

"Is that a very good idea?" Silk asked him as he too swung down from his saddle. "We might want to leave in a hurry." The little man was still wet and shivering.

"No," Belgarath said calmly. "If things go well, nothing in the city's going to be interested in giving us any trouble. If things don't go well, it's not going to matter anyway."

"I don't like unalterable commitments," Silk muttered sourly.

"You picked the wrong journey, then," Belgarath replied. "What we're about to do is just about as unalterable as things ever get. Once we start, there won't be any possible way to turn back."

"I still don't have to like it, do I? What now?"

"Garion and I are going to change into something a bit less conspicuous. You're an expert at moving about in the dark without being seen or heard, but we aren't that skilled at it."

"You're going to use sorcery—*this* close to Torak?" Silk asked him incredulously.

"We're going to be very quiet about it," Belgarath assured him. "A shape-change is directed almost entirely inward, so there isn't that much noise involved anyway." He turned to Garion. "We're going to do it slowly," he said. "That spreads out what little sound there is and makes it even fainter. Do you understand?"

"I think so, Grandfather."

"I'll go first. Watch me." The old man glanced at their horses. "Let's move away a bit. Horses are afraid of wolves. We don't want them to get hysterical and start crashing around."

They crept along the edge of the trees until they were some distance from the horses.

"This ought to be far enough," Belgarath said. "Now watch." He concentrated for a moment, and then his form began to shimmer and blur. The change-over was very gradual, and for several moments his face and the wolf's face seemed to coexist in the same place. The sound it made was only the faintest of whispers. Then it was done, and the great silver wolf sat on his haunches.

"Now you do it," he told Garion with the slight change of expression that is so much a part of the speech of wolves.

Garion concentrated very hard, holding the shape firmly in his mind. He did it so slowly that it seemed that he could actually feel the fur growing on his body.

Silk had been rubbing dirt on his face and hands to reduce the visibility of his skin. He looked at the two wolves, his eyes questioning.

Belgarath nodded once and led the way out onto the bare earth of the basin that sloped down toward the rotting ruins of Cthol Mishrak.

There were other shapes moving in the faint light, prowling, snuffling. Some of the shapes had a dog smell to them; others smelled faintly reptilian. Grolims, robed and cowled, stood watch on various hummocks and rocks, searching the darkness with their eyes and their minds for intruders.

The earth beneath Garion's paws felt dead. There was no growth, no life on this wasted heath. With Silk crouched low between them, the two wolves crept, belly low, toward the ruin, taking full advantage of rocky outcrops and eroded gullies. Their pace seemed excruciatingly slow to Garion, but Belgarath paid little attention to the passage of time. Occasionally, when they passed near one of the watching Grolims, they moved but one paw at a time. The minutes dragged by as they crept closer and closer to the broken City of Night.

Near the shattered wall, two of the hooded priests of Torak stood in quiet conversation. Their muted voices fell clearly upon Garion's intensely sharpened ears.

"The Hounds seem nervous tonight," one of them said.

"The storm," the other replied. "Bad weather always makes them edgy."

"I wonder what it's like to be a Hound," the first Grolim mused.

"If you like, perhaps they'll let you join them."

"I don't think I'm *that* curious."

Silk and the two wolves, moving as silently as smoke, passed no more than ten yards from the two idly chatting guards, and crept over the fallen stones into the dead City of Night. Once among the ruins, they were able to move faster. The shadows concealed their movements, and they flitted among the blasted stones in Belgarath's wake, moving steadily toward the center of the city where the stump of the iron tower now reared stark and black toward the murky sky.

The reek of rust, stagnation, and decay was much stronger, coming to Garion's wolf-sharp nose in almost overpowering waves. It was a gagging smell, and he clamped his muzzle shut and tried not to think about it.

"Who's there?" a voice came sharply from just ahead of them. A Grolim with a drawn sword stepped out into the rubble-strewn street, peering intently into the deep shadows where the three crouched, frozen into immobility. Garion sensed rather than heard or saw Silk's slow, deliberate reach toward the dagger sheathed at the back of his neck. Then the little man's arm swung sharply down, and his knife made a fluttering whistle as it sped with deadly accuracy, turning end for end as it flew.

The Grolim grunted, doubling over sharply, then he sighed and toppled forward, his sword clanging as it fell.

"Let's move!" Silk ran past the huddled form of the dead Grolim sprawled on the stones.

Garion smelled fresh blood as he loped past, and the smell brought a sudden, hot taste to his mouth.

They reached the massive tangle of twisted girders and crumpled plates that had been the iron tower and crept silently through the open doorway into the total blackness of the chamber within. The smell of rust was everywhere now; coupled with it was a smell of ancient, brooding evil. Garion stopped, sniffing nervously at the tainted air, feeling his hackles rising on his ruffed neck. With an effort, he suppressed the low growl that rose involuntarily in his throat.

He felt Belgarath's shoulder brush him and he followed the old wolf, guided now by scent alone in the utter blackness. At the far end of the huge, empty, iron room there was another doorway.

Belgarath stopped, and Garion felt again that faint brushing whisper as the old man slowly shifted back into the shape of a man. Garion clenched in his own will and let himself gradually flow back into his own form.

Silk was breathing a string of colorful curses, fervent but almost inaudible.

"What's the matter?" Belgarath whispered.

"I forgot to stop for my knife," Silk replied, grating his teeth together. "It's one of my favorites."

"What now, Grandfather?" Garion asked, his whisper hoarse.

"Just beyond this door, there's a flight of stairs leading down."

"What's at the bottom?"

"A cellar. It's a sort of tomb where Zedar's got Torak's body. Shall we go down?"

Garion sighed, then squared his shoulders. "I guess that's what we came for," he replied.

Chapter Twenty-Two

"You don't actually believe I'll accept that, do you, Zedar?"

Garion froze in the act of putting his hand on the iron door at the foot of the stairs.

"You can't evade your responsibility with the pretence of necessity," the voice beyond the door continued.

"Aren't we all driven by necessity, Polgara?" a stranger's voice replied with a kind of weary sadness. "I won't say that I was blameless, but wasn't my apostacy predestined? The universe has been divided against itself since the beginning of time, and now the two Prophecies rush toward each other for their final meeting when all will be resolved. Who can say that what I have done was not essential to that meeting?"

"That's an evasion, Zedar," Aunt Pol told him.

"What's *she* doing here?" Garion whispered to Belgarath.

"She's supposed to be here," Belgarath whispered back with an odd note of satisfaction. "Listen."

"I don't think we'll gain anything by wrangling with each

other, Polgara," Zedar the Apostate was saying. "We each believe that what we did was right. Neither of us could ever persuade the other to change sides at this point. Why don't we just let it go at that?"

"Very well, Zedar," Aunt Pol replied coolly.

"What now?" Silk breathed.

"There should be others in there, too," Belgarath answered softly. "Let's make sure before we go bursting in."

The iron door in front of them did not fit tightly, and faint light seeped through the cracks around the frame. Garion could make out Belgarath's intent face in that dim light.

"How's your father?" Zedar asked in a neutral tone.

"About the same as always. He's very angry with you, you know."

"That was to be expected, I suppose."

"He's finished eating, Lady Polgara," Garion heard Ce'Nedra say. He looked sharply at Belgarath, but the old man put one finger to his lips.

"Spread one of those pallets out for him, dear," Aunt Pol instructed, "and cover him with some blankets. It's very late, and he's sleepy."

"I'll do that," Durnik offered.

"Good," Belgarath breathed. "They're all here."

"How did they get here?" Silk whispered.

"I haven't the faintest idea, and I'm not going to worry about it. The important thing is that they're here."

"I'm glad you were able to rescue him from Ctuchik," Zedar said. "I grew rather fond of him during the years we spent together."

"Where did you find him?" Aunt Pol asked. "We've never been able to pin down what country he's from."

"I forgot precisely," Zedar answered, and his voice was faintly troubled. "Perhaps it was Camaar or Tol Honeth—or maybe some city on the other side of Mallorea. The details keep slipping away from me—almost as if I weren't supposed to examine them too closely."

"Try to remember," she said. "It might be important."

Zedar sighed. "If it amuses you," he said. He paused as if

thinking. "I'd grown restless for some reason," he began. "It was—oh, fifty or sixty years ago. My studies no longer interested me, and the bickering of the various Grolim factions began to irritate me. I took to wandering about—not really paying much attention to where I was. I must have crossed and crisscrossed the Kingdoms of the West and the Angarak Kingdoms a half-dozen times in those years.

"Anyway, I was passing through some city somewhere when the idea struck me all at once. We all know that the Orb will destroy anyone who touches it with the slightest trace of evil in his heart, but what would it do to someone who touched it in total innocence? I was stunned by the simplicity of the idea. The street I was on was full of people, and I needed quiet to consider this remarkable idea, so I turned a corner into some forgotten alley, and there the child was—almost as if he'd been waiting for me. He seemed to be about two years old at the time—old enough to walk and not much more. I held out my hand to him and said, 'I have a little errand for you, my boy.' He came to me and repeated the word, 'Errand.' It's the only word I've ever heard him say."

"What did the Orb do when he first touched it?" Aunt Pol asked him.

"It flickered. In some peculiar way it seemed to recognize him, and something seemed to pass between them when he laid his hand on it." He sighed. "No, Polgara, I don't know who the child is—or even what he is. For all I know, he may even be an illusion. The idea to use him in the first place came to me so suddenly that I sometimes wonder if perhaps it was placed in my mind. It's entirely possible, I suppose, that I didn't find *him*, but that he found *me*." He fell silent again.

There was a long pause on the other side of the iron door.

"Why, Zedar?" Aunt Pol asked him very quietly. "Why did you betray our Master?" Her voice was strangely compassionate.

"To save the Orb," he replied sadly. "At least, at first that was the idea. From the moment I first saw it, it owned me. After Torak took it from our Master, Belgarath and the others began making their plans to regain it by force, but I knew that if Aldur himself did not join his hand with theirs to strike directly at Torak, they would fail—and Aldur would not do that. I reasoned that if force must fail, then guile might succeed. I thought that by pretending allegiance to Torak, I might gain his confidence and steal it back from him."

"What happened, Zedar?" Her question was very direct.

There was another long, painful pause.

"Oh, Polgara!" Zedar's voice came in a strangled sob. "You cannot know! I was so sure of myself—so certain that I could keep a part of my mind free from Torak's domination—but I was wrong—wrong! His mind and will overwhelm me. He took me in his hand and he crushed out all of my resistance. The touch of his hand, Polgara!" There was horror in Zedar's voice. "It reaches down into the very depths of your soul. I know Torak for what he is—loathesome, twisted, evil beyond your understanding of the word—but when he calls me, I must go; and what he bids me do, I must do—even though my soul shrieks within me against it. Even now, as he sleeps, his fist is around my heart." There was another hoarse sob.

"Didn't you know that it's impossible to resist a God?" Aunt Pol asked in that same compassionate voice. "Was it pride, Zedar? Were you so sure of your power that you thought you could trick him—that you could conceal your intention from him?"

Zedar sighed. "Perhaps," he admitted. "Aldur was a gentle Master. He never brought his mind down on me, so I was not prepared for what Torak did to me. Torak is not gentle. What he wants, he takes—and if he must rip out your soul in the taking, it does not matter to him in the slightest. You'll discover his power, Polgara. Soon he'll awaken and he'll destroy Belgarion. Not even the Rivan King is a match for that awful mind. And then Torak will take you as his bride—as he has always said he would. Don't resist him, Polgara. Save yourself that agony. In the end, you'll go to him anyway. You'll go willingly—even eagerly."

There was a sudden scraping sound in the room beyond the iron door, and a quick rush of feet.

"Durnik!" Aunt Pol cried sharply. "No!"

"What's happening?" Garion demanded of Belgarath.

"*That's* what it means!" Belgarath gasped. "Get that door open!"

"Get back, you fool!" Zedar was shouting.

There was a sudden crash, the sound of bodies locked in struggle smashing into furniture.

"I warn you," Zedar cried again. "Get back!"

There was the sharp sound of a blow, of a fist striking solid bone.

"Zedar!" Belgarath roared, yanking at the iron door.

Then within the room there was a thunderous detonation.

"Durnik!" Aunt Pol shrieked.

In a sudden burst of fury, Belgarath raised his clenched hand, joined his flaming will with his arm and drove his fist at the locked door. The massive force of his blow ripped the iron door from its hinges as if it had been no more than paper.

The room beyond had a vaulted, curved ceiling supported by great iron girders, black with age. Garion seemed to see everything in the room at once with a curious kind of detachment, as if all emotion had been drained from him. He saw Ce'Nedra and Errand clinging to each other in fright beside one wall. Aunt Pol was standing as if locked in place, her eyes wide as she stared in stunned disbelief at the still form of Durnik the smith, who lay crumpled on the floor, and whose face had that deadly pale cast to it that could only mean one thing. A terrible flood of realization suddenly swept her face—a realization of an irrevocable loss. "No!" she cried out. "My Durnik— No!" She rushed to the fallen man, fell on her knees beside him and gathered his still form into her arms with a heartbroken wail of grief and despair.

And then Garion saw Zedar the Apostate for the first time. The sorcerer was also staring at Durnik's body. There was a desperate regret on his face—a knowledge that he had finally committed the one act that forever put him past all hope of redemption. "You fool," he muttered. "Why? Why did you make me kill you? That's the one thing above all others I didn't want to do."

Then Belgarath, as inexorable as death itself, lunged through the shattered remains of the door and rushed upon the man he had once called brother.

Zedar flinched back from the old sorcerer's awful rage. "I didn't mean to do it, Belgarath," he quavered, his hands raised to ward off Belgarath's rush. "The fool tried to attack me. He was—"

"You—" Belgarath grated at him from between teeth clenched with hate. "You—you—" But he was past speech. No word could contain his rage. He raised both arms and struck at Zedar's face with his fists. Zedar reeled back, but Belgarath was upon him, grappling, pounding at him with his hands.

Garion could feel flickers of will from one or the other of them; but caught up in emotions so powerful that they erased thought, neither was coherent enough to focus the force within him. And so, like two tavern brawlers, they rolled on the floor, kicking, gouging, pounding at each other, Belgarath consumed with fury and Zedar with fear and chagrin.

Desperately, the Apostate jerked a dagger from the sheath at his waist, and Belgarath seized his wrist in both hands and pounded it on the floor until the knife went skittering away. Then each struggled to reach the dagger, clawing and jerking at each other, their faces frozen into intense grimaces as each strove to reach the dagger first.

At some point during the frenzied seconds when they had burst into the room, Garion had, unthinking, drawn the great sword from its sheath across his back, but the Orb and the blade were cold and unresponsive in his hand as he stood watching the deadly struggle between the two sorcerers.

Belgarath's hands were locked about Zedar's throat, and Zedar, strangling, clawed desperately at the old man's arms. Belgarath's face was contorted into an animal snarl, his lips drawn back from clenched teeth as he throttled his ancient enemy. As if finally driven past all hope of sanity, he struggled to his feet, dragging Zedar up with him. Holding the Apostate by the throat with one hand, he began to rain blows on him with the other. Then, between one blow and the next, he swung his arm down and pointed at the stones beneath their feet. With a dreadful grinding, a great crack appeared, zigzagging across the floor. The rocks shrieked in protest as the crack widened. Still struggling, the two men toppled and fell into the yawning fissure. The earth seemed to shudder. With a terrible sound, the crack ground shut.

Incredulously, his mouth suddenly agape, Garion stared in stunned disbelief at the scarcely discernible crack through which the two men had fallen.

Ce'Nedra screamed, her hands going to her face in horror.

"Do something!" Silk shouted at Garion, but Garion could only stare at him in blank incomprehension.

"Polgara!" Silk said desperately, turning to Aunt Pol. Still incapacitated by her sudden, overwhelming grief, she could not respond, but knelt with Durnik's lifeless body in her arms, weeping uncontrollably as she rocked back and forth, holding him tightly against her.

From infinitely far beneath there was a sullen detonation, and then another. Even in the bowels of the earth, the deadly struggle continued.

As if compelled, Garion's eyes sought out the embrasure in the far wall; there in the dim light he could make out the recumbent form of Kal Torak. Strangely emotionless, Garion stared at the form of his enemy, meticulously noting every detail. He saw the black robe and the polished mask. And he saw Cthrek Goru, Torak's great black sword.

Although he did not—could not—move or even feel, a struggle, nonetheless, raged inside him—a struggle perhaps even more dreadful than that which had just plunged Belgarath and Zedar into the depths of the earth. The two forces which had first diverged and then turned and rushed at each other down the endless corridors of time had finally met within him. The EVENT which was the ultimate conclusion of the two Prophecies, had begun, and its first skirmishes were taking place within Garion's mind. Minute and very subtle adjustments were shifting some of his most deeply ingrained attitudes and perceptions.

Torak moved, stirring restlessly, as those same two forces met within *him*.

Dreadful flashes of the sleeping God's mind assailed Garion,

and he saw clearly the terrible subterfuge that lay behind Torak's offer of friendship and love. Had his fear of their duel
drawn him into yielding, fully half of creation would have
shimmered and vanished. More than that, what Torak had offered was not love but an enslavement so vile that it was beyond
imagining.

But he had not yielded. He had somehow evaded the overwhelming force of Torak's mind and had placed himself utterly
in the hands of the Prophecy that had drawn him here. With
an absolute denial of self, he had become the instrument of the
Prophecy. He was no longer afraid. Sword in hand, the Child
of Light awaited the moment when the Prophecy would release
him to join in deadly struggle with the Dark God.

Then, even as Silk desperately tried to arouse either Garion
or Polgara to action, the stones of the floor buckled upward,
and Belgarath rose from the earth.

Garion, still abstracted and bemused, saw that all traces of
the sometimes foolish old man he had known before were gone.
The thieving old storyteller had vanished. Even the irritable
old man who had led the quest for the Orb no longer existed.
In their place stood the form of Belgarath the sorcerer, the
Eternal Man, shimmering in the aura of his full power.

Chapter Twenty-Three

"WHERE IS ZEDAR?" Aunt Pol asked, raising her tear-streaked face from Durnik's lifeless body to stare with a dreadful intensity at her father.

"I left him down there," Belgarath replied bleakly.

"Dead?"

"No."

"Bring him back."

"Why?"

"To face me." Her eyes burned.

The old man shook his head. "No, Pol," he said to her. "You've never killed anyone. Let's leave it that way."

She gently lowered Durnik's body to the floor and rose to her feet, her pale face twisted with grief and an awful need. "Then *I* will go to him," she declared, raising both arms as if to strike at the earth beneath her feet.

"No," Belgarath told her, extending his own hand, "you will *not*."

They stood facing each other, locked in a dreadful, silent

struggle. Aunt Pol's look at first was one of annoyance at her father's interference. She raised one arm again to bring the force of her will crashing down at the earth, but once again Belgarath put forth his hand.

"Let me go, father."

"No."

She redoubled her efforts, twisting as if trying to free herself from his unseen restraint. "Let me go, old man," she cried.

"No. Don't do this, Pol. I don't want to hurt you."

She tried again, more desperately this time, but once again Belgarath smothered her will with his. His face hardened, and he set his jaw.

In a last effort, she flung the whole force of her mind against the barrier he had erected. Like some great rock, however, the old man remained firm. Finally her shoulders slumped, and she turned, knelt beside Durnik's body, and began to weep again.

"I'm sorry, Pol," he said gently. "I never wanted to have to do that. Are you all right?"

"How can you ask that?" she demanded brokenly, wringing her hands over Durnik's silent body.

"That's not what I meant."

She turned her back on him and buried her face in her hands.

"I don't think you could have reached him anyway, Pol," the old man told her. "You know as well as I that what one of us does, another cannot undo."

Silk, his ferretlike face shocked, spoke in a hushed voice. "What did you do to him?"

"I took him down until we came to solid rock. And then I sealed him up in it."

"Can't he just come up out of the earth the way you did?"

"No. That's impossible for him now. Sorcery is thought, and no man can exactly duplicate the thought of another. Zedar's imprisoned inside the rock forever—or until I choose to free him." The old man looked mournfully at Durnik's body. "And I don't think I'll chose to do that."

"He'll die, won't he?" Silk asked.

Belgarath shook his head. "No. That was part of what I did

to him. He'll lie inside the rock until the end of days."

"That's monstrous, Belgarath," Silk said in a sick voice.

"So was that," Belgarath replied grimly, pointing at Durnik.

Garion could hear what they were saying and could see them all quite clearly, but it seemed somehow that they were actually someplace else. The others in the underground crypt seemed to be on the periphery of his attention. For him there was only one other in the vaulted chamber, and that o er was Kal Torak, his enemy.

The restless stirring of the drowsing God became more evident. Garion's peculiarly multiple awareness—in part his own, in part derived from the Orb, and as ever overlaid by the consciousness which he had always called the dry voice in his mind—perceived in that stirring the pain that lay beneath the maimed God's movements. Torak was actually writhing as he half-slept. An injured man would heal in time, and his pain would gradually diminish and ultimately disappear, because injury was a part of the human condition. A man was born to be hurt from time to time, and the mechanism for recovery was born with him. A God, on the other hand, was invulnerable, and he had no need for the ability to heal. Thus it was with Torak. The fire which the Orb had loosed upon him when he had used it to crack the world still seared his flesh, and his pain had not diminished in the slightest down through all the endless centuries since his maiming. Behind that steel mask, the flesh of the Dragon-God's face still smoked, and his burned eye still boiled endlessly in its socket. Garion shuddered, almost pitying that perpetual agony.

The child, Errand, pulled himself free from Ce'Nedra's trembling arms and crossed the flagstone floor of the tomb, his small face intent. He stopped, bent and put his hand on Durnik's shoulder. Gently he shook the dead man as if trying to wake him. His little face became puzzled when the smith did not respond. He shook again, a bit harder, his eyes uncomprehending.

"Errand," Ce'Nedra called to him, her voice breaking, "come back. There's nothing we can do."

Errand looked at her, then back at Durnik. Then he gently

patted the smith's shoulder with a peculiar little gesture, sighed, and went back to the princess. She caught him suddenly in her arms and began to weep, burying her face against his small body. Once again with that same curious little gesture, he patted her flaming hair.

Then from the alcove in the far wall there came a long, rasping sigh, a shuddering expiration of breath. Garion looked sharply toward the alcove, his hand tightening on the hilt of his cold sword. Torak had turned his head, and his eyes were open. The hideous fire burned in the eye that was not as the God came awake.

Belgarath drew in his breath in a sharp hiss as Torak raised the charred stump of his left hand as if to brush away the last of his sleep, even as his right hand groped for the massive hilt of Cthrek Goru, his black sword. "Garion!" Belgarath said sharply.

But Garion, still locked in stasis by the forces focusing upon him, could only stare at the awakening God. A part of him struggled to shake free, and his hand trembled as he fought to lift his sword.

"*Not yet,*" the voice whispered.

"Garion!" Belgarath actually shouted this time. Then, in a move seemingly born of desperation, the old sorcerer lunged past the bemused young man to fling himself upon the still recumbent form of the Dark God.

Torak's hand released the hilt of his sword and almost contemptuously grasped the front of Belgarath's tunic, lifting the struggling old man from him as one might lift a child. The steel mask twisted into an ugly sneer as the God held the helpless sorcerer out from him. Then, like a great wind, the force of Torak's mind struck, hurling Belgarath across the room, ripping away the front of his tunic. Something glittered across Torak's knuckles, and Garion realized that it was the silver chain of Belgarath's amulet—the polished medallion of the standing wolf. In a very peculiar way the medallion had always been the center of Belgarath's power, and now it lay in the grip of his ancient enemy.

With a dreadfully slow deliberation, the Dark God rose from

his bier, towering over all of them, Cthrek Goru in his hand.

"Garion!" Ce'Nedra screamed. "Do something!"

With deadly pace Torak strode toward the dazed Belgarath, raising his sword. But Aunt Pol sprang to her feet and threw herself between them.

Slowly Torak lowered his sword, and then he smiled a loathsome smile. "My bride," he rasped in a horrid voice.

"Never, Torak," she declared.

He ignored her defiance. "Thou hast come to me at last, Polgara," he gloated.

"I have come to watch you die."

"Die, Polgara? Me? No, my bride, that is not why thou hast come. My will has drawn thee to me as was foretold. And now thou art mine. Come to me, my beloved."

"Never!"

"Never, Polgara?" There was a dreadful insinuation in the God's rasping voice. "Thou wilt submit to me, my bride. I will bend thee to my will. Thy struggles shall but make my victory over thee the sweeter. In the end, I will have thee. Come here."

So overwhelming was the force of his mind that she swayed almost as a tree sways in the grip of a great wind. "No," she gasped, closing her eyes and turning her face away sharply.

"Look at me, Polgara," he commanded, his voice almost purring. "I am thy fate. All that thou didst think to love before me shall fall away, and thou shalt love only me. Look at me."

Helplessly she turned her head and opened her eyes to stare at him. The hatred and defiance seemed to melt out of her, and a terrible fear came into her face.

"Thy will crumbles, my beloved," he told her. "Now come to me."

She *must* resist! All the confusion was gone now, and Garion understood at last. *This* was the real battle. If Aunt Pol succumbed, they were all lost. It had all been for this.

"*Help her,*" the voice within him said.

"*Aunt Pol!*" Garion threw the thought at her, "*Remember Durnik!*" He knew without knowing how he knew that this was the one thing that could sustain her in her deadly struggle. He ranged through his memory, throwing images of Durnik at her—of the smith's strong hands at work at his forge—of his serious eyes—of the quiet sound of his voice—and most of all of the good man's unspoken love for her, the love that had been the center of Durnik's entire life.

She had begun involuntarily to move, no more than a slight shifting of her weight in preparation for that first fatal step in response to Torak's overpowering command. Once she had made that step, she would be lost. But Garion's memories of Durnik struck her like a blow. Her shoulders, which had already begun to droop in defeat, suddenly straightened, and her eyes flashed with renewed defiance. "Never!" she told the expectantly waiting God. "I *will* not!"

Torak's face slowly stiffened. His eyes blazed as he brought the full, crushing force of his will to bear upon her, but she stood firmly against all that he could do, clinging to the memory of Durnik as if to something so solid that not even the will of the Dark God could tear her from it.

A look of baffled frustration contorted Torak's face as he perceived that she would never yield—that her love would be forever denied to him. She had won, and her victory was like a knife twisting slowly inside him. Thwarted, enraged, maddened by her now-unalterable will to resist, Torak raised his face and suddenly howled—a shocking, animallike sound of overwhelming frustration.

"Then perish both!" he raged. "Die with thy father!" And with that, he once more raised his deadly sword.

Unflinching, Aunt Pol faced the raging God.

"Now, Belgarion!" The voice cracked in Garion's mind.

The Orb, which had remained cold and dead throughout all the dreadful confrontation between Aunt Pol and the maimed God, suddenly flared into life, and the sword of the Rivan King exploded into fire, filling the crypt with an intense blue light. Garion leaped forward, extending his sword to catch the deadly blow which was already descending upon Aunt Pol's unprotected face.

The steel sound of blade against blade was like the striking of a great bell, and it rang within the crypt, shimmering and echoing from the walls. Torak's sword, deflected by the flaming blade, plowed a shower of sparks from the flagstone floor. The God's single eye widened as he recognized all in one glance the Rivan King, the flaming sword and the blazing Orb of Aldur. Garion saw in the look that Torak had already forgotten Aunt Pol and that now the maimed God's full attention was focused on *him*.

"And so thou hast come at last, Belgarion," the God greeted him gravely. "I have awaited thy coming since the beginning of days. Thy fate awaits thee here. Hail, Belgarion, and farewell." His arm lashed back, and he swung a vast blow, but Garion, without even thinking, raised his own sword and once again the crypt rang with the bell note of blade against blade.

"Thou art but a boy, Belgarion," Torak said. "Wilt thou pit thyself against the might and invincible will of a God? Submit to me, and I will spare thy life."

The will of the God of Angarak was now directed at *him*, and in that instant, Garion fully understood how hard Aunt Pol's struggle had been. He felt the terrible compulsion to obey draining the strength from him. But suddenly a vast chorus of voices rang down through all the centuries to him, crying out the single word, "No!" All the lives of all who preceeded him had been directed at this one moment, and those lives infused him now. Though he alone held Iron-grip's sword, Belgarion of Riva was *not* alone, and Torak's will could not sway him.

In a move of absolute defiance, Garion again raised his flaming sword.

"So be it, then," Torak roared. "To the death, Belgarion!"

At first it seemed but some trick of the flickering light that filled the tomb, but almost as soon as that thought occurred, Garion saw that Torak *was* growing larger, swelling upward, towering, expanding. With an awful wrenching sound, he shouldered aside the rusted iron roof of the tomb, bursting upward.

Once again without thinking, without even stopping to consider *how* to do it, Garion also began to expand, and he too exploded through the confining ceiling, shuddering away the rusty debris as he rose.

In open air among the decaying ruins of the City of Night the two titanic adversaries faced each other beneath the perpetual cloud that blotted out the sky.

"The conditions are met," the dry voice spoke through Garion's lips.

"So it would seem," another, equally unemotional voice came from Torak's steel-encased mouth.

"Do you wish to involve others?" Garion's voice asked.

"It hardly seems necessary. These two have sufficient capacity for what must be brought to bear upon them."

"Then let it be decided here."

"Agreed."

And with that Garion felt a sudden release as all constraint was removed from him. Torak, also released, raised Cthrek Goru, his lips drawn back in a snarl of hate.

Their struggle was immense. Rocks shattered beneath the colossal force of deflected blows. The sword of the Rivan King danced in blue flames, and Cthrek Goru, Torak's blade of shadows, swept a visible darkness with it at every blow. Beyond thought, beyond any emotion but blind hatred, the two swung and parried and lurched through the broken ruins, crushing all beneath them. The elements themselves erupted as the fight continued. The wind shrieked through the rotting city, tearing at the trembling stones. Lightning seethed about them, glaring and flickering. The earth rumbled and shook beneath their massive feet. The featureless cloud that had concealed the City of Night beneath its dark mantle for five millenia began to boil and race above them. Great patches of stars appeared and disappeared in the roiling middle of the surging cloud. The Grolims, both human and nonhuman, aghast at the towering struggle that had suddenly erputed in their very midst, fled shrieking in terror.

Garion's blows were directed at Torak's blind side, and the Dark God flinched from the fire of the Orb each time the flaming sword struck, but the shadow of Cthrek Goru put a deathly chill into Garion's blood each time it passed over him.

They were more evenly matched than Garion had imagined possible. Torak's advantage of size had been erased when they had both swelled into immensity, and Garion's inexperience was offset by Torak's maiming.

It was the uneven ground that betrayed Garion. Retreating before a sudden flurry of massive blows, he felt one heel catch on a heap of tumbled rock, and the rotten stones crumbled and rolled beneath his feet. Despite his scrambling attempt to keep his balance, he fell.

Torak's single eye blazed in triumph as he raised the dark sword. But, seizing his sword hilt in both hands, Garion raised his burning blade to meet that vast blow. When the swords struck, edge to edge, a huge shower of sparks cascaded down over Garion.

Again Torak raised Cthrek Goru, but a strange hunger flickered across his steel-encased face. "Yield!" he roared.

Garion stared up at the huge form towering over him, his mind racing.

"I have no wish to kill thee, boy," Torak said, almost pleading. "Yield and I will spare thy life."

And then Garion understood. His enemy was not trying to kill him, but was striving instead to force him to submit. Torak's driving need was for domination! *This* was where the real struggle between them lay!

"Throw down thy sword, Child of Light, and bow before me," the God commanded, and the force of his mind was like a crushing weight.

"I *will* not," Garion gasped, wrenching away from that awful compulsion. "You may kill me, but I will *not* yield."

Torak's face twisted as if his perpetual agony had been doubled by Garion's refusal. "Thou *must*," he almost sobbed. "Thou art helpless before me. Submit to me."

"No!" Garion shouted, and, taking advantage of Torak's chagrin at that violent rejection, he rolled out from under the shadow of Cthrek Goru and sprang to his feet. Everything was clear now, and he knew at last how he could win.

"Hear me, maimed and despised God," he grated from between clenched teeth. "You are nothing. Your people fear you, but they do not love you. You tried to deceive me into loving you; you tried to force Aunt Pol to love you; but I refuse you even as she did. You're a God, but you are nothing. In all the universe there is not one person—not one thing—that loves you. You are alone and empty, and even if you kill me, I will still win. Unloved and despised, you will howl out your miserable life to the end of days."

Garion's words struck the maimed God like blows, and the Orb, as if echoing those words, blazed anew, lashing at the Dragon-God with its consuming hatred. *This* was the EVENT for which the Universe had waited since the beginning of time. *This* was why Garion had come to this decaying ruin—not to fight Torak, but to reject him.

With an animal howl of anguish and rage, the Child of Dark raised Cthrek Goru above his head and ran at the Rivan King. Garion made no attempt to ward off the blow, but gripped the hilt of his flaming sword in both hands and, extending his blade before him, he lunged at his charging enemy.

It was so easy. The sword of the Rivan King slid into Torak's chest like a stick into water, and as it ran into the God's suddenly stiffening body, the power of the Orb surged up the flaring blade.

Torak's vast hand opened convulsively, and Cthrek Goru tumbled harmlessly from his grip. He opened his mouth to cry out, and blue flame gushed like blood from his mouth. He clawed at his face, ripping away the polished steel mask to reveal the hideously maimed features that had lain beneath. Tears started from his eyes, both the eye that was and the eye that was not, but the tears were also fire, for the sword of the Rivan King buried in his chest filled him with its flame.

He lurched backward. With a steely slither, the sword slid out of his body. But the fire the blade had ignited within him did not go out. He clutched at the gaping wound, and blue flame spurted out between his fingers, spattering in little burning pools among the rotting stones about him.

His maimed face, still streaked with fiery tears, contorted in agony. He lifted that burning face to the heaving sky and raised his vast arms. In mortal anguish, the stricken God cried to heaven, "Mother!" and the sound of his voice echoed from the farthest star.

He stood so for a frozen moment, his arms upraised in supplication, and then he tottered and fell dead at Garion's feet.

For an instant there was absolute silence. Then a howling cry started at Torak's dead lips, fading into unimaginable distance as the dark Prophecy fled, taking the inky shadow of Cthrek Goru with it.

Again there was silence. The racing clouds overhead stopped in their mad plunge, and the stars that had appeared among the tatters of that cloud went out. The entire universe shuddered— and stopped. There was a moment of absolute darkness as all light everywhere went out and all motion ceased. In that dreadful instant all that existed—all that had been, all that was, all that was yet to be was wrenched suddenly into the course of one Prophecy. Where there had always been two, there was now but one.

And then, faint at first, the wind began to blow, purging away the rotten stink of the City of Night, and the stars came on again like suddenly reilluminated jewels on the velvety throat of night. As the light returned, Garion stood wearily over the body of the God he had just killed. His sword still flickered blue in his hand, and the Orb exulted in the vaults of his mind. Vaguely he was aware that in that shuddering moment when all light had died, both he and Torak had returned to their normal size, but he was too tired to wonder about it.

From the shattered tomb not far away, Belgarath emerged, shaken and drawn. The broken chain of his medallion dangled from his tightly clenched hand, and he stopped to stare for a moment at Garion and the fallen God.

The wind moaned in the shattered ruins, and somewhere, far off in the night, the Hounds of Torak howled a mournful dirge for their fallen master.

Belgarath straightened his shoulders; then, in a gesture peculiarly like that which Torak had made in the moment of his death, he raised his arms to the sky.

"Master!" he cried out in a huge voice. "It is finished!"

Chapter Twenty-Four

IT WAS OVER, but there was a bitterness in the taste of Garion's victory. A man did not lightly kill a God, no matter how twisted or evil the God might be. And so Belgarion of Riva stood sadly over the body of his fallen enemy as the wind, smelling faintly of the approaching dawn, washed over the decaying ruins of the City of Night.

"Regrets, Garion?" Belgarath asked quietly, putting his hand on his grandson's shoulder.

Garion sighed. "No, Grandfather," he said. "I suppose not—not really. It had to be done, didn't it?"

Belgarath nodded gravely.

"It's just that he was so alone at the end. I took everything away from him before I killed him. I'm not very proud of that."

"As you say, it had to be done. It was the only way you could beat him."

"I just wish I could have left him something, that's all."

From the ruins of the shattered iron tower, a sad little procession emerged. Aunt Pol, Silk, and Ce'Nedra were bringing out the body of Durnik the smith, and walking gravely beside them came Errand.

A pang of almost unbearable grief ran through Garion. Durnik, his oldest friend, was pale and dead, and in that vast internal upheaval that had preceded the duel with Torak, Garion had not even been able to mourn.

"It was necessary, you understand," Belgarath said sadly.

"Why? Why did Durnik have to die, Grandfather?" Garion's voice was anguished, and tears stood openly in his eyes.

"Because his death gave your Aunt the will to resist Torak. That's always been the one flaw in the Prophecy—the possibility that Pol might yield. All Torak needed was one person to love him. It would have made him invincible."

"What would have happened if she had gone to him?"

"You'd have lost the fight. That's why Durnik had to die." The old man sighed regretfully. "I wish it could have been otherwise, but it was inevitable."

The three who had bore Durnik from the broken tomb gently laid his still form on the ground, and Ce'Nedra sadly joined Belgarath and Garion. Wordlessly, the tiny girl slipped her hand into Garion's, and the three of them stood, silently watching as Aunt Pol, past tears now, gently straightened Durnik's arms at his sides and then covered him with her cloak. She sat then upon the earth, took his head into her lap and almost absently stroked his hair, her head bowed over his in her grief.

"I can't bear it," Ce'Nedra suddenly sobbed, and she buried her face in Garion's shoulder and began to weep.

And then there was light where there had been only darkness before. As Garion stared, a single beam of brilliant blue light descended from the broken and tattered cloud rolling overhead. The entire ruin seemed bathed in its intense radiance as the light touched the earth. Like a great, glowing column, the beam of light reached down to the earth from the night sky, was joined by other beams, red and yellow and green and shades Garion could not even name. Like the colors at the foot of a sudden rainbow, the great columns of light stood side by side on the other side of Torak's fallen body. Then, indistinctly,

Garion perceived that a glowing, incandescent figure stood within the center of each column of light. The Gods had returned to mourn the passing of their brother. Garion recognized Aldur, and he could easily identify each of the others. Mara still wept, and dead-eyed Issa seemed to undulate, serpentlike, as he stood within his glowing column of pale green light. Nedra's face was shrewd, and Chaldan's proud. Belar, the blond-haired, boyish God of the Alorns had a roguish, impudent look about him, though his face, like those of his brothers, was sad at the death of Torak. The Gods had returned to earth in glowing light and with sound as well. The reeking air of Cthol Mishrak was suddenly alive with that sound as each colored beam of light gave off a different note, the notes joining in a harmony so profound that it seemed the answer to every question that had ever been asked.

And finally, joining the other columns of light, a single, blindingly white beam slowly descended, and within the center of that radiance stood the white-robed form of UL, that strange God whom Garion had seen once in Prolgu.

The figure of Aldur, still embraced in its glowing blue nimbus, approached the ancient God of Ulgo. "Father," Aldur said sadly, "our brother, thy son Torak, is slain."

Shimmering and incandescent, the form of UL, father of the other Gods, moved across the rubble-strewn ground to stand over the silent body of Torak. "I tried to turn thee from this path, my son," he said softly, and a single tear coursed its way down his eternal cheek. Then he turned back to Aldur. "Take up the form of thy brother, my son, and place it upon some more suitable resting place. It grieves me to see him lie so low upon the earth."

Aldur, joined by his brethren, took up the body of Torak and placed it upon a large block of stone lying amid the ancient ruins, and then, standing in a quiet gleaming circle about the bier, they mourned the passing of the God of Angarak.

Unafraid as always, seemingly not even aware that the glowing figures which had descended from the sky were not human, Errand walked quite confidently to the shining form of UL.

He reached out his small hand and tugged insistently at the God's robe. "Father," he said.

UL looked down at the small face.

"Father," Errand repeated, perhaps echoing Aldur, who had, in his use of that name, revealed at last the true identity of the God of Ulgo. "Father," the little boy said again. Then he turned and pointed at the silent form of Durnik. "Errand!" It was in some strange way more a command than a request.

The face of UL became troubled. "It is not possible, child," he replied.

"Father," the little boy insisted, "Errand."

Ul looked inquiringly at Garion, his eyes profoundly unsettled. "The child's request is serious," he said gravely, speaking not to Garion but to that other awareness, "and it places an obligation upon me—but it crosses the uncrossable boundary."

"The boundary must remain intact," the dry voice replied through Garion's lips. "Thy sons are passionate, Holy UL, and having once crossed this line, they may be tempted to do so again, and perhaps in one such crossing they may change that which must not be changed. Let us not provide the instrumentality whereby Destiny must once more follow two divergent paths."

UL sighed.

"Wilt thou and thy sons, however, lend of your power to *my* instrument so that *he* may cross the boundary?"

UL looked startled at that.

"Thus will the boundary be protected, and thy obligation shall be met. It can happen in no other way."

"Let it be as thou wilt," UL agreed. He turned then and a peculiar look passed between the father of the Gods and his eldest son, Aldur.

Aldur, still bathed in blue light, turned from his sad contemplation of his dead brother toward Aunt Pol, who was still bowed over Durnik's body.

"Be comforted, my daughter," he told her. "His sacrifice was for thee and for all mankind."

"That is slight comfort, Master," she replied, her eyes full of tears. "This was the best of men."

"All men die, my daughter, the best as well as the worst. In thy life thou hast seen this many times."

"Yes, Master, but this is different."

"In what way, beloved Polgara?" Aldur seemed to be pressing her for some reason.

Aunt Pol bit her lip. "Because I loved him, Master," she replied finally.

The faintest touch of a smile appeared on Aldur's lips. "Is that so difficult to say, my daughter?"

She could not answer, but bowed again over Durnik's lifeless form.

"Wouldst thou have us restore this man to thee, my daughter?" Aldur asked then.

Her face came up sharply. "That isn't possible, Master," she said. "Please don't toy with my grief like this."

"Let us however, consider that it *may* be possible," he told her. "Wouldst thou have us restore him?"

"With all my heart, Master."

"To what end? What task hast thou for this man that demands his restoration?"

She bit her lip again. "To be my husband, Master," she blurted finally with a trace of defiance in her voice.

"And was that also so very difficult to say? Art thou sure, however, that this love of thine derives not from thy grief, and that once this good man is restored, thy mind might not turn away from him? He *is*, thou must admit, most ordinary."

"Durnik has never been ordinary," she flared with sudden heat. "He is the best and bravest man in the world."

"I meant him no disrespect, Polgara, but no power doth infuse him. The force of the Will and the Word is not in him."

"Is that so important, Master?"

"Marriage must be a joining of equals, my daughter. How could this good, brave man be husband to thee, so long as *thy* power remains?"

She looked at him helplessly.

"Couldst thou, Polgara, limit thyself? Wouldst thou become his equal? With power no more than his?"

She stared at him, hesitated, then blurted the one word, "Yes."

Garion was shocked—not so much by Aunt Pol's acceptance but rather by Aldur's request. Aunt Pol's power was central to her very being. To remove it from her would leave her with nothing. What would she be without it? How could she even live without it? It was a cruel price to demand, and Garion had believed that Aldur was a kindly God.

"I will accept thy sacrifice, Polgara," Aldur was saying. "I will speak with my father and my brothers. For good and proper reasons, we have denied ourselves this power, and we must all agree to it before any of us might attempt this violation of the natural order of things." And he returned to the sorrowful gathering about Torak's bier.

"How could he do that?" Garion, his arm still about Ce'Nedra, demanded of his grandfather.

"Do what?"

"Ask her to give up her power like that? It will destroy her."

"She's much stronger than you think, Garion," Belgarath assured him, "and Aldur's reasoning is sound. No marriage could survive that kind of inequality."

Among the glowing Gods, however, one angry voice was raised. "No!" It was Mara, the weeping God of the Marags, who were no more. "Why should one man be restored when all my slaughtered children still lie cold and dead? Did Aldur hear *my* pleas? Did he come to *my* aid when my children died? I will not consent."

"I hadn't counted on that," Belgarath muttered. "I'd better take steps before this goes any further." He crossed the littered ground and bowed respectfully. "Forgive my intrusion," he said, "but would my Master's brother accept a woman of the Marags as a gift in exchange for his aid in restoring Durnik?"

Mara's tears, which had been perpetual, suddenly stopped, and his face became incredulous. "A Marag woman?" he demanded sharply. "None such exist. I would have known in my heart if one of my children had survived in Maragor."

"Of a certainty, Lord Mara," Belgarath agreed quickly. "But what of those few who were carried *out* of Maragor to dwell in perpetual slavery?"

"Knowest thou of such a one, Belgarath?" Mara asked with a desperate eagerness.

The old man nodded. "We discovered her in the slave pens beneath Rak Cthol, Lord Mara. Her name is Taiba. She is but one, but a race may be restored by such a one as she—particularly if she be watched over by a loving God."

"Where is Taiba, my daughter?"

"In the care of Relg, the Ulgo," Belgarath replied. "They seem quite attached to each other," he added blandly.

Mara looked at him thoughtfully. "A race may not be restored by one," he said, "even in the care of the most loving God. It requires two." He turned to UL. "Wilt thou give me this Ulgo, Father?" he asked. "He shall become the sire of my people."

UL gave Belgarath a rather penetrating look. "Thou knowest that Relg hath another duty to perform," he said pointedly.

Belgarath's expression was almost impish. "I'm certain that the Gorim and I can work out the details, Most Holy," he declared with utmost self-confidence.

"Aren't you forgetting something, Belgarath?" Silk asked diffidently, as if not wanting to intrude. "Relg has this little problem, remember?"

Belgarath gave the little man a hard look.

"I just thought I ought to mention it," Silk said innocently.

Mara looked sharply at them. "What is this?"

"A minor difficulty, Lord Mara," Belgarath said quickly. "One I'm certain Taiba can overcome. I have the utmost confidence in her in that particular area."

"I will have the truth of this," Mara said firmly.

Belgarath sighed and gave Silk another grim look. "Relg is a zealot, Lord Mara," he explained. "For religious reasons, he avoids certain—ah—forms of human contact."

"Fatherhood is his destiny," UL said. "From him will issue

a special child. I will explain this to him. He is an obedient man, and he will put aside his aversions for my sake."

"Then thou wilt give him to me, Father?" Mara asked eagerly.

"He is thine—with but one restriction—of which we will speak later."

"Let us see to this brave Sendar, then," Mara said, and all traces of his weeping were now gone.

"*Belgarion,*" the voice in Garion's mind said.

"*What?*"

"*The restoration of your friend is in your hands now.*"

"*Me? Why me?*"

"*Must you always say that? Do you want Durnik's life restored?*"

"*Of course, but I can't do it. I wouldn't even know where to begin.*"

"*You did it before. Remember the colt in the cave of the Gods?*"

Garion had almost forgotten that.

"*You are my instrument, Belgarion. I can keep you from making mistakes—most of the time anyway. Just relax; I'll show you what to do.*"

Garion was already moving without conscious volition. He let his arm fall from about Ce'Nedra's shoulders, and, his sword still in his hand, he walked slowly toward Aunt Pol and Durnik's body. He looked once into her eyes as she sat with the dead man's head in her lap, and then he knelt beside the body.

"For me, Garion," she murmured to him.

"If I can, Aunt Pol," he said. Then, without knowing why, he laid the sword of the Rivan King upon the ground and took hold of the Orb at its pommel. With a faint click, the Orb came free in his hand. Errand, smiling now, approached from the other side and also knelt, taking up Durnik's lifeless hand in his. Holding the Orb in both hands, Garion reached out and put it against the dead man's chest. He was faintly conscious of the fact that the Gods had gathered about in a circle and that they had reached out their arms, palm to palm, forming an unbroken ring. Within that circle, a great light began to pulsate, and the Orb, as if in answer, glowed between his hands.

The blank wall he had seen once before was there again, still black, impenetrable, and silent. As he had before in the cave of the Gods, Garion pushed tentatively against the substance of death itself, striving to reach through and pull his friend back into the world of the living.

It was different this time. The colt he had brought to life in the cave had never lived except within its mother's body. Its death had been as tenuous as its life, and it lay but a short distance beyond the barrier. Durnik, however, had been a man full grown, and his death, like his life, was far more profound. With all his strength, Garion pushed. He could feel the enormous force of the combined wills of the Gods joining with his in the silent struggle, but the barrier would not yield.

"Use the Orb!" the voice commanded.

This time Garion focused all the power, his own and that of the Gods upon the round stone between his hands. It flickered, then glowed, then flickered again.

"Help me!" Garion commanded it.

As if suddenly understanding, the Orb flared into a coruscating eruption of colored light. The barrier was weakening.

With an encouraging little smile, Errand reached out and laid one hand upon the blazing Orb.

The barrier broke. Durnik's chest heaved, and he coughed once.

With profoundly respectful expression upon their eternal faces, the Gods stepped back. Aunt Pol cried out in sudden relief and clasped her arms about Durnik, cradling him against her.

"Errand," the child said to Garion with a peculiar note of satisfaction. Garion stumbled to his feet, exhausted by the struggle and nearly staggering as he moved away.

"Are you all right?" Ce'Nedra demanded of him, even as she ducked her head beneath his arm and firmly pulled it about her tiny shoulders.

He nodded, though his knees almost buckled.

"Lean on me," she told him.

He was about to protest, but she put her hand firmly to his

lips. "Don't argue, Garion," she told him. "You know that I love you and that you're going to be leaning on me for the rest of your life anyway, so you might as well get used to the idea."

"I think my life's going to be different now, Master," Belgarath was saying to Aldur. "Pol's always been there, ready to come when I called her—not always willingly, perhaps—but she always came. Now she'll have other concerns." He sighed. "I suppose our children all grow up and get married sometime."

"This particular pose doth not become thee, my son," Aldur told him.

Belgarath grinned. "I've never been able to slip anything past you, Master," he said. Then his face grew serious again. "Polgara's been almost like a son to me," he told Aldur, "but perhaps it's time that I let her be a woman. I've denied her that for too long."

"As it seems best to thee, my son," Aldur said. "And now, I pray thee, go apart a little way and permit us our family grief." He looked at Torak's body lying on the bier and then at Garion. "I have but one more task for thee, Belgarion," he said. "Take the Orb and place it upon my brother's breast."

"Yes, Master," Garion replied immediately. He removed his arm from about Ce'Nedra's shoulders and walked to the bier, trying not to look at the dead God's seared and twisted face. He reached out and laid the round blue stone upon the motionless chest of Kal Torak. Then he stepped back. Once again his little princess wormed her way beneath his arm and clasped him about the waist. It was not unpleasant, but he had the brief, irrational thought that things would be awkward if she were going to insist on this close embrace for the rest of their lives.

Once again the Gods formed their circle, and once again the Orb began to glow. Gradually, the seared face started to change, its maiming slowly disappearing. The light surrounding the Gods and the bier grew stronger, and the glow of the Orb became incandescent. The last Garion saw of the face of Torak, it was calm, composed and unmarked. It was a beautiful face, but it was nonetheless still a dead face.

And then the light grew so intense that Garion could no longer look at it. When it subsided, and when Garion looked back at the bier, the Gods and the body of Torak were gone. Only the Orb remained, glowing slightly as it lay on the rough stone.

Errand, once again with that confident look, went to the bier. Standing on his tiptoes, he reached across the block to retrieve the glowing stone. Then he carried it to Garion. "Errand, Belgarion," he said firmly, handing the Orb back, and in their touch as the Orb exchanged hands, Garion felt something profoundly different.

Drawn together by what had happened, the little group silently gathered about Aunt Pol and Durnik. To the east, the sky had begun to lighten, and the rosy blush of dawn touched the few last remaining tatters of the cloud that had covered Cthol Mishrak. The events of the dreadful night had been titanic, but now the night was nearly over, and they stood together, not speaking as they watched the dawn.

The storm that had raged through the long night had passed. For years beyond counting, the universe had been divided against itself, but now it was one again. If there were such things as beginnings, this was a beginning. And so it was, through broken cloud, that the sun rose on the morning of the first day.

Epilogue

THE ISLE OF
THE WINDS

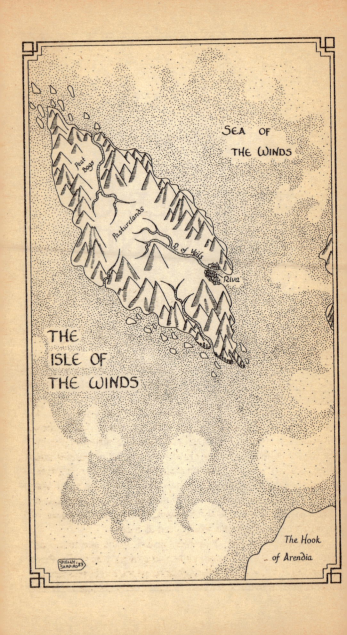

SEA OF
THE WINDS

Peat
Bogs

Pasturelands

R. of Veils

Riva

THE
ISLE OF
THE WINDS

The Hook
of Arendia

SHELLY
SHAPIRO

Chapter Twenty-Five

BELGARION OF RIVA slept very fitfully the night before his wedding. Had he and Ce'Nedra been married in some simple, private little ceremony shortly after his meeting with Torak, things might have gone more smoothly. At that time both he and his flightly little princess had been too tired and too overwhelmed by the events which had taken place to be anything but absolutely honest with each other. During those few short days he had found her to be almost a different person. She had watched his every move with a kind of patient adoration, and she was forever touching him—his hair, his face, his arms—her fingers gentle and curious. The peculiar way she had of coming up to him, no matter who was present or what was going on, and worming her way into the circle of his arm had been, on the whole, rather nice.

Those days had not, however, lasted. Once she had reassured herself that he was all right and that he was really there and not some figment of her imagination which might be snatched away at any moment, Ce'Nedra had gradually changed. He felt somehow like a possession; following her initial delight in ownership, his princess had rather deliberately embarked upon some grand plan of alteration.

And now the day upon which her possession of him was to be formalized was only hours away. His sleep came in fits and starts with dreams mingling peculiarly with memories as he dipped in and out of sleep like a sea bird skimming across the waves.

He was at Faldor's farm again. Even in his sleep he could hear the ringing of Durnik's hammer and smell the odors coming from Aunt Pol's kitchen. Rundorig was there—and Zubrette—and Doroon—and there was Brill, creeping around a corner. He half-woke and turned restlessly in the royal bed. That wasn't possible. Doroon was dead, drowned in the River Mardu, and Brill had vanished forever over the parapet of mile-high Rak Cthol.

And then he was in the palace at Sthiss Tor, and Salmissra, her blatant nudity glowing through her filmy gown, was touching his face with her cold fingers.

But Salmissra was no longer a woman. He had watched her himself as she had changed into a serpent.

Grul the Eldrak hammered at the frozen ground with his iron-shod club, bellowing, "Come 'Grat, fight!" and Ce'Nedra was screaming.

In the chaotic world of dreams half-mixed with memories he saw Ctuchik, his face contorted with horror, exploding once more into nothingness in the hanging turret at Rak Cthol.

And then he stood once again in the decaying ruin of Cthol Mishrak, his sword ablaze, and watched as Torak raised his arms to the rolling cloud, weeping tears of fire, and once again he heard the stricken God's final cry, "Mother!"

He stirred, half-rousing and shuddering as he always did when that dream recurred, but dipped almost immediately into sleep again.

He was standing on the deck of Barak's ship just off the Mallorean coast, listening as King Anheg explained why Barak was chained to the mast.

"We had to do it, Belgarath," the coarse-faced monarch said

mournfully. "Right during the middle of that storm, he turned into a *bear*! He drove the crew to row toward Mallorea all night long, and then, just before daybreak, he turned back into a man again."

"Unchain him, Anheg," Belgarath said disgustedly. "He's not going to turn into a bear again—not as long as Garion's safe and well."

Garion rolled over and sat up. *That* had been a startling revelation. There had been a purpose behind Barak's periodic alterations.

"You're Garion's defender," Belgarath had explained to the big man. "That's why you were born. Any time Garion was in mortal danger, you changed into a bear in order to protect him."

"You mean to say that I'm a sorcerer?" Barak had demanded incredulously.

"Hardly. The shape-change isn't all that difficult, and you didn't do it consciously. The Prophecy did the work, not you."

Barak had spent the rest of the voyage back to Mishrak ac Thull trying to come up with a tastefully understated way to add that concept to his coat of arms.

Garion climbed out of his high, canopied bed and went to the window. The stars in the spring sky looked down at the sleeping city of Rivan and at the dark waters of the Sea of the Winds beyond the harbor. There was no sign that dawn was anywhere near yet. Garion sighed, poured himself a drink of water from the pitcher on the table, and went back to bed and his troubled sleep.

He was at Thull Zelik, and Hettar and Mandorallen were reporting on the activities of 'Zakath, the Mallorean Emperor. "He's laying siege to Rak Goska right now," hawk-faced Hettar was saying. There had been a peculiar softening in Hettar's face since Garion had last seen him, as if something very significant had happened. The tall Algar turned to Garion. "Eventually you're going to have to do something about 'Zakath," he said. "I don't think you want him roaming around at will in this part of the world."

"Why me?" Garion asked without thinking.

"You're Overlord of the West, remember?"

Once again Garion awoke. Sooner or later he *would* have to deal with 'Zakath; there was no question about that. Maybe after the wedding, he'd have time to consider the matter. That thought, however, stopped him. Strangely, he had no conception of anything that might happen after the wedding. It stood before him like some huge door that led into a place he had never been. 'Zakath would have to wait. Garion had to get through the wedding first.

Half asleep, somewhere between dreaming and remembering, Garion relived a significant little exchange between himself and her Imperial Highness.

"It's stupid, Ce'Nedra," he was protesting. "I'm not going to fight anybody, so why should I ride in waving my sword?"

"They deserve to see you, Garion," she explained as if talking to a child. "They left their homes and rode into battle at your summons."

"I didn't summon anybody."

"I did it in your behalf. They're a very good army, really, and I raised them all by myself. Aren't you proud of me?"

"I didn't ask you to do that."

"You were too proud to ask. That's one of your failings, Garion. You must never be too proud to ask the people who love you for help. Every man in the army loves you. They followed me because of you. Is it too much trouble for the great Overlord of the West to reward his faithful soldiers with just a little bit of a display or appreciation? Or have you become too grand and lofty for simple gratitude?"

"You're twisting things, Ce'Nedra. You do that a lot, you know."

But Ce'Nedra had already moved on as if the entire matter were settled. "And of course you *will* wear your crown—and some nice armor. I think a mail shirt would be appropriate."

"I'm not going to make a clown of myself just to satisfy your urges toward cheap theatricality."

Her eyes filled. Her lower lip trembled. "You don't love me any more," she accused him in a quavering little voice.

Garion groaned even in his sleep. It *always* came down to

that. She won every single argument with that artful bit of deception. He *knew* it was not genuine. He *knew* that she only did it to get her own way, but he was absolutely defenseless against it. It might have nothing whatsoever to do with the matter under discussion, but she always managed to twist things around until she could unleash that devastating accusation, and all hope of his winning even the smallest point was immediately lost. Where had she learned to be so heartlessly dishonest?

And so it was that Garion, dressed in mail, wearing his crown and self-consciously holding his flaming sword aloft, had ridden into the forts atop the eastern escarpment to the thunderous cheers of Ce'Nedra's army.

So much had happened since Garion and Silk and Belgarath had crept from the citadel at Riva the previous spring. The young king lay musing in his high, canopied bed, having almost given up on sleep. Ce'Nedra *had* in fact raised an army. As he had heard more of the details, he had been more and more astonished—not only by her audacity but also by the enormous amount of energy and sheer will she had expended in the process. She had been guided and assisted, certainly, but the initial concept had been hers. His admiration for her was tinged slightly with apprehension. He was going to marry a very strong-minded young woman—and one who was not overly troubled by scruples.

He rolled over and punched at his pillow, hoping somehow by that familiar act to bring on more normal sleep, but once again he slipped into restless dreaming. Relg and Taiba were walking toward him, and they were holding hands!

And then he was at the Stronghold, sitting at Adara's bedside. His beautiful cousin was even paler than he remembered, and she had a persistent, racking cough. Even as the two of them talked, Aunt Pol was taking steps to remedy the last complications of the wound which had so nearly claimed the girl's life.

"I was mortified, of course," Adara was saying. "I'd taken so much care to conceal it from him, and now I'd gone and blurted it out to him, and I wasn't even dying."

"Hettar?" Garion said again. He'd already said it three times.

"If you don't stop that, Garion, I'm going to be cross with you," Adara said quite firmly.

"I'm sorry," he apologized quickly. "It's just that I've never considered him in that light. He's a good friend, but I never thought of him as particularly loveable. He's so—I don't know—implacable, I suppose."

"I have certain reasons to believe that may change," Adara said with a faint blush. Then she began to cough again.

"Drink this, dear," Aunt Pol ordered, coming to the bedside with a fuming cup.

"It's going to taste awful," Garion warned his cousin.

"That will do, Garion," Aunt Pol told him. "I can manage this without the helpful comments."

And then he was in the caves beneath Prolgu, standing beside Relg as the Gorim performed the simple ceremony uniting the zealot and the Marag woman who had so totally changed Relg's life. Garion sensed another presence in the underground chamber, and he wondered if anyone had yet told Relg about the bargain that had been struck in Cthol Mishrak. He'd thought about saying something himself, but had decided against it. All things considered, it might be best to let Relg adjust to one thing at a time. Marriage to Taiba was probably going to be enough of a shock to the fanatic's system for now. Garion could feel Mara's gloating exultation as the ceremony concluded. The weeping God no longer wept.

It was useless, Garion decided. He was not going to be able to sleep—at least not the kind of sleep that would do him any good. He threw off the covers and pulled on his robe. The fire in his fireplace had been banked for the night, and he stirred it up again. Then he sat in the chair in front of it, staring pensively into the dancing flames.

Even if his wedding to Ce'Nedra had taken place immediately upon their arrival back at Riva, things might still have turned out all right, but the arrangements for a royal wedding of this magnitude were far too complex to be made overnight, and many of those who were to be honored guests were still recuperating from wounds received during the battle of Thull Mardu.

The interim had given Ce'Nedra time to embark upon a full-blown plan of modification. She had, it appeared, a certain concept of him—some ideal which only she could perceive—and she was absolutely determined to cram him into that mold despite all his objections and protests. Nothing could make her relent in her singleminded drive to make him over. It was so unfair. He was quite content to accept her exactly as she was. She had her flaws—many of them—but he was willing to take the good with the bad. Why couldn't she extend him the same courtesy? But each time he tried to put his foot down and absolutely refuse one of her whims, her eyes would fill with tears, her lip would tremble, and the fatal, "You don't love me any more," would drop quaveringly upon him. Belgarion of Riva had considered flight several times during that long winter.

Now it was spring again, and the storms which isolated the Isle of the Winds during the winter months were past. The day which Garion felt would never come had suddenly rushed upon him. Today was the day in which he would take the Imperial Princess Ce'Nedra to wife, and it was too late to run.

He knew that if he brooded about it much longer, he'd push himself over the edge into total panic, and so he stood up and quickly dressed himself in plain tunic and hose, ignoring the more ostentatious garments which his valet—at Ce'Nedra's explicit instructions—had laid out for him.

It was about an hour before daylight as the young king of Riva opened the door to the royal apartment and slipped into the silent corridor outside.

He wandered for a time through the dim, empty halls of the Citadel, and then, inevitably, his undirected steps led him to Aunt Pol's door. She was already awake and seated by her fire with a cup of fragrant tea in her hands. She wore a deep blue dressing gown, and her dark hair flowed down across her shoulders in a lustrous wave.

"You're up early," she noted.

"I couldn't sleep."

"You should have. You have a very full day ahead of you."

"I know. That's why I couldn't sleep."

"Tea?"

"No, thanks." He sat in the carved chair on the other side of the fireplace. "Everything's changing, Aunt Pol," he said after a moment of thoughtful silence. "After today, nothing will ever be the same again, will it?"

"Probably not," she said, "but that doesn't necessarily mean that it will be a change for the worse."

"How do *you* feel about the idea of getting married?"

"A bit nervous," she admitted calmly.

"You?"

"I've never been married before either, Garion."

Something had been bothering him about that. "Was it really such a good idea, Aunt Pol?" he asked her. "I mean, arranging to have you and Durnik get married on the same day as Ce'Nedra and I? What I'm trying to say is that you're the most important woman in the world. Shouldn't your wedding be a special occasion?"

"That was what we were trying to avoid, Garion," she replied. "Durnik and I decided that we wanted our wedding to be private, and we hope that it will be lost in all the confusion and ceremony that's going to surround yours."

"How is he? I haven't seen him for several days now."

"He's still a bit strange. I don't think he'll ever be the same man we all knew."

"He's all right, isn't he?" Garion's question was concerned.

"He's fine, Garion. He's just a bit different, that's all. Something happened to him that's never happened to any other man, and it changed him. He's as practical as ever, but now he looks at the other side of things as well. I think I rather like that."

"Do you *really* have to leave Riva?" he asked suddenly. "You and Durnik could stay here in the Citadel."

"We want our own place, Garion," she told him. "We need to be alone with each other. Besides, if I were here, every time you and Ce'Nedra had a squabble, I'd have one or both of you hammering on my door. I've done my best to raise you two. Now you're going to have to work things out on your own."

"Where will you go?"

"To the Vale. My mother's cottage is still standing there. It's a very solid house. All it needs is new thatching on the roof and new doors and windows. Durnik will know how to take care of that, and it will be a good place for Errand to grow up."

"Errand? You're taking him with you?"

"Someone has to care for him, and I've grown used to having a small boy around. Besides, father and I've decided that we'd like for him to be some distance from the Orb. He's still the only one beside you who can touch it. Someone at some time might seize upon that and try to use him in the same way Zedar did."

"What'd be the point? I mean, Torak's gone now. What good would the Orb do anybody else?"

She looked at him very gravely, and the white lock of her brow seemed to glow in the soft light. "I don't believe that was the only reason for the Orb's existence, Garion," she told him seriously. "Something hasn't been completed yet."

"What? What else is there left to do?"

"We don't know. The Mrin Codex does not end with the meeting between the Child of Light and the Child of Dark. You're the Guardian of the Orb now, and it's still as important as ever, so don't just put it on the back shelf of a closet somewhere and forget about it. Be watchful, and don't let ordinary affairs dull your mind. Keeping the Orb is still your first duty—and I'm not going to be here to remind you about it every day."

He didn't want to think about that. "What will you do if somebody comes to the Vale and tries to take Errand away? You won't be able to protect him, now that—" He faltered to a stop. He had not spoken to her about that.

"Go ahead and say it, Garion," she said directly. "Let's look it right in the face. You were going to say now that I no longer have any power."

"What's it like, Aunt Pol? Is it like losing something—a sort of emptiness, maybe?"

"I feel the same as always, dear. Of course I haven't tried

to *do* anything since I agreed to give it up. It might be painful if I tried to make something happen and failed. I don't think I'd care for the experience, so I simply haven't tried." She shrugged. "That part of my life is over, so I'll just have to put it behind me. Errand will be safe, though. Beldin's in the Vale—and the twins. That's enough power in one place to keep away anything that might want to harm him."

"Why's Durnik spending so much time with Grandfather?" Garion asked suddenly. "Ever since we got back to Riva, they've been together just about every minute they were awake."

She gave him a knowing smile. "I imagine they're preparing some surprise for me," she replied. "Some suitable wedding present. They both tend to be a trifle transparent."

"What is it?" Garion asked curiously.

"I haven't the slightest idea—and I wouldn't dream of trying to find out. Whatever it is, they've both worked too hard at it for me to spoil it for them by snooping around." She glanced at the window where the first light of dawn was appearing. "Perhaps you'd better run along now, dear," she suggested. "I have to start getting ready. This is a very special day for me, too, and I really want to look my best."

"You could never look anything less than beautiful, Aunt Pol," he told her sincerely.

"Why thank you, Garion." She smiled at him, looking somehow almost girlish. "But I'd rather not take the chance." She gave him an appraising glance and touched his cheek. "Why don't you visit the baths, dear," she suggested, "and wash your hair and get somebody to shave you."

"I can do that myself, Aunt Pol."

"That's not a good idea, Garion. You're a little nervous today, and you don't want to put a razor to your face when your hands are trembling."

He laughed a bit ruefully, kissed her, and started toward the door. Then he stopped and turned back toward her. "I love you, Aunt Pol," he said simply.

"Yes, dear, I know. I love you, too."

After he had visited the baths, Garion went looking for

Lelldorin. Among the matters that had finally been settled was the marital status of the young Asturian and his semiofficial bride. Ariana had finally despaired of Lelldorin's ever making the first move on his own and had solved the entire problem by simply moving in with him. She had been quite firm about it. Garion gathered that Lelldorin's resistance had faded rather quickly. His expression of late had been somewhat more foolish than usual, and Ariana's had been, although radiant, just a trifle smug. In a peculiar way, they closely resembled Relg and Taiba in that respect. Since his wedding, Relg's expression had been one of almost perpetual astonishment, while Taiba's had that same smugness that marked Ariana's. Garion wondered if he might not awaken tomorrow morning to see that same self-satisfied little smirk on Ce'Nedra's lips.

There was a purpose to Garion's search for his Asturian friend. As a result of one of Ce'Nedra's whims, their wedding was going to be followed by a grand ball, and Lelldorin had been teaching Garion how to dance.

The idea of the ball had been greeted with enthusiasm by all the ladies; the men, however, had not been universal in their approval. Barak had been particularly vehement in his objections. "You want *me* to get in the middle of the floor and dance?" he had demanded of the princess in an outraged tone of voice. "What's wrong with all of us just getting drunk? That's the normal way to celebrate a wedding."

"You'll be just fine," Ce'Nedra had told him, patting his cheek in that infuriating way of hers. "And you will do it, won't you, Barak—for me?" And she had insincerely fluttered her eyelashes at him.

Barak had stamped away, muttering curses under his breath.

Garion found Lelldorin and Ariana doting on each other across the breakfast table in their rooms.

"Wilt thou take breakfast with us, your Majesty?" Ariana inquired politely.

"Thanks all the same, my Lady," Garion declined, "but I don't seem to have much appetite today."

"Nerves," Lelldorin observed sagely.

"I think I've got most of it," Garion rushed to the core of his problem, "but that crossover baffles me. My feet keep getting all tangled up."

Lelldorin immediately fetched a lute, and with Ariana's help walked Garion through the complex procedure.

"Thou art becoming most skilled, your Majesty," Ariana complimented him at the end of the lesson.

"All I want to do is get through it without tripping and falling on my face in public."

"The princess would surely support thee, shouldst thou stumble."

"I'm not sure about that. She might enjoy watching me make a fool of myself."

"How little thou knowest of women." Ariana gave Lelldorin an adoring look—a look he fatuously returned.

"Will you two stop that?" Garion demanded irritably. "Can't you wait until you're alone to carry on that way?"

"My heart is too full of love for me to hide it, Garion," Lelldorin said extravagantly.

"So I've noticed," Garion said dryly. "I've got to go see Silk, so I'll leave you two to your amusements."

Ariana blushed, then smiled. "Might we take that as a royal command, your Majesty?" she asked archly.

Garion fled.

Silk had arrived from the east late the previous evening, and Garion was anxious for news. He found the little Drasnian lingering over a breakfast of partridge and hot, spiced wine.

"Isn't that a little heavy for breakfast?" Garion asked him.

"I've never been that partial to gruel first thing in the morning," Silk replied. "Gruel's the sort of thing a man has to work himself up to."

Garion went directly to the point. "What's happening in Cthol Murgos?"

"'Zakath is still laying siege to Rak Goska," Silk reported. "He's transporting in more troops, though. It's pretty obvious that he's going to strike into southern Cthol Murgos as soon as the ground's firm enough to move an army."

"Are the Thulls with him?"

"Only a few. Most of them are concentrating on finding the few Grolims left in their kingdom. I always thought Thulls were a stupid people, but you'd be amazed at how creative they can be when it comes to finding new and interesting ways for Grolims to die."

"We're going to have to keep an eye on 'Zakath," Garion said. "I wouldn't want him to come creeping up on me from the south."

"I think you can count on him not to creep," Silk said. "He sent you a message of congratulations, incidentally."

"He did *what*?"

"He's a civilized man, Garion—*and* a politician. He was badly shaken by the fact that you killed Torak. I think he's actually afraid of you, so he wants to stay on your good side—at least until he finishes up in southern Cthol Murgos."

"Who's in command of the Murgos, now that Taur Urgas is dead?"

"Urgit, his third son by his second wife. There was the usual squabble over the succession by the various sons of Taur Urgas's assorted wives. The fatalities were numerous, I understand."

"What kind of man is Urgit?"

"He's a schemer. I don't think he's any match for 'Zakath, but he'll keep the Malloreans busy for ten or twenty years. By then, 'Zakath may be too old and tired of war to give you any problems."

"Let's hope so."

"Oh, I almost forgot. Hettar married your cousin last week."

"Adara? I thought she was ill."

"Not that much, apparently. They're coming to your wedding—along with Cho-Hag and Silar."

"Is *everybody* getting married?"

Silk laughed. "Not *me*, my young friend. In spite of this universal plunge toward matrimony, *I* still haven't lost my senses. If worse comes to worst, I still know how to run. The Algars should arrive sometime this morning. They met Korodullin's entourage, and they're all coming together. Their ship was right behind mine when we left Camaar."

"Was Mandorallen with them?"

Silk nodded. "Along with the Baroness of Vo Ebor. The Baron's still much too ill to travel. I think he's hoping that he'll die, to leave the way clear for his wife and Mandorallen."

Garion sighed.

"Don't let it make you unhappy, Garion," Silk advised. "Arends actually enjoy that kind of misery. Mandorallen's perfectly content to suffer nobly."

"That's a rotten thing to say," Garion accused the little man.

Silk shrugged. "I'm a rotten sort of person," he admitted.

"Where are you going after—" Garion left it hanging.

"After I see you safely married?" Silk suggested pleasantly. "As soon as I recover from all the drinking I'll do tonight, I'll be off for Gar og Nadrak. There's a great deal of opportunity in the new situation there. I've been in contact with Yarblek. He and I are going to form a partnership."

"With Yarblek?"

"He's not so bad—if you keep an eye on him—and he's very shrewd. We'll probably do rather well together."

"I can imagine." Garion laughed. "One of you is bad enough all by himself, but with the two of you acting together, no honest merchant's going to escape with his skin."

Silk grinned wickedly. "That was sort of what we had in mind."

"I imagine that you'll get very rich."

"I suppose I could learn to live with that." Silk's eyes took on a distant look. "That's not really what it's all about, though," he noted. "It's a game. The money's just a way of keeping score. It's the game that's important."

"It seems to me that you told me that once before."

"Nothing's changed since then, Garion," Silk told him with a laugh.

Aunt Pol's wedding to Durnik took place later that morning in a small, private chapel in the west wing of the Citadel. There were but few guests. Belgarath and the twins, Beltira and Belkira, were there of course, and Silk and Barak. Aunt Pol, beautiful in a deep blue velvet gown, was attended by Queen Layla, and Garion stood with Durnik. The ceremony was performed by the hunchbacked Beldin, dressed for once in decent clothing and with a strangely gentle expression on his ugly face.

Garion's emotions were very complex during the ceremony. He realized with a sharp little pang that Aunt Pol would no longer be exclusively his. An elemental, childish part of him resented that. He was, however, pleased that it was Durnik whom she was marrying. If anyone deserved her, it was Durnik. The good, plain man's eyes were filled with absolute love, and he obviously could not take them from her face. Aunt Pol herself was gravely radiant as she stood at Durnik's side.

As Garion stepped back while the two exchanged vows, he heard a faint rustle. Just inside the door of the chapel, in a hooded cloak that covered her from head to foot and wearing a heavy veil that covered her face, stood Princess Ce'Nedra. She had made a large issue of the fact that by an ancient Tolnedran custom, Garion was not supposed to see her before their wedding on this day, and the cloak and veil provided her with the illusion of invisibility. He could imagine her wrestling with the problem until she had come up with this solution. Nothing could have kept her from Polgara's wedding, but all the niceties and formalities had to be observed. Garion smiled slightly as he turned back to the ceremony.

It was the expression on Beldin's face that made him turn again to look sharply toward the back of the chapel—an expression of surprise that turned to calm recognition. At first Garion saw nothing, but then a faint movement up among the rafters caught his eye. The pale, ghostly shape of a snowy owl perched on one of the dark beams, watching as Aunt Pol and Durnik were married.

When the ceremony was concluded and after Durnik had respectfully and rather nervously kissed his bride, the white owl spread her pinions to circle the chapel in ghostly silence. She hovered briefly as if in silent benediction over the happy couple; then with two soft beats of her wings, she moved through the breathless air to Belgarath. The old sorcerer resolutely averted his eyes.

"You may as well look at her, father," Aunt Pol told him. "She won't leave until you recognize her."

Belgarath sighed then, and looked directly at the oddly luminous bird hovering in the air before him. "I still miss you," he said very simply. "Even after all this time."

The owl regarded him with her golden, unblinking eyes for a moment, then flickered and vanished.

"What an absolutely astonishing thing," Queen Layla gasped.

"We're astonishing people, Layla," Aunt Pol replied, "and we have a number of peculiar friends—and relatives." She smiled then, her arm closely linked in Durnik's. "Besides," she added with a twinkle in her eye, "you wouldn't really expect a girl to get married without her mother in attendance, would you?"

Following the wedding, they all walked through the corridors of the Citadel back to the central fortress and stopped outside the door of Aunt Pol's private apartment. Garion was about to follow Silk and Barak as, after a few brief congratulations, they moved on down the hallway, but Belgarath put his hand on his grandson's arm. "Stay a moment," the old man said.

"I don't think we should intrude, Grandfather," Garion said nervously.

"We'll only stay for a few minutes," Belgarath assured him. The old man's lips were actually quivering with a suppressed mirth. "There's something I want you to see."

One of Aunt Pol's eyebrows raised questioningly as her father and Garion followed into the apartment. "Are we responding to some ancient and obscure custom, father?" she asked.

"No, Pol," he replied innocently. "Garion and I only want to toast your happiness, that's all."

"What exactly are you up to, Old Wolf?" she asked him, but her eyes had an amused look in them.

"Do I have to be up to something?"

"You usually are, father." She did, however, fetch four crystal goblets and a decanter of fine old Tolnedran wine.

"The four of us started all this together quite a long time ago," Belgarath recalled. "Perhaps, before we all separate, we should take a moment to remember that we've come a long way since then, and some rather strange things have happened to us. We've all changed in one way or another, I think."

"You haven't changed all that much, father," Aunt Pol said meaningfully. "Would you get to the point?"

Belgarath's eyes were twinkling openly now with some huge, suppressed mirth. "Durnik has something for you," he said.

Durnik swallowed hard. "Now?" he asked Belgarath apprehensively.

Belgarath nodded.

"I know how much you love beautiful things—like that bird over there," Durnik said to Aunt Pol, looking at the crystal wren Garion had given her the previous year. "I wanted to give you something like that, too—only I can't work in glass or in gemstones. I'm a metalsmith, so I have to work in steel." He had been unwrapping something covered in plain cloth. What he produced finally was an intricately wrought steel rose, just beginning to open. The details were exquisite, and the flower glowed with a burnished life of its own.

"Why, Durnik," Aunt Pol said, genuinely pleased. "How very lovely."

Durnik, however, did not give her the rose yet. "It has no color, though," he noted a bit critically, "and no fragrance." He glanced nervously at Belgarath.

"Do it," the old man told him. "The way I showed you."

Durnik turned back to Aunt Pol, still holding the burnished rose in his hand. "I really have nothing to give you, my Pol," he told her humbly, "except an honest heart—and this." He held out the rose in his hand, and his face took on an expression of intense concentration.

Garion heard it very clearly. It was a familiar, rushing surge of whispered sound, filled with a peculiarly bell-like shimmer. The polished rose in Durnik's outstretched hand seemed to pulsate slightly, and then gradually it began to change. The outsides of the petals were as white as new snow, but the insides, where the flower was just opening, were a deep, blushing red. When Durnik finished, he held a living flower out to Aunt Pol, its petals beaded with dew.

Aunt Pol gasped as she stared incredulously at the rose. It was unlike any flower that had ever existed. With a trembling hand she took it from him, her eyes filled with sudden tears. "How is it possible?" she asked in an awed voice.

"Durnik's a very special man now," Belgarath told her. "So far as I know, he's the only man who ever died and then lived again. That could not help changing him—at least a little. But then, I suspect that there's always been a poet lurking under the surface of our good, practical friend. Maybe the only real difference is that now he has a way of letting that poet out."

Durnik, looking just a bit embarrassed, touched the rose with a tentative finger. "It does have one advantage, my Pol," he noted. "The steel is still in it, so it will never fade or wilt. It will stay just as it is now. Even in the middle of winter, you'll have at least one flower."

"Oh, Durnik!" she cried, embracing him.

Durnik looked a bit abashed as he awkwardly returned her embrace. "If you really like it, I could make you some others," he told her. "A whole garden of them, I suppose. It's not really all that hard, once you get the hang of it."

Aunt Pol's eyes, however, had suddenly widened. With one arm still about Durnik, she turned slightly to look at the crystal wren perched upon its glass twig. "Fly," she said, and the glowing bird spread its wings and flew to her outstretched hand. Curiously it inspected the rose, dipped its beak into a dew drop, and then it lifted its head and began to sing a trilling little song. Gently Aunt Pol raised her hand aloft, and the crystal bird soared back to its glass twig. The echo of its song still hung in the silent air.

"I expect it's time for Garion and me to be going," Belgarath said, his face rather sentimental and misty.

Aunt Pol, however, had quite obviously realized something. Her eyes narrowed slightly, then went very wide. "Just a moment, Old Wolf," she said to Belgarath with a faint hint of steel in her voice. "You knew about this from the very beginning, didn't you?"

"About what, Pol?" he asked innocently.

"That Durnik—that I—" For the first time in his life Garion saw her at a loss for words. "You knew!" she flared.

"Naturally. As soon as Durnik woke up, I could feel something different in him. I'm surprised you didn't feel it yourself. I had to work with him a bit to bring it out, though."

"Why didn't you tell me?"

"You didn't ask, Pol."

"You—I—" With an enormous effort she gained control of herself. "All of these months you let me go on thinking that my power was gone, and it was there all the time! It was still there, and you put me through all of that?"

"Oh, really, Pol. If you'd just stopped to think, you'd have realized that you can't give it up like that. Once it's there, it's there."

"But our Master said—"

Belgarath raised one hand. "If you'll just stop and remember, Pol, all he really asked was if you'd be willing to limit your independence in marriage and go through life with no more power than Durnik has. Since there's no way he could remove *your* power, he obviously had something else in mind."

"You let me believe—"

"I have no control over what you believe, Pol," he replied in his most reasonable tone of voice.

"You tricked me!"

"No, Pol," he corrected, "you tricked yourself." Then he smiled fondly at her. "Now, before you go off into a tirade, think about it for a moment. All things considered, it didn't really hurt you, did it? And isn't it really nicer to find out about it this way?" His smile became a grin. "You can even consider it my wedding present to you, if you'd like," he added.

She stared at him for a moment, obviously wanting to be cross about the whole thing, but the look he returned her was impish. The confrontation between them had been obscure, but he had quite obviously won this time. Finally, no longer able to maintain even the fiction of anger, she laughed helplessly and put her hand affectionately on his arm. "You're a dreadful old man, father," she told him.

"I know," he admitted. "Coming, Garion?"

Once they were in the hall outside, Belgarath began to chuckle.

"What's so funny?" Garion asked him.

"I've been waiting for that moment for months," his grandfather said, still chortling. "Did you see her face when she finally realized what had happened? She's been moping around with that look of noble self-sacrifice for all this time, and then she suddenly finds out that it was absolutely unnecessary." His face took on a wicked little smirk. "Your Aunt's always been just a little too sure of herself, you know. Maybe it was good for her to go for a little while thinking that she was just an ordinary person. It might give her some perspective."

"She was right." Garion laughed. "You *are* a dreadful old man."

Belgarath grinned. "One does one's best."

They went along the hallway to the royal apartment where the clothes Garion was to wear for his wedding were already laid out.

"Grandfather," Garion said, sitting down to pull off his boots, "there's something I've been meaning to ask you. Just before Torak died, he called out to his mother."

Belgarath, tankard in hand, nodded.

"Who is his mother?"

"The universe," the old man replied.

"I don't understand."

Belgarath scratched thoughtfully at his short, white beard. "As I understand it, each of the Gods began as an idea in the mind of UL, the father of the Gods, but it was the universe that brought them forth. It's very complicated. I don't understand it entirely myself. Anyway, as he was dying, Torak cried out to the one thing that he felt still loved him. He was wrong, of course. UL and the other Gods *did* still love him, even though they knew that he had become twisted and totally evil. And the universe grieved for him."

"The universe?"

"Didn't you feel it? That instant when everything stopped and all the lights went out?"

"I thought that was just me."

"No, Garion. For that single instant all the light in the universe went out, and everything stopped moving—everything—everywhere. A part of that was the grief of the universe for her dead son."

Garion thought about that. "He had to die, though, didn't he?"

Belgarath nodded. "It was the only way that things could get back on the right course. Torak had to die so that things could go toward what they're supposed to. Otherwise, everything would have ultimately wound up in chaos."

A sudden strange thought struck Garion. "Grandfather," he said, "who is Errand?"

"I don't know," Belgarath replied. "Perhaps he's just a strange little boy. Perhaps he's something else. You'd probably better start changing clothes."

"I was trying not to think about that."

"Oh, come now. This is the happiest day of your life."

"Really?"

"It might help if you keep saying that to yourself."

By general consent, the Gorim of Ulgo had been selected to perform the ceremony uniting Garion and Ce'Nedra in marriage. The frail, saintly old man had made the journey from Prolgu in short, easy stages, carried by litter through the caves to Sendaria, then conveyed in King Fulrach's royal carriage to the city of Sendar and thence by ship to Riva. The revelation of the fact that the God of the Ulgos was the father of the other Gods had struck theological circles like a thunderclap. Entire libraries of turgid philosophical speculation had instantly become obsolete, and priests everywhere now stumbled about in a state of shock. Grodeg, the High Priest of Belar, fainted dead away at the news. The towering ecclesiastic, already crippled for life by the wounds he had received during the battle of Thull Mardu, did not take this final blow well. When he recovered from his swoon, his attendants found that his mind had reverted to childhood, and he spent his days now surrounded by toys and brightly colored bits of string.

The royal wedding, of course, took place in the Hall of the Rivan King, and everyone was there. King Rhodar was in crimson, King Anheg in blue. King Fulrach wore brown, and King Cho-Hag the customary Algar black. Brand, the Rivan Warder, his face made even more somber by the death of his youngest son, was dressed in Rivan gray. There were other royal visitors as well. Ran Borune XXIII in his gold-colored mantle was strangely jovial as he bantered with the shaven-headed Sadi. Oddly enough, the two of them got on well together. The possibilities of the new situation in the west appealed to them both, and they were obviously moving toward an accommodation of some sort. King Korodullin wore royal purple and stood about with the other kings—although he spoke but little. The blow to his head during the battle of Thull Mardu had affected his hearing, and the young king of Arendia was obviously uncomfortable in company.

In the very center of the gathered monarchs stood King Drosta lek Thun of Gar og Nadrak, wearing a curiously un-attractive yellow doublet. The nervous, emaciated king of the Nadraks spoke in short little bursts, and when he laughed, there was a shrill quality in his voice. King Drosta made many arrangements that afternoon—some of which he even intended to honor.

Belgarion of Riva, of course, did not participate in those discussions—which was probably just as well. The Rivan King's mind was a trifle distracted at that moment. Dressed all in blue, he paced nervously in a nearby antechamber where he and Lelldorin awaited the fanfare which was to summon them into the great hall. "I wish this was all over," he said for the sixth time.

"Just be patient, Garion," Lelldorin advised him again.

"What are they *doing* out there?"

"Probably waiting for word that her Highness is ready. At this particular time, she's far more important than you are. That's the way weddings are, you know."

"You're the lucky one. You and Ariana just ran off and got married without all this fuss."

Lelldorin laughed ruefully. "I didn't really escape it, Garion," he said, "just postponed it for a while. All the preparations here have inflamed my Ariana. As soon as we return to Arendia, she wants us to have a proper wedding."

"What is it about weddings that does such strange things to the female mind?"

"Who can say?" Lelldorin shrugged. "A woman's mind is a mystery—as you'll soon discover."

Garion gave him a sour look and adjusted his crown once again. "I wish it were all over," he said again.

In time the fanfare echoed through the Hall of the Rivan King, the door opened, and, trembling visibly, Garion adjusted his crown one last time and marched out to meet his fate. Although he knew most of the people in the hall, the faces around him were all a blur as he and Lelldorin walked past the peat fires glowing in the pits in the floor toward the throne where his great sword once more hung in its proper place with the Orb of Aldur glowing on its pommel.

The hall was hung with buntings and banners, and there was a vast profusion of spring flowers. The wedding guests, in silks, satins, and brightly colored brocades, seemed themselves almost like some flower garden as they twisted and strained to watch the entrance of the royal bridegroom.

Awaiting him before the throne stood the white-robed old Gorim of Ulgo, a smile on his gentle face. "Greetings, Belgarion," the Gorim murmured as Garion mounted the steps.

"Holy Gorim," Garion replied with a nervous bow.

"Be tranquil, my son," the Gorim advised, noting Garion's shaking hands.

"I'm trying, Holy One."

The brazen horns sounded yet another fanfare, and the door at the back of the hall swung wide. The Imperial Princess Ce'Nedra, dressed in her creamy, pearl-studded wedding gown, stood in the doorway with her cousin Xera at her side. She was stunning. Her flaming hair streamed down across one shoulder of her gown, and she wore the varicolored golden circlet of which she had always been so fond. Her face was demure, and a delicate little blush colored her cheeks. She kept her eyes downcast, although once she flickered a quick glance at Garion, and he saw the little twinkle that lurked behind her thick lashes. He knew then with absolute certainty that all that demure modesty was a pose. She stood long enough to allow all to look their fill at her perfection before, accompanied by the sound of gently cascading harps, she came down the aisle to meet her quivering bridegroom. In a ceremony Garion thought just a trifle overdone, Barak's two little daughters preceded the bride, strewing her path with flowers.

When she reached the dais, Ce'Nedra rather impulsively kissed the kindly old Gorim's cheek and then took her place at Garion's side. There was a fragrance about her that was strangely flowerlike—a fragrance that for some reason made Garion's knees tremble.

The Gorim looked out at the assemblage and began to speak. "We are gathered today," he began, "to witness the last unraveling of the Prophecy which has guided all our lives through the deadliest of peril and brought us safely to this happy moment. As foretold, the Rivan King has returned. He has met our ancient foe and he has prevailed. His reward stands radiant at his side."

Reward? Garion had not considered it in precisely that light before. He thought about it a bit as the Gorim continued, but it didn't really help all that much. He felt a sharp little nudge in his ribs.

"Pay attention," Ce'Nedra whispered.

It got down to the questions and answers shortly after that. Garion's voice cracked slightly, but that was only to be expected. Ce'Nedra's voice, however, was clear and firm. Couldn't she at least *pretend* to be nervous—just a little?

The rings which they exchanged were carried on a small velvet cushion by Errand. The child took his duties quite seriously, but even on *his* small face there was that slightly amused look. Garion resented that. Was *everyone* secretly laughing at him?

The ceremony concluded with the Gorim's benediction,

which Garion did not hear. The Orb of Aldur, glowing with an insufferable smugness, filled his ears with its song of jubilation during the Gorim's blessing, adding its own peculiar congratulations.

Ce'Nedra had turned to him. "Well?" she whispered.

"Well what?" he whispered back.

"Aren't you going to kiss me?"

"Here? In front of everybody?"

"It's customary."

"It's a stupid custom."

"Just do it, Garion," she said with a warm little smile of encouragement. "We can discuss it later."

Garion tried for a certain dignity in the kiss—a kind of chaste formality in keeping with the general tone of the occasion. Ce'Nedra, however, would have none of that. She threw herself into the business with an enthusiasm which Garion found slightly alarming. Her arms locked about his neck and her lips were glued to his. He irrationally wondered just how far she intended to go with this. His knees were already beginning to buckle.

The cheer which resounded through the hall saved him. The trouble with kissing in public was that one was never sure just how long one should keep it up. If it were too short, people might suspect a lack of regard; if it were too long, they might begin to snicker. Grinning rather foolishly, Belgarion of Riva turned to face the wedding guests.

The wedding ball and the supper which was part of it immediately followed the ceremony. Chatting gaily, the wedding guests trooped through a long corridor to a brightly decorated hall which had been converted into a grand ballroom ablaze with candles. The orchestra was composed of Rivan musicians under the direction of a fussy Arendish concertmaster, who strove mightily to keep the independent Rivans from improvising on those melodies which pleased them.

This was the part Garion had dreaded the most. The first dance was to be a solo affair featuring the royal couple. He was expected to march Ce'Nedra to the center of the floor and perform in public. With a sudden horror, he realized—even

as he and his radiant bride went to the center of the room—
that he had forgotten everything Lelldorin had taught him.

The dance which was popular at that particular season in
the courts of the south was graceful and quite intricate. The
partners were to face in the same direction, the man behind
and slightly to one side of the woman. Their arms were supposed to be extended and their hands joined. Garion managed
that part without too much trouble. It was all those quick, tiny
little steps in time to the music that had him worried.

In spite of everything, though, he did quite well. The fragrance of Ce'Nedra's hair, however, continued to work on him,
and he noted that his hands trembled visibly as the two of them
danced. At the end of the first melody, the wedding guests
applauded enthusiastically; as the orchestra took up the second
tune, they all joined in, and the floor was filled with whirling
colors as the dance became general.

"I guess we didn't do too badly," Garion murmured.

"We were just fine," Ce'Nedra assured him.

They continued to dance.

"Garion," she said after a few moments.

"Yes?"

"Do you really love me?"

"Of course I do. What a silly thing to ask."

"Silly?"

"Wrong word," he amended quickly. "Sorry."

"Garion," she said after a few more measures.

"Yes?"

"I love you too, you know."

"Of course I know."

"Of course? Aren't you taking a bit much for granted?"

"Why are we arguing?" he asked rather plaintively.

"We aren't arguing, Garion," she told him loftily. "We're
discussing."

"Oh," he said. "That's all right then."

As was expected, the royal couple danced with everyone.
Ce'Nedra was passed from king to king like some royal prize,
and Garion escorted queens and ladies alike to the center of
the floor for the obligatory few measures. Tiny blond Queen

Porenn of Drasnia gave him excellent advice, as did the stately Queen Islena of Cherek. Plump little Queen Layla was motherly—even a bit giddy. Queen Silar gravely congratulated him, and Mayaserana of Arendia suggested that he'd dance better if he weren't quite so stiff. Barak's wife, Merel, dressed in rich green brocade, gave him the best advice of all. "You'll fight with each other, of course," she told him as they danced, "but never go to sleep angry. That was always *my* mistake."

And finally Garion danced with his cousin Adara.

"Are you happy?" he asked her.

"More than you could ever imagine," she replied with a gentle smile.

"Then everything worked out for the best, didn't it?"

"Yes, Garion. It's as if it had all been fated to happen. Everything feels so right, somehow."

"It's possible that it *was* fated," Garion mused. "I sometimes think we have very little control over our own lives—I know I don't."

She smiled. "Very deep thoughts for a bridegroom on his wedding day." Then her face grew gravely serious. "Don't let Ce'Nedra drive you to distraction," she advised. "And don't always give in to her."

"You've heard about what's been happening?"

She nodded. "Don't take it too seriously, Garion. She's been testing you, that's all."

"Are you trying to say that I *still* have to prove something?"

"With Ce'Nedra—probably every day. I know your little princess, Garion. All she really wants is for you to prove that you love her—and don't be afraid to say it to her. I think you'll be surprised at how agreeable she'll be if you just take the trouble to tell her that you love her—frequently."

"She knows that already."

"But you have to tell her."

"How often do you think I ought to say it?"

"Oh, probably every hour or so."

He was almost certain that she was joking.

"I've noticed that Sendars are a reserved sort of people," she told him. "That isn't going to work with Ce'Nedra. You're going to have to put your upbringing aside and come right out and say it. It will be worth the trouble, believe me."

"I'll try," he promised her.

She laughed and lightly kissed his cheek. "Poor Garion," she said.

"Why poor Garion?"

"You still have so much to learn."

The dance continued.

Exhausted finally and famished by their efforts, Garion and his bride made their way to the groaning table and sat down to take their wedding supper. The supper was quite special. Two days before the wedding, Aunt Pol had calmly marched into the royal kitchen and had taken charge. As a result, everything was perfect. The smells from the heavily laden table were overwhelming. King Rhodar absolutely could not pass by without just one more nibble.

The music and the dance continued, and Garion watched, relieved that he had escaped the floor. His eyes sought out old friends in the crowd. Barak, huge but strangely gentle, danced with Merel, his wife. They looked very good together. Lelldorin danced with Ariana, and their eyes were lost in each others' faces. Relg and Taiba did not dance, but sat together in a secluded corner. They were, Garion noted, holding hands. Relg's expression was still slightly startled, but he did not look unhappy.

Near the center of the floor, Hettar and Adara danced with the innate grace of those who spend their lives on horseback. Hettar's hawklike face was different somehow, and Adara was flushed with happiness. Garion decided that it might be a good time to try Adara's advice. He leaned toward Ce'Nedra's pink little ear and cleared his throat. "I love you," he whispered. It was difficult the first time, so he tried it again—just to get the feel of it. "I love you," he whispered again. It was easier the second time.

The effect on his princess was electrifying. She blushed sudden rosy red, and her eyes went very wide and somehow defenseless. Her entire heart seemed to be in those eyes. She appeared unable to speak, but reached out instead gently t touch his face. As he returned her gaze, he was quite amazed at the change that the simple phrase had made in her. Adara, it appeared, had been right. He stored that bit of information away rather carefully, feeling more confident than he had in months.

The hall was filled with colors as the guests danced in celebration of the royal wedding. There were, however, a few faces that did not reflect the general happiness. Near the center of the floor, Mandorallen danced with the Lady Nerina, Baroness of Vo Ebor, and their faces mirrored that tragedy which was still central to their lives. Not far from them, Silk danced with Queen Porenn. The little man's face bore once again that same bitter, self-mocking expression Garion had first seen in King Anheg's palace in Val Alorn.

Garion sighed.

"Melancholy already, my husband?" Ce'Nedra asked him with a little twinkle. Once again, even as they sat, she ducked her head beneath his arm and drew it about her in that peculiar way of hers. She smelled very good, and he noted that she was very soft and warm.

"I was just remembering a few things," he replied to her question.

"Good. Try to get that all out of the way now. I wouldn't want it interfering later."

Garion's face turned bright red, and Ce'Nedra laughed a wicked little laugh. "I think that perhaps later is not much further off," she said then. "You must dance with Lady Polgara, and I will dance with your grandfather. And then I think it will be time for us to retire. It's been a very full day."

"I *am* a bit tired," Garion agreed.

"Your day isn't over yet, Belgarion of Riva," she told him pointedly.

Feeling a bit peculiar about it, Garion approached Aunt Pol where she and Durnik sat watching the dance. "Will you dance with me, Aunt Polgara?" he asked with a formal little bow.

She looked at him a bit quizzically. "So you've finally admitted it," she said.

"Admitted what?"

"Who I really am."

"I've known."

"But you've never called me by my full name before, Garion," she pointed out, rising and gently smoothing back his hair. "I think it might be a rather significant step."

They danced together in the glowing candlelight to the music of lutes and pipes. Polgara's steps were more measured and slow than the dance Lelldorin had so painstakingly taught to Garion. She had reached back, Garion realized, into the dim past, and she led him through the stately measures of a dance she had learned centuries before, during her sojourn with the Wacite Arends. Together they moved through the slow, graceful, and somehow melancholy measures of a dance which had vanished forever some twenty-five centuries before, to live on only in Polgara's memory.

Ce'Nedra was blushing furiously when Belgarath returned her to Garion for their last dance. The old man grinned impishly, bowed to his daughter and took her hands to lead her as well. The four of them danced not far from each other, and Garion clearly heard his Aunt's question. "Have we done well, father?"

Belgarath's smile was quite genuine. "Why yes, Polgara," he replied. "As a matter of fact, I think we've done very well indeed."

"Then it was all worth it, wasn't it, father?"

"Yes, Pol, it really was."

They danced on.

"What did he say to you?" Garion whispered to Ce'Nedra. She blushed. "Never mind. Maybe I'll tell you—later."

There was that word again.

The dance ended, and an expectant hush fell over the crowd. Ce'Nedra went to her father, kissed him lightly, and then returned. "Well?" she said to Garion.

"Well what?"

She laughed. "Oh, you're impossible." Then she took his hand and very firmly led him from the hall.

* * *

It was quite late—perhaps two hours past midnight. Belgarath the Sorcerer was in a whimsical mood as he wandered about the deserted halls of the Rivan Citadel with a tankard in his hand. Belgarath had done a bit of celebrating, and he was feeling decidedly mellow—though not nearly as much as many of the other wedding guests, who had already mellowed themselves into insensibility.

The old man stopped once to examine a guard who was snoring in a doorway, sprawled in a puddle of spilled ale. Then, humming rather tunelessly and adding a couple of skipping little dance steps as he proceeded down the hall, the white-bearded old sorcerer made his way in the general direction of the ballroom, where he was certain there was a bit of ale left.

As he passed the Hall of the Rivan King, he noted that the door was ajar and that there was a light inside. Curious, he stuck his head through the doorway to see if anyone might be about. The Hall was deserted, and the light infusing it came from the Orb of Aldur, resting on the pommel of the sword of the Rivan King.

"Oh," Belgarath said to the stone, "it's you." Then the old man walked a trifle unsteadily down the aisle to the foot of the dais. "Well, old friend," he said, squinting up at the Orb, "I see they've all gone off and left you alone too."

The Orb flickered its recognition of him.

Belgarath sat down heavily on the edge of the dais and took a drink of ale. "We've come a long way together, haven't we?" he said to the Orb in a conversational tone.

The Orb ignored him.

"I wish you weren't so serious about things all the time. You're a very stodgy companion." The old man took another drink.

They were silent for a while, and Belgarath pulled off one of his boots, sighed and wriggled his toes contentedly.

"You really don't understand any of this, do you, my friend?" he asked the Orb finally. "In spite of everything, you still have the soul of a stone. You understand hate and loyalty and un-swerving commitment, but you can't comprehend the more human feelings—compassion, friendship, love—love most of all, I think. It's sort of a shame that you don't understand, really, because those were the things that finally decided all this. They've been mixed up in it from the very beginning— but then you wouldn't know about that, would you?"

The Orb continued to ignore him, its attention obviously elsewhere.

"What *are* you concentrating on so hard?" the old man asked curiously.

The Orb, which had glowed with a bright blue radiance flickered again, and its blue became suddenly infused with a pale pink which steadily grew more and more pronounced until the stone was actually blushing.

Belgarath cast one twinkling glance in the general direction of the royal apartment. "Oh," he said, understanding. Then he began to chuckle.

The Orb blushed even brighter.

Belgarath laughed, pulled his boot back on and rose unsteadily to his feet. "Perhaps you understand more than I thought you did," he said to the stone. He drained the last few drops from his tankard. "I'd really like to stay and discuss it," he said, "but I've run out of ale. I'm sure you'll excuse me." Then he went back up the broad aisle.

When he reached the doorway, he stopped and cast one amused glance back at the still furiously blushing Orb. Then he chuckled again and went out, quietly closing the door behind him.

Thus concludes *The Belgariad*,
which began with *Pawn of Prophecy*.
And while History, unlike mortal pen,
does not cease, the records beyond this point
remain as yet unrevealed.

About the Author

David Eddings was born in Spokane, Washington, in 1931, and was raised in the Puget Sound area north of Seattle. He received a Bachelor of Arts degree from Reed College in Portland, Oregon, in 1954 and a Master of Arts degree from the University of Washington in 1961. He has served in the United States Army, worked as a buyer for the Boeing Company, has been a grocery clerk, and has taught English. He has lived in many parts of the United States.

His first novel, *High Hunt* (published by Putnam in 1973), was a contemporary adventure story. The field of fantasy has always been of interest to him, however, and he turned to *The Belgariad* in an effort to develop certain technical and philosophical ideas concerning that genre.

Eddings currently resides with his wife, Leigh, in the northwest.